ABERDEEN
CITY LIBRARIES

THE BROKER

In his final hours in the Oval Office the outgoing President grants a controversial last minute pardon to Joel Backman, a notorious Washington power broker who has spent the last six years in a federal prison. What no one knows is that the President issues the pardon only after receiving enormous pressure from the CIA. It seems that Backman, in his heyday, may have obtained secrets that compromise the world's most sophisticated satellite surveillance system.

Backman is quietly smuggled out of the country, given a new name, a new identity and a new home in Italy. When he has settled into his new life, the CIA will leak his whereabouts to the Israelis, the Russians, the Chinese and the Saudis. Then the CIA will sit back and watch. The question is not whether Backman will survive – there's no chance of that. The question the CIA needs answered is, who will kill him?

THE BROKER

John Grisham

WINDSOR
PARAGON

First published 2005
by
Century
This Large Print edition published 2005
by
BBC Audiobooks Ltd by arrangement with
Random House Ltd
ISBN 1 4056 1093 X (Windsor Hardcover)
ISBN 1 4056 2081 1   (Paragon Softcover)

British Library Cataloguing in Publication Data available

Printed and bound in Great Britain by
Antony Rowe Ltd., Chippenham, Wiltshire

1

In the waning hours of a presidency that was destined to arouse less interest from historians than any since perhaps that of William Henry Harrison (thirty-one days from inauguration to death), Arthur Morgan huddled in the Oval Office with his last remaining friend and pondered his final decisions. At that moment he felt as though he'd botched every decision in the previous four years, and he was not overly confident that he could, somehow, so late in the game, get things right. His friend wasn't so sure either, though, as always, he said little and whatever he did say was what the President wanted to hear.

They were about pardons—desperate pleas from thieves and embezzlers and liars, some still in jail and some who'd never served time but who nonetheless wanted their good names cleared and their beloved rights restored. All claimed to be friends, or friends of friends, or die-hard supporters, though only a few had ever gotten the chance to proclaim their support before that eleventh hour. How sad that after four tumultuous years of leading the free world it would all fizzle into one miserable pile of requests from a bunch of crooks. Which thieves should be allowed to steal again? That was the momentous question facing the President as the hours crept by.

The last friend was Critz, an old fraternity pal from their days at Cornell when Morgan ran the student government while Critz stuffed the ballot boxes. In the past four years, Critz had served as press secretary, chief of staff, national security advisor, and even secretary of state, though that appointment lasted for only three months and was hastily rescinded when Critz's unique style of diplomacy nearly ignited World War III. Critz's last appointment had taken place the previous October, in the final frantic weeks of the reelection onslaught. With the polls showing President Morgan trailing badly in at least forty states, Critz seized control of the campaign and managed to alienate the rest of the country, except, arguably, Alaska.

It had been a historic election; never before had an incumbent president received so few electoral votes. Three to be exact, all from Alaska, the only state Morgan had not visited, at Critz's advice. Five hundred and thirty-five for the challenger, three for President Morgan. The word 'landslide' did not even begin to capture the enormity of the shellacking.

Once the votes were counted, the challenger, following bad advice, decided to contest the results in Alaska. Why not go for all 538 electoral votes? he reasoned. Never again would a candidate for the presidency have the opportunity to completely whitewash his opponent, to throw the mother of all shutouts. For six weeks the President suffered even more while lawsuits raged in Alaska. When the supreme court there eventually awarded him the state's three electoral votes, he and Critz had a very quiet bottle of champagne.

President Morgan had become enamored of Alaska, even though the certified results gave him a scant seventeen-vote margin.

He should have avoided more states.

He even lost Delaware, his home, where the once-enlightened electorate had allowed him to serve eight wonderful years as governor. Just as he had never found the time to visit Alaska, his opponent had totally ignored Delaware—no organization to speak of, no television ads, not a single campaign stop. And his opponent still took 52 percent of the vote!

Critz sat in a thick leather chair and held a notepad with a list of a hundred things that needed to be done immediately. He watched his President move slowly from one window to the next, peering into the darkness, dreaming of what might have been. The man was depressed and humiliated. At fifty-eight his life was over, his career a wreck, his marriage crumbling. Mrs. Morgan had already moved back to Wilmington and was openly laughing at the idea of living in a cabin in Alaska. Critz had secret doubts about his friend's ability to hunt and fish for the rest of his life, but the prospect of living two thousand miles from Mrs. Morgan was very appealing. They might have carried Nebraska if the rather blue-blooded First Lady had not referred to the football team as the 'Sooners.'

The Nebraska Sooners!

Overnight, Morgan fell so far in the polls in both Nebraska and Oklahoma that he never recovered.

And in Texas she took a bite of prizewinning chili and began vomiting. As she was rushed to the hospital a microphone captured her still-famous words: 'How can you backward people eat such a putrid mess?'

Nebraska has five electoral votes. Texas has

thirty-four. Insulting the local football team was a mistake they could have survived. But no candidate could overcome such a belittling description of Texas chili.

What a campaign! Critz was tempted to write a book. Someone needed to record the disaster.

Their partnership of almost forty years was ending. Critz had lined up a job with a defense contractor for $200,000 a year, and he would hit the lecture circuit at $50,000 a speech if anybody was desperate enough to pay it. After dedicating his life to public service, he was broke and aging quickly and anxious to make a buck.

The President had sold his handsome home in Georgetown for a huge profit. He'd bought a small ranch in Alaska, where the people evidently admired him. He planned to spend the rest of his days there, hunting, fishing, perhaps writing his memoirs. Whatever he did in Alaska, it would have nothing to do with politics and Washington. He would not be the senior statesman, the grand old man of anybody's party, the sage voice of experience. No farewell tours, convention speeches, endowed chairs of political science. No presidential library. The people had spoken with a clear and thunderous voice. If they didn't want him, then he could certainly live without them.

'We need to make a decision about Cuccinello,' Critz said. The President was still standing at a window, looking at nothing in the darkness, still pondering Delaware. 'Who?'

'Figgy Cuccinello, that movie director who was indicted for having sex with a young starlet.'

'How young?'

'Fifteen, I think.'

4

'That's pretty young.'

'Yes, it is. He fled to Argentina, where he's been for ten years. Now he's homesick, wants to come back and start making dreadful movies again. He says his art is calling him home.'

'Perhaps the young girls are calling him home.'

'That too.'

'Seventeen wouldn't bother me. Fifteen's too young.'

'His offer is up to five million.'

The President turned and looked at Critz. 'He's offering five million for a pardon?'

'Yes, and he needs to move quickly. The money has to be wired out of Switzerland. It's three in the morning over there.'

'Where would it go?'

'We have accounts offshore. It's easy.'

'What would the press do?'

'It would be ugly.'

'It's always ugly.'

'This would be especially ugly.'

'I really don't care about the press,' Morgan said.

Then why did you ask? Critz wanted to say.

'Can the money be traced?' the President asked and turned back to the window.

'No.'

With his right hand, the President began scratching the back of his neck, something he always did when wrestling with a difficult decision. Ten minutes before he almost nuked North Korea, he'd scratched until the skin broke and blood oozed onto the collar of his white shirt. 'The answer is no,' he said. 'Fifteen is too young.'

Without a knock, the door opened and Artie

5

Morgan, the President's son, barged in holding a Heineken in one hand and some papers in the other. 'Just talked to the CIA,' he said casually. He wore faded jeans and no socks. 'Maynard's on the way over.' He dumped the papers on the desk and left the room, slamming the door behind him.

Artie would take the $5 million without hesitation, Critz thought to himself, regardless of the girl's age. Fifteen was certainly not too young for Artie. They might have carried Kansas if Artie hadn't been caught in a Topeka motel room with three cheerleaders, the oldest of whom was seventeen. A grandstanding prosecutor had finally dropped the charges—two days after the election—when all three girls signed affidavits claiming they had not had sex with Artie. They were about to, in fact had been just seconds away from all manner of frolicking, when one of their mothers knocked on the motel room door and prevented an orgy.

The President sat in his leather rocker and pretended to flip through some useless papers. 'What's the latest on Backman?' he asked.

*   *   *

In his eighteen years as director of the CIA, Teddy Maynard had been to the White House less than ten times. And never for dinner (he always declined for health reasons), and never to say howdy to a foreign hotshot (he couldn't have cared less). Back when he could walk, he had occasionally stopped by to confer with whoever happened to be president, and perhaps one or two of his policy makers. Now, since he was in a wheelchair, his conversations with the White House were by

6

phone. Twice, a vice president had actually been driven out to Langley to meet with Mr. Maynard.

The only advantage of being in a wheelchair was that it provided a wonderful excuse to go or stay or do whatever he damn well pleased. No one wanted to push around an old crippled man.

A spy for almost fifty years, he now preferred the luxury of looking directly behind himself when he moved about. He traveled in an unmarked white van—bulletproof glass, lead walls, two heavily armed boys perched behind the heavily armed driver—with his wheelchair clamped to the floor in the rear and facing back, so that Teddy could see the traffic that could not see him. Two other vans followed at a distance, and any misguided attempt to get near the director would be instantly terminated. None was expected. Most of the world thought Teddy Maynard was either dead or idling away his final days in some secret nursing home where old spies were sent to die.

Teddy wanted it that way.

He was wrapped in a heavy gray quilt, and tended to by Hoby, his faithful aide. As the van moved along the Beltway at a constant sixty miles an hour, Teddy sipped green tea poured from a thermos by Hoby, and watched the cars behind them. Hoby sat next to the wheelchair on a leather stool made especially for him.

A sip of tea and Teddy said, 'Where's Backman right now?'

'In his cell,' Hoby answered.

'And our people are with the warden?'

'They're sitting in his office, waiting.'

Another sip from a paper cup, one carefully guarded with both hands. The hands were frail, veiny, the color of skim milk, as if they had already died and were patiently waiting for the rest of the body. 'How long will it take to get him out of the country?'

'About four hours.'

'And the plan is in place?'

'Everything is ready. We're waiting on the green light.'

'I hope this moron can see it my way.'

                    *   *   *

Critz and the moron were staring at the walls of the Oval Office, their heavy silence broken occasionally by a comment about Joel Backman. They had to talk about something, because neither would mention what was really on his mind.

Can this be happening?

Is this finally the end?

Forty years. From Cornell to the Oval Office. The end was so abrupt that they had not had enough time to properly prepare for it. They had been counting on four more years. Four years of glory as they carefully crafted a legacy, then rode gallantly into the sunset.

Though it was late, it seemed to grow even darker outside. The windows that overlooked the Rose Garden were black. A clock above the fireplace could almost be heard as it ticked nonstop in its final countdown.

'What will the press do if I pardon Backman?' the President asked, not for the first time.

'Go berserk.'

'That might be fun.'

'You won't be around.'

'No, I won't.' After the transfer of power at noon the next day, his escape from Washington would begin with a private jet (owned by an oil company) to an old friend's villa on the island of Barbados. At Morgan's instructions, the televisions had been removed from the villa, no newspapers or magazines would be delivered, and all phones had been unplugged. He would have no contact with anyone, not even Critz, and especially not Mrs. Morgan, for at least a month. He wouldn't care if Washington burned. In fact, he secretly hoped that it would.

After Barbados, he would sneak up to his cabin in Alaska, and there he would continue to ignore the world as the winter passed and he waited on spring.

'Should we pardon him?' the President asked.

'Probably,' Critz said.

The President had shifted to the 'we' mode now, something he invariably did when a potentially unpopular decision was at hand. For the easy ones, it was always 'I.' When he needed a crutch, and especially when he would need someone to blame, he opened up the decision-making process and included Critz.

Critz had been taking the blame for forty years, and though he was certainly used to it, he was nonetheless tired of it. He said, 'There's a very good chance we wouldn't be here had it not been for Joel Backman.'

'You may be right about that,' the President said. He had always maintained that he had been elected because of his brilliant campaigning, charismatic personality, uncanny grasp of the issues, and clear vision for America. To finally

9

admit that he owed anything to Joel Backman was almost shocking.

But Critz was too calloused, and too tired, to be shocked.

Six years ago, the Backman scandal had engulfed much of Washington and eventually tainted the White House. A cloud appeared over a popular president, paving the way for Arthur Morgan to stumble his way into the White House.

Now that he was stumbling out, he relished the idea of one last arbitrary slap in the face to the Washington establishment that had shunned him for four years. A reprieve for Joel Backman would rattle the walls of every office building in D.C. and shock the press into a blathering frenzy. Morgan liked the idea. While he sunned away on Barbados, the city would gridlock once again as congressmen demanded hearings and prosecutors performed for the cameras and the insufferable talking heads prattled nonstop on cable news.

The President smiled into the darkness.

*   *   *

On the Arlington Memorial Bridge, over the Potomac River, Hoby refilled the director's paper cup with green tea. 'Thank you,' Teddy said softly. 'What's our boy doing tomorrow when he leaves office?' he asked.

'Fleeing the country.'

'He should've left sooner.'

'He plans to spend a month in the Caribbean, licking his wounds, ignoring the world, pouting, waiting for someone to show some interest.'

'And Mrs. Morgan?'

10

'She's already back in Delaware playing bridge.'

'Are they splitting?'

'If he's smart. Who knows?'

Teddy took a careful sip of tea. 'So what's our leverage if Morgan balks?'

'I don't think he'll balk. The preliminary talks have gone well. Critz seems to be on board. He has a much better feel of things now than Morgan. Critz knows that they would've never seen the Oval Office had it not been for the Backman scandal.'

'As I said, what's our leverage if he balks?'

'None, really. He's an idiot, but he's a clean one.'

They turned off Constitution Avenue onto 18th Street and were soon entering the east gate of the White House. Men with machine guns materialized from the darkness, then Secret Service agents in black trench coats stopped the van. Code words were used, radios squawked, and within minutes Teddy was being lowered from the van. Inside, a cursory search of his wheelchair revealed nothing but a crippled and bundled-up old man.

*   *   *

Artie, minus the Heineken, and again without knocking, poked his head through the door and announced: 'Maynard's here.'

'So he's alive,' the President said.

'Barely.'

'Then roll him in.'

Hoby and a deputy named Priddy followed the wheelchair into the Oval Office. The President and Critz welcomed their guests and directed them to the sitting area in front of the fireplace. Though

11

Maynard avoided the White House, Priddy practically lived there, briefing the President every morning on intelligence matters.

As they settled in, Teddy glanced around the room, as if looking for bugs and listening devices. He was almost certain there were none; that practice had ended with Watergate. Nixon laid enough wire in the White House to juice a small city, but, of course, he paid for it. Teddy, however, was wired. Carefully hidden above the axle of his wheelchair, just inches below his seat, was a powerful recorder that would capture every sound made during the next thirty minutes.

He tried to smile at President Morgan, but he wanted to say something like: You are without a doubt the most limited politician I have ever encountered. Only in America could a moron like you make it to the top.

President Morgan smiled at Teddy Maynard, but he wanted to say something like: I should have fired you four years ago. Your agency has been a constant embarrassment to this country.

Teddy: I was shocked when you carried a single state, albeit by seventeen votes.

Morgan: You couldn't find a terrorist if he advertised on a billboard.

Teddy: Happy fishing. You'll get even fewer trout than votes.

Morgan: Why didn't you just die, like everyone promised me you would?

Teddy: Presidents come and go, but I never leave.

Morgan: It was Critz who wanted to keep you. Thank him for your job. I wanted to sack your ass two weeks after my inauguration.

12

Critz said loudly, 'Coffee anyone?'

Teddy said, 'No,' and as soon as that was established, Hoby and Priddy likewise declined. And because the CIA wanted no coffee, President Morgan said, 'Yes, black with two sugars.' Critz nodded at a secretary who was waiting in a half-opened side door.

He turned back to the gathering and said, 'We don't have a lot of time.'

Teddy said quickly, 'I'm here to discuss Joel Backman.'

'Yes, that's why you're here,' the President said.

'As you know,' Teddy continued, almost ignoring the President, 'Mr. Backman went to prison without saying a word. He still carries some secrets that, frankly, could compromise national security.'

'You can't kill him,' Critz blurted.

'We cannot target American citizens, Mr. Critz. It's against the law. We prefer that someone else do it.'

'I don't follow,' the President said.

'Here's the plan. If you pardon Mr. Backman, and if he accepts the pardon, then we will have him out of the country in a matter of hours. He must agree to spend the rest of his life in hiding. This should not be a problem because there are several people who would like to see him dead, and he knows it. We'll relocate him to a foreign country, probably in Europe where he'll be easier to watch. He'll have a new identity. He'll be a free man, and with time people will forget about Joel Backman.'

'That's not the end of the story,' Critz said.

'No. We'll wait, perhaps a year or so, then we'll leak the word in the right places. They'll find Mr.

Backman, and they'll kill him, and when they do so, many of our questions will be answered.'

A long pause as Teddy looked at Critz, then the President. When he was convinced they were thoroughly confused, he continued. 'It's a very simple plan, gentlemen. It's a question of who kills him.'

'So you'll be watching?' Critz asked.

'Very closely.'

'Who's after him?' the President asked.

Teddy refolded his veiny hands and recoiled a bit, then he looked down his long nose like a schoolteacher addressing his little third graders. 'Perhaps the Russians, the Chinese, maybe the Israelis. There could be others.'

Of course there were others, but no one expected Teddy to reveal everything he knew. He never had; never would, regardless of who was president and regardless of how much time he had left in the Oval Office. They came and went, some for four years, others for eight. Some loved the espionage, others were only concerned with the latest polls. Morgan had been particularly inept at foreign policy, and with a few hours remaining in his administration, Teddy certainly was not going to divulge any more than was necessary to get the pardon.

'Why would Backman take such a deal?' Critz asked.

'He may not,' Teddy answered. 'But he's been in solitary confinement for six years. That's twenty-three hours a day in a tiny cell. One hour of sunshine. Three showers a week. Bad food—they say he's lost sixty pounds. I hear he's not doing too well.'

14

Two months ago, after the landslide, when Teddy Maynard conceived this pardon scheme, he had pulled a few of his many strings and Backman's confinement had grown much worse. The temperature in his cell was lowered ten degrees, and for the past month he'd had a terrible cough. His food, bland at best, had been run through the processor again and was being served cold. His toilet flushed about half the time. The guards woke him up at all hours of the night. His phone privileges were curtailed. The law library that he used twice a week was suddenly off-limits. Backman, a lawyer, knew his rights, and he was threatening all manner of litigation against the prison and the government, though he had yet to file suit. The fight was taking its toll. He was demanding sleeping pills and Prozac.

'You want me to pardon Joel Backman so you can arrange for him to be murdered?' the President asked.

'Yes,' Teddy said bluntly. 'But we won't actually arrange it.'

'But it'll happen.'

'Yes.'

'And his death will be in the best interests of our national security?'

'I firmly believe that.'

2

The isolation wing at Rudley Federal Correctional Facility had forty identical cells, each a twelve-foot square with no windows, no bars, green-painted concrete floors and cinder-block walls, and a door that was solid metal with a narrow slot at the bottom for food trays and a small open peephole for the guards to have a look occasionally. The wing was filled with government informants, drug snitches, Mafia misfits, a couple of spies—men who needed to be locked away because there were plenty of folks back home who would gladly slice their throats. Most of the forty inmates in protective custody at Rudley had requested the I-wing.

Joel Backman was trying to sleep when two guards clanged open his door and switched on his light. 'The warden wants you,' one said, and there was no elaboration. They rode in silence in a prison van across the frigid Oklahoma prairie, past other buildings holding less-secure criminals, until they arrived at the administration building. Backman, handcuffed for no apparent reason, was hurried inside, up two flights of stairs, then down a long hall to the big office where lights were on and something important was going down. He saw a clock on a wall; it was almost 11:00 p.m.

He'd never met the warden, which was not at all unusual. For many good reasons the warden didn't circulate. He wasn't running for office, nor was he concerned with motivating the troops. With him were three other suits, all earnest-looking men

16

who'd been chatting for some time. Though smoking was strictly prohibited in offices owned by the U.S. government, an ashtray was full and a thick fog hung close to the ceiling.

With absolutely no introduction, the warden said, 'Sit over there, Mr. Backman.'

'A pleasure to meet you,' Backman said as he looked at the other men in the room. 'Why, exactly, am I here?'

'We'll discuss that.'

'Could you please remove these handcuffs? I promise not to kill anyone.'

The warden snapped at the nearest guard, who quickly found a key and freed Backman. The guard then scrambled out of the room, slamming the door behind him, much to the displeasure of the warden, a very nervous man.

He pointed and said, 'This is Special Agent Adair of the FBI. This is Mr. Knabe from the Justice Department. And this is Mr. Sizemore, also from Washington.'

None of the three moved in the direction of Mr. Backman, who was still standing and looking quite perplexed. He nodded at them, in a halfhearted effort to be polite. His efforts were not returned.

'Please sit,' the warden said, and Backman finally took a chair. 'Thank you. As you know, Mr. Backman, a new president is about to be sworn in. President Morgan is on the way out. Right now he is in the Oval Office wrestling with the decision of whether to grant you a full pardon.'

Backman was suddenly seized with a violent cough, one brought on in part by the near arctic temperature in his cell and in part by the shock of the word 'pardon.'

17

Mr. Knabe from Justice handed him a bottle of water, which he gulped and splashed down his chin and finally managed to stifle the cough. 'A pardon?' he mumbled.

'A full pardon, with some strings attached.'

'But why?'

'I don't know why, Mr. Backman, nor is it my business to understand what's happening. I'm just the messenger.'

Mr. Sizemore, introduced simply as 'from Washington,' but without the baggage of title or affiliation, said, 'It's a deal, Mr. Backman. In return for a full pardon, you must agree to leave the country, never return, and live with a new identity in a place where no one can find you.'

No problem there, thought Backman. He didn't want to be found.

'But why?' he mumbled again. The bottle of water in his left hand could actually be seen shaking.

As Mr. Sizemore from Washington watched it shake, he studied Joel Backman, from his closely cropped gray hair to his battered dime-store running shoes, with his black prison-issue socks, and couldn't help but recall the image of the man in his prior life. A magazine cover came to mind. A fancy photo of Joel Backman in a black Italian suit, impeccably tailored and detailed and groomed and looking at the camera with as much smugness as humanly possible. The hair was longer and darker, the handsome face was fleshy and wrinkle free, the waistline was thick and spoke of many power lunches and four-hour dinners. He loved wine and women and sports cars. He had a jet, a yacht, a place in Vail, all of which he'd been quite eager to

18

talk about. The bold caption above his head read:
THE BROKER—IS THIS THE SECOND MOST POWERFUL
MAN IN WASHINGTON?

The magazine was in Mr. Sizemore's briefcase,
along with a thick file on Joel Backman. He'd
scoured it on the flight from Washington to Tulsa.

According to the magazine article, the broker's
income at the time was reported to be in excess of
$10 million a year, though he'd been coy with the
reporter. The law firm he founded had two
hundred lawyers, small by Washington standards,
but without a doubt the most powerful in political
circles. It was a lobbying machine, not a place
where real lawyers practiced their craft. More like
a bordello for rich companies and foreign
governments.

Oh, how the mighty have fallen, Mr. Sizemore
thought to himself as he watched the bottle shake.

'I don't understand,' Backman managed to
whisper.

'And we don't have time to explain,' Mr.
Sizemore said. 'It's a quick deal, Mr. Backman.
Unfortunately, you don't have time to contemplate
things. A snap decision is required. Yes or no. You
want to stay here, or you want to live with another
name on the other side of the world?'

'Where?'

'We don't know where, but we'll figure it out.'

'Will I be safe?'

'Only you can answer that question, Mr.
Backman.'

As Mr. Backman pondered his own question,
he shook even more.

'When will I leave?' he asked slowly. His voice
was regaining strength for the moment, but

19

another violent cough was always waiting.

'Immediately,' said Mr. Sizemore, who had seized control of the meeting and relegated the warden, the FBI, and the Justice Department to being spectators.

'You mean, like, right now?'

'You will not return to your cell.'

'Oh darn,' Backman said, and the others couldn't help but smile.

'There's a guard waiting by your cell,' the warden said. 'He'll bring whatever you want.'

'There's always a guard waiting by my cell,' Backman snapped at the warden. 'If it's that sadistic little bastard Sloan, tell him to take my razor blades and slash his own wrists.'

Everyone swallowed hard and waited for the words to escape through the heating vents. Instead, they cut through the polluted air and rattled around the room for a moment.

Mr. Sizemore cleared his throat, reshuffled his weight from the left buttock to the right, and said, 'There are some gentlemen waiting in the Oval Office, Mr. Backman. Are you going to accept the deal?'

'The President is waiting on me?'

'You could say that.'

'He owes me. I put him there.'

'This really is not the time to debate such matters, Mr. Backman,' Mr. Sizemore said calmly.

'Is he returning the favor?'

'I'm not privy to the President's thoughts.'

'You're assuming he has the ability to think.'

'I'll just call and tell them the answer is no.'

'Wait.'

Backman drained the bottle of water and asked

20

for another. He wiped his mouth with a sleeve, then said, 'Is it like a witness protection program, something like that?'

'It's not an official program, Mr. Backman. But, from time to time, we find it necessary to hide people.'

'How often do you lose one?'

'Not too often.'

'Not too often? So there's no guarantee I'll be safe.'

'Nothing is guaranteed. But your odds are good.'

Backman looked at the warden and said, 'How many years do I have left here, Lester?'

Lester was jolted back into the conversation. No one called him Lester, a name he hated and avoided. The nameplate on his desk declared him to be L. Howard Cass. 'Fourteen years, and you can address me as Warden Cass.'

'Cass my ass. Odds are I'll be dead in three. A combination of malnutrition, hypothermia, and negligent health care should do it. Lester here runs a really tight ship, boys.'

'Can we move along?' Mr. Sizemore said.

'Of course I'll take the deal,' Backman said. 'What fool wouldn't?'

Mr. Knabe from Justice finally moved. He opened a briefcase and said, 'Here's the paperwork.'

'Who do you work for?' Backman asked Mr. Sizemore.

'The President of the United States.'

'Well, tell him I didn't vote for him because I was locked away. But I certainly would have, if given the chance. And tell him I said thanks, okay?'

'Sure.'

*　　　*　　　*

Hoby poured another cup of green tea, decaffeinated now because it was almost midnight, and handed it to Teddy, who was wrapped in a blanket and staring at the traffic behind them. They were on Constitution Avenue, leaving downtown, almost to the Roosevelt Bridge. The old man took a sip and said, 'Morgan is too stupid to be selling pardons. Critz, however, worries me.'

'There's a new account on the island of Nevis,' Hoby said. 'It popped up two weeks ago, opened by an obscure company owned by Floyd Dunlap.'

'And who's he?'

'One of Morgan's fund-raisers.'

'Why Nevis?'

'It's the current hot spot for offshore activity.'

'And we're covering it?'

'We're all over it. Any transfers should take place in the next forty-eight hours.'

Teddy nodded slightly and glanced to his left for a partial look at the Kennedy Center. 'Where's Backman?'

'He's leaving prison.'

Teddy smiled and sipped his tea. They crossed the bridge in silence, and when the Potomac was behind them, he finally said, 'Who'll get him?'

'Does it really matter?'

'No, it doesn't. But it will be quite enjoyable watching the contest.'

*　　　*　　　*

Wearing a well-worn but starched and pressed khaki military uniform, with all the patches and badges removed, and shiny black combat boots and a heavy navy parka with a hood that he pulled snugly around his head, Joel Backman strutted out of the Rudley Federal Correctional Facility at five minutes after midnight, fourteen years ahead of schedule. He had been there, in solitary confinement, for six years, and upon leaving he carried with him a small canvas bag with a few books and some photos. He did not look back.

He was fifty-two years old, divorced, broke, thoroughly estranged from two of his three children and thoroughly forgotten by every friend he'd ever made. Not a single one had bothered to maintain a correspondence beyond the first year of his confinement. An old girlfriend, one of the countless secretaries he'd chased around his plush offices, had written for ten months, until it was reported in *The Washington Post* that the FBI had decided it was unlikely that Joel Backman had looted his firm and his clients of the millions that had first been rumored. Who wants to be pen pals with a broke lawyer in prison? A wealthy one, maybe.

His mother wrote him occasionally, but she was ninety-one years old and living in a low-rent nursing home near Oakland, and with each letter he got the impression it would be her last. He wrote her once a week, but doubted if she was able to read anything, and he was almost certain that no one on staff had the time or interest to read to her. She always said, 'Thanks for the letter,' but never mentioned anything he'd said. He sent her cards on special occasions. In one of her letters she had confessed that no one else remembered her birthday.

The boots were very heavy. As he plodded along the sidewalk he realized that he'd spent most of the past six years in his socks, no shoes. Funny the things you think about when you get sprung with no warning. When was the last time he'd worn boots? And how soon could he shuck the damn things?

He stopped for a second and looked toward the sky. For one hour each day, he'd been allowed to roam a small patch of grass outside his prison wing. Always alone, always watched by a guard, as if he, Joel Backman, a former lawyer who'd never fired a gun in anger, might suddenly become dangerous and maim someone. The 'garden' was lined with ten feet of chain-link topped with razor wire. Beyond it was an empty drainage canal, and beyond that was an endless, treeless prairie that stretched to Texas, he presumed.

Mr. Sizemore and Agent Adair were his escorts. They led him to a dark green sport-utility vehicle that, though unmarked, practically screamed 'government issue' to anyone looking. Joel crawled into the backseat, alone, and began praying. He closed his eyes tightly, gritted his teeth, and asked God to please allow the engine to start, the wheels to move, the gates to open, the paperwork to be sufficient; please, God, no cruel jokes. This is not a dream, God, please!

Twenty minutes later, Sizemore spoke first. 'Say, Mr. Backman, are you hungry?'

Mr. Backman had ceased praying and had begun crying. The vehicle had been moving steadily, though he had not opened his eyes. He

24

was lying on the rear seat, fighting his emotions and losing badly.

'Sure,' he managed to say. He sat up and looked outside. They were on an interstate highway, a green sign flew by—Perry Exit. They stopped in the parking lot of a pancake house, less than a quarter of a mile from the interstate. Big trucks were in the distance, their diesel engines grinding along. Joel watched them for a second, and listened. He glanced upward again and saw a half-moon.

'Are we in a hurry?' he asked Sizemore as they entered the restaurant.

'We're on schedule,' came the reply.

They sat at a table near the front window, with Joel looking out. He ordered french toast and fruit, nothing heavy because he was afraid his system was too accustomed to the gruel he'd been living on. Conversation was stiff; the two government boys were programmed to say little and were thoroughly incapable of small talk. Not that Joel wanted to hear anything they had to say.

He tried not to smile. Sizemore would report later that Backman glanced occasionally at the door and seemed to keep a close eye on the other customers. He did not appear to be frightened; quite the contrary. As the minutes dragged on and the shock wore off, he seemed to adjust quickly and became somewhat animated. He devoured two orders of french toast and had four cups of black coffee.

*　　　*　　　*

A few minutes after 4:00 a.m. they entered the

25

gates of Fort Summit, near Brinkley, Texas. Backman was taken to the base hospital and examined by two physicians. Except for a head cold and the cough, and general gauntness, he wasn't in bad shape. He was then taken to a hangar where he met a Colonel Gantner, who instantly became his best friend. At Gantner's instructions, and under his close supervision, Joel changed into a green army jumpsuit with the name HERZOG stenciled above the right pocket. 'Is that me?' Joel asked, looking at the name.

'It is for the next forty-eight hours,' Gantner said.

'And my rank?'

'Major.'

'Not bad.'

At some point during this quick briefing, Mr. Sizemore from Washington and Agent Adair slipped away, never to be seen again by Joel Backman. With the first hint of sunlight, Joel stepped through the rear hatch of a C-130 cargo plane and followed Gantner to the upper level, to a small bunk room where six other soldiers were preparing for a long flight.

'Take that bunk,' Gantner said, pointing to one close to the floor.

'Can I ask where we're going?' Joel whispered.

'You can ask, but I can't answer.'

'Just curious.'

'I'll brief you before we land.'

'And when might that be?'

'In about fourteen hours.'

With no windows to distract him, Joel situated himself on his bunk, pulled a blanket over his head, and was snoring by takeoff.

3

Critz slept a few hours, then left home long before the inauguration mess began. Just after dawn, he and his wife were whisked off to London on one of his new employer's many private jets. He was to spend two weeks there, then return to the grind of the Beltway as a new lobbyist playing a very old game. He hated the idea. For years he'd watched the losers cross the street and start new careers twisting the arms of their former colleagues, selling their souls to anyone with enough money to buy whatever influence they advertised. It was such a rotten business. He was sick of the political life, but, sadly, he knew nothing else.

He'd make some speeches, maybe write a book, hang on for a few years hoping someone remembered him. But Critz knew how quickly the once powerful are forgotten in Washington.

President Morgan and Director Maynard had agreed to sit on the Backman story for twenty-four hours, until well after the inauguration. Morgan didn't care; he'd be in Barbados. Critz, however, did not feel bound by any agreement, especially one made with the likes of Teddy Maynard. After a long dinner with lots of wine, sometime around 2:00 a.m. in London, he called a White House correspondent for CBS and whispered the basics of the Backman pardon. As he predicted, CBS broke the story during its early-morning gossip hour, and before 8:00 a.m. the news was roaring around D.C.

Joel Backman had been given a full and unconditional pardon at the eleventh hour!

There were no details of his release. When last
heard from, he'd been tucked away in a maximum-
security facility in Oklahoma.

In a very nervous city, the day began with the
pardon storming onto center stage and competing
with a new President and his first full day in office.

*   *   *

The bankrupt law firm of Pratt & Bolling now
found itself on Massachusetts Avenue, four blocks
north of Dupont Circle; not a bad location, but not
nearly as classy as the old place on New York
Avenue. A few years earlier, when Joel Backman
was in charge—it was Backman, Pratt & Bolling
then—he had insisted on paying the highest rent in
town so he could stand at the vast windows of his
vast office on the eighth floor and look down at the
White House.

Now the White House was nowhere in sight;
there were no power offices with grand vistas; the
building had three floors, not eight. And the firm
had shrunk from two hundred highly paid lawyers to about thirty struggling ones. The first
bankruptcy—commonly referred to within the
offices as Backman I—had decimated the firm, but
it had also miraculously kept its partners out of
prison. Backman II had been caused by three years
of vicious infighting and suing among the survivors.
The firm's competitors were fond of saying that
Pratt & Bolling spent more time suing itself than
those it was hired to sue.

Early that morning, though, the competitors
were quiet. Joel Backman was a free man. The
broker was loose. Would he make a comeback? Was

28

he returning to Washington? Was it all true? Surely not.

Kim Bolling was currently locked away in alcohol rehab, and from there he would be sent straight to a private mental facility for many years. The unbearable strain of the last six years had driven him over the edge, to a point of no return. The task of dealing with the latest nightmare from Joel Backman fell into the rather large lap of Carl Pratt.

It had been Pratt who had uttered the fateful 'I do' twenty-two years earlier when Backman had proposed a marriage of their two small firms. It had been Pratt who had labored strenuously for sixteen years to clean up behind Backman as the firm expanded and the fees poured in and all ethical boundaries were blurred beyond recognition. It had been Pratt who'd fought weekly with his partner, but who, over time, had come to enjoy the fruits of their enormous success.

And it had been Carl Pratt who'd come so close to a federal prosecution himself, just before Joel Backman heroically took the fall for everyone. Backman's plea agreement, and the agreement that exculpated the firm's other partners, required a fine of $10 million, thus leading directly to the first bankruptcy—Backman I.

But bankruptcy was better than jail, Pratt reminded himself almost daily. He lumbered around his sparse office early that morning, mumbling to himself and trying desperately to believe that the news was simply not true. He stood at his small window and gazed at the gray brick building next door, and asked himself how it could happen. How could a broke, disbarred, disgraced

29

former lawyer/lobbyist convince a lame-duck president to grant a last-minute pardon?

By the time Joel Backman went to prison, he was probably the most famous white-collar criminal in America. Everybody wanted to see him hang from the gallows.

But, Pratt conceded to himself, if anyone in the world could pull off such a miracle, it was Joel Backman.

Pratt worked the phones for a few minutes, tapping into his extensive network of Washington gossipmongers and know-it-alls. An old friend who'd somehow managed to survive in the Executive Department under four presidents—two from each party—finally confirmed the truth.

'Where is he?' Pratt asked urgently, as if Backman might resurrect himself in D.C. at any moment.

'No one knows,' came the reply.

Pratt locked his door and fought the urge to open the office bottle of vodka. He had been forty-nine years old when his partner was sent to prison for twenty years with no parole, and he often wondered what he would do when he was sixty-nine and Backman got out.

At that moment, Pratt felt as though he'd been cheated out of fourteen years.

*　　　*　　　*

The courtroom had been so crowded that the judge postponed the hearing for two hours until the demand for seating could be organized and somewhat prioritized. Every prominent news organization in the country was screaming for a

30

place to sit or stand. Big shots from Justice, the FBI, the Pentagon, the CIA, the NSA, the White House, and Capitol Hill were pressing for seats, all claiming that their best interests would be served if they could be present to watch the lynching of Joel Backman. When the defendant finally appeared in the tense courtroom, the crowd suddenly froze and the only sound was that of the court reporter prepping his steno machine.

Backman was led to the defense table, where his small army of lawyers packed tightly around him as if bullets were expected from the mob in the gallery. Gunfire would not have been a surprise, though the security rivaled that of a presidential visit. In the first row directly behind the defense table sat Carl Pratt and a dozen or so other partners, or soon-to-be-former partners, of Mr. Backman. They had been searched most aggressively, and for good reason. Though they seethed with hatred for the man, they were also pulling for him. If his plea agreement fell through because of a last-second hitch or disagreement, then they would be fair game again, with nasty trials just around the corner.

At least they were sitting on the front row, out with the spectators, and not at the defense table where the crooks were kept. At least they were alive. Eight days earlier, Jacy Hubbard, one of their trophy partners, had been found dead in Arlington National Cemetery, in a contrived suicide that few people believed. Hubbard had been a former senator from Texas who had given up his seat after twenty-four years for the sole, though unannounced, purpose of offering his significant influence to the highest bidder. Of course Joel

31

Backman would never allow such a big fish to escape his net, so he and the rest of Backman, Pratt & Bolling had hired Hubbard for a million bucks a year because good ol' Jacy could get himself into the Oval Office anytime he wanted.

Hubbard's death had worked wonders in helping Joel Backman to see the government's point of view. The logjam that had delayed the plea negotiations was suddenly broken. Not only would Backman accept twenty years, he wanted to do it quickly. He was anxious for protective custody!

The government's lawyer that day was a high-ranking career prosecutor from Justice, and with such a big and prestigious crowd he could not help but grandstand. He simply couldn't use one word when three would suffice; there were too many people out there. He was onstage, a rare moment in a long dull career, when the nation happened to be watching. With a savage blandness he launched into a reading of the indictment, and it was quickly apparent that he possessed almost no talent at theatrics, virtually no flair for drama, though he tried mightily. After eight minutes of stultifying monologue, the judge, peering sleepily over reading glasses, said, 'Would you speed it up, sir, and lower your voice at the same time.'

There were eighteen counts, alleging crimes ranging from espionage to treason. When they were all read, Joel Backman was so thoroughly vilified that he belonged in the same league with Hitler. His lawyer immediately reminded the court, and everyone else present, that nothing in the indictment had been proven, that it was in fact just a recitation of one side of the case, the government's heavily slanted view of things. He

32

explained that his client would be pleading guilty to only four of the eighteen counts—unauthorized possession of military documents. The judge then read the lengthy plea agreement, and for twenty minutes nothing was said. The artists on the front row sketched the scene with a fury, their images bearing almost no likeness to reality.

Hiding on the back row, seated with strangers, was Neal Backman, Joel's oldest son. He was, at that moment, still an associate with Backman, Pratt & Bolling, but that was about to change. He watched the proceedings in a state of shock, unable to believe that his once powerful father was pleading guilty and about to be buried in the federal penal system.

The defendant was eventually herded to the bench, where he looked up as proudly as possible and faced the judge. With lawyers whispering in both ears, he pled guilty to his four counts, then was led back to his seat. He managed to avoid eye contact with everyone.

A sentencing date was set for the following month. As Backman was handcuffed and taken away, it became obvious to those present that he would not be forced to divulge his secrets, that he would indeed be incarcerated for a very long time while his conspiracies faded away. The crowd slowly broke up. The reporters got half the story they wanted. The big men from the agencies left without speaking—some were pleased that secrets had been protected, others were furious that crimes were being hidden. Carl Pratt and the other beleaguered partners headed for the nearest bar.

*   *   *

33

The first reporter called the office just before 9:00 a.m. Pratt had already alerted his secretary that such calls were expected. She was to tell everyone that he was to be busy in court on some lengthy matter and might not be back in the office for months. Soon the phone lines were gridlocked and a seemingly productive day was shot to hell. Every lawyer and other employee dropped everything and whispered of nothing but the Backman news. Several watched the front door, half expecting the ghost to come looking for them.

Behind a locked door and alone, Pratt sipped a Bloody Mary and watched the nonstop news on cable. Thankfully, a busload of Danish tourists had been kidnapped in the Philippines, otherwise Joel Backman would have been the top story. But he was running a close second, as all kinds of experts were brought in, powdered up, and placed in the studio under the lights where they prattled on about the man's legendary sins.

A former Pentagon chief called the pardon 'a potential blow to our national security.' A retired federal judge, looking every day of his ninety-plus years, called it, predictably, 'a miscarriage of justice.' A rookie senator from Vermont admitted he knew little about the Backman scandal but he was nonetheless enthusiastic about being on live cable and said he planned to call for all sorts of investigations. An unnamed White House official said the new President was 'quite disturbed' by the pardon and planned to review it, whatever that meant.

And on and on. Pratt mixed a second Bloody Mary.

Going for the gore, a 'correspondent'—not simply a 'reporter'—dug up a piece on Senator Jacy Hubbard, and Pratt reached for the remote. He turned up the volume when a large photo of Hubbard's face was flashed on the screen. The former senator had been found dead with a bullet in the head the week before Backman pled guilty. What appeared at first to be a suicide was later called suspicious, though no suspect had ever been identified. The pistol was unmarked and probably stolen. Hubbard had been an active hunter but had never used handguns. The powder residue on his right hand was suspicious. An autopsy revealed a stout concentration of alcohol and barbiturates in his system. The alcohol could certainly be predicted but Hubbard had never been known to use drugs. He'd been seen a few hours earlier with an attractive young lady at a Georgetown bar, which was fairly typical.

The prevailing theory was that the lady slipped him enough drugs to knock him out, then handed him over to the professional killers. He was hauled to a remote section of the Arlington National Cemetery and shot once in the head. His body came to rest on the grave of his brother, a decorated Vietnam hero. A nice touch, but those who knew him well claimed he seldom talked about his family and many knew nothing of the dead brother.

The unspoken theory was that Hubbard was killed by the same people who wanted a shot at Joel Backman. And for years afterward Carl Pratt and Kim Bolling paid serious money for professional bodyguards just in case their names were on the same list. Evidently, they were not.

The details of the fateful deal that nailed Backman and killed Hubbard had been handled by those two, and with time Pratt had loosened the security around himself, though he still carried a Ruger with him everywhere.

*   *   *

But Backman was far away, with the distance growing every minute. Oddly enough, he, too, was thinking of Jacy Hubbard and the people who might have killed him. He had plenty of time to think—fourteen hours in a fold-down bunk on a rattling cargo plane did much to deaden the senses, for a normal person anyway. But for a freshly released former convict who'd just walked out of six years in solitary lockdown, the flight was quite stimulating.

Whoever killed Jacy Hubbard would want very much to kill Joel Backman, and as he bumped along at 24,000 feet he pondered some serious questions. Who had lobbied for his pardon? Where did they plan to hide him? Who, exactly, were 'they'?

Pleasant questions, really. Less than twenty-four hours earlier his questions had been: Are they trying to starve me to death? Freeze me? Am I slowly losing my mind in this twelve-by-twelve cell? Or losing it rapidly? Will I ever see my grandchildren? Do I want to?

He liked the new questions better, troubling as they were. At least he would be able to walk down a street somewhere and breathe the air and feel the sun and perhaps stop at a café and sip a strong coffee.

He'd had a client once, a wealthy cocaine importer who'd been snared in a DEA sting. The client had been such a valuable catch that the feds offered him a new life with a new name and a new face if he would squeal on the Colombians. Squeal he did, and after surgery he was reborn on the north side of Chicago, where he ran a small bookshop. Joel had dropped in one day years later and found the client sporting a goatee, smoking a pipe, looking rather cerebral and earthy. He had a new wife and three stepchildren, and the Colombians never had a clue.

It's a big world out there. Hiding is not that difficult.

Joel closed his eyes, grew still, listened to the steady hum of the four engines, and tried to tell himself that wherever he was headed he would not live like a man on the run. He would adapt, he would survive, he would not live in fear.

There was a muted conversation under way two bunks down, two soldiers swapping stories about all the girls they'd had. He thought of Mo the mob snitch who, for the last four years, had occupied the cell next to Joel's, and who, for about twenty-two hours a day, was the only human he could chat with. He couldn't see him, but they could hear each other through a vent. Mo didn't miss his family, his friends, his neighborhood, or food or drink or sunshine. All Mo talked about was sex. He told long, elaborate stories about his escapades. He told jokes, some of the dirtiest Joel had ever heard. He even wrote poems about old lovers and orgies and fantasies.

He wouldn't miss Mo and his imagination.

Unwillingly, he dozed off again.

Colonel Gantner was shaking him, whispering loudly, 'Major Herzog, Major Herzog. We need to talk.' Backman squeezed out of his bunk, and followed the colonel along the dark cramped aisle between the bunks and into a small room, somewhere closer to the cockpit. 'Take a seat,' Gantner said. They huddled over a small metal table.

Gantner was holding a file. 'Here's the deal,' he began. 'We land in about an hour. The plan is for you to be sick, so sick that an ambulance from the base hospital will meet the plane at the landing field. The Italian authorities will do their usual quick inspection of the paperwork, and they might actually take a look at you. Probably not. We'll be at a U.S. military base, and soldiers come and go all the time. I have a passport for you. I'll do the talking with the Italians, then you'll be taken by ambulance to the hospital.'

'Italians?'

'Yes. Ever hear of the Aviano Air Base?'

'No.'

'Didn't think so. It's been around in U.S. hands since we ran the Germans off in 1945. It's in the northeast part of Italy, near the Alps.'

'Sounds lovely.'

'It's okay, but it's a base.'

'How long will I be there?'

'That's not my decision. My job is to get you from this airplane to the base hospital. There, someone else takes over. Take a look at this bio for Major Herzog, just in case.'

Joel spent a few minutes reading the fictional history of Major Herzog and memorizing the details on the fake passport.

38

'Remember, you're very ill and sedated,' Gantner said. 'Just pretend you're in a coma.'

'I've been in one for six years.'

'Would you like some coffee?'

'What time is it where we're going?'

Gantner looked at his watch and did a quick calculation. 'We should land around one a.m.'

'I'd love some coffee.'

Gantner gave him a paper cup and a thermos, and disappeared.

After two cups, Joel felt the engines reduce power. He returned to his bunk and tried to close his eyes.

*   *   *

As the C-130 rolled to a stop, an air force ambulance backed itself close to the rear hatch. The troops ambled off, most still half asleep. A stretcher carrying Major Herzog rolled down the gateway and was carefully lifted into the ambulance. The nearest Italian official was sitting inside a U.S. military jeep, watching things halfheartedly and trying to stay warm. The ambulance pulled away, in no particular hurry, and five minutes later Major Herzog was rolled into the small base hospital and tucked away in a tiny room on the second floor where two military policemen guarded his door.

4

Fortunately for Backman, though he had no way of knowing and no reason to care, at the eleventh hour President Morgan also pardoned an aging billionaire who'd escaped prison by fleeing the country. The billionaire, an immigrant from some Slavic state who'd had the option of redoing his name upon his arrival decades earlier, had chosen in his youth the title of Duke Mongo. The Duke had given trainloads of money to Morgan's presidential campaign. When it was revealed that he'd spent his career evading taxes it was also revealed he'd spent several nights in the Lincoln Bedroom, where, over a friendly nightcap, he and the President discussed pending indictments. According to the third person present for the nightcap, a young tart who was currently serving as the Duke's fifth wife, the President promised to throw his weight around over at the IRS and call off the dogs. Didn't happen. The indictment was thirty-eight pages long, and before it rolled off the printer the billionaire, minus wife number five, took up residence in Uruguay where he thumbed his nose north while living in a palace with soon-to-be wife number six.

Now he wanted to come home so he could die with dignity, die as a real patriot, and be buried on his Thoroughbred farm just outside Lexington, Kentucky. Critz cut the deal, and minutes after signing the pardon for Joel Backman, President Morgan granted complete clemency to Duke Mongo.

It took a day for the news to leak—the pardons, for good reason, were not publicized by the White House—and the press went insane. Here was a man who cheated the federal government out of $600 million over a twenty-year period, a crook who deserved to be locked away forever, and he was about to fly home in his mammoth jet and spend his final days in obscene luxury. The Backman story, sensational as it was, now had serious competition from not only the kidnapped Danish tourists but also the country's largest tax cheater.

But it was still a hot item. Most of the major morning papers along the East Coast ran a picture of 'The Broker' somewhere on the front page. Most ran long stories about his scandal, his guilty plea, and now his pardon.

Carl Pratt read them all online, in a huge messy office he kept above his garage in northwest Washington. He used the place to hide, to stay away from the wars that raged within his firm, to avoid the partners he couldn't stand. He could drink there and no one would care. He could throw things, and curse at the walls, and do whatever he damn well pleased because it was his sanctuary.

The Backman file was in a large cardboard storage box, one he kept hidden in a closet. Now it was on a worktable, and Pratt was going through it for the first time in many years. He'd saved everything—news articles, photos, interoffice memos, sensitive notes he'd taken, copies of the indictments, Jacy Hubbard's autopsy report.

What a miserable history.

*   *   *

41

In January of 1996, three young Pakistani computer scientists made an astounding discovery. Working in a hot, cramped flat on the top floor of an apartment building on the outskirts of Karachi, the three linked together a series of Hewlett-Packard computers they'd purchased online with a government grant. Their new 'supercomputer' was then wired to a sophisticated military satellite telephone, one also provided by the government. The entire operation was secret and funded off the books by the military. Their objective was simple: to locate, and then try to access, a new Indian spy satellite hovering three hundred miles above Pakistan. If they successfully tapped into the satellite, then they hoped to monitor its surveillance. A secondary dream was to try to manipulate it.

The stolen intelligence was at first exciting, then proved to be virtually useless. The new Indian 'eyes' were doing much the same thing the old ones had been doing for ten years—taking thousands of photographs of the same military installations. Pakistani satellites had been sending back photos of Indian army bases and troop movements for the same ten years. The two countries could swap pictures and learn nothing.

But another satellite was accidentally discovered, then another and another. They were neither Pakistani nor Indian, and they were not supposed to be where they were found—each about three hundred miles above the earth, moving north-northeast at a constant speed of 120 miles per hour, and each maintaining a distance of four hundred miles from the other. Over ten days, the terribly excited hackers monitored the movements of at least six different satellites, all apparently part of the same system, as they slowly approached from the Arabian Peninsula, swept through the skies over Afghanistan and Pakistan, then headed off for western China.

They told no one, but instead managed to procure a more powerful satellite telephone from the military, claiming it was needed to follow up some unfinished work with the Indian surveillance. After a month of methodical, twenty-four-hour monitoring, they had pieced together a global web of nine identical satellites, all linked to each other, and all carefully designed to be invisible to everyone except the men who launched them.

They code-named their discovery Neptune.

The three young wizards had been educated in the United States. The leader was Safi Mirza, a former Stanford graduate assistant who'd worked briefly at Breedin Corp, a renegade U.S. defense contractor that specialized in satellite systems. Fazal Sharif had an advanced degree in computer science from Georgia Tech.

The third and youngest member of the Neptune gang was Farooq Khan, and it was Farooq who finally wrote the software that penetrated the first Neptune satellite. Once inside its computer system, Farooq began downloading intelligence so sensitive that he and Fazal and Safi knew they were entering no-man's-land. There were clear color pictures of terrorist training camps in Afghanistan, and government limousines in Beijing. Neptune could listen as Chinese pilots bantered back and forth at twenty thousand feet, and it could watch a suspicious fishing boat as it docked in Yemen.

43

Neptune followed an armored truck, presumably Castro's, through the streets of Havana. And in a live video feed that shocked the three, Arafat himself was clearly seen stepping into an alley in his compound in Gaza, lighting a cigarette, then urinating.

For two sleepless days, the three peeked inside the satellites as they crossed Pakistan. The software was in English, and with Neptune's preoccupation with the Middle East, Asia, and China, it was easy to assume Neptune belonged to the United States, with Britain and Israel a distant second and third. Perhaps it was a joint U.S.-Israeli secret.

After two days of eavesdropping, they fled the apartment and reorganized their little cell in a friend's farmhouse ten miles outside of Karachi. The discovery was exciting enough, but they, and Safi in particular, wanted to go one step further. He was quite confident he could manipulate the system.

His first success was watching Fazal Sharif read a newspaper. To protect the identity of their location, Fazal took a bus into downtown Karachi, and wearing a green cap and sunglasses, he bought a newspaper and sat on a park bench near a certain intersection. With Farooq feeding commands through a ramped-up sat-phone, a Neptune satellite found Fazal, zoomed down close enough to pick off the headlines of his newspaper, and relayed it all back to the farmhouse where it was watched in muted disbelief.

The electro-optical imaging relays to Earth were of the highest resolution known to technology at that time, down to about four feet—equal to the sharpest images produced by U.S. military reconnaissance satellites and about twice as sharp as the best European and American commercial satellites.

For weeks and months, the three worked nonstop writing home-brewed software for their discovery. They discarded much of what they wrote, but as they fine-tuned the successful programs they became even more amazed at Neptune's possibilities.

Eighteen months after they first discovered Neptune, the three had, on four Jaz 2-gigabyte disks, a software program that not only increased the speed at which Neptune communicated with its numerous contacts on Earth but also allowed Neptune to jam many of the navigation, communications, and reconnaissance satellites already in orbit. For lack of a better code name, they called their program JAM.

Though the system they called Neptune belonged to someone else, the three conspirators were able to control it, to thoroughly manipulate it, and even to render it useless. A bitter fight erupted. Safi and Fazal got greedy and wanted to sell JAM to the highest bidder. Farooq saw nothing but trouble with their creation. He wanted to give it to the Pakistani military and wash his hands of the entire matter.

In September of 1998, Safi and Fazal traveled to Washington and spent a frustrating month trying to penetrate military intelligence through Pakistani contacts. Then a friend told them about Joel Backman, the man who could open any door in Washington.

But getting in his door was a challenge. The broker was a very important man with important clients and lots of significant people demanding small segments of his time. His flat fee for a one-hour consultation with a new client was $5,000 and that was for those lucky enough to be looked upon with favor by the great man. Safi borrowed $2,000 from an uncle in Chicago and promised to pay Mr. Backman the rest in ninety days. Documents in court later revealed that their first meeting took place on October 24, 1998, in the offices of Backman, Pratt & Bolling. The meeting would eventually destroy the lives of everyone present.

Backman at first had seemed skeptical of JAM and its incredible capabilities. Or perhaps he'd grasped its potential immediately and chosen to play it sly with his new clients. Safi and Fazal dreamed of selling JAM to the Pentagon for a fortune, whatever Mr. Backman thought their product might fetch. And if anyone in Washington could get a fortune for JAM, it was Joel Backman.

Early on, he had called in Jacy Hubbard, his million-dollar mouthpiece who still played golf once a week with the President and went barhopping with big shots on Capitol Hill. He was colorful, flamboyant, combative, thrice-divorced, and quite fond of expensive whiskeys—especially when purchased by lobbyists. He had survived politically only because he was known as the dirtiest campaigner in the history of the U.S. Senate, no small feat. He was known to be anti-Semitic, and during the course of his career he developed close ties with the Saudis. Very close. One of many ethics investigations revealed a $1 million campaign contribution from a prince, the same one Hubbard went skiing with in Austria.

Initially, Hubbard and Backman argued over

46

the best way to market JAM. Hubbard wanted to peddle it to the Saudis, who, he was convinced, would pay $1 billion for it. Backman had taken the rather provincial view that such a dangerous product should be kept at home. Hubbard was convinced he could cut a deal with the Saudis in which they would promise that JAM would never be used against the United States, their ostensible ally. Backman was afraid of the Israelis—their powerful friends in the United States, their military, and, most important, their secret spy services.

At that time Backman, Pratt & Bolling represented many foreign companies and governments. In fact, the firm was 'the' address for anyone looking for instant clout in Washington. Pay their frightening fees, and you had yourself access. Its endless list of clients included the Japanese steel industry, the South Korean government, the Saudis, most of the Caribbean banking conspiracy, the current regime in Panama, a Bolivian farming cooperative that grew nothing but cocaine, and on and on. There were many legitimate clients, and many that were not so clean.

The rumor about JAM slowly leaked around their offices. It could potentially be the largest fee the firm had yet seen, and there had been some startling ones. As weeks passed, other partners in the firm presented varying scenarios for the marketing of JAM. The notion of patriotism was slowly forgotten—there was simply too much money out there! The firm represented a Dutch company that built avionics for the Chinese air force, and with that entrée a lucrative deal could be struck with the Beijing government. The South

Koreans would rest easier if they knew exactly what was happening to the north. The Syrians would hand over their national treasury for the ability to neutralize Israeli military communications. A certain drug cartel would pay billions for the ability to track DEA interdiction efforts.

Each day Joel Backman and his band of greedy lawyers grew richer. In the firm's largest offices, they talked of little else.

*   *   *

The doctor was rather brusque and appeared to have little time for his new patient. It was, after all, a military hospital. With scarcely a word he checked the pulse, heart, lungs, blood pressure, reflexes, and so on, then from out of the blue announced, 'I think you're dehydrated.'

'How's that?' Backman asked.

'Happens a lot with long flights. We'll start a drip. You'll be okay in twenty-four hours.'

'You mean, like an IV?'

'That's it.'

'I don't do IVs.'

'Beg your pardon.'

'I didn't stutter. I don't do needles.'

'We took a sample of your blood.'

'Yeah, that was blood going out, not something coming in. Forget it, Doc, I'm not doing an IV.'

'But you're dehydrated.'

'I don't feel dehydrated.'

'I'm the doctor, and I say you're dehydrated.'

'Then give me a glass of water.'

Half an hour later, a nurse entered with a big smile and a handful of medications. Joel said no to the sleeping pills, and when she sort of waved a hypodermic he said, 'What's that?'

'Ryax.'

'What the hell is Ryax?'

'It's a muscle relaxer.'

'Well, it just so happens that my muscles are very relaxed right now. I haven't complained of unrelaxed muscles. I haven't been diagnosed with unrelaxed muscles. No one has asked me if my muscles are relaxed. So you can take that Ryax and stick it up your own ass and we'll both be relaxed and happier.'

She almost dropped the needle. After a long painful pause in which she was completely speechless, she managed to utter, 'I'll check with the doctor.'

'You do that. On second thought, why don't you poke him in his rather fat ass. He's the one who needs to relax.' But she was already out of the room.

On the other side of the base, a Sergeant McAuliffe pecked on his keyboard and sent a message to the Pentagon. From there it was sent almost immediately to Langley where it was read by Julia Javier, a veteran who'd been selected by Director Maynard himself to handle the Backman matter. Less than ten minutes after the Ryax incident, Ms. Javier stared at her monitor, mumbled the word 'Dammit,' then walked upstairs.

As usual, Teddy Maynard was sitting at the end of a long table, wrapped in a quilt, reading one of the countless summaries that got piled on his desk every hour.

Ms. Javier said, 'Just heard from Aviano. Our boy is refusing all medications. Won't take an IV.

49

Won't take a pill.'

'Can't they put something in his food?' Teddy said at low volume.

'He's not eating.'

'What's he saying?'

'That his stomach is upset.'

'Is that possible?'

'He's not spending time on the toilet. Hard to say.'

'Is he taking liquids?'

'They took him a glass of water, which he refused. Insisted on bottled water only. When he got one, he inspected the cap to make sure the seal had not been broken.'

Teddy shoved the current report away and rubbed his eyes with his knuckles. The first plan had been to sedate Backman in the hospital, with either an IV or a regular injection, knock him out cold, keep him drugged for two days, then slowly bring him back with some delightful blends of their most up-to-date narcotics. After a few days in a haze, they would start the sodium pentothal treatment, the truth serum, which, when used with their veteran interrogators, always produced whatever they were after.

The first plan was easy and foolproof. The second one would take months and success was far from guaranteed.

'He's got big secrets, doesn't he?' Teddy said.

'No doubt.'

'But we knew that, didn't we?'

'Yes, we did.'

5

Two of Joel Backman's three children had already abandoned him when the scandal broke. Neal, the oldest, had written his father at least twice a month, though in the early days of the sentence the letters had been quite difficult to write.

Neal had been a twenty-five-year-old rookie associate at the Backman firm when his father went to prison. Though he knew little about JAM and Neptune, he was nonetheless harassed by the FBI and eventually indicted by federal prosecutors.

Joel's abrupt decision to plead guilty was aided mightily by what happened to Jacy Hubbard, but it was also pushed along by the mistreatment of his son by the authorities. All charges against Neal were dropped in the deal. When his father left for twenty years, Neal was immediately terminated by Carl Pratt and escorted from the firm's offices by armed security. The Backman name was a curse, and employment was impossible around Washington. A pal from law school had an uncle who was a retired judge, and after calls here and there Neal landed in the small town of Culpeper, Virginia, working in a five-man firm and thankful for the opportunity.

He craved the anonymity. He thought about changing his name. He refused to discuss his father. He did title work, wrote wills and deeds, and settled nicely into the routine of small-town living. He eventually met and married a local girl and they quickly produced a daughter, Joel's second grandchild, and the only one he had a

51

photo of.

Neal read about his father's release in the *Post*. He discussed it at length with his wife, and briefly with the partners of his firm. The story might be causing earthquakes in D.C., but the tremors had not reached Culpeper. No one seemed to know or care. He wasn't the broker's son; he was simply Neal Backman, one of many lawyers in a small Southern town.

A judge pulled him aside after a hearing and said, 'Where are they hiding your old man?'

To which Neal replied respectfully, 'Not one of my favorite subjects, Your Honor.' And that was the end of the conversation.

On the surface, nothing changed in Culpeper. Neal went about his business as if the pardon had been granted to a man he didn't know. He waited on a phone call; somewhere down the road his father would eventually check in.

*　　　*　　　*

After repeated demands, the supervising nurse passed the hat and collected almost three bucks in change. This was delivered to the patient they still called Major Herzog, an increasingly cranky sort whose condition was no doubt worsening because of hunger. Major Herzog took the money and proceeded directly to the vending machines he'd found on the second floor, and there he bought three small bags of Fritos corn chips and two Dr Peppers. All were consumed within minutes, and an hour later he was on the toilet with raging diarrhea.

But at least he wasn't quite as hungry, nor was

he drugged and saying things he shouldn't say.

Though technically a free man, fully pardoned and all that, he was still confined to a facility owned by the U.S. government, and still living in a room not much larger than his cell at Rudley. The food there had been dreadful, but at least he could eat it without fear of being sedated. Now he was living on corn chips and sodas. The nurses were only slightly friendlier than the guards who tormented him. The doctors just wanted to dope him, following orders from above, he was certain. Somewhere close by was a little torture chamber where they were waiting to pounce on him after the drugs had worked their miracles.

He longed for the outside, for fresh air and sunshine, for plenty of food, for a little human contact with someone not wearing a uniform. And after two very long days he got it.

A stone-faced young man named Stennett appeared in his room on the third day and began pleasantly by saying, 'Okay, Backman, here's the deal. My name's Stennett.'

He tossed a file on the blankets, on Joel's legs, next to some old magazines that were being read for the third time. Joel opened the file. 'Marco Lazzeri?'

'That's you, pal, a full-blown Italian now. That's your birth certificate and national ID card. Memorize all the info as soon as possible.'

'Memorize it? I can't even read it.'

'Then learn. We're leaving in about three hours. You'll be taken to a nearby city where you'll meet your new best friend who'll hold your hand for a few days.'

'A few days?'

'Maybe a month, depends on how well you make the transition.'

Joel laid down the file and stared at Stennett. 'Who do you work for?'

'If I told you, then I'd have to kill you.'

'Very funny. The CIA?'

'The USA, that's all I can say, and that's all you need to know.'

Joel looked at the metal-framed window, complete with a lock, and said, 'I didn't notice a passport in the file.'

'Yes, well, that's because you're not going anywhere, Marco. You're about to live a very quiet life. Your neighbors will think you were born in Milan but raised in Canada, thus the bad Italian you're about to learn. If you get the urge to travel, then things could get very dangerous for you.'

'Dangerous?'

'Come on, Marco. Don't play games with me. There are some really nasty people in this world who'd love to find you. Do what we tell you, and they won't.'

'I don't know a word of Italian.'

'Sure you do—pizza, spaghetti, caffè latte, bravo, opera, mamma mia. You'll catch on. The quicker you learn and the better you learn, the safer you'll be. You'll have a tutor.'

'I don't have a dime.'

'That's what they say. None that they could find, anyway.' He pulled some bills out of his pocket and laid them on the file. 'While you were tucked away, Italy abandoned the lira and adopted the euro. There's a hundred of them. One euro is about a dollar. I'll be back in an hour with some clothes. In the file is a small dictionary, two hundred of your first words in Italian. I suggest you get busy.'

An hour later Stennett was back with a shirt, slacks, jacket, shoes, and socks, all of the Italian variety. 'Buon giorno,' he said.

'Hello to you,' Backman said.

'What's the word for car?'

'Macchina.'

'Good, Marco. It's time to get in the macchina.'

Another silent gentleman was behind the wheel of the compact, nondescript Fiat. Joel folded himself into the backseat with a canvas bag that held his net worth. Stennett sat in the front. The air was cold and damp and a thin layer of snow barely covered the ground. When they passed through the gates of the Aviano Air Base, Joel Backman had the first twinge of freedom, though the slight wave of excitement was heavily layered with apprehension.

He watched the road signs carefully; not a word from the front seat. They were on Route 251, a two-lane highway, headed south, he thought. The traffic soon grew heavy as they approached the city of Pordenone.

'What's the population of Pordenone?' Joel asked, breaking the thick silence.

'Fifty thousand,' Stennett said.

'This is northern Italy, right?'

'Northeast.'

'How far away are the Alps?'

Stennett nodded in the general direction of his right and said, 'About forty miles that way. On a clear day, you can see them.'

'Can we stop for a coffee somewhere?' Joel asked.

'No, we, uh, are not authorized to stop.'

So far the driver appeared to be completely deaf.

They skirted around the northern edge of Pordenone and were soon on A28, a four-lane where everyone but the truckers appeared to be very late for work. Small cars whizzed by them while they puttered along at a mere one hundred kilometers per hour. Stennett unfolded an Italian newspaper, *La Repubblica*, and blocked half the windshield with it.

Joel was very content to ride in silence and gaze at the countryside flying by. The rolling plain appeared to be very fertile, though it was late January and the fields were empty. Occasionally, above a terraced hillside, an ancient villa could be seen.

He'd actually rented one once. A dozen or so years earlier, wife number two had threatened to walk out if he didn't take her somewhere for a long vacation. Joel was working eighty hours a week with time to spare for even more work. He preferred to live at the office, and judging by the way things were going at home, life would've certainly been more peaceful there. A divorce, however, would've cost too much money, so Joel announced to everyone that he and his dear wife would spend a month in Tuscany. He acted as though it had all been his idea—'a monthlong wine and culinary adventure through the heart of Chianti!'

They found a fourteenth-century monastery near the medieval village of San Gimignano, complete with housekeepers and cooks, even a chauffeur. But on the fourth day of the adventure,

56

Joel received the alarming news that the Senate Appropriations Committee was considering deleting a provision that would wipe out $2 billion for one of his defense-contractor clients. He flew home on a chartered jet and went to work whipping the Senate back into shape. Wife number two stayed behind, where, as he would later learn, she began sleeping with the young chauffeur. For the next week he called daily and promised to return to the villa to finish their vacation, but after the second week she stopped taking his calls.

The appropriations bill was put back together in fine fashion.

A month later she filed for divorce, a raucous contest that would eventually cost him over three million bucks.

And she was his favorite of the three. They were all gone now, all scattered forever. The first, the mother of two of his children, had remarried twice since Joel, and her current husband had gotten rich selling liquid fertilizer in third world countries. She had actually written him in prison, a cruel little note in which she praised the judicial system for finally dealing with one of its biggest crooks.

He couldn't blame her. She packed up after catching him with a secretary, the bimbo that became wife number two.

Wife number three had jumped ship soon after his indictment.

What a sloppy life. Fifty-two years, and what's to show for a career of bilking clients, chasing secretaries around the office, putting the squeeze on slimy little politicians, working seven days a week, ignoring three surprisingly stable children, crafting the public image, building the boundless ego, pursuing money money money? What are the rewards for the reckless pursuit of the great American dream?

Six years in prison. And now a fake name because the old one is so dangerous. And about a hundred dollars in his pocket.

Marco? How could he look himself in the mirror every morning and say, 'Buon giorno, Marco'?

Sure beat the hell out of 'Good morning, Mr. Felon.'

Stennett didn't as much read the newspaper as he wrestled with it. Under his perusal, it jerked and popped and wrinkled, and at times the driver glanced over in frustration.

A sign said Venice was sixty kilometers to the south, and Joel decided to break the monotony. 'I'd like to live in Venice, if that's all right with the White House.'

The driver flinched and Stennett's newspaper dropped six inches. The air in the small car was tense for a moment until Stennett managed a grunt and a shrug. 'Sorry,' he said.

'I really need to pee,' Joel said. 'Can you get authorization to stop for a potty break?'

They stopped north of the town of Conegliano, at a modern roadside servizio. Stennett bought a round of corporate espressos. Joel took his to the front window where he watched the traffic speed by while he listened to a young couple snipe at each other in Italian. He heard none of the two hundred words he'd tried to memorize. It seemed an impossible task.

Stennett appeared by his side and watched the

traffic. 'Have you spent much time in Italy?' he asked.

'A month once, in Tuscany.'

'Really? A whole month? Must've been nice.'

'Four days actually, but my wife stayed for a month. She met some friends. How about you? Is this one of your hangouts?'

'I move around.' His face was as vague as his answer. He sipped from the tiny cup and said, 'Conegliano, known for its Prosecco.'

'The Italian answer to champagne,' Joel said.

'Yes. You're a drinking man?'

'Haven't touched a drop in six years.'

'They didn't serve it in prison?'

'Nope.'

'And now?'

'I'll ease back into it. It was a bad habit once.'

'We'd better go.'

'How much longer?'

'Not far.'

Stennett headed for the door, but Joel stopped him. 'Hey, look, I'm really hungry. Could I get a sandwich for the road?'

Stennett looked at rack of ready-made panini. 'Sure.'

'How about two?'

'No problem.'

A27 led south to Treviso, and when it became apparent they would not bypass the city, Joel began to assume the ride was about to end. The driver slowed, made two exits, and they were soon bouncing through the narrow streets of the city.

'What's the population of Treviso?' Joel asked.

'Eighty-five thousand,' Stennett answered.

'What do you know about the city?'

'It's a prosperous little city that hasn't changed much in five hundred years. It was once a staunch ally of Venice back when these towns all fought with each other. We bombed the hell out of it in World War Two. A nice place, not too many tourists.'

A good place to hide, Joel thought. 'Is this my stop?'

'Could be.'

A tall clock tower beckoned all the traffic into the center of the city where it inched along around the Piazza dei Signori. Scooters and mopeds zipped between cars, their drivers seemingly fearless. Joel soaked in the quaint little shops—the tabaccheria with racks of newspapers blocking the door, the farmacia with its neon green cross, the butcher with all manner of hams hanging in the window, and of course the tiny sidewalk cafés where all tables were taken with people who appeared content to sit and read and gossip and sip espresso for hours. It was almost 11:00 a.m. What could those people possibly do for a living if they broke for coffee an hour before lunch?

It would be his challenge to find out, he decided.

The nameless driver wheeled into a temporary parking place. Stennett pecked numbers on a cell phone, waited, then spoke quickly in Italian. When he was finished, he pointed through the windshield and said, 'You see that café over there, under the red-and-white awning? Caffè Donati?'

Joel strained from the backseat and said, 'Yeah, I got it.'

'Walk in the front door, past the bar on your right, on to the back where there are eight tables.

60

Have a seat, order a coffee, and wait.'

'Wait for what?'

'A man will approach you after about ten minutes. You will do what he says.'

'And if I don't?'

'Don't play games, Mr. Backman. We'll be watching.'

'Who is this man?'

'Your new best friend. Follow him, and you'll probably survive. Try something stupid, and you won't last a month.' Stennett said this with a certain smugness, as if he might enjoy being the one who rubbed out poor Marco.

'So it's adios for us, huh?' Joel said, gathering his bag.

'Arrivederci, Marco, not adios. You have your paperwork?'

'Yes.'

'Then arrivederci.'

Joel slowly got out of the car and began walking away. He fought the urge to glance over his shoulder to make sure Stennett, his protector, was paying attention and still back there, shielding him from the unknown. But he did not turn around. Instead, he tried to look as normal as possible as he strolled down the street carrying a canvas bag, the only canvas bag he saw at that moment in the center of Treviso.

Stennett was watching, of course. And who else? Certainly his new best friend was over there somewhere, partially hiding behind a newspaper, giving signals to Stennett and the rest of the static. Joel stopped for a second in front of the tabaccheria and scanned the headlines of the Italian newspapers, though he understood not a single word. He stopped because he could stop, because he was a free man with the power and the right to stop wherever he wanted, and to start moving whenever he chose to.

He entered Caffè Donati and was greeted with a soft 'Buon giorno' from the young man wiping off the bar.

'Buon giorno,' Joel managed in reply, his first real words to a real Italian. To prevent further conversation, he kept walking, past the bar, past a circular stairway where a sign pointed to a café upstairs, past a large counter filled with beautiful pastries. The back room was dark and cramped and choking under a fog of cigarette smoke. He sat down at one of two empty tables and ignored the glances of the other patrons. He was terrified of the waiter, terrified of trying to order, terrified of being unmasked so early in his flight, and so he just sat with his head down and read his new identity papers.

'Buon giorno,' the young lady said at his left shoulder.

'Buon giorno,' Joel managed to reply. And before she could rattle off anything on the menu, he said, 'Espresso.' She smiled, said something thoroughly incomprehensible, to which he replied, 'No.'

It worked, she left, and for Joel it was a major victory. No one stared at him as if he was some ignorant foreigner. When she brought the espresso he said, 'Grazie,' very softly, and she actually smiled at him. He sipped it slowly, not knowing how long it would have to last, not wanting to finish it so he might be forced to order something else.

Italian whirled around him, the soft incessant

chatter of friends gossiping at a rapid-fire pace. Did English sound this fast? Probably so. The idea of learning the language well enough to be able to understand what was being said around him seemed thoroughly impossible. He looked at his paltry little list of two hundred words, then for a few minutes tried desperately to hear a single one of them spoken.

The waitress happened by and asked a question. He gave his standard reply of 'No,' and again it worked.

So Joel Backman was having an espresso in a small bar on Via Verde, at the Piazza dei Signori, in the center of Treviso, in the Veneto, in northeast Italy, while back at Rudley Federal Correctional Facility his old pals were still locked down in protective isolation with lousy food and watery coffee and sadistic guards and silly rules and years to go before they could even dream of life on the outside.

Contrary to previous plans, Joel Backman would not die behind bars at Rudley. He would not wither away in mind and body and spirit. He had cheated his tormentors out of fourteen years, and now he sat unshackled in a quaint café an hour from Venice.

Why was he thinking of prison? Because you can't just walk away from six years of anything without the aftershocks. You carry some of the past with you, regardless of how unpleasant it was. The horror of prison made his sudden release so sweet. It would take time, and he promised himself to focus on the present. Don't even think about the future.

Listen to the sounds, the rapid chatter of

friends, the laughter, the guy over there whispering into a cell phone, the pretty waitress calling into the kitchen. Take in the smells—the cigarette smoke, the rich coffee, the fresh pastries, the warmth of an ancient little room where locals had been meeting for centuries.

And he asked himself for the hundredth time, Why, exactly, was he here? Why had he been whisked away from prison, then out of the country? A pardon is one thing, but why a full-blown international getaway? Why not hand him his walking papers, let him say so long to dear ol' Rudley and live his life, same as all the other freshly pardoned criminals?

He had a hunch. He could venture a fairly accurate guess.

And it terrified him.

Luigi appeared from nowhere.

6

Luigi was in his early thirties, with dark sad eyes and dark hair half covering his ears, and at least four days' worth of stubble on his face. He was bundled in some type of heavy barn jacket that, along with the unshaven face, gave him a handsome peasant look. He ordered an espresso and smiled a lot. Joel immediately noticed that his hands and nails were clean, his teeth were straight. The barn jacket and whiskers were part of the act. Luigi had probably gone to Harvard.

His perfect English was accented just enough to convince anyone that he was really an Italian. He

64

said he was from Milan. His Italian father was a diplomat who took his American wife and their two children around the world in service to his country. Joel was assuming Luigi knew plenty about him, so he prodded to learn what he could about his new handler.

He didn't learn much. Marriage—none. College—Bologna. Studies in the United States—yes, somewhere in the Midwest. Job—government. Which government—couldn't say. He had an easy smile that he used to deflect questions he didn't want to answer. Joel was dealing with a professional, and he knew it.

'I take it you know a thing or two about me,' Joel said.

The smile, the perfect teeth. The sad eyes almost closed when he smiled. The ladies were all over this guy. 'I've seen the file.'

'The file? The file on me wouldn't fit in this room.'

'I've seen the file.'

'Okay, how long did Jacy Hubbard serve in the U.S. Senate?'

'Too long, I'd say. Look, Marco, we're not going to relive the past. We have too much to do now.'

'Can I have another name? I'm not crazy about Marco.'

'It wasn't my choice.'

'Well, who picked Marco?'

'I don't know. It wasn't me. You ask a lot of useless questions.'

'I was a lawyer for twenty-five years. It's an old habit.'

Luigi drained what was left of his espresso and

placed some euros on the table. 'Let's go for a walk,' he said, standing. Joel lifted his canvas bag and followed his handler out of the café, onto the sidewalk, and down a side street with less traffic. They had walked only a few steps when Luigi stopped in front of the Albergo Campeol. 'This is your first stop,' he said.

'What is it?' Joel asked. It was a four-story stucco building wedged between two others. Colorful flags hung above the portico.

'A nice little hotel. "Albergo" means hotel. You can also use the word 'hotel' if you want, but in the smaller cities they like to say albergo.'

'So it's an easy language.' Joel was looking up and down the cramped street—evidently his new neighborhood.

'Easier than English.'

'We'll see. How many do you speak?'

'Five or six.'

They entered and walked through the small foyer. Luigi nodded knowingly at the clerk behind the front desk. Joel managed a passable 'Buon giorno' but kept walking, hoping to avoid a more involved reply. They climbed three flights of stairs and walked to the end of a narrow hallway. Luigi had the key to room 30, a simple but nicely appointed suite with windows on three sides and a view of a canal below.

'This is the nicest one,' Luigi said. 'Nothing fancy, but adequate.'

'You should've seen my last room.' Joel tossed his bag on the bed and began opening curtains.

Luigi opened the door to the very small closet. 'Look here. You have four shirts, four slacks, two jackets, two pairs of shoes, all in your size. Plus a

66

heavy wool overcoat—it gets quite cold here in Treviso.' Joel stared at his new wardrobe. The clothes were hanging perfectly, all pressed and ready to wear. The colors were subdued, tasteful, and every shirt could be worn with every jacket and pair of slacks. He finally shrugged and said, 'Thanks.'

'In the drawer over there you'll find a belt, socks, underwear, everything you'll need. In the bathroom you'll find all the necessary toiletries.'

'What can I say?'

'And here on the desk are two sets of glasses.' Luigi picked up a pair of glasses and held them to the light. The small rectangular lenses were secured by thin black metal, very European frames. 'Armani,' Luigi said, with a trace of pride.

'Reading glasses?'

'Yes, and no. I suggest you wear them every moment you're outside this room. Part of the disguise, Marco. Part of the new you.'

'You should've met the old one.'

'No thanks. Appearance is very important to Italians, especially those of us from here in the north. Your attire, your glasses, your haircut, everything must be put together properly or you will get noticed.'

Joel was suddenly self-conscious, but, then, what the hell. He'd been wearing prison garb for longer than he cared to remember. Back in the glory days he routinely dropped $3,000 for a finely tailored suit.

Luigi was still lecturing. 'No shorts, no black socks and white sneakers, no polyester slacks, no golf shirts, and please don't start getting fat.'

'How do you say 'Kiss my ass' in Italian?'

'We'll get to that later. Habits and customs are important. They're easy to learn and quite enjoyable. For example, never order cappuccino after ten-thirty in the morning. But an espresso can be ordered at any hour of the day. Did you know that?'

'I did not.'

'Only tourists order cappuccino after lunch or dinner. A disgrace. All that milk on a full stomach.' For a moment Luigi frowned as if he might just vomit for good measure.

Joel raised his right hand and said, 'I swear I'll never do it.'

'Have a seat,' Luigi said, waving at the small desk and its two chairs. They sat down and tried to get comfortable. He continued: 'First, the room. It's in my name, but the staff thinks that a Canadian businessman will be staying here for a couple of weeks.'

'A couple of weeks?'

'Yes, then you'll move to another location.' Luigi said this as ominously as possible, as if squads of assassins were already in Treviso, looking for Joel Backman. 'From this moment on, you will be leaving a trail. Keep that in mind: everything you do, everyone you meet—they're all part of your trail. The secret of survival is to leave behind as few tracks as possible. Speak to very few people, including the clerk at the front desk and the housekeeper. Hotel personnel watch their guests, and they have good memories. Six months from now someone might come to this very hotel and start asking questions about you. He might have a photograph. He might offer bribes. And the clerk might suddenly remember you, and the fact that you spoke almost no Italian.'

'I have a question.'

'I have very few answers.'

'Why here? Why a country where I cannot speak the language? Why not England or Australia, someplace where I could blend in easier?'

'That decision was made by someone else, Marco. Not me.'

'That's what I figured.'

'Then why did you ask?'

'I don't know. Can I apply for a transfer?'

'Another useless question.'

'A bad joke, not a bad question.'

'Can we continue?'

'Yes.'

'For the first few days I will take you to lunch and dinner. We'll move around, always going to different places. Treviso is a nice city with lots of cafés and we'll try them all. You must start thinking of the day when I will not be here. Be careful who you meet.'

'I have another question.'

'Yes, Marco.'

'It's about money. I really don't like being broke. Are you guys planning to give me an allowance or something? I'll wash your car and do other chores.'

'What is allowance?'

'Cash, okay? Money in my pocket.'

'Don't worry about money. For now, I take care of the bills. You will not be hungry.'

'All right.'

Luigi reached deep in the barn jacket and pulled out a cell phone. 'This is for you.'

'And who, exactly, am I going to call?'

'Me, if you need something. My number is on the back.'

Joel took the phone and laid it on the desk. 'I'm hungry. I've been dreaming of a long lunch with pasta and wine and dessert, and of course espresso, certainly not cappuccino at this hour, then perhaps the required siesta. I've been in Italy for four days now, and I've had nothing but corn chips and sandwiches. What do you say?'

Luigi glanced at his watch. 'I know just the place, but first some more business. You speak no Italian, right?'

Joel rolled his eyes and exhaled mightily in frustration. Then he tried to smile and said, 'No, I've never had the occasion to learn Italian, or French, or German, or anything else. I'm an American, okay, Luigi? My country is larger than all of Europe combined. All you need is English over there.'

'You're Canadian, remember?'

'Okay, whatever, but we're isolated. Just us and the Americans.'

'My job is to keep you safe.'

'Thank you.'

'And to help us do that, you need to learn a lot of Italian as quickly as possible.'

'I understand.'

'You will have a tutor, a young student by the name of Ermanno. You will study with him in the morning and again in the afternoon. The work will be difficult.'

'For how long?'

'As long as it takes. That depends on you. If you work hard, then in three or four months you should be on your own.'

'How long did it take you to learn English?'

'My mother is American. We spoke English at home, Italian everywhere else.'

'That's cheating. What else do you speak?'

'Spanish, French, a few more. Ermanno is an excellent teacher. The classroom is just down the street.'

'Not here, in the hotel?'

'No, no, Marco. You must think about your trail. What would the bellboy or the housekeeper say if a young man spent four hours a day in this room with you?'

'God forbid.'

'The housekeeper would listen at the door and hear your lessons. She would whisper to her supervisor. Within a day or two the entire staff would know that the Canadian businessman is studying intensely. Four hours a day!'

'Gotcha. Now about lunch.'

Leaving the hotel, Joel managed to smile at the clerk, a janitor, and the bell captain without uttering a word. They walked one block to the center of Treviso, the Piazza dei Signori, the main square lined with arcades and cafés. It was noon and the foot traffic was heavier as the locals hurried about for lunch. The air was getting colder, though Joel was quite comfortable tucked inside his new wool overcoat. He tried his best to look Italian.

'Inside or outside?' Luigi asked.

'Inside,' Joel said, and they ducked into the Caffè Beltrame, overlooking the piazza. A brick oven near the front was heating the place, and the aroma of the daily feast was steaming from the rear. Luigi and the headwaiter both spoke at the

71

same time, then they laughed, then a table was found by a front window.

'We're in luck,' Luigi said as they took off their coats and sat down. 'The special today is faraona con polenta.'

'And what might that be?'

'Guinea fowl with polenta.'

'What else?'

Luigi was studying one of the blackboards hanging from a rough-hewn crossbeam. 'Panzerotti di funghi al burro—fried mushroom pastries. Conchiglie con cavalfiori—pasta shells with cauliflower. Spiedino di carne misto alla griglia—grilled shish kabob of mixed meats.'

'I'll have it all.'

'Their house wine is pretty good.'

'I prefer red.'

Within minutes the café was crowded with locals, all of whom seemed to know each other. A jolly little man with a dirty white apron sped by the table, slowed just long enough to make eye contact with Joel, and wrote down nothing as Luigi spat out a long list of what they wanted to eat. A jug of house wine arrived with a bowl of warm olive oil and a platter of sliced focaccia, and Joel began eating. Luigi was busy explaining the complexities of lunch and breakfast, the customs and traditions and mistakes made by tourists trying to pass themselves off as authentic Italians.

With Luigi, everything would be a learning experience.

Though Joel sipped and savored the first glass of wine, the alcohol went straight to his brain. A wonderful warmth and numbness embraced his body. He was free, many years ahead of schedule, and sitting in a rustic little café in an Italian town he'd never heard of, drinking a nice local wine, and inhaling the smells of a delicious feast. He smiled at Luigi as the explanations continued, but at some point Joel drifted into another world.

*   *   *

Ermanno claimed to be twenty-three years old but looked no more than sixteen. He was tall and painfully thin, and with sandy hair and hazel eyes he looked more German than Italian. He was also very shy and quite nervous, and Joel did not like the first impression.

They met Ermanno at his tiny apartment, on the third floor of an ill-kept building six blocks or so from Joel's hotel. There were three small rooms—kitchen, bedroom, living area—all sparsely furnished, but then Ermanno was a student so such surroundings were not unexpected. But the place looked as though he had just moved in and might be moving out at any minute.

They sat around a small desk in the center of the living room. There was no television. The room was cold and dimly lit, and Joel couldn't help but feel as if he had been placed in some underground highway where fugitives are kept alive and moved about in secret. The warmth of a two-hour lunch was fading quickly.

His tutor's nervousness didn't help matters.

When Ermanno was unable to take control of the meeting, Luigi quickly stepped in and kicked things off. He suggested that they study each morning from 9:00 a.m. to 11:00 a.m., break for two hours, then resume around 1:30 and study until

73

they were tired. This seemed to suit Ermanno and Joel, who thought about asking the obvious: If my new guy here is a student, how does he have the time to teach me all day long? But he let it pass. He'd pursue it later.

Oh, the questions he was accumulating.

Ermanno eventually relaxed and described the language course. When he spoke slowly, his accent was not intrusive. But when he rushed things, as he was prone to do, his English might as well have been Italian. Once Luigi interrupted and said, 'Ermanno, it's important to speak very slowly, at least in the first few days.'

'Thank you,' Joel said, like a true smartass.

Ermanno's cheeks actually reddened and he offered a very timid 'Sorry.'

He handed over the first batch of study aids— course book number one, along with a small tape player and two cassettes. 'The tapes follow the book,' he said, very slowly. 'Tonight, you should study chapter one and listen to each tape several times. Tomorrow we'll begin there.'

'It will be very intense,' Luigi added, applying more pressure, as if more was needed.

'Where did you learn English?' Joel asked.

'At the university,' Ermanno said. 'In Bologna.'

'So you haven't studied in the United States?'

'Yes, I have,' he said, shooting a quick nervous glance at Luigi, as if whatever happened in the States was something he preferred not to talk about. Unlike Luigi, Ermanno was an easy read, obviously not a professional.

'Where?' Joel asked, probing, seeing how much he could get.

'Furman,' Ermanno said. 'A small school in

South Carolina.'

'When were you there?'

Luigi came to the rescue, clearing his throat. 'You will have plenty of time for this small talk later. It is important for you to forget English, Marco. From this day forward, you will live in a world of Italian. Everything you touch has an Italian name for it. Every thought must be translated. In one week you'll be ordering in restaurants. In two weeks you'll be dreaming in Italian. It's total, absolute immersion in the language and culture, and there's no turning back.'

'Can we start at eight in the morning?' Joel asked.

Ermanno glanced and fidgeted, finally said, 'Perhaps eight-thirty.'

'Good, I'll be here at eight-thirty.'

They left the apartment and strolled back to the Piazza dei Signori. It was mid-afternoon, traffic was noticeably quieter, the sidewalks almost deserted. Luigi stopped in front of the Trattoria del Monte. He nodded at the door, said, 'I'll meet you here at eight for dinner, okay?'

'Yes, okay.'

'You know where your hotel is?'

'Yes, the albergo.'

'And you have a map of the city?'

'Yes.'

'Good. You're on your own, Marco.' And with that Luigi ducked into an alley and disappeared. Joel watched him for a second, then continued his walk to the main square.

He felt very much alone. Four days after leaving Rudley, he was finally free and unaccompanied, perhaps unobserved, though he

75

doubted it. He decided immediately that he would move around the city, go about his business, as if no one was watching him. And he further decided, as he pretended to examine the items in the window of a small leather shop, that he would not live the rest of his life glancing over his shoulder.

They wouldn't find him.

He drifted until he found himself at Piazza San Vito, a small square where two churches had been sitting for seven hundred years. The Santa Lucia and San Vito were both closed, but, according to the ancient brass plate, they would reopen from 4:00 p.m. to 6:00 p.m. What kind of place closes from noon to four?

The bars weren't closed, just empty. He finally mustered the courage to sneak into one. He pulled up a stool, held his breath, and said the word 'Birra' when the bartender got close.

The bartender shot something back, waited for a response, and for a split second Joel was tempted to bolt. But he saw the tap, pointed at it as if it was perfectly clear what he wanted, and the bartender reached for an empty mug.

The first beer in six years. It was cool, heavy, tasty, and he savored every drop. A soap opera rattled from a television somewhere at the end of the bar. He listened to it from time to time, understood not a single word, and worked hard to convince himself that he could master the language. As he was making the decision to leave and drift back to his hotel, he looked through the front window.

Stennett walked by.

Joel ordered another beer.

7

The Backman affair had been closely chronicled by Dan Sandberg, a veteran of *The Washington Post*. In 1998, he'd broken the story about certain highly classified papers leaving the Pentagon without authorization. The FBI investigation that soon followed kept him busy for half a year, during which he filed eighteen stories, most of them on the front page. He had reliable contacts at the CIA and the FBI. He knew the partners at Backman, Pratt & Bolling and had spent time in their offices. He hounded the Justice Department for information. He'd been in the courtroom the day Backman hurriedly pled guilty and disappeared.

A year later he'd written one of two books about the scandal. His sold a respectable 24,000 copies in hardback, the other about half of that.

Along the way, Sandberg built some key relationships. One in particular grew into a valuable, if quite unexpected, source. A month before Jacy Hubbard's death, Carl Pratt, then very much under indictment, as were most of the senior partners of the firm, had contacted Sandberg and arranged a meeting. They eventually met more than a dozen times while the scandal ran its course, and in the ensuing years had become drinking buddies. They sneaked away at least twice year to exchange gossip.

Three days after the pardon story first broke, Sandberg called Pratt and arranged a meeting at their favorite place, a college bar near Georgetown University.

Pratt looked awful, as if he'd been drinking for days. He ordered vodka; Sandberg stuck with beer.

'So where's your boy?' Sandberg asked with a grin.

'He's not in prison anymore, that's for sure.' Pratt took a near lethal slug of the vodka and smacked his lips.

'No word from him?'

'None. Not me, not anyone at the firm.'

'Would you be surprised if he called or stopped by?'

'Yes and no. Nothing surprises me with Backman.' More vodka. 'If he never set foot in D.C. again, I wouldn't be surprised. If he showed up tomorrow and announced the opening of a new law firm, I wouldn't be surprised.'

'The pardon surprised you.'

'Yes, but that wasn't Backman's deal, was it?'

'I doubt it.' A coed walked by and Sandberg gave her a look. Twice-divorced, he was always on the prowl. He sipped his beer and said, 'He can't practice law, can he? I thought they yanked his license.'

'That wouldn't stop Backman. He'd call it 'government relations' or 'consulting' or something else. It's lobbying, that's his speciality, and you don't need a license for that. Hell, half the lawyers in this city couldn't find the nearest courthouse. But they can damned sure find Capitol Hill.'

'What about clients?'

'It's not gonna happen. Backman ain't coming back to D.C. Unless you've heard something different?'

'I've heard nothing. He vanished. Nobody at the prison is talking. I can't get a word from the

78

penal folks.'

'What's your theory?' Pratt asked, then drained his glass and seemed poised for more.

'I found out today that Teddy Maynard went to the White House late on the nineteenth. Only someone like Teddy could squeeze it out of Morgan. Backman walked away, probably with an escort, and vanished.'

'Witness protection?'

'Something like that. The CIA has hidden people before. They have to. There's nothing official on the books, but they have the resources.'

'So why hide Backman?'

'Revenge. Remember Aldrich Ames, the biggest mole in CIA history?'

'Sure.'

'Now locked away securely in a federal pen. Don't you know the CIA would love to have a crack at him? They can't do it because it's against the law—they cannot target a U.S. citizen, either here or abroad.'

'Backman wasn't a CIA mole. Hell, he hated Teddy Maynard, and the feeling was very mutual.'

'Maynard won't kill him. He'll just set things up so someone else will have the pleasure.'

Pratt was getting to his feet. 'You want another one of those?' he asked, pointing at the beer.

'Later, maybe.' Sandberg picked up his pint for the second time and took a drink.

When Pratt returned with a double vodka, he sat down and said, 'So you think Backman's days are numbered?'

'You asked my theory. Let me hear yours.'

A reasonable pull on the vodka, then, 'Same result, but from a slightly different angle.' Pratt stuck his finger in the drink, stirred it, then licked his finger, thinking for a few seconds. 'Off the record, okay?'

'Of course.' They had talked so much over the years that everything was off the record.

'There was an eight-day period between Hubbard's death and Backman's plea. It was a very scary time. Both Kim Bolling and I were under FBI protection, around the clock, around the block, everywhere. Quite odd, really. The FBI was doing its best to send us to prison forever and at the same time felt compelled to protect us.' A sip, as he glanced around to see if any of the college students were eavesdropping. They were not. 'There were some threats, some serious movements by the same people who killed Jacy Hubbard. The FBI debriefed us later, months after Backman was gone and things settled down. We felt a bit safer, but Bolling and I paid armed security for two years afterward. I still glance in the rearview mirror. Poor Kim has lost his mind.'

'Who made the threats?'

'The same people who'd love to find Joel Backman.'

'Who?'

'Backman and Hubbard had made a deal to sell their little product to the Saudis for a trainload of money. Very pricey, but far less than the cost of building a brand-new satellite system. The deal fell through. Hubbard gets himself killed. Backman hurries off to jail, and the Saudis are not happy at all. Neither are the Israelis, because they wanted to make a deal too. Plus, they were furious that Hubbard and Backman would deal with the Saudis.' He paused and took a drink, as if he needed the fortitude to finish the story. 'Then you have the folks who built the system in the first place.'

'The Russians?'

'Probably not. Jacy Hubbard loved Asian girls. He was last seen leaving a bar with a gorgeous young leggy thing, long black hair, round face, from somewhere on the other side of the world. Red China uses thousands of people here to gather information. All their U.S. students, businessmen, diplomats, this place is crawling with Chinese who are snooping around. Plus, their intelligence service has some very effective agents. For a matter like this, they wouldn't hesitate to go after Hubbard and Backman.'

'You're sure it's Red China?'

'No one's sure, okay? Maybe Backman knows, but he never told anyone. Keep in mind, the CIA didn't even know about the system. They got caught with their pants down, and ol' Teddy's still trying to catch up.'

'Fun and games for Teddy, huh?'

'Absolutely. He fed Morgan a line about national security. Morgan, no surprise, falls for it. Backman walks. Teddy sneaks him out of the country, then watches to see who shows up with a gun. It's a no-lose game for Teddy.'

'It's brilliant.'

'It's beyond brilliant, Dan. Think about it. When Joel Backman meets his maker, no one will ever know about it. No one knows where he is now. No one will know who he is when his body is found.'

'If it's found.'

'Exactly.'

'And Backman knows this?'

Pratt drained the second drink and wiped his mouth with a sleeve. He was frowning. 'Backman's not stupid by any measure. But a lot of what we know came to light after he went away. He survived six years in prison, he probably figures he can survive anything.'

*   *   *

Critz ducked into a pub not far from the Connaught Hotel in London. A light rain grew steadier and he needed a place to stay dry. Mrs. Critz was back at the small apartment that was on loan from their new employer, so Critz had the luxury of sitting in a crowded pub where no one knew him and knocking back a couple of pints. A week in London now with a week to go before he pushed himself back across the Atlantic, back to D.C. where he would take a miserable job lobbying for a company that made, among other hardware, defective missiles that the Pentagon hated but nonetheless would be forced to buy because the company had all the right lobbyists.

He found an empty booth, one partially visible through a fog of tobacco smoke, and wedged himself into it and settled in behind his pint. How nice it was to drink alone without the worry of being spotted by someone who would rush over and say, 'Hey, Critz, what were you idiots thinking with that Berman veto?' Yakety-yakety-yak.

He absorbed the cheery British voices of neighbors coming and going. He didn't even mind the smoke. He was alone and unknown and he quietly reveled in his privacy.

His anonymity was not complete, however. From behind him a small man wearing a battered sailor's cap appeared and fell into the booth across the table, startling Critz.

'Mind if I join you, Mr. Critz?' the sailor said with a smile that revealed large yellow teeth. Critz would remember the dingy teeth.

'Have a seat,' Critz said warily. 'You got a name?'

'Ben.' He wasn't British, and English was not his native tongue. Ben was about thirty, with dark hair, dark brown eyes, and a long pointed nose that made him rather Greek-looking.

'No last name, huh?' Critz took a sip from his glass and said, 'How, exactly, do you know my name?'

'I know everything about you.'

'Didn't realize I was that famous.'

'I wouldn't call it fame, Mr. Critz. I'll be brief. I work for some people who desperately want to find Joel Backman. They'll pay serious money, cash. Cash in a box, or cash in a Swiss bank, doesn't matter. It can be done quickly, within hours. You tell us where he is, you get a million bucks, no one will ever know.'

'How did you find me?'

'It was simple, Mr. Critz. We're, let's say, professionals.'

'Spies?'

'It's not important. We are who we are, and we're going to find Mr. Backman. The question is, do you want the million bucks?'

'I don't know where he is.'

'But you can find out.'

'Maybe.'

'Do you want to do business?'

'Not for a million bucks.'

'Then how much?'

'I'll have to think about it.'

'Then think quickly.'

'And if I can't get the information?'

'Then we'll never see you again. This meeting never took place. It's very simple.'

Critz took a long pull on his pint and contemplated things. 'Okay, let's say I'm able to get this information—I'm not too optimistic—but what if I get lucky? Then what?'

'Take a Lufthansa flight from Dulles to Amsterdam, first class. Check into the Amstel Hotel on Biddenham Street. We'll find you, just like we found you here.'

Critz paused and committed the details to memory. 'When?' he asked.

'As soon as possible, Mr. Critz. There are others looking for him.'

Ben vanished as quickly as he had materialized, leaving Critz to peer through the smoke and wonder if he'd just witnessed a dream. He left the pub an hour later, with his face hidden under an umbrella, certain that he was being watched.

Would they watch him in Washington too? He had the unsettling feeling that they would.

8

The siesta didn't work. The wine at lunch and the two afternoon beers didn't help. There was simply too much to think about.

Besides, he was too rested; there was too much sleep in his system. Six years in solitary confinement reduces the human body to such a passive state that sleep becomes a principal activity. After the first few months at Rudley, Joel was getting eight hours a night and a hard nap after lunch, which was understandable since he'd slept so little during the previous twenty years when he was holding the republic together during the day and chasing skirts till dawn. After a year he could count on nine, sometimes ten hours of sleep. There was little else to do but read and watch television. Out of boredom, he once conducted a survey, one of his many clandestine polls, by passing a sheet of paper from cell to cell while the guards were themselves napping, and of the thirty-seven respondents on his block the average was eleven hours of sleep a day. Mo, the Mafia snitch, claimed sixteen hours and could often be heard snoring at noon. Mad Cow Miller registered the lowest at just three hours, but the poor guy had lost his mind years earlier and so Joel was forced to discount his responses to the survey.

There were bouts of insomnia, long periods of staring into the darkness and thinking about the mistakes and the children and grandchildren, about the humiliation of the past and the fear of the future. And there were weeks when sleeping pills were delivered to his cell, one at a time, but they never worked. Joel always suspected they were nothing more than placebos.

But in six years there had been too much sleep. Now his body was well rested. His mind was working overtime.

He slowly got up from the bed where he'd been lying for an hour, unable to close his eyes, and walked to the small table where he picked up the cell phone Luigi had given him. He took it to the window, punched the numbers taped to its back, and after four rings he heard a familiar voice.

'Ciao, Marco. Come stai?'

'Just checking to see if this thing works,' Joel said.

'You think I'd give you a defective phone?' Luigi asked.

'No, of course not.'

'How was your nap?'

'Uh, nice, very nice. I'll see you at dinner.'

'Ciao.'

Where was Luigi? Lurking nearby with a phone in his pocket, just waiting for Joel to call? Watching the hotel? If Stennett and the driver were still in Treviso, along with Luigi and Ermanno, that would add up to four 'friends' of some variety assigned to keep tabs on Joel Backman.

He gripped the phone and wondered who else out there knew about the call. Who else was listening? He glanced at the street below and wondered who was down there. Only Luigi?

He dismissed those thoughts and sat at the table. He wanted some coffee, maybe a double espresso to get the nerves buzzing, certainly not a cappuccino because of the late hour, but he wasn't ready to pick up the phone and place an order. He could handle the 'Hello' and the 'Coffee,' but there would be a flood of other words he did not yet know.

How can a man survive without strong coffee? His favorite secretary had once brought forth his first cup of some jolting Turkish brew at exactly six-thirty every morning, six days a week. He'd almost married her. By ten each morning, the broker was so wired he was throwing things and yelling at subordinates and juggling three calls at once while senators were on hold.

The flashback did not please him. They seldom did. There were plenty of them, and for six years in solitary he'd waged a ferocious mental war to purge his past.

Back to the coffee, which he was afraid to order because he was afraid of the language. Joel Backman had never feared a damn thing, and if he could keep track of three hundred pieces of legislation moving through the maze of Congress, and if he could make one hundred phone calls a day while rarely looking at a Rolodex or a directory, then he could certainly learn enough Italian to order coffee. He arranged Ermanno's study materials neatly on the table and looked at the synopsis. He checked the batteries in the small tape player and fiddled with the tapes. The first page of lesson one was a rather crude color drawing of a family living room with Mom and Pop and the kids watching television. The objects were labeled in both English and Italian—door and porta, sofa and sofà, window and finestra, painting and quadro, and so on. The boy was ragazzo, the mother was madre, the old man teetering on a cane in the corner was the grandfather, or il nonno.

A few pages later was the kitchen, then the bedroom, then the bath. After an hour, still without coffee, Joel was walking softly around his room pointing and whispering the name of everything he saw: bed, letto; lamp, lampada; clock, orologio; soap, sapone. There were a few verbs thrown in for caution: •to speak, parlare; to eat, mangiare; to drink, bere; to think, pensare. He stood before the small mirror (specchio) in his bathroom (bagno) and tried to convince himself that he was really Marco. Marco Lazzeri. 'Sono Marco, sono Marco,' he repeated. I am Marco. I am Marco. Silly at first, but that must be put aside. The stakes were too high to cling to an old name that could get him killed. If being Marco would save his neck, then Marco he was.

Marco. Marco. Marco.

He began looking for words that were not in the drawings. In his new dictionary he found carta igienica for toilet paper, guanciale for pillow, soffitto for ceiling. Everything had a new name, every object in his room, in his own little world, everything he could see at that moment became something new. Over and over, as his eyes bounced from one article to another, he uttered the Italian word.

And what about himself? He had a brain, cervello. He touched a hand, mano; an arm, braccio; a leg, gamba. He had to breathe, respirare; see, vedere; touch, toccare; hear, sentire; sleep, dormire; dream, sognare. He was digressing now, and he caught himself. Tomorrow Ermanno would begin with lesson one, the first blast of vocabulary with emphasis on the basics: greetings and salutations, polite talk, numbers one through a hundred, the days of the week, the months of the year, even the alphabet. The verbs to be (essere) and to have (avere) were both conjugated in the present, simple past, and future.

When it was time for dinner, Marco had memorized all of the first lesson and had listened to the tape of it a dozen times. He stepped into the very cool night and walked happily in the general direction of Trattoria del Monte, where he knew Luigi would be waiting with a choice table and some excellent suggestions from the menu. On the street, and still reeling from several hours of rote memorization, he noticed a scooter, a bike, a dog, a set of twin girls, and he was hit hard with the reality that he knew none of those words in his new language.

All of it had been left in his hotel room.

With food waiting, though, he plowed ahead, undaunted and still confident that he, Marco, could become a somewhat respectable Italian. At a table in the corner, he greeted Luigi with a flourish. 'Buona sera, signore, come sta?'

'Sto bene, grazie, e tu?' Luigi said with an approving smile. Fine, thanks, and you?

'Molto bene, grazie,' Marco said. Very well, thank you.

'So you've been studying?' Luigi said.

'Yes, there's nothing else to do.'

Before Marco could unwrap his napkin, a waiter stopped by with a straw-covered flask of the house red. He quickly poured two glasses and then disappeared. 'Ermanno is a very good teacher,' Luigi was saying.

'You've used him before?' Marco asked

casually.

'Yes.'

'So how often do you bring in someone like me and turn him into an Italian?'

Luigi gave a smile and said, 'From time to time.'

'That's hard to believe.'

'Believe what you want, Marco. It's all fiction.'

'You talk like a spy.'

A shrug, no real response.

'Who do you work for, Luigi?'

'Who do you think?'

'You're part of the alphabet—CIA, FBI, NSA. Maybe some obscure branch of military intelligence.'

'Do you enjoy meeting me in these nice little restaurants?' Luigi asked.

'Do I have a choice?'

'Yes. If you keep asking these questions, then we'll stop meeting. And when we stop meeting, your life, shaky as it is, will become even more fragile.'

'I thought your job was to keep me alive.'

'It is. So stop asking questions about me. I assure you there are no answers.'

As if he were on the payroll, the waiter appeared with perfect timing and dropped two large menus between them, effectively changing whatever course the conversation was taking. Marco frowned at the list of dishes and was once again reminded of how far his Italian had to go. At the bottom he recognized the words caffè, vino, and birra.

'What looks good?' he asked.

'The chef is from Siena, so he likes Tuscan

90

dishes. The risotto with porcini mushrooms is great for a first course. I've had the steak florentine, outstanding.'

Marco closed his menu and savored the aroma from the kitchen. 'I'll take both.'

Luigi closed his too and waved at the waiter. After he ordered, they sipped the wine for a few minutes in silence. 'A few years ago,' Luigi began, 'I woke up one morning in a small hotel room in Istanbul. Alone, with about five hundred dollars in my pocket. And a fake passport. I didn't speak a single word of Turkish. My handler was in the city, but if I contacted him then I would be forced to find a new career. In exactly ten months I was supposed to return to the same hotel to meet a friend who would take me out of the country.'

'Sounds like basic CIA training.'

'Wrong part of the alphabet,' he said, then paused, took a sip, and continued. 'Since I enjoy eating, I learned to survive. I absorbed the language, the culture, everything around me. I managed quite nicely, blended in with the surroundings, and ten months later when I met my friend I had more than a thousand dollars.'

'Italian, English, French, Spanish, Turkish—what else?'

'Russian. They dropped me in Stalingrad for a year.'

Marco almost asked who 'they' might be, but he let it pass. There would be no answer; besides, he thought he knew.

'So I've been dropped here?' Marco asked.

The waiter plunked down a basket of mixed breads and a small bowl of olive oil. Luigi began dipping and eating, and the question was either

91

forgotten or ignored. More food followed, a small tray of ham and salami with olives, and the conversation lagged. Luigi was a spy, or a counterspy, or an operative, or an agent of some strain, or simply a handler or a contact, or maybe a stringer, but he was first and foremost an Italian. All the training possible could not divert his attention from the challenge at hand when the table was covered.

As he ate, he changed subjects. He explained the rigors of a proper Italian dinner. First, the anitpasti—usually a plate of mixed meats, such as they had before them. Then the first course, primi, which is usually a reasonably sized serving of pasta, rice, soup, or polenta, the purpose of which is to sort of limber up the stomach in preparation for the main course, the secondi—a hearty dish of meat, fish, pork, chicken, or lamb. Be careful with desserts, he warned ominously, glancing around to make sure the waiter wasn't listening. He shook his head sadly as he explained that many good restaurants now buy them off premises, and they're loaded with so much sugar or cheap liqueur that they practically rot your teeth out.

Marco managed to appear sufficiently shocked at this national scandal.

'Learn the word "gelato,"' he said, his eyes glowing again.

'Ice cream,' Marco said.

'Bravo. The best in the world. There's a gelateria down the street. We'll go there after dinner.'

*   *   *

Room service terminated at midnight. At 11:55, Marco slowly picked up the phone and punched number four twice. He swallowed deeply, then held his breath. He'd been practicing the dialogue for thirty minutes.

After a few lazy rings, during which time he almost hung up twice, a sleepy voice answered and said, 'Buona sera.'

Marco closed his eyes and plunged ahead. 'Buona sera. Vorrei un caffè, per favore. Un espresso doppio.'

'Sì, latte e zucchero?' Milk and sugar?

'No, senza latte e zucchero.'

'Sì, cinque minuti.'

'Grazie.' Marco quickly hung up before risking further dialogue, though given the enthusiasm on the other end he doubted it seriously. He jumped to his feet, pumped a fist in the air, and patted himself on the back for completing his first conversation in Italian. No hitches whatsoever. Both parties understood all of what the other said.

At 1:00 a.m., he was still sipping his double espresso, savoring it even though it was no longer warm. He was in the middle of lesson three, and with sleep not even a distant thought, he was thinking of maybe devouring the entire textbook for his first session with Ermanno.

*   *   *

He knocked on the apartment door ten minutes early. It was a control thing. Though he tried to resist it, he found himself impulsively reverting to his old ways. He preferred to be the one who decided when the lesson would begin. Ten minutes early or twenty minutes late, the time was not important. As he waited in the dingy hallway he flashed back to a high-level meeting he'd once hosted in his enormous conference room. It was packed with corporate executives and honchos from several federal agencies, all summoned there by the broker. Though the conference room was fifty steps down the hall from his own office, he made his entrance twenty minutes late, apologizing and explaining that he'd been on the phone with the office of the prime minister of some minor country.

Petty, petty, petty. The games he played.

Ermanno was seemingly unimpressed. He made his student wait at least five minutes before he opened the door with a timid smile and a friendly 'Buon giorno, Signor Lazzeri.'

'Buon giorno, Ermanno. Come stai?'

'Molto bene, grazie, e tu?'

'Molto bene, grazie.'

Ermanno opened the door wider, and with the sweep of a hand said, 'Prego.' Please come in.

Marco stepped inside and was once again struck by how sparse and temporary everything looked. He placed his books on the small table in the center of the front room and decided to keep his coat on. The temperature was about forty outside and not much warmer in this tiny apartment.

'Vorrebbe un caffè?' Ermanno asked. Would you like a coffee?

'Sì, grazie.' He'd slept about two hours, from four to six, then he'd showered, dressed, and ventured into the streets of Treviso, where he'd found an early bar where the old gentlemen gathered and had their espressos and all talked at once. He wanted more coffee, but what he really needed was a bite to eat. A croissant or a muffin or something of that variety, something he had not yet learned the name of. He decided he could hold off hunger until noon, when he would once again meet Luigi for another foray into Italian cuisine.

'You are a student, right?' he asked when Ermanno returned from the kitchen with two small cups.

'Non inglese, Marco, non inglese.'

And that was the end of English. An abrupt end; a harsh, final farewell to the mother tongue. Ermanno sat on one side of the table, Marco on the other, and at exactly eight-thirty they, together, turned to page one of lesson one. Marco read the first dialogue in Italian, Ermanno gently made corrections, though he was quite impressed with his student's preparation. The vocabulary was thoroughly memorized, but the accent needed work. An hour later, Ermanno began pointing at various objects around the room—rug, book, magazine, chair, quilt, curtains, radio, floor, wall, backpack—and Marco responded with ease. With an improving accent, he rattled off the entire list of polite expressions—good day, how are you, fine thanks, please, see you later, goodbye, good night—and thirty others. He rattled off the days of the week and the months of the year. Lesson one was completed after only two hours and Ermanno asked if they needed a break. 'No.' They turned to lesson two, with another page of vocabulary that Marco had already mastered and more dialogue that he delivered quite impressively.

'You've been studying,' Ermanno mumbled in

English.

'Non inglese, Ermanno, non inglese,' Marco corrected him. The game was on—who could show more intensity. By noon, the teacher was exhausted and ready for a break, and they were both relieved to hear the knock on the door and the voice of Luigi outside in the hallway. He entered and saw the two of them squared off across the small, littered table, as if they'd been arm wrestling for several hours.

'Come va?' Luigi asked. How's it going?

Ermanno gave him a weary look and said, 'Molto intenso.' Very intense.

'Vorrei pranzare,' Marco announced, slowly rising to his feet. I'd like some lunch.

Marco was hoping for a nice lunch with some English thrown in to make things easier and perhaps relieve the mental strain of trying to translate every word he heard. However, after Ermanno's glowing summary of the morning session, Luigi was inspired to continue the immersion through the meal, or at least the first part of it. The menu contained not a word of English, and after Luigi explained each dish in incomprehensible Italian, Marco threw up his hands and said, 'That's it. I'm not speaking or listening to Italian for the next hour.'

'What about your lunch?'

'I'll eat yours.' He gulped the red wine and tried to relax.

'Okay then. I suppose we can do English for one hour.'

'Grazie,' Marco said before he caught himself.

9

Midway through the morning session the following day, Marco abruptly changed direction. In the middle of a particularly tedious piece of dialogue he ditched the Italian and said, 'You're not a student.'

Ermanno looked up from the study guide, paused for a moment, then said, 'Non inglese, Marco. Soltanto Italiano.' Only Italian.

'I'm tired of Italian right now, okay? You're not a student.'

Deceit was difficult for Ermanno, and he paused a bit too long. 'I am,' he said, without much conviction.

'No, I don't think so. You're obviously not taking classes, otherwise you wouldn't be able to spend all day teaching me.'

'Maybe I have classes at night. Why does it matter?'

'You're not taking classes anywhere. There are no books here, no student newspaper, none of the usual crap that students leave lying around everywhere.'

'Perhaps it's in the other room.'

'Let me see.'

'Why? Why is it important?'

'Because I think you work for the same people Luigi works for.'

'And what if I do?'

'I want to know who they are.'

'Suppose I don't know? Why should you be concerned? Your task is to learn the language.'

97

'How long have you lived here, in this apartment?'

'I don't have to answer your questions.'

'See, I think you got here last week; that this is a safe house of some sort; that you're not really who you say you are.'

'Then that would make two of us.' Ermanno suddenly stood and walked through the tiny kitchen to the rear of the apartment. He returned with some papers, which he slid in front of Marco. It was a registration packet from the University of Bologna, with a mailing label listing the name of Ermanno Rosconi, at the address where they were now sitting.

'I resume classes soon,' Ermanno said. 'Would you like some more coffee?'

Marco was scanning the forms, comprehending just enough to get the message. 'Yes, please,' he said. It was just paperwork—easily faked. But if it was a forgery, it was a very good one. Ermanno disappeared into the kitchen and began running water.

Marco shoved his chair back and said, 'I'm going for a walk around the block. I need to clear my head.'

*   *   *

The routine changed at dinner. Luigi met him in front of a tobacco shop facing the Piazza dei Signori, and they strolled along a busy alley as shopkeepers were closing up. It was already dark and very cold, and smartly bundled businessmen hurried home, their heads covered with hats and scarves.

Luigi had his gloved hands buried deep in the wool pockets of his knee-length rough fabric duster, one that could've been handed down by his grandfather or purchased last week in Milan at some hideously expensive designer shop. Regardless, he wore it stylishly, and once again Marco was envious of the casual elegance of his handler.

Luigi was in no hurry and seemed to enjoy the cold. He offered a few comments in Italian, but Marco refused to play along. 'English, Luigi,' he said twice. 'I need English.'

'All right. How was your second day of class?'

'Good. Ermanno's okay. No sense of humor, but an adequate teacher.'

'You're making progress?'

'How could I not make progress?'

'Ermanno tells me you have an ear for the language.'

'Ermanno is a bad con man and you know it. I'm working hard because a lot depends on it. I'm drilled by him six hours a day, then I spend three hours at night cramming. Progress is inevitable.'

'You work very hard,' Luigi repeated. He suddenly stopped and looked at what appeared to be a small deli. 'This, Marco, is dinner.'

Marco stared with disapproval. The storefront was no more than fifteen feet across. Three tables were crammed in the window and the place appeared to be packed. 'Are you sure?' Marco asked.

'Yes, it's very good. Lighter food, sandwiches and stuff. You're eating by yourself. I'm not going in.'

Marco looked at him and started to protest,

99

then he caught himself and smiled as if he gladly accepted the challenge.

'The menu is on a chalkboard above the cashier, no English. Order first, pay, then pick up your food at the far end of the counter, which is not a bad to place to sit if you can get a stool. Tip is included.'

Marco asked, 'What's the specialty of the house?'

'The ham and artichoke pizza is delicious. So are the panini. I'll meet you over there, by the fountain, in one hour.'

Marco gritted his teeth and entered the café, very alone. As he waited behind two young ladies he desperately searched the chalkboard for something he could pronounce. Forget taste. What was important was the ordering and paying. Fortunately, the cashier was a middle-aged lady who enjoyed smiling. Marco gave her a friendly 'Buona sera,' and before she could shoot something back he ordered a 'panino prosciutto e formaggio'—ham and cheese sandwich—and a Coca-Cola.

Good ol' Coca-Cola. The same in any language.

The register rattled and she offered a blur of words that he did not understand. But he kept smiling and said, 'Sì,' then handed over a twenty-euro bill, certainly enough to cover things and bring back some change. It worked. With the change was a ticket. 'Numero sessantasette,' she said. Number sixty-seven.

He held the ticket and moved slowly along the counter toward the kitchen. No one gawked at him, no one seemed to notice. Was he actually passing himself off as an Italian, a real local? Or was it so obvious that he was an alien that the locals didn't bother to look? He had quickly developed the habit of evaluating how other men were dressed, and he judged himself to be in the game. As Luigi had told him, the men of northern Italy were much more concerned with style and appearance than Americans. There were more jackets and tailored slacks, more sweaters and ties. Much less denim, and virtually no sweatshirts or other signs of indifference to appearance.

Luigi, or whoever had put together his wardrobe, one no doubt paid for by the American taxpayers, had done a fine job. For a man who'd worn the same prison garb for six years, Marco was quickly adjusting to things Italian.

He watched the plates of food as they popped up along the counter near the grill. After about ten minutes, a thick sandwich appeared. A server grabbed it, snatched off a ticket, and yelled, 'Numero sessantasette.' Marco stepped forward without a word and produced his ticket. The soft drink came next. He found a seat at a small corner table and thoroughly enjoyed the solitude of his dinner. The deli was loud and crowded, a neighborhood place where many of the customers knew each other. Their greetings involved hugs and kisses and long hellos, even longer goodbyes. Waiting in line to order caused no problems, though the Italians seemed to struggle with the basic concept of one standing behind the other. Back home there would've been sharp words from the customers and perhaps swearing from the cashier.

In a country where a three-hundred-year-old house is considered new, time has a different

101

meaning. Food is to be enjoyed, even in a small deli with few tables. Those seated close to Joel seemed poised to take hours to digest their pizza and sandwiches. There was simply too much talking to do!

The brain-dead pace of prison life had flattened all his edges. He'd kept his sanity by reading eight books a week, but even that exercise had been for escape and not necessarily for learning. Two days of intensive memorizing, conjugating, pronouncing, and listening like he'd never listened before left him mentally exhausted.

So he absorbed the roar of Italian without trying to understand any of it. He enjoyed its rhythm and cadence and laughter. He caught a word every now and then, especially in the greetings and farewells, and considered this to be progress of some sort. Watching the families and friends made him lonely, though he refused to dwell on it. Loneliness was twenty-three hours a day in a small cell with little mail and nothing but a cheap paperback to keep him company. He'd seen loneliness; this was a day at the beach.

He tried hard to linger over his ham and cheese, but he could only stretch it so far. He reminded himself to order fries the next time because fries can be toyed with until long after they're cold, thus extending the meal far beyond what would be considered normal back home. Reluctantly, he surrendered his table. Almost an hour after he entered the café, he left the warmth of it and walked to the fountain where the water had been turned off so it wouldn't freeze. Luigi strolled up a few minutes later, as if he'd been loitering in the shadows, waiting. He had the nerve to suggest a gelato, an ice cream, but Marco was already shivering. They walked to the hotel and said good night.

*   *   *

Luigi's field supervisor had diplomatic cover at the U.S. consulate in Milan. His name was Whitaker, and Backman was the least of his priorities. Backman was not involved in intelligence, or counterintelligence, and Whitaker had a full load in those arenas without having to worry about an ex–Washington power broker who'd been stashed away in Italy. But he dutifully prepared his daily summaries and sent them to Langley. There they were received and reviewed by Julia Javier, the veteran with access to Mr. Maynard himself. It was because of Ms. Javier's watchful eye that Whitaker was so diligent in Milan. Otherwise, the daily summaries may not have been so prompt.

Teddy wanted a briefing.

Ms. Javier was summoned to his office on the seventh floor, to the 'Teddy Wing,' as it was known throughout Langley. She entered his 'station,' as he preferred it to be called, and once again found him parked at the end of a long wide conference table, sitting high in his jacked-up wheelchair, bundled in blankets from the chest down, wearing his standard black suit, peering over stacks of summaries, with Hoby hovering nearby ready to fetch another cup of the wretched green tea that Teddy was convinced was keeping him alive.

He was barely alive, but then Julia Javier had been thinking that for years now.

Since she didn't drink coffee and wouldn't

touch the tea, nothing was offered. She took her customary seat to his right, sort of the witness chair that all visitors were expected to take—his right ear caught much more than his left—and he managed a very tired 'Hello, Julia.'

Hoby, as always, sat across from her and prepared to take notes. Every sound in the 'station' was being captured by some of the most sophisticated recording devices modern technology had created, but Hoby nonetheless went through the charade of writing it all down.

'Brief me on Backman,' Teddy said. A verbal report such as this was expected to be concise, to the point, with not a single unnecessary word thrown in.

Julia looked at her notes, cleared her throat, and began speaking for the hidden recorders. 'He's in place in Treviso, a nice little town in northern Italy. Been there for three full days, seems to be making the adjustment quite well. Our agent is in complete contact, and the language tutor is a local who's doing a nice job. Backman has no money and no passport, and so far has been quite willing to stick close to the agent. He has not used the phone in his hotel room, nor has he tried to use his cell phone for anything other than to call our agent. He has shown no desire to explore or to wander about. Evidently, the habits learned in prison are hard to break. He's staying close to his hotel. When he's not being tutored or eating, he stays in his room and studies Italian.'

'How is his language?'

'Not bad. He's fifty-two years old, so it won't be quick.'

'I learned Arabic when I was sixty,' Teddy said

proudly, as if sixty was a century ago.

'Yes, I know,' she said. Everyone at Langley knew it. 'He is studying extremely hard and making progress, but it's only been three days. The tutor is impressed.'

'What does he talk about?'

'Not the past, not old friends and old enemies. Nothing that would interest us. He's closed that off, for now anyway. Idle conversation tends to be about his new home, the culture and language.'

'His mood?'

'He just walked out of prison fourteen years early and he's having long meals and good wine. He's quite happy. Doesn't appear to be homesick, but of course he doesn't really have a home. Never talks about his family.'

'His health?'

'Seems fine. The cough is gone. Appears to be sleeping. No complaints.'

'How much does he drink?'

'He's careful. Enjoys wine at lunch and dinner and a beer in a nearby bar, but nothing excessive.'

'Let's try and crank up the booze, okay? See if he'll talk more.'

'That's our plan.'

'How secure is he?'

'Everything's bugged—phones, room, language lessons, lunches, dinners. Even his shoes have mikes. Both pairs. His overcoat has a Peak 30 sewn into the lining. We can track him virtually anywhere.'

'So you can't lose him?'

'He's a lawyer, not a spy. As of now, he seems very content to enjoy his freedom and do what he's told.'

'He's not stupid, though. Remember that, Julia. Backman knows there are some very nasty people who would love to find him.'

'True, but right now he's like a toddler clinging to his mother.'

'So he feels safe?'

'Under the circumstances, yes.'

'Then let's give him a scare.'

'Now?'

'Yes.' Teddy rubbed his eyes and took a sip of tea. 'What about his son?'

'Level-three surveillance, not much happening in Culpeper, Virginia. If Backman tries to contact anyone, it will be Neal Backman. But we'll know it in Italy before we know it in Culpeper.'

'His son is the only person he trusts,' Teddy said, stating what Julia had said many times.

'Very true.'

After a long pause he said, 'Anything else, Julia?'

'He's writing a letter to his mother in Oakland.'

Teddy gave a quick smile. 'How nice. Do we have it?'

'Yes, our agent took a picture of it yesterday, we just got it. Backman hides it in between the pages of a local tourism magazine in his hotel room.'

'How long is it?'

'Two good paragraphs. Evidently a work in progress.'

'Read it to me,' Teddy said as he leaned his head back against his wheelchair and closed his eyes.

Julia shuffled papers and pushed up her reading glasses. 'No date, handwritten, which is a chore because Backman's penmanship is lousy. "Dear Mother: I'm not sure when or if you will ever receive this letter. I'm not sure if I will ever mail it, which could affect whether or not you get it. At any rate, I'm out of prison and doing better. In my last letter I said things were going well in the flat country of Oklahoma. I had no idea at that time that I would be pardoned by the President. It happened so quickly that I still find it hard to believe." Second paragraph. "I'm living on the other side of the world, I can't say where because this would upset some people. I would prefer to be in the United States, but that is not possible. I had no say in the matter. It's not a great life but it's certainly better than the one I had a week ago. I was dying in prison, in spite of what I said in my letters. Didn't want to worry you. Here, I'm free, and that's the most important thing in the world. I can walk down the street, eat in a café, come and go as I please, do pretty much whatever I want. Freedom, Mother, something I dreamed of for years and thought was impossible." '

She laid it down and said, 'That's as far as he's gotten.'

Teddy opened his eyes and said, 'You think he's stupid enough to mail a letter to his mother?'

'No. But he's been writing her once a week for a long time. It's a habit, and it's probably therapeutic. He has to talk to somebody.'

'Are we still watching her mail?'

'Yes, what little she receives.'

'Very well. Scare the hell out of him, then report back.'

'Yes sir.' Julia gathered her papers and left the office. Teddy picked up a summary and adjusted

107

his reading glasses. Hoby went to a small kitchen nearby.

Backman's mother's phone had been tapped in the nursing home in Oakland, and so far it had revealed nothing. The day the pardon was announced two very old friends had called with lots of questions and some subdued congratulations, but Mrs. Backman had been so bewildered she was eventually sedated and napped for hours. None of her grandchildren—the three produced by Joel and his various wives—had called her in the past six months.

Lydia Backman had survived two strokes and was confined to a wheelchair. When her son was at his pinnacle she lived in relative luxury in a spacious condo with a full-time nurse. His conviction had forced her to give up the good life and live in a nursing home with a hundred others.

Surely Backman would not try to contact her.

10

After a few days of dreaming about the money, Critz began spending it, at least mentally. With all that cash, he wouldn't be forced to work for the sleazy defense contractor, nor would he be forced to hustle audiences on the lecture circuit. (He wasn't convinced the audiences were out there to begin with, in spite of what his lecture agent had promised him.)

Critz was thinking about retirement! Somewhere far away from Washington and all the enemies he'd made there, somewhere on a beach with a sailboat nearby. Or maybe he'd move to Switzerland and stay close to his new fortune buried in his new bank, all wonderfully tax free and growing by the day.

He made a phone call and got the flat in London for a few more days. He encouraged Mrs. Critz to shop more aggressively. She, too, was tired of Washington and deserved an easier life.

Partly because of his greedy enthusiasm, and partly because of his natural ineptitude, and also because of his lack of sophistication in intelligence matters, Critz blundered badly from the start. For such an old hand at the Washington game, his mistakes were inexcusable.

First, he used the phone in his borrowed flat, thus making it easy for someone to nail down his exact location. He called Jeb Priddy, the CIA liaison who had been stationed in the White House during the last four years. Priddy was still at his post but expected to be called back to Langley soon. The new President was settling in, things were chaotic, and so on, according to Priddy, who seemed slightly irritated by the call. He and Critz had never been close, and Priddy knew immediately that the guy was fishing. Critz eventually said he was trying to find an old pal, a senior CIA analyst he'd once played a lot of golf with. Name was Daly, Addison Daly, and he'd left Washington for a stint in Asia. Did Priddy perhaps know where he was now?

Addison Daly was tucked away at Langley and Priddy knew him well. 'I know the name,' Priddy said. 'Maybe I can find him. Where can I reach you?'

Critz gave him the number at the flat. Priddy

called Addison Daly and passed along his suspicions. Daly turned on his recorder and called London on a secure line. Critz answered the phone and went overboard with his delight at hearing from an old friend. He rambled on about how wonderful life was after the White House, after all those years playing the political game, how nice it was being a private citizen. He was anxious to renew old friendships and get serious about his golf game.

Daly played along well. He offered that he, too, was contemplating retirement—almost thirty years in the service—and that he caught himself looking forward to an easier life.

How's Teddy these days? Critz wanted to know. And how's the new president? What's the mood in Washington with the new administration?

Nothing changes much, Daly mused, just another bunch of fools. By the way, how's former president Morgan?

Critz didn't know, hadn't talked to him, in fact might not talk to him for many weeks. As the conversation was winding down, Critz said with a clumsy laugh, 'Don't guess anybody's seen Joel Backman?'

Daly managed to laugh too—it was all a big joke. 'No,' he said, 'I think the boy's well hidden.'

'He should be.'

Critz promised to call as soon as he returned to D.C. They'd play eighteen holes at one of the good clubs, then have a drink, just like in the old days!

What old days? Daly asked himself after he hung up.

An hour later, the phone conversation was played for Teddy Maynard.

Since the first two calls had been somewhat encouraging, Critz pressed on. He'd always been one to work the phones like a maniac. He subscribed to the shotgun theory—fill the air with calls and something will happen. A rough plan was coming together. Another old pal had once been a senior staffer to the chairman of the Senate Intelligence Committee, and though he was now a well-connected lobbyist, he had, allegedly, maintained close ties to the CIA.

They talked politics and golf and eventually, much to Critz's delight, the pal asked what, exactly, was President Morgan thinking when he pardoned Duke Mongo, the biggest tax evader in the history of America? Critz claimed to have been opposed to the pardon but managed to steer the conversation along to the other controversial reprieve. 'What's the gossip on Backman?' he asked.

'You were there,' answered his pal.

'Yes, but where did Maynard stash him? That's the big question.'

'So it was a CIA job?' his friend asked.

'Of course,' Critz said with the voice of authority. Who else could sneak him out of the country in the middle of the night?

'That's interesting,' said his pal, who then became very quiet. Critz insisted on a lunch the following week, and that's where they left the conversation.

As Critz feverishly worked the phone, he marveled once again at his endless list of contacts. Power did have its rewards.

*　　　*　　　*

Joel, or Marco, said goodbye to Ermanno at five-thirty in the afternoon, completing a three-hour session that had gone virtually nonstop. Both were exhausted.

The chilly air helped clear his head as he walked the narrow streets of Treviso. For the second day, he dropped by a small corner bar and ordered a beer. He sat in the window and watched the locals hurry about, some rushing home from work, others shopping quickly for dinner. The bar was warm and smoky, and Marco once again drifted back to prison. He couldn't help himself—the change had been too drastic, the freedom too sudden. There was still the lingering fear that he would wake up and find himself locked in the cell with some unseen prankster laughing hysterically in the distance.

After the beer he had an espresso, and after that he stepped into the darkness and shoved both hands deep into his pockets. When he turned the corner and saw his hotel, he also saw Luigi pacing nervously along the sidewalk, smoking a cigarette. As Marco crossed the street, Luigi came after him. 'We are leaving, immediately,' he said.

'Why?' Marco asked, glancing around, looking for bad guys.

'I'll explain later. There's a travel bag on your bed. Pack your things as quickly as possible. I'll wait here.'

'What if I don't want to leave?' Marco asked.

Luigi clutched his left wrist, thought for a quick second, then gave a very tight smile. 'Then you might not last twenty-four hours,' he said as ominously as possible. 'Please trust me.'

Marco raced up the stairs and down the hall,

and was almost to his room before he realized that the sharp pain in his stomach was not from heavy breathing but from fear.

What had happened? What had Luigi seen or heard, or been told? Who, exactly, was Luigi in the first place and who was he taking orders from? As Marco yanked his clothes out of the tiny closet and flung them toward the bed, he asked all these questions, and many more. When everything was packed, he sat for a moment and tried to collect his thoughts. He took deep breaths, exhaled slowly, told himself that whatever was happening was just part of the game.

Would he be running forever? Always packing in a hurry, fleeing one room in search of another? It still beat the hell out of prison, but it would take its toll.

And how could anyone possibly have found him this soon? He'd been in Treviso only four days.

When his composure was somewhat restored, he walked slowly down the hall, down the stairs, through the lobby where he nodded at the gawking clerk but said nothing, and out the front door. Luigi snatched his bag and tossed it into the trunk of a compact Fiat. They were on the outskirts of Treviso before a word was spoken.

'Okay, Luigi, what's up?' Marco asked.

'A change of scenery.'

'Got that. Why?'

'Some very good reasons.'

'Oh, well, that explains everything.'

Luigi drove with his left hand, shifted gears frantically with his right, and kept the accelerator as close to the floor as possible while ignoring the brakes. Marco was already perplexed as to how a

113

race of people could spend two and a half leisurely hours over lunch, then hop in a car for a ten-minute drive across town at breakneck speed.

They drove an hour, generally in a southward direction, avoiding the highways by clinging to the back roads. 'Is someone behind us?' Marco asked more than once as they sped around tight curves on two wheels.

Luigi just shook his head. His eyes were narrow, his eyebrows pinched together, his jaw clenched tightly when the cigarette wasn't near. He somehow managed to drive like a maniac while smoking calmly and never glancing behind them. He was determined not to speak, and that reinforced Marco's determination to have a conversation.

'You're just trying to scare me, aren't you, Luigi? We're playing the spy game—you're the master, I'm the poor schmuck with the secrets. Scare the hell out of me and keep me dependent and loyal. I know what you're doing.'

'Who killed Jacy Hubbard?' Luigi asked, barely moving his lips.

Backman suddenly wanted to go quiet. The mere mention of Hubbard made him freeze for a second. The name always brought the same flashback: a police photo of Jacy slumped against his brother's grave, the left side of his head blown away, blood everywhere—on the tombstone, on his white shirt. Everywhere.

'You have the file,' Backman said. 'It was a suicide.'

'Oh yes. And if you believed that, then why did you decide to plead guilty and beg for protective custody in prison?'

'I was scared. Suicides can be contagious.'

'Very true.'

'So you're saying that the boys who did the Hubbard suicide are after me?'

Luigi confirmed it with a shrug.

'And somehow they found out I was hiding in Treviso?'

'It's best not to take chances.'

He would not get the details, if, in fact, there were any. He tried not to, but he instinctively glanced over his shoulder and saw the dark road behind them. Luigi looked into his rearview mirror, and managed a satisfactory smile, as if to say: They're back there, somewhere.

Joel sank a few inches in his seat and closed his eyes. Two of his clients had died first. Safi Mirza had been knifed outside a Georgetown nightclub three months after he hired Backman and handed over the only copy of JAM. The knife wounds were severe enough, but a poison had been injected, probably with the thrust of the blade. No witnesses. No clues. A very unsolved murder, but one of many in D.C. A month later Fazal Sharif had disappeared in Karachi, and was presumed dead.

JAM was indeed worth a billion dollars, but no one would ever enjoy the money.

*   *   *

In 1998, Backman, Pratt & Bolling had hired Jacy Hubbard for $1 million a year. The marketing of JAM was his first big challenge. To prove his worth, Hubbard bullied and bribed his way into the Pentagon in a clumsy and ill-fated effort to confirm the existence of the Neptune satellite system. Some documents—doctored but still classified—were smuggled out by a Hubbard mole who was reporting everything to his superiors. The highly sensitive papers purported to show the existence of Gamma Net, a fictitious Star Wars–like surveillance system with unheard-of capabilities. Once Hubbard 'confirmed' that the three young Pakistanis were indeed correct—their Neptune was a U.S. project—he proudly reported his findings to Joel Backman and they were in business.

Since Gamma Net was supposedly the creation of the U.S. military, JAM was worth even more. The truth was that neither the Pentagon nor the CIA knew about Neptune.

The Pentagon then leaked its own fiction—a fabricated breach of security by a mole working for ex-senator Jacy Hubbard and his powerful new boss, the broker himself. The scandal erupted. The FBI raided the offices of Backman, Pratt & Bolling in the middle of the night, found the Pentagon documents that everyone presumed to be authentic, and within forty-eight hours a highly motivated team of federal prosecutors had issued indictments against every partner in the firm.

The killings soon followed, with no clues as to who was behind them. The Pentagon brilliantly neutralized Hubbard and Backman without tipping its hand as to whether it actually owned and created the satellite system. Gamma Net or Neptune, or whatever, was effectively shielded under the impenetrable web of 'military secrets.'

Backman the lawyer wanted a trial, especially if the Pentagon documents were questionable, but Backman the defendant wanted to avoid a fate similar to Hubbard's.

If Luigi's mad dash out of Treviso was designed to frighten him, then the plan suddenly began working. For the first time since his pardon, Joel missed the safety of his little cell in maximum security.

The city of Padua was ahead, its lights and traffic growing by the mile. 'What's the population of Padua?' Marco asked, his first words in half an hour.

'Two hundred thousand. Why do Americans always want to know the population of every village and city?'

'Didn't realize it was a problem.'

'Are you hungry?'

The dull throbbing in his stomach was from fear, not hunger, but he said 'Sure' anyway. They ate a pizza at a neighborhood bar just beyond the outer ring of Padua, and were quickly back in the car and headed south.

They slept that night in a tiny country inn— eight closet-sized rooms—that had been in the same family since Roman times. There was no sign advertising the place; it was one of Luigi's stopovers. The nearest road was narrow, neglected, and virtually free of any vehicle built after 1970. Bologna was not far away.

Luigi was next door, through a thick stone wall that went back for centuries. When Joel Backman/ Marco Lazzeri crawled under the blankets and finally got warm, he couldn't see a flicker of light anywhere. Total blackness. And total quiet. It was so quiet he couldn't close his eyes for a long time.

11

After the fifth report that Critz had called with questions about Joel Backman, Teddy Maynard threw a rare tantrum. The fool was in London, working the phones furiously, for some reason trying to find someone, anyone, who might lead him to information about Backman.

'Someone's offered Critz money,' Teddy barked at Wigline, an assistant deputy director.

'But there's no way Critz can find out where Backman is,' Wigline said.

'He shouldn't be trying. He'll only complicate matters. He must be neutralized.'

Wigline glanced at Hoby, who had suddenly stopped his note-taking. 'What are you saying, Teddy?'

'Neutralize him.'

'He's a U.S. citizen.'

'I know that! He's also compromising an operation. There is precedent. We've done it before.' He didn't bother to tell them what the precedent was, but they assumed that since Teddy often created his own precedents, then it would do no good to argue the matter.

Hoby nodded as if to say: Yes, we've done it before.

Wigline clenched his jaw and said, 'I assume you want it done now.'

'As soon as possible,' Teddy said. 'Show me a plan in two hours.'

They watched Critz as he left his borrowed apartment and began his long, late-afternoon walk, one that usually ended with a few pints. After half an hour at a languid pace he neared Leicester Square and entered the Dog and Duck, the same pub as the day before.

He was on his second pint at the far end of the main bar, first floor, before the stool next to him cleared and an agent named Greenlaw wedged in and yelled for a beer.

'Mind if I smoke?' Greenlaw asked Critz, who shrugged and said, 'This ain't America.'

'A Yank, huh?' Greenlaw said.

'Yep.'

'Live here?'

'No, just visiting.' Critz was concentrating on the bottles on the wall beyond the bar, avoiding eye contact, wanting no part of the conversation. He had quickly come to adore the solitude of a crowded pub. He loved to sit and drink and listen to the rapid banter of the Brits and know that not a soul had a clue as to who he was. He was, though, still wondering about the little guy named Ben. If they were watching him, they were doing a great job of staying in the shadows.

Greenlaw gulped his beer in an effort to catch up with Critz. It was crucial to order the next two at the same time. He puffed a cigarette, then added his smoke to the cloud above them. 'I've been here for a year,' he said.

Critz nodded without looking. Get lost.

'I don't mind driving on the wrong side, or the lousy weather, but what really bugs me here are the sports. You ever watch a cricket match? Lasts for four days.'

Critz managed to grunt and offer a lame 'Such a stupid sport.'

119

'It's either soccer or cricket, and these people go nuts over both. I just survived the winter here without the NFL. It was pure misery.'

Critz was a loyal Redskins season-ticket holder and few things in life excited him as much as his beloved team. Greenlaw was a casual fan but had spent the day memorizing statistics in a CIA safe house north of London. If football didn't work, then politics would be next. If that didn't work, there was a fine-looking lady waiting outside, though Critz did not have a reputation as a philanderer.

Critz was suddenly homesick. Sitting in a pub, far from home, far from the frenzy of the Super Bowl—two days away and virtually ignored by the British press—he could hear the crowd and feel the excitement. If the Redskins had survived the playoffs, he would not be drinking pints in London. He would be at the Super Bowl, fifty-yard-line seats, furnished by one of the many corporations he could lean on.

He looked at Greenlaw and said, 'Patriots or Packers?'

'My team didn't make it, but I always pull for the NFC.'

'Me too. Who's your team?'

And that was perhaps the most fatal question Robert Critz would ever ask. When Greenlaw answered, 'Redskins,' Critz actually smiled and wanted to talk. They spent a few minutes establishing pedigree—how long each had been a Redskins fan, the great games they'd seen, the great players, the Super Bowl championships. Greenlaw ordered another round and both seemed ready to replay old games for hours. Critz had talked to so few Yanks in London, and this guy was certainly an easy one to get on with.

Greenlaw excused himself and went to find the restroom. It was upstairs, the size of a broom closet, a one-holer like so many johns in London. He latched the door for a few seconds of privacy and quickly whipped out a cell phone to report his progress. The plan was in place. The team was just down the street, waiting. Three men and the fine-looking lady.

Halfway through his fourth pint, and with a polite disagreement under way over Sonny Jurgensen's touchdown-to-interception ratio, Critz finally needed to pee. He asked directions and disappeared. Greenlaw deftly dropped into Critz's glass one small white tablet of Rohypnol—a strong, tasteless, odorless sedative. When Mr. Redskins returned he was refreshed and ready to drink. They talked about John Riggins and Joe Gibbs and thoroughly enjoyed themselves as poor Critz's chin began to drop.

'Wow,' he said, his tongue already thick. 'I'd better be going. Old lady is waiting.'

'Yeah, me too,' Greenlaw said, raising his glass. 'Drink up.'

They drained their pints and stood to leave; Critz in front, Greenlaw waiting to catch him. They made it through the crowd packed around the front door and onto the sidewalk where a cold wind revived Critz, but only for a second. He forgot about his new pal, and in less than twenty steps was wobbling on rubbery legs and grasping for a lamp pole. Greenlaw grabbed him as he was falling, and for the benefit of a young couple passing by said loudly, 'Dammit, Fred, you're drunk again.'

Fred was far beyond drunk. A car appeared from nowhere and slowed by the sidewalk. A back door swung open, and Greenlaw shoveled a half-dead Critz into the rear seat. The first stop was a warehouse eight blocks away. There Critz, thoroughly unconscious now, was transferred to a small unmarked panel truck with a double rear door. While Critz lay on the floor of the van, an agent used a hypodermic needle and injected him with a massive dose of very pure heroin. The presence of heroin always squelched the autopsy results, at the family's insistence of course.

With Critz barely breathing, the van left the warehouse and drove to Whitcomb Street, not far from his apartment. The killing required three vehicles—the van, followed by a large and heavy Mercedes, and a trail car driven by a real Brit who would hang around and chat with the police. The trail car's primary purpose was to keep the traffic as far behind the Mercedes as possible.

On the third pass, with all three drivers talking to each other, and with two agents, including the fine-looking lady, hiding on the sidewalk and also listening, the rear doors of the van were shoved open, Critz fell onto the street, the Mercedes aimed for his head and got it with a sickening thump, then everyone disappeared but the Brit in the trail car. He slammed on his brakes, jumped out and ran to the poor drunk who'd just stumbled into the street and been run over, and looked around quickly for other witnesses.

There were none, but a taxi was approaching in the other lane. He flagged it down, and soon other traffic stopped. Before long, a crowd was gathering and the police arrived. The Brit in the trail car may have been the first on the scene, but he saw very little. He saw the man stumble between those two parked cars over there, into the street, and get hit by a large black car. Or maybe it was dark green. Not sure of the make or model. Never thought about looking at the license plates. No clue as to the description of the hit-and-run driver. He was too shocked by the sight of the drunk suddenly appearing at the edge of the street.

By the time the body of Bob Critz was loaded into an ambulance for the trip to the morgue, Greenlaw, the fine-looking lady, and two other members of the team were on a train leaving London and headed for Paris. They would scatter for a few weeks, then return to England, their home base.

*   *   *

Marco wanted breakfast primarily because he could smell it—ham and sausages on the grill somewhere deep in the main house—but Luigi was anxious to move on. 'There are other guests and everyone eats at the same table,' he explained as they hurriedly threw their bags in his car. 'Remember, you're leaving a trail, and the signora forgets nothing.'

They sped down the country lane in search of wider roads.

'Where are we going?' Marco asked.

'We'll see.'

'Stop playing games with me!' he growled and Luigi actually flinched. 'I'm a perfectly free man who could get out of this car anytime I want!'

'Yes, but—'

123

'Stop threatening me! Every time I ask a question you give me these vague threats about how I won't last twenty-four hours on my own. I want to know what's going on. Where are we headed? How long will we be there? How long will you be around? Give me some answers, Luigi, or I'll disappear.'

Luigi turned onto a four-lane and a sign said that Bologna was thirty kilometers ahead. He waited for the tension to ease a bit, then said, 'We're going to Bologna for a few days. Ermanno will meet us there. You will continue your lessons. You'll be placed in a safe house for several months. Then I'll disappear and you'll be on your own.'

'Thank you. Why was that so difficult?'

'The plan changes.'

'I knew Ermanno wasn't a student.'

'He is a student. He's also part of the plan.'

'Do you realize how ridiculous the plan is? Think about it, Luigi. Someone is spending all this time and money trying to teach me another language and another culture. Why not just put me back on the cargo plane and stash me in some place like New Zealand?'

'That's a great idea, Marco, but I'm not making those decisions.'

'Marco my ass. Every time I look in the mirror and say Marco I want to laugh.'

'This is not funny. Do you know Robert Critz?'

Marco paused for a moment. 'I met him a few times over the years. Never had much use for him. Just another political hack, like me, I guess.'

'Close friend of President Morgan, chief of staff, campaign director.'

'So?'

124

'He was killed last night in London. That makes five people who've died because of you—Jacy Hubbard, the three Pakistanis, now Critz. The killing hasn't stopped, Marco, nor will it. Please be patient with me. I'm only trying to protect you.'

Marco slammed his head into the headrest and closed his eyes. He could not begin to put the pieces together.

They made a quick exit and stopped for gas. Luigi returned to the car with two small cups of strong coffee. 'Coffee to go,' Marco said pleasantly. 'I figured such evils would be banned in Italy.'

'Fast food is creeping in. It's very sad.'

'Just blame the Americans. Everybody else does.'

Before long they were inching through the rush hour traffic on the outskirts of Bologna. Luigi was saying, 'Our best cars are made around here, you know. Ferraris, Lamborghinis, Maseratis, all the great sports cars.'

'Can I have one?'

'It's not in the budget, sorry.'

'What, exactly, is in the budget?'

'A very quiet, simple life.'

'That's what I thought.'

'Much better than your last one.'

Marco sipped his coffee and watched the traffic. 'Didn't you study here?'

'Yes. The university is a thousand years old. One of the finest in the world. I'll show it to you later.'

They exited the main thoroughfare and wound through a gritty suburb. The streets became shorter and narrower and Luigi seemed to know the place well. They followed the signs pointing them toward the center of the city, and the university. Luigi suddenly swerved, jumped a curb, and wedged the Fiat into a slot barely wide enough for a motorcycle. 'Let's eat something,' he said, and, once they managed to squeeze themselves out of the car, they were on the sidewalk, walking quickly through the cool air.

*   *   *

Marco's next hiding place was a dingy hotel a few blocks from the outer edge of the old city. 'Budget cuts already,' he mumbled as he followed Luigi through the cramped lobby to the stairs.

'It's just for a few days,' Luigi said.

'Then what?' Marco was struggling with his bags up the narrow stairway. Luigi was carrying nothing. Thankfully the room was on the second floor, a rather small space with a tiny bed and curtains that hadn't been opened in days.

'I like Treviso better,' Marco said, staring at the walls.

Luigi yanked open the curtains. The sunlight helped only slightly. 'Not bad,' he said, without conviction.

'My prison cell was nicer.'

'You complain a lot.'

'With good reason.'

'Unpack. I'll meet you downstairs in ten minutes. Ermanno is waiting.'

Ermanno appeared as rattled as Marco by the sudden change in location. He was harried and unsettled, as if he'd chased them all night from Treviso. They walked with him a few blocks to a run-down apartment building. No elevators were evident, so they climbed four flights of stairs and entered a tiny, two-room flat that had even less furniture than the apartment in Treviso. Ermanno had obviously packed in a hurry and unpacked even faster.

'Your dump's worse than mine,' Marco said, taking it in.

Spread on a narrow table and waiting for action were the study materials they'd used the day before.

'I'll be back for lunch,' Luigi said, and quickly disappeared.

'Andiamo a studiare,' Ermanno announced. Let's study.

'I've already forgotten everything.'

'But we had a good session yesterday.'

'Can't we just go to a bar and drink? I'm really not in the mood for this.' But Ermanno had assumed his position across the table and was turning pages in his manual. Marco reluctantly settled into the seat across from him.

*   *   *

Lunch and dinner were forgettable. Both were quick snacks in fake trattorias, the Italian version of fast food. Luigi was in a foul mood and insisted, quite harshly at times, that they speak only Italian. Luigi spoke slowly, clearly, and repeated everything four times until Marco figured it out, then he moved along to the next phrase. It was impossible to enjoy food under such pressure.

At midnight, Marco was in his bed, in his cold room, wrapped tightly with the thin blanket, sipping orange juice he had ordered himself, and

127

memorizing list after list of verbs and adjectives.

What could Robert Critz have possibly done to get himself killed by people who might also be looking for Joel Backman? The question itself was too bizarre to ask. He couldn't begin to contemplate an answer. He assumed Critz was present when the pardon was granted; ex-president Morgan was incapable of making such a decision by himself. Beyond that, though, it was impossible to see Critz involved at a higher level. He had proven for decades that he was nothing more than a good hatchet man. Very few people trusted him.

But if people were still dying, then it was urgent that he learn the verbs and adjectives scattered on his bed. Language meant survival, and movement. Luigi and Ermanno would soon disappear, and Marco Lazzeri would be left to fend for himself.

12

Marco escaped his claustrophobic room, or 'apartment' as it was called, and went for a long walk at daybreak. The sidewalks were almost as damp as the frigid air. With a pocket map Luigi had given him, all in Italian of course, he made his way into the old city, and once past the ruins of the ancient walls at Porta San Donato, he headed west on Via Irnerio along the north edge of the university section of Bologna. The sidewalks were centuries old and covered with what appeared to be miles of arching porticoes.

Evidently street life began late in the university

section. An occasional car passed, then a bike or two, but the foot traffic was still asleep. Luigi had explained that Bologna had a history of left-wing, communist leanings. It was a rich history, one that Luigi promised to explore with him.

Ahead Marco saw a small green neon sign that was indifferently advertising the Bar Fontana, and as he walked toward it he soon picked up the scent of strong coffee. The bar was wedged tightly into the corner of an ancient building—but then they were all ancient. The door opened reluctantly, and once inside Marco almost smiled at the aromas—coffee, cigarettes, pastries, breakfast on a grill in the rear. Then the fear hit, the usual apprehension of trying to order in an unknown language.

Bar Fontana was not for students, or for women. The crowd was his age, fifty and up, somewhat oddly dressed, with enough pipes and beards to identify it as a hangout for faculty. One or two glanced his way, but in the center of a university with 100,000 students it was difficult for anyone to draw attention.

Marco got the last small table near the back, and when he finally nestled into his spot with his back to the wall he was practically shoulder to shoulder with his new neighbors, both of whom were lost in their morning papers and neither of whom appeared to notice him. In one of Luigi's lectures on Italian culture he had explained the concept of space in Europe and how it differed significantly from that in the States. Space is shared in Europe, not protected. Tables are shared, the air evidently is shared because smoking bothers no one. Cars, houses, buses, apartments, cafés—so many important aspects of life are smaller, thus more cramped, thus more willingly shared. It's not offensive to go nose to nose with an acquaintance during routine conversation because no space is being violated. Talk with your hands, hug, embrace, even kiss at times.

Even for a friendly people, such familiarity was difficult for Americans to understand.

And Marco was not yet prepared to yield too much space. He picked up the wrinkled menu on the table and quickly settled on the first thing he recognized. Just as the waiter stopped and glanced down at him he said, with all the ease he could possibly exude, 'Espresso, e un panino al formaggio.' A small cheese sandwich.

The waiter nodded his approval. Not a single person glanced over to check out his accented Italian. No newspapers dipped to see who he might be. No one cared. They heard accents all the time. As he placed the menu back on the table, Marco Lazzeri decided that he probably liked Bologna, even if it turned out to be a nest for Communists. With so many students and faculty coming and going, and from all over the world, foreigners were accepted as part of the culture. Perhaps it was rather cool to have an accent and dress differently. Perhaps it was okay to openly study the language.

One sign of a foreigner was that he noticed everything, his eyes darting around as if he knew he was trespassing into a new culture and didn't want to get caught. Marco would not be caught taking in the sights in the Bar Fontana. He removed a booklet of vocabulary sheets and tried mightily to ignore the people and scenes he wanted to watch. Verbs, verbs, verbs. Ermanno kept saying that to master Italian, or any Romance language for that

130

matter, you had to know the verbs. The booklet had one thousand of the basic verbs, and Ermanno claimed that it was a good starting point.

As tedious as rote memorization was, Marco was finding an odd pleasure in it. He found it quite satisfying to zip through four pages—one hundred verbs, or nouns, or anything for that matter—and not miss a one. When he got one wrong, or missed a pronunciation, he went back to the beginning and punished himself by starting over. He had conquered three hundred verbs when his coffee and sandwich arrived. He took a sip, went back to work as if the food was much less important than the vocab, and was somewhere over four hundred when Rudolph arrived.

The chair on the other side of Marco's small round table was vacant, and this caught the attention of a short fat man, dressed entirely in faded black, with wild bunches of gray frizzy hair protruding from all parts of his head, some of it barely suppressed by a black beret that somehow managed to stay aboard. 'Buon giorno. È libera?' he asked politely, gesturing toward the chair. Marco wasn't sure what he said but it was obvious what he wanted. Then he caught the word 'libera' and assumed it meant 'free' or 'vacant.'

'Sì,' Marco managed with no accent, and the man removed a long black cape, draped it over the chair, then maneuvered himself into position. When he came to rest they were less than three feet apart. Space is different here, Marco kept telling himself. The man placed a copy of *L'Unità* on the table, making it rock back and forth. For an instant Marco was worried about his espresso. To avoid conversation, he buried himself even deeper into Ermanno's verbs.

'American?' his new friend said, in English with no foreign accent.

Marco lowered the booklet and looked into the glowing eyes not far away. 'Close. Canadian. How'd you know?'

He nodded at the booklet and said, 'English to Italian vocabulary. You don't look British, so I figure you're American.' Judging by his accent, he was probably not from the upper Midwest. Not from New York or New Jersey; not from Texas or the South, or Appalachia, or New Orleans. As vast sections of the country were eliminated, Marco was beginning to think of California. And he was beginning to get very nervous. The lying would soon start, and he hadn't practiced enough.

'And where are you from?' he asked.

'Last stop was Austin, Texas. That was thirty years ago. Name's Rudolph.'

'Good morning, Rudolph, a pleasure. I'm Marco.' They were in kindergarten where only first names were needed. 'You don't sound Texan.'

'Thank God for that,' he said with a pleasant laugh, one that barely revealed his mouth. 'Originally from San Francisco.'

The waiter leaned in and Rudolph ordered black coffee, then something else in rapid Italian. The waiter had a follow-up, as did Rudolph, and Marco understood none of it.

'What brings you to Bologna?' Rudolph asked. He seemed anxious to chat; probably rare that he cornered a fellow North American in his favorite café.

Marco lowered his booklet and said, 'Just traveling around Italy for a year, seeing the sights, trying to pick up some of the language.'

Half of Rudolph's face was covered with an unkempt gray beard that began fairly high up the cheekbones and sprang in all directions. Most of his nose was visible, as was part of his mouth. For some odd reason, one that no one would ever understand because no one would ever dare ask such a ridiculous question, he had developed the habit of shaving a small round spot under his lower lip and comprising most of his upper chin. Other than that sacred ground, the wild frizzy whiskers were allowed to run free and apparently go unwashed. The top of his head was pretty much the same—acres of untouched bright gray brush sprouting from all around the beret.

Because so many of his features were masked, his eyes got all the attention. They were dark green and projected rays that, from under a set of thick sagging eyebrows, took in everything.

'How long in Bologna?' Rudolph asked.

'Got here yesterday. I have no schedule. And you, what brings you here?' Marco was anxious to keep the conversation away from himself.

The eyes danced and never blinked. 'I've been here for thirty years. I'm a professor at the university.'

Marco finally took a bite of his cheese sandwich, partly out of hunger, but more importantly to keep Rudolph talking.

'Where's your home?' he asked.

Following the script, Marco said, 'Toronto. Grandparents immigrated there from Milan. I have Italian blood but never learned the language.'

'The language is not hard,' Rudolph said, and his coffee arrived. He grabbed the small cup and thrust it deep into the beard. Evidently it found his mouth. He smacked his lips and leaned forward a bit as though he wanted to talk. 'You don't sound Canadian,' he said, and those eyes appeared to be laughing at him.

Marco was struggling under the labor of looking, acting, and sounding Italian. He'd had no time to even think about putting on Canadian airs. How, exactly, does one sound Canadian? He took another bite, a huge one, and through his food said, 'Can't help that. How did you get here from Austin?'

'A long story.'

Marco shrugged as if he had plenty of time.

'I was once a young professor at the University of Texas law school. When they found out I was a Communist they began pressuring me to leave. I fought them. They fought back. I got louder, especially in the classroom. Communists didn't fare too well in Texas in the early seventies, doubt if much has changed. They denied me tenure, ran me out of town, so I came here to Bologna, the heart of Italian communism.'

'What do you teach here?'

'Jurisprudence. Law. Radical left-wing legal theories.'

A powdered brioche of some sort arrived and Rudolph ate half of it with the first bite. A few crumbs dropped from the depths of his beard.

'Still a Communist?' Marco asked.

'Of course. Always. Why would I change?'

'Seems to have run its course, don't you think? Not such a great idea after all. I mean, look at what a mess Russia is in because of Stalin and his legacy. And North Korea, they're starving there while the

134

dictator builds nuclear warheads. Cuba is fifty years behind the rest of the world. The Sandinistas were voted out in Nicaragua. China is turning to free market capitalism because the old system broke down. It really doesn't work, does it?'

The brioche had lost its appeal; the green eyes were narrow. Marco could see a tirade coming, probably one laced with obscenities in both English and Italian. He glanced around quickly and realized that there was a very good chance the Communists had him outnumbered in the Bar Fontana.

And what had capitalism done for him?

Much to his credit, Rudolph smiled and shrugged and said with an air of nostalgia, 'Maybe so, but it sure was fun being a Communist thirty years ago, especially in Texas. Those were the days.'

Marco nodded at the newspaper and said, 'Ever read papers from home?'

'Home is here, my friend. I became an Italian citizen and haven't been back to the States in twenty years.'

Backman was relieved. He had not seen American newspapers since his release, but he assumed there had been coverage. Probably old photos as well. His past seemed safe from Rudolph.

Marco wondered if that was his future—Italian citizenship. If any at all. Fast-forward twenty years, and would he still be drifting through Italy, not exactly glancing over his shoulder but always thinking about it?

'You said "home,"' Rudolph interrupted. 'Is that the U.S. or Canada?'

Marco smiled and nodded to a far-off place.

'Over there, I guess.' A small mistake, but one that should not have been made. To quickly shift to another subject, he said, 'This is my first visit to Bologna. Didn't know it was the center of Italian communism.'

Rudolph lowered his cup and made a smacking sound with his partially concealed lips. Then with both hands he gently pawed his beard backward, much like an old cat slicking down his whiskers. 'Bologna is a lot of things, my friend,' he said, as if a lengthy lecture was starting. 'It's always been the center of free thought and intellectual activity in Italy, thus its first nickname, la dotta, which means the learned. Then it became the home of the political left and received its second nickname, la rossa, the red. And the Bolognesi have always been very serious about their food. They believe, and they're probably right, that this is the stomach of Italy. Thus, the third nickname of la grassa, the fat, an affectionate term because you won't see many overweight people here. Me, I was fat when I arrived.' He patted his stomach proudly with one hand while finishing off the brioche with the other.

A frightening question suddenly hit Marco: Was it possible that Rudolph was part of the static? Was he a teammate of Luigi and Ermanno and Stennett and whoever else was out there in the shadows working so hard to keep Joel Backman alive? Surely not. Surely he was what he said he was—a professor. An oddball, a misfit, an aging Communist who'd found a better life somewhere else.

The thought passed, but it was not forgotten. Marco finished his little sandwich and decided they'd talked enough. He suddenly had a train to catch for another day of sightseeing. He managed to extricate himself from the table and got a fond farewell from Rudolph. 'I'm here every morning,' he said. 'Come back when you can stay longer.'

'Grazie,' Marco said. 'Arrivederci.'

Outside the café, Via Irnerio was stirring to life as small delivery vans began their routes. Two of the drivers yelled at each other, probably friendly obscenities Marco would never understand. He hustled away from the café just in case old Rudolph thought of something else to ask him and came charging out. He turned down a side street, Via Capo di Lucca—he was learning that they were well marked and easy to find on his map—and zigzagged his way toward the center. He passed another cozy little café, then backtracked and ducked inside for a cappuccino.

No Communists bothered him there, no one seemed to even notice him. Marco and Joel Backman savored the moment—the delicious strong drink, the warm thick air, the quiet laughter of those doing the talking. Right now not a single person in the world knew exactly where he was, and it was indeed an exhilarating feeling.

*   *   *

At Marco's insistence, the morning sessions were beginning at eight, not thirty minutes later. Ermanno, the student, still needed long hours of hard sleep but he couldn't argue with his pupil's intensity. Marco arrived for each lesson with his vocabulary lists thoroughly memorized, his situational dialogues perfected, and his urgent desire to absorb the language barely under control.

At one point he suggested they begin at seven.

The morning he met Rudolph, Marco studied intensely for two uninterrupted hours, then abruptly said, 'Vorrei vedere l'università.' I'd like to see the university.

'Quando?' Ermanno asked. When?

'Adesso. Andiamo a fare una passeggiata.' Now. Let's go for a walk.

'Penso che dobbiamo studiare.' I think we should study.

'Sì. Possiamo studiare a camminando.' We can study while we're walking.

Marco was already on his feet, grabbing his coat. They left the depressing building and headed in the general direction of the university.

'Questa via, come si chiama?' Ermanno asked. What's the name of this street?

'È Via Donati,' Marco answered without looking for a street sign.

They stopped in front of a small crowded shop and Ermanno asked, 'Che tipo di negozio è questo?' What kind of store is this?

'Una tabaccheria.' A tobacco store.

'Che cosa puoi comprare in questo negozio?' What can you buy here?

'Posso comprare molte cose. Giornali, riviste, francobolli, sigarette.' I can buy many things. Newspapers, magazines, stamps, cigarettes.

The session became a roving game of name that thing. Ermanno would point and say, 'Cosa è quello?' What's that? A bike, a policeman, a blue car, a city bus, a bench, a garbage can, a student, a telephone booth, a small dog, a café, a pastry shop. Except for a lamppost, Marco was quick with the Italian word for each. And the all-important verbs—walking, talking, seeing, studying, buying, thinking, chatting, breathing, eating, drinking, hurrying, driving—the list was endless and Marco had the proper translations at his disposal.

A few minutes after ten, and the university was finally coming to life. Ermanno explained that there was no central campus, no American-style quadrangle lined with trees and such. The Università degli Studi was found in dozens of handsome old buildings, some five hundred years old, most of them packed end to end along Via Zamboni, though over the centuries the school had grown and now covered an entire section of Bologna.

The Italian lesson was forgotten for a block or two as they were swept along in wave of students hustling to and from their classes. Marco caught himself looking for an old man with bright gray hair—his favorite Communist, his first real acquaintance since walking out of prison. He had already made up his mind to see Rudolph again.

At 22 Via Zamboni, Marco stopped and gazed at a sign between the door and a window: FACOLTÀ DI GIURISPRUDENZA.

'Is this the law school?' he asked.

'Sì.'

Rudolph was somewhere inside, no doubt spreading left-wing dissent among his impressionable students.

They ambled on, in no hurry as they continued to play name that thing and enjoy the energy of the street.

13

The lezione-a-piedi—lesson on foot—continued the next day when Marco revolted after an hour of tedious grammar straight from the textbook and demanded to go for a walk.

'Ma, deve imparare la grammatica,' Ermanno insisted. You must learn grammar.

Marco was already putting on his coat. 'That's where you're wrong, Ermanno. I need real conversation, not sentence structure.'

'Sono io l'insegnante.' I am the teacher.

'Let's go. Andiamo. Bologna is waiting. The streets are filled with happy young people, the air is alive with the sounds of your language, all just waiting for me to absorb.' When Ermanno hesitated, Marco smiled at him and said, 'Please, my friend. I've been locked in a small cell about the size of this apartment for six years. You can't expect me to stay here. There's a vibrant city out there. Let's go explore it.'

Outside the air was clear and brisk, not a cloud anywhere, a gorgeous winter day that drew every warm-blooded Bolognese into the streets for errands and long-winded chats with old friends. Pockets of intense conversation materialized as sleepy-eyed students greeted each other and housewives gathered to trade the gossip. Elderly gentlemen dressed in coats and ties shook hands and then all talked at once. Street merchants called out with their latest bargains.

But for Ermanno it was not a walk in the park. If his student wanted conversation, then he would certainly earn it. He pointed to a policeman and said to Marco, in Italian of course, 'Go to that policeman and ask directions for the Piazza Maggiore. Get them right, then repeat them to me.'

Marco walked very slowly, whispering some words, trying to recall others. Always start with a smile and the proper greeting. 'Buon giorno,' he said, almost holding his breath.

'Buon giorno,' answered the policeman.

'Mi può aiutare?' Can you help me?

'Certamente.' Certainly.

'Sono Canadese. Non parlo molto bene.' I'm Canadian. I don't speak Italian very well.

'Allora.' Okay. The policeman was still smiling, now quite anxious to help.

'Dov'è la Piazza Maggiore?'

The policeman turned and gazed into the distance, toward the central part of Bologna. He cleared his throat and Marco braced for the torrent of directions. Just a few feet away and listening to every sound was Ermanno.

With a beautifully slow cadence, he said in Italian, and pointing of course the way they all do, 'It's not too far away. Take this street, turn at the next right, that's Via Zamboni, follow it until you see the two towers. Turn on Via Rizzoli, and go for three blocks.'

Marco listened as hard as possible, then tried to repeat each phrase. The policeman patiently went through the exercise again. Marco thanked him, repeated as much as he could to himself, then unloaded it on Ermanno.

'Non c'è male,' he said. Not bad. The fun was just starting. As Marco was enjoying his little triumph, Ermanno was searching for the next unsuspecting tutor. He found him in an old man shuffling by on a cane and with a thick newspaper under his arm. 'Ask him where he bought the newspaper,' he instructed his student.

Marco took his time, followed the gentleman for a few steps, and when he thought he had the words together he said, 'Buon giorno, scusi.' The old man stopped and stared, and for a moment looked as though he might lift his cane and whack it across Marco's head. He did not offer the customary 'Buon giorno.'

'Dov'è ha comprato questo giornale?' Where did you buy this newspaper?

The old man looked at the newspaper as if it were contraband, then looked at Marco as if he'd cursed him. He jerked his head to the left and said something like, 'Over there.' And his part of the conversation was over. As he shuffled away, Ermanno eased beside Marco and said in English, 'Not much for conversation, huh?'

'I guess not.'

They stepped inside a small café, where Marco ordered a simple espresso for himself. Ermanno could not be content with simple things; instead he wanted regular coffee with sugar but without cream, and a small cherry pastry, and he made Marco order everything and get it perfect. At their table, Ermanno laid out several euro notes of various denominations, along with the coins for fifty cents and one euro, and they practiced numbers and counting. He then decided he wanted another regular coffee, this time with no sugar but just a little cream. Marco took two euros and came back with the coffee. He counted the change.

142

After the brief break, they were back on the street, drifting along Via San Vitale, one of the main avenues of the university, with porticoes covering the sidewalks on both sides and thousands of students jostling to early classes. The street was crammed with bicycles, the preferred mode of getting around. Ermanno had been studying for three years in Bologna, so he said, though Marco believed little of what he heard from either his tutor or his handler.

'This is Piazza Verdi,' Ermanno said, nodding to a small plaza where a protest of some sort was stuttering to a start. A long-haired relic from the seventies was adjusting a microphone, no doubt prepping for a screeching denunciation of American misdeeds somewhere. His cohorts were trying to unravel a large, badly painted homemade banner with a slogan not even Ermanno could understand. But they were too early. The students were half asleep and more concerned with being late for class.

'What's their problem?' Marco asked as they walked by.

'I'm not sure. Something to do with the World Bank. There's always a demonstration here.'

They walked on, flowing with the young crowd, picking their way through the foot traffic, and headed generally to il centro.

Luigi met them for lunch at a restaurant called Testerino, near the university. With American taxpayers footing the bill, he ordered often and with no regard for price. Ermanno, the broke student, seemed ill at ease with such extravagance, but, being an Italian, he eventually warmed to the idea of a long lunch. It lasted for two hours and not

143

a single word of English was spoken. The Italian was slow, methodical, and often repeated, but it never yielded to English. Marco found it difficult to enjoy a fine meal when his brain was working overtime to hear, grasp, digest, understand, and plot a response to the last phrase thrown at him. Often the last phrase had passed over his head with only a word or two being somewhat recognizable when the whole thing was suddenly chased by another. And his two friends were not just chatting for the fun of it. If they caught the slightest hint that Marco was not following, that he was simply nodding so they would keep talking so he could eat a bite, then they stopped abruptly and said, 'Che cosa ho detto?' What did I say?

Marco would chew for a few seconds, buying time to think of something—in Italian dammit!—that might get him off the hook. He was learning to listen, though, to catch the key words. Both of his friends had repeatedly said that he would always understand much more than he could say.

The food saved him. Of particular importance was the distinction between tortellini (small pasta stuffed with pork) and tortelloni (larger pasta stuffed with ricotta cheese). The chef, upon realizing that Marco was a Canadian very curious about Bolognese cuisine, insisted on serving both dishes. As always, Luigi explained that both were exclusively the creations of the great chefs of Bologna.

Marco simply ate, trying his best to devour the delicious servings while avoiding the Italian language.

After two hours, Marco insisted on a break. He finished his second espresso and said goodbye. He left them in front of the restaurant and walked away, alone, his ears ringing and his head spinning from the workout.

*   *   *

He made a two-block loop off Via Rizzoli. Then he did it again to make sure no one was following. The long porticoed walkways were ideal for ducking and hiding. When they were thick with students again he crossed Piazza Verdi, where the World Bank protest had yielded to a fiery speech that, for a moment, made Marco quite happy he could not understand Italian. He stopped at 22 Via Zamboni and once again looked at the massive wooden door that led to the law school. He walked through it and tried his best to appear as if this was his turf. No directory was in sight, but a student bulletin board advertised apartments, books, companionship, almost everything, it seemed, including a summer studies program at Wake Forest Law School.

Through the hallway, the building yielded to an open courtyard where students were milling around, chatting on cell phones, smoking, waiting for classes.

A stairway to his left caught his attention. He climbed to the third floor, where he finally located a directory of sorts. He understood the word 'uffici,' and followed a corridor past two classrooms until he found the faculty offices. Most had names, a few did not. The last belonged to Rudolph Viscovitch, so far the only non-Italian name in the building. Marco knocked and no one answered. He twisted the knob but the door was locked. He

145

quickly removed from his coat pocket a sheet of paper he'd taken from the Albergo Campeol in Treviso and scribbled a note:

Dear Rudolph: I was wandering around the campus, stumbled upon your office and wanted to say hello. Maybe I'll catch you again at the Bar Fontana. Enjoyed our chat yesterday. Nice to hear English occasionally. Your Canadian friend, Marco Lazzeri

He slid it under the door and walked down the stairs behind a group of students. Back on Via Zamboni, he drifted along with no particular destination in mind. He stopped for a gelato, then slowly made his way back to his hotel. His dark little room was too cold for a nap. He promised himself again that he would complain to his handler. Lunch had cost more than three nights' worth of his room. Surely Luigi and those above him could spring for a nicer place.

He dragged himself back to Ermanno's cupboard-sized apartment for the afternoon session.

*   *   *

Luigi waited patiently at Bologna Centrale for the nonstop Eurostar from Milano. The train station was relatively quiet, the lull before the five o'clock rush hour. At 3:35, precisely on schedule, the sleek bullet blew in for a quick stop and Whitaker bounced off.

Since Whitaker never smiled, they barely said hello. After a cursory handshake was complete, they walked to Luigi's Fiat. 'How's our boy?' Whitaker asked as soon as he slammed the door.

'Doing fine,' Luigi said as he started the engine and drove away. 'He's studying hard. There's not much else for him to do.'

'And he's staying close?'

'Yes. He likes to walk around the city, but he's afraid to venture too far. Plus, he has no money.'

'Keep him broke. How's his Italian?'

'He's learning rapidly.' They were on the Via dell' Indipendenza, a wide avenue that was taking them directly south, into the center of the city. 'Very motivated.'

'Is he scared?'

'I think so.'

'He's smart, and he's a manipulator, Luigi, don't forget that. And because he's smart, he's also very frightened. He knows the danger.'

'I told him about Critz.'

'And?'

'He was bewildered.'

'Did it scare him?'

'Yes, I think so. Who got Critz?'

'I'm assuming we did, but you never know. Is the safe house ready?'

'Yes.'

'Good. Let's see Marco's apartment.'

Via Fondazza was a quiet residential street in the southeast section of the old city, a few blocks south of the university section. As in the rest of Bologna, the walkways on both sides of the street were covered with porticoes. Doors to the homes and apartments opened directly onto the sidewalks. Most had building directories on brass plaques next to intercoms, but the one at 112 Via Fondazza did not. It was unmarked and had been for the three years it had been leased to a mysterious businessman in Milan who paid the rent but seldom used it. Whitaker had not seen it in more than a year; not that it was much of an attraction. It was a simple apartment of about six hundred square feet; four rooms with basic furnishings that cost 1,200 euros a month. It was a safe house, nothing more or less; one of three currently under his control in northern Italy.

There were two bedrooms, a tiny kitchen, and a living area with a sofa, a desk, two leather chairs, no television. Luigi pointed to the phone and they discussed, in near coded language, the bugging device that had been installed and could never be detected. There were two hidden mikes in each room, powerful little collectors that missed no human sound. There were also two microscopic cameras—one hidden in a crack of an old tile high above the den, and from there it offered a view of the front door. The other was hidden in a cheap light fixture hanging from a kitchen wall, with a clear view of the rear door.

They would not be watching his bedroom, and Luigi said he was relieved by that. If Marco managed to find a woman willing to visit him, they could catch her coming and going with the camera in the den, and that was certainly enough for Luigi. If he got really bored, he could hit a switch and listen for fun.

The safe house was bordered to the south by another apartment, with a thick stone wall separating the two. Luigi was staying there, hiding next door in a five-room flat slightly larger than Marco's. His rear door opened into a small garden that could not be seen from the safe house, thus concealing his movements. His kitchen had been converted into a high-tech snooping room where he could switch on a camera anytime he wanted and take a look at what was happening next door.

'Will they study here?' Whitaker asked.

'Yes. I think it's secure enough. Plus I can monitor things.'

Whitaker walked through each room again. When he'd seen enough he said, 'Everything's set up next door?'

'Everything. I've spent the last two nights there. We're ready.'

'How soon can you move him?'

'This afternoon.'

'Very well. Let's go see the boy.'

They walked north along Via Fondazza until it came to an end, then northwest along a wider avenue, Strada Maggiore. The rendezvous point was a small café called Lestre's. Luigi found a newspaper and sat alone at a table. Whitaker found another newspaper and sat nearby, each man ignoring the other. At precisely four-thirty, Ermanno and his student stopped by for a quick espresso with Luigi.

When the greetings were exchanged and the coats removed, Luigi asked, 'Are you tired of Italian, Marco?'

'I'm sick of it,' Marco replied with a smile.

'Good. Let's talk English.'

'God bless you,' Marco said.

Whitaker sat five feet away, partially hidden behind a newspaper, smoking a cigarette as if he had no interest in anyone around him. He of course knew of Ermanno, but had never actually seen him. Marco was another story.

Whitaker had been in Washington for a stint at Langley a dozen or so years earlier, back when everyone knew the broker. He remembered Joel Backman as a political force who spent almost as much time cultivating his oversized image as he did representing his important clients. He'd been the epitome of money and power, the perfect fat cat who could bully and cajole and throw around enough money to get whatever he wanted.

Amazing what six years in prison could do. He was very thin now, and looking quite European behind the Armani eyewear. He had the beginnings of a salt-and-pepper goatee. Whitaker was certain that virtually no one from back home could walk into Lestre's at that moment and identify Joel Backman.

Marco caught the man five feet away glancing over one time too often but thought nothing of it. They were chatting in English, and perhaps few people did so, at Lestre's anyway. Nearer the university, one could hear several languages in every coffee shop.

Ermanno excused himself after one espresso. A few minutes later Whitaker left too. He walked a few blocks and found an Internet café, one he'd used before. He plugged in his laptop, got online, and typed a message to Julia Javier at Langley:

Fondazza flat is ready to go, should move in tonight. Laid eyes on our man, having a coffee with our friends. Would not have known him otherwise. Adjusting nicely to a new life. All is in order here; no problems whatsoever.

After dark, the Fiat stopped in the middle of Via
Fondazza, and its contents were quickly unloaded.
Marco packed light because he owned practically
nothing. Two bags of clothes and some Italian
study books, and he was completely mobile. When
he stepped into his new apartment, the first thing
he noticed was that it was sufficiently heated. 'This
is more like it,' he said to Luigi.

'I'll move the car. Have a look around.'

He looked around, counted four rooms with
nice furnishings, nothing extravagant but a huge
step up from the last place. Life was improving—
ten days ago he'd been in prison.

Luigi returned in a rush. 'What do you think?'

'I'll keep it. Thank you.'

'Don't mention it.'

'And thank the folks in Washington too.'

'Did you see the kitchen?' Luigi asked, flipping
on a light switch.

'Yes, it's perfect. How long do I stay here,
Luigi?'

'I don't make those decisions. You know that.'

'I know.'

They were back in the den. 'A couple of things,'
Luigi said. 'First, Ermanno will come here each day
to study. Eight until eleven, then two until five or
whenever you wish to stop.'

'Wonderful. Please get the boy a new flat,
would you? His dump is an embarrassment to the
American taxpayers.'

'Second, this is a very quiet street, mainly
apartments. Come and go quickly, don't chat with

your neighbors, don't make any friends. Remember, Marco, you are leaving a trail. Make it wide enough and someone will find you.'

'I heard you the first ten times.'

'Then hear me again.'

'Relax, Luigi. My neighbors will never see me, I promise. I like it here. It's much nicer than my prison cell.'

14

The memorial service for Robert Critz was held in a country club–like mausoleum in a ritzy suburb of Philadelphia, the city of his birth but a place he'd avoided for at least the past thirty years. He died without a will and without a thought as to his final arrangements, leaving poor Mrs. Critz with the burden of not only getting him home from London but then deciding how to properly dispose of him. A son pressed the idea of cremation and a rather neat interment in a marble vault, one shielded from the weather. By that point Mrs. Critz would have agreed to almost any plan. Flying seven hours across the Atlantic (in coach) with her husband's remains somewhere below her, in a rather stark air-transport box made especially for dead humans, had nearly pushed her over the edge. And then there had been the chaos at the airport when no one was there to greet her and take charge. What a mess!

The service was by invitation only, a condition laid down by former president Arthur Morgan, who, after only two weeks on Barbados, was quite unwilling to return and be seen by anyone. If he was truly saddened by the death of his lifelong friend, he didn't show it. He'd haggled over the details of the service with the Critz family until he was almost asked to stay away. The date had been moved because of Morgan. The order of service didn't suit him. He reluctantly agreed to deliver a eulogy, but only if it could be very brief. Truth was, he'd never liked Mrs. Critz and she'd never liked him.

To the small circle of friends and family, it seemed implausible that Robert Critz would get so drunk in a London pub that he would stagger into a busy street and fall in front of a car. When the autopsy revealed a significant level of heroin, Mrs. Critz had become so distraught that she insisted that the report be sealed and buried. She had refused to tell even her children about the narcotic. She was absolutely certain her husband had never touched an illicit drug—he drank too much but few people knew it—but she nonetheless was determined to protect his good name.

The London police had readily agreed to lock away the autopsy findings and close the case. They had their questions all right, but they had many other cases to keep them busy, and they also had a widow who couldn't wait to get home and put it all behind her.

The service began at two on a Thursday afternoon—the time also dictated by Morgan so that the private jet could fly nonstop from Barbados to Philly International—and lasted for an hour. Eighty-two people had been invited, and fifty-one showed up, a fair majority of them more curious to see President Morgan than to say

153

goodbye to ol' Critz. A semi-Protestant minister of some variety presided. Critz had not seen the inside of a church in forty years, except for weddings and funerals. The minister was faced with the difficult task of bringing to life the memory of a man he'd never met, and though he tried gamely he failed completely. He read from the book of Psalms. He offered a generic prayer that would've fit a deacon or a serial killer. He offered soothing words to the family, but, again, they were total strangers to him.

Rather than a heart-warming send-off, the service was as cold as the gray marble walls of the faux chapel. Morgan, with a bronze tan too ridiculous for February, attempted to humor the small crowd with some anecdotes about his old pal, but he came off as a man going through the motions and wanting desperately to get back on the jet.

Hours in the Caribbean sun had convinced Morgan that the blame for his disastrous reelection campaign could be placed squarely at the feet of Robert Critz. He'd told no one of this conclusion; there really was no one to confide in since the beach mansion was deserted except for him and the staff of natives. But he'd already begun to carry a grudge, to question the friendship.

He didn't linger when the service finally ran out of gas and came to an end. He offered obligatory hugs to Mrs. Critz and her children, spoke briefly with some old friends, promised to see them in a few weeks, then rushed away with his mandatory Secret Service escort. News cameras had been stationed along a fence outside the grounds, but they caught no glimpse of the former president. He

154

was ducking in the rear of one of two black vans. Five hours later he was by the pool watching another Caribbean sunset.

Though the memorial drew a small crowd, it nonetheless was being keenly observed by others. While it was actually in progress, Teddy Maynard had a list of all fifty-one people in attendance. There was no one suspicious. No name raised an eyebrow.

The killing was clean. The autopsy was buried, thanks in part to Mrs. Critz, and thanks also in part to strings pulled at levels much higher than the London police. The body was now ashes and the world would quickly forget about Robert Critz. His idiotic foray into the Backman disappearance had ended with no damage to the plan.

The FBI had tried, and failed, to mount a hidden camera inside the chapel. The owner had balked, then refused to bend despite enormous pressure. He did allow hidden cameras outside, and these provided close shots of all the mourners as they entered and left. The live feeds were edited, the list of fifty-one quickly compiled, and an hour after the service ended the director was given a briefing.

*   *   *

The day before the death of Robert Critz, the FBI received some startling information. It was completely unexpected, unsolicited, and delivered by a desperate corporate crook staring at forty years in a federal prison. He'd been the manager of a large mutual fund who had been caught skimming fees; just another Wall Street scandal

155

involving only a few billion bucks. But his mutual fund was owned by an international banking cabal, and over the years the crook had worked his way into the inner core of the organization. The fund was so profitable, thanks in no small measure to his talent for skimming, that the profits could not be ignored. He was voted onto the board of directors and given a luxury condo in Bermuda, the corporate headquarters for his very secretive company.

In his desperation to avoid spending the rest of his life in prison, he became willing to share secrets. Banking secrets. Offshore dirt. He claimed he could prove that former president Morgan, during his last day in office, had sold at least one pardon for $3 million. The money had been wired from a bank on Grand Cayman to a bank in Singapore, both banks being secretly controlled by the cabal he'd just left. The money was still hiding in Singapore, in an account opened by a shell corporation that was really owned by an old crony of Morgan's. The money, according to the snitch, was intended for Morgan's use.

When the wire transfers and the accounts were confirmed by the FBI, a deal was suddenly put on the table. The crook was now facing only two years of light house arrest. Cash for a presidential pardon was such a sensational crime that it became a high priority at the Hoover Building.

The informant was unable to identify whose money had left Grand Cayman, but it seemed quite obvious to the FBI that only two of the people pardoned by Morgan had the potential of paying such a bribe. The first and likeliest was Duke Mongo, the geriatric billionaire who held the record for the most dollars illegally hidden from the IRS, at least by an individual. The corporate category was still open for debate. However, the informant felt strongly that Mongo was not involved because he had a long, ugly history with the banks in question. He preferred the Swiss, and this was verified by the FBI.

The second suspect was, of course, Joel Backman. Such a bribe would not be unexpected from an operator like Backman. And while the FBI had believed for many years that he had not hidden a fortune, there had always been doubt. When he was the broker he had relationships with banks in both Switzerland and the Caribbean. He had a web of shadowy friends, contacts in important places. Bribes, payoffs, campaign contributions, lobbying fees—it was all familiar turf for the broker.

The director of the FBI was an embattled soul named Anthony Price. Three years earlier he had been appointed by President Morgan, who then tried to fire him six months later. Price begged for more time and got it, but the two fought constantly. For some reason he could never quite remember, Price had also decided to prove his manhood by crossing swords with Teddy Maynard. Teddy hadn't lost many battles in the CIA's secret war with the FBI, and he certainly wasn't frightened by Anthony Price, the latest in a long line of lame ducks.

But Teddy didn't know about the cash-for-pardon conspiracy that now consumed the director of the FBI. The new President had vowed to get rid of Anthony Price and revamp his agency. He'd also promised to finally put Maynard out to pasture, but such threats had been heard many times in Washington.

Price suddenly had a beautiful opportunity to secure his job, and possibly eliminate Maynard at the same time. He went to the White House and briefed the national security advisor, who'd been confirmed the day before, on the suspicious account in Singapore. He strongly implicated former president Morgan in the scheme. He argued that Joel Backman should be located and hauled back to the United States for questioning and possible indictment. If proven to be true, it would be an earthshaking scandal, unique and truly historic.

The national security advisor listened intently. After the briefing, he walked directly to the office of the vice president, cleared out the staffers, locked the door, and unloaded everything he'd just heard. Together, they told the President.

As usual, there was no love lost between the new man in the Oval Office and his predecessor. Their campaign had been loaded with the same mean-spiritedness and dirty tricks that have become standard behavior in American politics. Even after a landslide of historic proportions and the thrill of reaching the White House, the new President was unwilling to rise above the mud. He adored the idea of once again humiliating Arthur Morgan. He could see himself, after a sensational trial and conviction, stepping in at the last minute with a pardon of his own to salvage the image of the presidency.

What a moment!

At six the following morning, the vice president was driven in his usual armed caravan to the CIA headquarters at Langley. Director Maynard had been summoned to the White House, but, suspecting some ploy, had begged off, claiming he was suffering from vertigo and confined to his office by his doctors. He often slept and ate there, especially when his vertigo was in high gear and kept him dizzy. Vertigo was one of his many handy ailments.

The meeting was brief. Teddy was sitting at the end of his long conference table, in his wheelchair, wrapped tightly in blankets, with Hoby at his side. The vice president entered with only one aide, and after some awkward chitchat about the new administration and such, he said, 'Mr. Maynard, I'm here on behalf of the President.'

'Of course you are,' Teddy said with a very tight smile. He was expecting to be fired; finally, after eighteen years and numerous threats, this was it. Finally, a president with the stones to replace Teddy Maynard. He had prepped Hoby for the moment. As they waited for the vice president, Teddy had laid out his fears.

Hoby was scribbling on his customary legal pad, waiting to write the words he'd been dreading for many years: Mr. Maynard, the President requests your resignation.

Instead, the vice president said something completely unexpected. 'Mr. Maynard, the President wants to know about Joel Backman.'

Nothing made Teddy Maynard flinch. 'What about him?' he said without hesitation.

'He wants to know where he is and how long it will take to bring him home.'

'Why?'

'I can't say.'

'Then neither can I.'

'It's very important to the President.'

'I appreciate that. But Mr. Backman is very important to our operations right now.'

The vice president blinked first. He glanced at his aide, who was consumed with his own note-taking and completely useless. They would not under any circumstances tell the CIA about the wire transfers and the bribes for pardons. Teddy would figure out a way to use that information to his advantage. He would steal their little nugget and survive yet another day. No sir, Teddy would either play ball with them or finally get himself fired.

The vice president inched forward on his elbows and said, 'The President is not going to compromise on this, Mr. Maynard. He will have this information, and he'll have it very soon. Otherwise, he will ask for your resignation.'

'He won't get it.'

'Need I remind you that you serve at his pleasure?'

'You need not.'

'Very well. The lines are clear. You come to the White House with the Backman file and discuss it with us at length, or the CIA will soon have a new director.'

'Such bluntness is rare among your breed, sir, with all due respect.'

'I'll take that as a compliment.'

The meeting was over.

*   *   *

Leaking like an old dike, the Hoover Building practically sprayed gossip onto the streets of Washington. And there to collect it was, among

160

many others, Dan Sandberg of *The Washington Post*. His sources, though, were far better than those of the average investigative journalist, and it wasn't long before he picked up the scent of the pardon scandal. He worked an old mole in the new White House and got a partial confirmation. The outline of the story began to take shape, but Sandberg knew the hard details would be virtually impossible to confirm. He stood no chance of seeing the wire-transfer records.

But if it happened to be true—a sitting president selling pardons for some serious retirement cash—Sandberg could not imagine a bigger story. A former president indicted, put on trial, maybe convicted and sent to jail. It was unthinkable.

He was at his landfill of a desk when the call came from London. It was an old friend, another hard-charging reporter who wrote for *The Guardian*. They talked a few minutes about the new administration, which was the official topic in Washington. It was, after all, early February with heavy snow on the ground and Congress mired in its annual committee work. Life was relatively slow and there was little else to talk about.

'Anything on the death of Bob Critz?' his friend asked.

'No, just a funeral yesterday,' Sandberg replied. 'Why?'

'A few questions about how the poor chap went down, you know. That, and we can't get near the autopsy.'

'What kind of questions? I thought it was open-and-shut.'

'Maybe, but it got shut really fast. Nothing

concrete, mind you, just fishing to see if there's anything amiss over there.'

'I'll make some calls,' Sandberg said, already very suspicious.

'Do that. Let's talk in a day or so.'

Sandberg hung up and stared at his blank computer monitor. Critz would certainly have been present when the last-minute pardons were granted by Morgan. Given their paranoia, there was a good chance that only Critz was in the Oval Office with Morgan when the decisions were made and the paperwork signed.

Perhaps Critz knew too much.

Three hours later, Sandberg left Dulles for London.

15

Long before dawn, Marco once again awoke in a strange bed in a strange place, and for a long time worked hard gathering his thoughts—recalling his movements, analyzing his bizarre situation, planning the day ahead, trying to forget his past while trying to predict what might happen in the next twelve hours. Sleep was fitful at best. He had dozed for a few hours; it felt like four or five but he couldn't be sure because his rather warm little room was completely dark. He removed the earphones; as usual, he'd fallen asleep sometime after midnight with happy Italian dialogue ringing in his ears.

He was thankful for the heat. They'd frozen him at Rudley and his last hotel stop had been just

162

as cold. The new apartment had thick walls and windows and a heating system that worked overtime. When he decided the day was properly organized, he slowly placed his feet on the very warm tile floor and again thanked Luigi for the change of residence.

How long he might stay here was uncertain, like most of the future they'd planned for him. He switched on the light and checked his watch— almost five. In the bathroom he switched on another light and studied himself in the mirror. The growth under his nose and along the sides of his mouth and covering his chin was coming in quite a bit grayer than he had hoped. In fact, after a week of cultivation, it was now obvious that his goatee would be at least 90 percent gray, with just a few lonely specks of dark brown thrown in. What the hell. He was fifty-two years old. It was part of the disguise and looked quite distinctive. With the thin face, hollow cheeks, short haircut, and little funky rectangular designer eyeglass frames, he could easily pass for Marco Lazzeri on any street in Bologna. Or Milan or Florence or all the other places he wanted to visit.

An hour later he stepped outside, under the cold, silent porticoes built by laborers who'd been dead for three hundred years. The wind was sharp and biting, and once again he reminded himself to complain to his handler about the lack of proper winter clothing. Marco didn't read papers and didn't watch television and thus had no idea about weather forecasts. But it was certainly getting colder.

He hustled along under the low porticoes of Via Fondazza, headed toward the university, the only person moving about. He refused to use the map tucked away in his pocket. If he got lost he might pull it out and concede a momentary defeat, but he was determined to learn the city by walking and observing. Thirty minutes later, with the sun finally showing some life, he emerged onto Via Irnerio on the northern edge of the university section. Two blocks east and he saw the pale green sign for Bar Fontana. Through the front window he saw a shock of gray hair. Rudolph was already there.

Out of habit, Marco waited for a moment. He glanced down Via Irnerio, from the direction he'd just come, waiting for someone to sneak out of the shadows like a silent bloodhound. When no one appeared, he went inside.

'My friend Marco,' Rudolph said with a smile as they exchanged greetings. 'Please sit.'

The café was half full, with the same academic types buried in their morning papers, lost in their own worlds. Marco ordered a cappuccino while Rudolph refilled his meerschaum pipe. A pleasant aroma engulfed their little corner of the place.

'Got your note the other day,' Rudolph was saying as he shot a cloud of pipe smoke across the table. 'Sorry I missed you. So where have you been?'

Marco had been nowhere, but as the laid-back Canadian tourist with Italian roots he had put together a mock itinerary. 'A few days in Florence,' he said.

'Ah, what a beautiful city.'

They talked about Florence for a while, with Marco rambling on about the sites and art and history of a place he knew only from a cheap

164

guidebook Ermanno had loaned him. It was in Italian, of course, which meant he'd labored hours with a dictionary translating it into something he could kick back and forth with Rudolph as if he'd spent weeks there.

The tables grew crowded and the latecomers packed around the bar. Luigi had explained to him early on that in Europe when you get a table, it's yours for the day. No one is rushed out the door so someone can be seated. A cup of coffee, a newspaper, something to smoke, and it doesn't matter how long you hold a table while others come and go.

They ordered another round and Rudolph repacked his pipe. For the first time Marco noticed tobacco stains on the wild whiskers closest to his mouth. On the table were three morning newspapers, all Italian.

'Is there a good English newspaper here in Bologna?' Marco asked.

'Why do you ask?'

'Oh, I don't know. Sometimes I'd like to know what's happening across the ocean.'

'I'll pick up the *Herald Tribune* occasionally. It makes me so happy that I live here, away from all the crime and traffic and pollution and politicians and scandals. U.S. society is so rotten. And the government is the height of hypocrisy—the world's brightest democracy. Hah! Congress is bought and paid for by the rich.'

When he looked as though he wanted to spit, Rudolph suddenly sucked on his pipe and began grinding away on the stem. Marco held his breath, waiting for another venomous assault on the United States. A moment passed; they both sipped

165

coffee.

'I hate the U.S. government,' Rudolph grumbled bitterly.

Attaboy, thought Marco. 'What about the Canadian?' he asked.

'I give you higher marks. Slightly higher.'

Marco pretended to be relieved and decided to change the subject. He said he was thinking of going to Venice next. Of course, Rudolph had been there many times and had lots of advice. Marco actually took notes, as if he couldn't wait to hop a train. And then there was Milano, though Rudolph wasn't too keen on it because of all the 'right-wing fascists' lurking there. 'It was Mussolini's center of power, you know,' he said, leaning in low as if the other Communists in Bar Fontana might erupt in violence at the very mention of the little dictator's name.

When it became apparent that Rudolph was willing to sit and talk through most of the morning, Marco began his exit. They agreed to meet at the same place, same time, the following Monday.

A light snow had begun, enough to leave tracks for the delivery vans on Via Irnerio. As Marco left the warm café behind, he once again marveled at the foresight of Bologna's ancient city planners who designed some twenty miles of covered sidewalks in the old town. He went a few blocks farther east and turned south on Via dell' Indipendenza, a wide elegant avenue built in the 1870s so the higher classes who lived in the center would have an easy walk to the train station north of town. When he crossed Via Marsala he stepped in a pile of shoveled snow and flinched as the frozen mush soaked his right foot.

166

He cursed Luigi for his inadequate wardrobe—
if it was going to snow then common sense would
dictate that a person needed some boots. This led
to a lengthy internal tirade about the lack of
funding Marco felt he was receiving from whoever
in hell was in charge of his current cover. They'd
dumped him in Bologna, Italy, and they were
obviously spending a fair amount on language
lessons and safe houses and personnel and
certainly food to keep him alive. In his opinion,
they were wasting valuable time and money. The
better plan would be to sneak him into London or
Sydney where there were lots of Americans and
everyone spoke English. He could blend in much
easier.

The man himself strode alongside him. 'Buon
giorno,' Luigi said.

Marco stopped, smiled, offered a handshake
and said, 'Well, buon giorno, Luigi. Are you
following me again?'

'No. I was out for a walk, saw you pass on the
other side of the street. I love the snow, Marco.
How about you?'

They were walking again, at a leisurely pace.
Marco wanted to believe his friend, but he doubted
if their meeting was an accident. 'It's okay. It's
much prettier here in Bologna than in Washington,
D.C., during rush hour traffic. What, exactly, do
you do all day long, Luigi? Mind if I ask?'

'Not at all. You can ask all you want.'

'That's what I figured. Look, I have two
complaints. Actually three.'

'No surprise. Have you had coffee?'

'Yes, but I'll take some more.'

Luigi nodded to a small corner café just ahead.

They stepped inside and found all the tables taken, so they stood along the crowded bar and sipped espresso. 'What's the first complaint?' Luigi said in a low voice.

Marco moved closer, they were practically nose to nose. 'The first two complaints are closely related. First, it's the money. I don't want a lot, but I would like to have some sort of stipend. No one likes to be broke, Luigi. I'd feel better if I had a little cash in my pocket and knew I didn't have to hoard it.'

'How much?'

'Oh, I don't know. I haven't negotiated an allowance in a long time. What about a hundred euros a week for starters. That way I can buy newspapers, books, magazines, food—you know, just the basics. Uncle Sam's paying my rent and I'm very grateful. Come to think of it, he's been paying my rent for the past six years.'

'You could still be in prison, you know.'

'Oh, thank you, Luigi. I hadn't thought of that.'

'I'm sorry, that was unkind on my—'

'Listen, Luigi, I'm lucky to be here, okay. But, at the same time, I am now a fully pardoned citizen of some country, not sure which one, but I have the right to be treated with a little dignity. I don't like being broke, and I don't like begging for money. I want the promise of a hundred euros a week.'

'I'll see what I can do.'

'Thank you.'

'The second complaint?'

'I would like some money so I can buy some clothes. Right now my feet are freezing because it's snowing outside and I don't have proper footwear. I'd also like a heavier coat, perhaps a couple of sweaters.'

'I'll get them.'

'No, I want to buy them, Luigi. Get me the cash and I'll do my own shopping. It's not asking too much.'

'I'll try.'

They backed away a few inches and each took a sip. 'The third complaint?' Luigi said.

'It's Ermanno. He's losing interest very fast. We spend six hours a day together and he's getting bored with the whole thing.'

Luigi rolled his eyes in frustration. 'I can't just snap my fingers and find another language teacher, Marco.'

'You teach me. I like you, Luigi, we have good times together. You know Ermanno is dull. He's young and wants to be in school. But you would be a great teacher.'

'I am not a teacher.'

'Then please find someone else. Ermanno doesn't want to do it. I'm afraid I'm not making much progress.'

Luigi looked away and watched two elderly gentlemen enter and shuffle by. 'I think he's leaving anyway,' he said. 'Like you said, he really wants to go back to school.'

'How long will my lessons last?'

Luigi shook his head as if he had no idea. 'That's not my decision.'

'I have a fourth complaint.'

'Five, six, seven. Let's hear them all, then maybe we could go a week with no complaints.'

'You've heard it before, Luigi. It's sort of my standing objection.'

'Is that a lawyer thing?'

169

'You've watched too much American television. I really want to be transferred to London. There are ten million people there, they all speak English. I won't waste ten hours a day trying to learn a language. Don't get me wrong, Luigi, I love Italian. The more I study, the more beautiful it becomes. But, come on, if you're going to hide me, then stash me someplace where I can survive.'

'I've already passed this along, Marco. I'm not making these decisions.'

'I know, I know. Just keep the pressure on, please.'

'Let's go.'

The snow was heavier as they left the café and resumed their walk under the covered sidewalk. Smartly dressed businessmen hustled by them on the way to work. The early shoppers were out—mainly housewives headed for the market. The street itself was busy as small cars and scooters dodged the city buses and tried to avoid the accumulating slush.

'How often does it snow here?' Marco asked.

'A few times each winter. Not much, and we have these lovely porticoes to keep us dry.'

'Good call.'

'Some date back a thousand years. We have more than any other city in the world, did you know that?'

'No. I have very little to read, Luigi. If I had some money then I could buy books, then I could read and learn such things.'

'I'll have the money at lunch.'

'And where is lunch?'

'Ristorante Cesarina, Via San Stefano, one o'clock?'

'How can I refuse?'

         *   *   *

Luigi was sitting with a woman at a table near the front of the restaurant when Marco entered, five minutes early. A serious conversation had just been interrupted. The woman stood, reluctantly, and offered a limp hand and a somber face as Luigi introduced her as Signora Francesca Ferro. She was attractive, in her mid-forties, perhaps a bit too old for Luigi, who tended to gawk at the university girls. She radiated an air of sophisticated irritation. Marco wanted to say: Excuse me, but I was invited here for lunch.

As they settled into their seats Marco noticed what was left of two fully smoked cigarettes in the ashtray. Luigi's water glass was almost completely empty. The two had been sitting there for at least twenty minutes. In very deliberate Italian, Luigi said to Marco, 'Signora Ferro is a language teacher and a local guide.' Pause, to which Marco offered a weak 'Sì.'

He glanced at the signora and smiled, to which she responded with a forced smile of her own. She appeared to be bored with him already.

Luigi continued in Italian. 'She is your new Italian teacher. Ermanno will teach you in the mornings, and Signora Ferro in the afternoons.' Marco understood all of it. He managed a fake smile in her direction and said, 'Va bene.' That's good.

'Ermanno wants to resume his studies at the university next week,' Luigi said.

'I thought so,' Marco said in English.

171

Francesca fired up another cigarette and crunched her full red lips around it. She exhaled a huge cloud of smoke and said, 'So, how is your Italian?' It was a rich, almost husky voice, one no doubt enriched by years of smoking. Her English was slow, very refined, and without an accent.

'Terrible,' Marco said.

'He's doing fine,' Luigi said. The waiter delivered a bottle of mineral water and handed over three menus. La signora disappeared behind hers. Marco followed her lead. A long silent spell followed as they contemplated food and ignored each other.

When the menus finally came down she said to Marco, 'I'd like to hear you order in Italian.'

'No problem,' he said. He'd found some things he could pronounce without drawing laughter. The waiter appeared with his pen and Marco said, 'Sì, allora, vorrei un'insalata di pomodori, e una mezza porzione di lasagna.' Yes, okay, I'd like a salad with tomatoes and a half portion of lasagna. Once again he was very thankful for transatlantic goodies such as spaghetti, lasagna, ravioli, and pizza.

'Non c'è male,' she said. Not bad.

She and Luigi stopped smoking when the salads arrived. Eating gave them a break in the awkward conversation. No wine was ordered, though much was needed.

His past, her present, and Luigi's shadowy occupation were all off-limits, so they bobbed and weaved through the meal with light talk about the weather, almost all of it mercifully in English.

When the espressos were finished Luigi grabbed the check and they hurried from the restaurant. In the process, and while Francesca

172

wasn't looking, he slid an envelope to Marco and whispered, 'Here are some euros.'

'Grazie.'

The snow was gone, the sun was up and bright. Luigi left them at the Piazza Maggiore and vanished, as only he could do. They walked in silence for a while, until she said, 'Che cosa vorrebbe vedere?' What would you like to see?

Marco had yet to step inside the main cathedral, the Basilica di San Petronio. They walked to its sweeping front steps and stopped. 'It's both beautiful and sad,' she said in English, with the first hint of a British accent. 'It was conceived by the city council as a civic temple, not a cathedral, in direct opposition to the pope in Rome. The original design was for it to be even larger than Saint Peter's Cathedral, but along the way the plans fell short. Rome opposed it, and diverted money elsewhere, some of which went to the founding of the university.'

'When was it built?' Marco asked.

'Say that in Italian,' she instructed.

'I can't.'

'Then listen: 'Quando è stata costruita?' Repeat that for me.'

Marco repeated it four times before she was satisfied.

'I don't believe in books or tapes or such things,' she said as they continued to gaze upward at the vast cathedral. 'I believe in conversation, and more conversation. To learn to speak the language, then you have to speak it, over and over and over, just like when you were a child.'

'Where did you learn English?' he asked.

'I can't answer that. I've been instructed to say

173

nothing about my past. And yours too.'

For a split second, Marco came very close to turning around and walking away. He was sick of people who couldn't talk to him, who dodged his questions, who acted as if the whole world was filled with spies. He was sick of the games.

He was a free man, he kept telling himself, completely able to come and go and make whatever decision he felt like. If he got sick of Luigi and Ermanno and now Signora Ferro, then he could tell the whole bunch, in Italian, to choke on a panino.

'It was begun in 1390, and things went smoothly for the first hundred years or so,' she said. The bottom third of the façade was a handsome pink marble; the upper two-thirds was an ugly brown brick that hadn't been layered with the marble. 'Then it fell on hard times. Obviously, the outside was never completed.'

'It's not particularly pretty.'

'No, but it's quite intriguing. Would you like to see the inside?'

What else was he supposed to do for the next three hours? 'Certamente,' he said.

They climbed the steps and stopped at the front door. She looked at a sign and said, 'Mi dica.' Tell me. 'What time does the church close?'

Marco frowned hard, rehearsed some words, and said, 'La chiesa chiude alle sei.' The church closes at six.

'Ripeta.'

He repeated it three times before she allowed him to stop, and they stepped inside. 'It's named in honor of Petronio, the patron saint of Bologna,' she said softly. The central floor of the cathedral

174

was big enough for a hockey match with large crowds on both sides. 'It's huge,' Marco said, in awe.

'Yes, and this is about one-fourth of the original design. Again, the pope got worried and applied some pressure. It cost a tremendous amount of public money, and eventually the people got tired of building.'

'It's still very impressive.' Marco was aware that they were chatting in English, which suited him fine.

'Would you like the long tour or the short one?' she asked. Though the inside was almost as cold as the outside, Signora Ferro seemed to be thawing just a bit.

'You're the teacher,' he said.

They drifted to the left and waited for a small group of Japanese tourists to finish studying a large marble crypt. Other than the Japanese, the cathedral was empty. It was a Friday in February, not exactly peak tourist season. Later in the afternoon he would learn that Francesca's very seasonal tourist work was quite slow in the winter months. That confession was the only bit of personal data she divulged.

Because business was so slow, she felt no urge to race through the Basilica di San Petronio. They saw all twenty-two side chapels and looked at most of the paintings, sculptures, glasswork, and frescoes. The chapels were built over the centuries by wealthy Bolognese families who paid handsomely for commemorative art. Their construction was a history of the city, and Francesca knew every detail. She showed him the well-preserved skull of Saint Petronio himself sitting proudly on an altar, and an astrological clock created in 1655 by two scientists who relied directly on Galileo's studies at the university.

Though sometimes bored with the intricacies of paintings and sculptures, and inundated with names and dates, Marco gamely held on as the tour inched around the massive structure. Her voice captivated him, her rich slow delivery, her perfectly refined English.

Long after the Japanese had abandoned the cathedral, they made it back to the front door and she said, 'Had enough?'

'Yes.'

They stepped outside and she immediately lit a cigarette.

'How about some coffee?' he said.

'I know just the place.'

He followed her across the street to Via Clavature; a few steps down and they ducked into Rosa Rose. 'It's the best cappuccino around the square,' she assured him as she ordered two at the bar. He started to ask her about the Italian prohibition of drinking cappuccino after ten-thirty in the morning, but let it pass. As they waited she carefully removed her leather gloves, scarf, overcoat. Perhaps this coffee would last for a while.

They took a table near the front window. She stirred in two sugars until things were just perfect. She hadn't smiled in the past three hours, and Marco was not expecting one now.

'I have a copy of the materials you're using with the other tutor,' she said, reaching for the cigarettes.

'Ermanno.'

'Whoever, I don't know him. I suggest that each

176

afternoon we do conversation based on what you have covered that morning.'

He was in no position to argue with whatever she was suggesting. 'Fine,' he said with a shrug.

She lit a cigarette, then sipped the coffee.

'What did Luigi tell you about me?' Marco asked.

'Not much. You're a Canadian. You're taking a long vacation through Italy and you want to study the language. Is that true?'

'Are you asking personal questions?'

'No, I simply asked if that was true.'

'It's true.'

'It's not my business to worry about such matters.'

'I didn't ask you to worry.'

He saw her as the stoic witness on the stand, sitting arrogantly in front of the jury, thoroughly convinced that she would not bend or break regardless of the barrage of cross-examination. She had mastered the distracted pouty look so popular among European women. She held the cigarette close to her face, her eyes studying everything on the sidewalk and seeing nothing.

Idle chitchat was not one of her specialties.

'Are you married?' he asked, the first hint of cross-examination.

A grunt, a fake smile. 'I have my orders, Mr. Lazzeri.'

'Please call me Marco. And what should I call you?'

'Signora Ferro will do for now.'

'But you're ten years younger than me.'

'Things are more formal here, Mr. Lazzeri.'

'Evidently.'

177

She snubbed out the cigarette, took another sip, and got down to business. 'Today is your free day, Mr. Lazzeri. We've done English for the last time. Next lesson, we do nothing but Italian.'

'Fine, but I'd like for you to keep one thing in mind. You're not doing me any favors, okay? You're getting paid. This is your profession. I'm a Canadian tourist with plenty of time, and if we don't get along, then I'll find someone else to study with.'

'Have I offended you?'

'You could smile more.'

She nodded slightly and her eyes were instantly moist. She looked away, through the window, and said, 'I have so little to smile about.'

16

The shops along Via Rizzoli opened at 10:00 a.m. on Saturday and Marco was waiting, studying the merchandise in the windows. With the five hundred fresh euros in his pocket, he swallowed hard, told himself he had no choice but to go in and survive his first real shopping experience in Italian. He'd memorized words and phrases until he fell asleep, but as the door closed behind him he prayed for a nice young clerk who spoke perfect English.

Not a word. It was an older gentleman with a warm smile. In less than fifteen minutes, Marco had pointed and stuttered and, at times, done quite nicely when asking sizes and prices. He left with a pair of modestly priced and youthful-looking hiking boots, the style he'd seen occasionally around the university when the weather was bad, and a black waterproof parka with a hood that rolled up in the collar. And he left with almost three hundred euros in his pocket. Hoarding cash was his newest priority.

He hustled back to his apartment, changed into the boots and the parka, then left again. The thirty-minute walk to Bologna Centrale took almost an hour with the snaking and circuitous route he used. He never looked behind him, but instead would duck into a café and study the foot traffic, or suddenly stop at a pastry shop and admire the delicacies while watching the reflections in the glass. If they were following, he didn't want them to know he was suspicious. And the practice was important. Luigi had told him more than once that soon he would be gone, and Marco Lazzeri would be left alone in the world.

The question was, how much could he trust Luigi? Neither Marco Lazzeri nor Joel Backman trusted anyone.

There was a moment of anxiety at the train station when he walked inside, saw the crowd, studied the overhead schedules of arrivals and departures, and looked about desperately for the ticket window. By habit, he also searched for anything in English. But he was learning to shove the anxiety aside and push on. He waited in line and when a window was open he stepped up quickly, smiled at the little lady on the other side of the glass, offered a pleasant 'Buon giorno,' and said, 'Vado a Milano.' I'm going to Milan.

She was already nodding.

'Alle tredici e venti,' he said. At 1:20.

'Sì, cinquanta euro,' she said. Fifty euros.

He gave her a one-hundred-euro bill because he wanted the change, then walked away clutching his ticket and patting himself on the back. With an hour to kill, he left the station and wandered down Via Boldrini two blocks until he found a café. He had a panino and a beer and enjoyed both while watching the sidewalk, expecting to see no one of any interest.

The Eurostar arrived precisely on schedule, and Marco followed the crowd as it hurried on board. It was his first train ride in Europe and he wasn't exactly sure of the protocol. He'd studied his ticket over lunch and saw nothing to indicate a seat assignment. Selection appeared to be random and haphazard and he grabbed the first available window seat. His car was less than half full when the train began moving, at exactly 1:20.

They were soon out of Bologna and the countryside was flying by. The rail track followed M4, the main auto route from Milano to Parma, Bologna, Ancona, and the entire eastern coast of Italy. After half an hour, Marco was disappointed in the scenery. It was hard to appreciate when zipping along at one hundred miles an hour; things were rather blurry and a handsome landscape was gone in a flash. And there were too many factories bunched along the line, near the transportation routes.

He soon realized why he was the only person in his car who was remotely interested in things outside. Those above the age of thirty were lost in newspapers and magazines and looked completely at ease, even bored. The younger ones were sound asleep. After a while Marco nodded off too.

The conductor woke him, saying something

180

completely incomprehensible in Italian. He caught the word 'biglietto' on the second or third try and quickly handed over his ticket. The conductor scowled at it as if he might toss poor Marco off at the next bridge, then abruptly marked it with a punch and gave it back with a wide toothy grin.

An hour later a rush of gibberish over the loudspeaker announced something to do with Milano, and the scenery began to change dramatically. The sprawling city soon engulfed them as the train slowed, then stopped, then moved again. It passed block after block of postwar apartment buildings packed tightly together, with wide avenues separating them. Ermanno's guidebook gave the population of Milano at four million; an important city, the unofficial capital of northern Italy, the country's center for finance, fashion, publishing, and industry. A hard-working industrial city with, of course, a beautiful center and a cathedral worth the visit.

The tracks multiplied and fanned out as they entered the sprawling rail yards of Milano Centrale. They came to a stop under the vast dome of the station, and when Marco stepped onto the platform he was startled at the sheer size of the place. As he walked along the platform he counted at least a dozen other tracks lined in perfect rows, most with trains waiting patiently for their passengers. He stopped at the end, in the frenzy of thousands of people coming and going, and studied the departures: Stuttgart, Rome, Florence, Madrid, Paris, Berlin, Geneva.

All of Europe was within his reach, just a few hours away.

He followed the signs down to the front

entrance and found the taxi stand, where he waited in line briefly before he hopped in the backseat of a small white Renault. 'Aeroporto Malpensa,' he said to the driver. They crawled through heavy Milano traffic until they reached the perimeter. Twenty minutes later they left the autostrada for the airport. 'Quale compagnia aerea?' the driver said over his shoulder. Which airline?

'Lufthansa,' Marco said. At Terminal 2 the cab found a spot at the curb, and Marco turned loose another forty euros. The automatic doors opened to a mass of people, and he was thankful he had no plane to catch. He checked the departures and found what he wanted—a direct flight to Dulles. He circled around the terminal until he found the Lufthansa check-in desk. A long line was waiting, but with typical German efficiency things were moving quickly.

The first prospect was an attractive redhead of about twenty-five who appeared to be traveling alone, which was something he preferred. Anyone with a partner might be tempted to talk about the strange man back at the airport with his rather odd request. She was second in line at the business-class desk. As he watched her he also spotted prospect number two: a denim-clad student with long scruffy hair, unshaven face, well-worn backpack, and a University of Toledo sweatshirt—the perfect fit. He was well back in the line, listening to music on bright yellow headphones.

Marco followed the redhead as she left the counter with her boarding card and carry-on bags. The flight was still two hours away, so she drifted through the crowd to the duty-free shop, where she stopped to inspect the latest in Swiss watches.

Seeing nothing to buy, she wandered around the corner to a newsstand and bought two fashion magazines. As she was headed to the gate, and the first security checkpoint, Marco sucked in his gut and made his move. 'Excuse me, miss, excuse me.' She couldn't help but turn and look at him, but she was too suspicious to say anything.

'Are you by chance going to Dulles?' he asked with a huge smile and the pretense of being out of breath, as if he'd just sprinted to catch her.

'Yes,' she snapped. No smile. American.

'So was I, but my passport has just been stolen. Don't know when I'll get home.' He was pulling an envelope out of his pocket. 'This is a birthday card for my father. Could you please drop it in the box when you get to Dulles? His birthday is next Tuesday, and I'm afraid I won't make it. Please.'

She looked at both him and the envelope suspiciously. It was just a birthday card, not a bomb or a gun.

He was yanking something else out of his pocket. 'Sorry, there's no stamp. Here's a euro. Please, if you don't mind.'

The face finally cracked, and she almost smiled. 'Sure,' she said, taking both the envelope and the euro and placing them in her purse.

'Thank you so much,' Marco said, ready to burst into tears. 'It's his ninetieth birthday. Thank you.'

'Sure, no problem,' she said.

The kid with the yellow headphones was more complicated. He, too, was an American, and he also fell for the lost passport story. But when Marco tried to hand over the envelope, he looked around warily as if they might be breaking the law.

183

'I don't know, man,' he said, taking a step back. 'I don't think so.'

Marco knew better than to push. He backed away and said as sarcastically as possible, 'Have a nice flight.'

Mrs. Ruby Ausberry of York, Pennsylvania, was one of the last passengers at check-in. She had taught world history in high school for forty years and was now having a delightful time spending her retirement funds traveling to places she'd only seen in textbooks. This was the last leg of a three-week adventure through most of Turkey. She was in Milano only for a connecting flight from Istanbul to Washington. The nice gentleman approached her with a desperate smile and explained that his passport had just been stolen. He would miss his father's ninetieth birthday. She gladly took the card and placed it in her bag. She cleared security and walked a quarter of a mile to the gate, where she found a seat and made herself a nest.

Behind her, less than fifteen feet away, the redhead reached a decision. It could be one of those letter bombs after all. It certainly didn't seem thick enough to carry explosives, but what did she know about such things? There was a waste can near the window—a sleek chrome can with a chrome top (they were, after all, in Milano)—and she casually walked over and dropped the letter into the garbage.

What if it explodes there? she wondered as she sat back down. It was too late. She wasn't about to go over and fish it out. And if she did, then what? Track down someone in a uniform and try to explain in English that there was a chance she was holding a letter bomb? Come on, she told herself.

184

She grabbed her carry-on and moved to the other side of the gate, as far away as possible from the waste can. And she couldn't keep her eyes off it.

The conspiracy grew. She was the first one on the 747 when they began boarding. Only with a glass of champagne did she finally relax. She'd watch CNN as soon as she got home to Baltimore. She was convinced there would be carnage at Milano's Malpensa airport.

Marco's taxi ride back to Milano Centrale cost forty-five euros, but he didn't question the driver. Why bother? The return ticket to Bologna was the same—fifty euros. After a day of shopping and traveling he was down to around one hundred euros. His little stash of cash was dwindling rapidly.

It was almost dark when the train slowed at the station in Bologna. Marco was just another weary traveler when he stepped onto the platform, but he was silently bursting with pride at the day's accomplishments. He'd purchased clothing, bought rail tickets, survived the madness of both the train station and the airport in Milano, hired two cabs, and delivered his mail, a rather full day without a hint of anyone knowing who or where he was.

And he'd never been asked to show a passport or any type of identification.

*   *   *

Luigi had taken a different train, the 11:45 express to Milano. But he stepped off at Parma and got lost in the crowd. He found a cab and took a short ride to the meeting place, a favorite café. He waited almost an hour for Whitaker, who had missed one train in Milano and caught the next one. As usual,

Whitaker was in a foul mood, which was made even worse by having to meet on a Saturday. They ordered quickly and as soon as the waiter was gone, Whitaker said, 'I don't like this woman.'

'Francesca?'

'Yes, the travel guide. We've never used her before, right?'

'Right. Relax, she's fine. She doesn't have a clue.'

'What does she look like?'

'Reasonably attractive.'

'Reasonably attractive can mean anything, Luigi. How old is she?'

'I never ask that question. Forty-five is a good guess.'

'Is she married?'

'Yes, no children. She married an older man who's in very bad health. He's dying.'

As always, Whitaker was scribbling notes, thinking about the next question. 'Dying? Why is he dying?'

'I think it's cancer. I didn't ask a lot of questions.'

'Perhaps you should ask more questions.'

'Perhaps she doesn't want to talk about certain things—her age and her dying husband.'

'Where'd you find her?'

'It wasn't easy. Language tutors are not exactly lined up like taxi drivers. A friend recommended her. I asked around. She has a good reputation in the city. And she's available. It's almost impossible to find a tutor willing to spend three hours every day with a student.'

'Every day?'

'Most weekdays. She agreed to work every

afternoon for the next month or so. It's the slow season for guides. She might have a job once or twice a week, but she'll try to be on call. Relax, she's good.'

'What's her fee?'

'Two hundred euros a week, until spring when tourism picks up.'

Whitaker rolled his eyes as if the money would come directly from his salary. 'Marco's costing too much,' he said, almost to himself.

'Marco has a great idea. He wants to go to Australia or New Zealand or someplace where the language won't be a problem.'

'He wants a transfer?'

'Yes, and I think it's a great idea. Let's dump him on someone else.'

'That's not our decision, is it, Luigi?'

'I guess not.'

The salads arrived and they were quiet for a moment. Then Whitaker said, 'I still don't like this woman. Keep looking for someone else.'

'There is no one else. What are you afraid of?'

'Marco has a history with women, okay? There's always the potential for romance. She could complicate things.'

'I've warned her. And she needs the money.'

'She's broke?'

'I get the impression things are very tight. It's the slow season, and her husband is not working.'

Whitaker almost smiled, as if this was good news. He stuffed a large wedge of tomato in his mouth and chomped on it while peering around the trattoria to see if anyone was eavesdropping on their hushed conversation in English. When he was finally able to swallow, he said, 'Let's talk about e-mail. Marco was never much of a hacker. Back in his glory days he lived on the phone—had four or five of them in his office, two in his car, one in his pocket—always juggling three conversations at once. He bragged about charging five thousand bucks just to take a phone call from a new client, that sort of crap. Never used the computer. Those who worked for him have said that he occasionally read e-mails. He rarely sent them, and when he did it was always through a secretary. His office was high-tech, but he hired people to do the grunt work. He was too much of a big shot.'

'What about prison?'

'No evidence of e-mail. He had a laptop which he used only for letters, never e-mail. It looks as though everyone abandoned him when he took the fall. He wrote occasionally to his mother and his son, but always used regular mail.'

'Sounds completely illiterate.'

'Sounds like it, but Langley's concerned that he might try and contact someone on the outside. He can't do it by phone, at least not now. He has no address he can use, so mail is probably out of the question.'

'He'd be stupid to mail a letter,' Luigi said. 'It might divulge his whereabouts.'

'Exactly. Same for the phone, fax, everything but e-mail.'

'We can track e-mail.'

'Most of it, but there are ways around it.'

'He has no computer and no money to buy one.'

'I know, but, hypothetically, he could sneak into an Internet café, use a coded account, send the e-mail, then clean his trail, pay a small fee for the rental, and walk away.'

'Sure, but who's gonna teach him how to do that?'

'He can learn. He can find a book. It's unlikely, but there's always a chance.'

'I'm sweeping his apartment every day,' Luigi said. 'Every inch of it. If he buys a book or lays down a receipt, I'll know it.'

'Scope out the Internet cafés in the neighborhood. There are several of them in Bologna now.'

'I know them.'

'Where's Marco right now?'

'I don't know. It's Saturday, a day off. He's probably roaming the streets of Bologna, enjoying his freedom.'

'And he's still scared?'

'He's terrified.'

*　　　*　　　*

Mrs. Ruby Ausberry took a mild sedative and slept for six of the eight hours it took to fly from Milano to Dulles International. The lukewarm coffee they served before landing did little to clear the cobwebs, and as the 747 taxied to the gate she dozed off again. She forgot about the birthday card as they were herded onto the cattle cars on the tarmac and driven to the main terminal. She forgot about it as she waited with the mob to claim her baggage and plod through customs. And she forgot about it when she saw her beloved granddaughter waiting for her at the arrival exit.

She forgot about it until she was safely at home in York, Pennsylvania, and shuffling through her shoulder bag for a souvenir. 'Oh my,' she said as the card fell onto the kitchen table. 'I was supposed to drop this off at the airport.' Then she told her granddaughter the story of the poor guy in the Milan airport who'd just lost his passport and would miss his father's ninetieth birthday.

Her granddaughter looked at the envelope. 'Doesn't look like a birthday card,' she said. She studied the address: R. N. Backman, Attorney at Law, 412 Main Street, Culpeper, Virginia, 22701.

'There's no return address,' the granddaughter said.

'I'll mail it first thing in the morning,' Mrs. Ausberry said. 'I hope it arrives before the birthday.'

17

At ten Monday morning in Singapore, the mysterious $3 million sitting in the account of Old Stone Group, Ltd, made an electronic exit and began a quiet journey to the other side of the world. Nine hours later, when the doors of the Galleon Bank and Trust opened on the Caribbean island of Saint Christopher, the money arrived promptly and was deposited in a numbered account with no name. Normally it would have been a completely anonymous transaction, one of several thousand that Monday morning, but Old Stone now had the full attention of the FBI. The bank in Singapore was cooperating fully. The bank on Saint Christopher was not, though it would soon get the opportunity to participate.

When Director Anthony Price arrived in his office at the Hoover Building before dawn on Monday, the hot memo was waiting. He canceled everything planned for that morning. He huddled with his team and waited for the money to land on Saint Christopher.

Then he called the vice president.

It took four hours of undiplomatic arm-breaking to shake the information loose on Saint Christopher. At first the bankers refused to budge, but what small quasi-nation can withstand the full might and fury of the world's only superpower? When the vice president threatened the prime minister with economic and banking sanctions that would destroy what little economy the island was clinging to, he finally knuckled under and turned on his bankers.

The numbered account could be directly traced to Artie Morgan, the thirty-one-year-old son of the former president. He'd been in and out of the Oval Office during the final hours of his father's administration, sipping Heinekens and occasionally dispensing advice to both Critz and the President.

The scandal was ripening by the hour.

From Grand Cayman to Singapore and now to Saint Christopher, the wiring bore the telltale signs of an amateur trying to cover his tracks. A professional would've split the money eight ways and parked it in several different banks in different countries, and the wires would've been months apart. But even a rookie like Artie should've been able to hide the cash. The offshore banks he selected were secretive enough to protect him. The break for the feds had been the mutual-fund crook desperate to avoid prison.

191

However, there was still no evidence as to the source of the money. In his last three days in office, President Morgan granted twenty-two pardons. All went unnoticed except two: Joel Backman and Duke Mongo. The FBI was hard at work digging for financial dirt on the other twenty. Who had $3 million? Who had the resources to get it? Every friend, family member, and business associate was being scrutinized by the feds.

A preliminary analysis repeated what was already known. Mongo had billions and was certainly corrupt enough to bribe anyone. Backman, too, could pull it off. A third possibility was a former New Jersey state legislator whose family made a bundle in government road contracts. Twelve years earlier he'd gone to 'federal camp' for a few months and now wanted his rights restored.

The President was off in Europe, in the middle of his get-acquainted tour, his first victory lap around the world. He wouldn't be back for three days, and the vice president decided to wait. They would watch the money, double- and triple-check the facts and details, and when he returned they would brief him with an airtight case. A cash-for-pardon scandal would electrify the country. It would humiliate the opposition party and weaken its resolve in Congress. It would ensure that Anthony Price would head the FBI for a few more years. It would finally send old Teddy Maynard off to the retirement home. There was simply no downside to the launching of a full federal blitz against an unsuspecting ex-president.

* * *

His tutor was waiting in the back pew of the Basilica di San Francesco. She was still bundled, with her gloved hands stuck partially in the pockets of her heavy overcoat. It was snowing again outside, and in the vast, cold, empty sanctuary the temperature was not much warmer. He sat beside her and offered a soft 'Buon giorno.'

She acknowledged him with just enough of a smile to be considered polite, and said, 'Buon giorno.' He kept his hands in his pockets too, and for a long time they sat like two frozen hikers hiding from the weather. As usual, her face was sad and her thoughts were on something other than this bumbling Canadian businessman who wanted to speak her language. She was aloof and distracted and Marco was fed up with her attitude. Ermanno was losing interest by the day. Francesca was barely tolerable. Luigi was always back there, lurking and watching, but he, too, seemed to be losing interest in the game.

Marco was beginning to think that the break was about to happen. Cut the lifeline and set him adrift to sink or swim on his own. So be it. He'd been free for almost a month. He'd learned enough Italian to survive. He could certainly learn more by himself.

'So how old is this one?' he said after it became apparent that he was expected to speak first.

She shifted slightly, cleared her throat, took her hands out of her pockets, as if he'd awakened her from a deep sleep. 'It was begun in 1236 by some Franciscan monks. Thirty years later the main sanctuary here was complete.'

'A rush job.'

'Yes, quite fast. Over the centuries the chapels sort of sprang up along both sides. The sacristy was built, then the bell tower. The French, under Napoleon, deconsecrated it in 1798 and turned it into a customs house. In 1886 it was converted back to a church, then restored in 1928. When Bologna was bombed by the Allies its façade was extensively damaged. It's had a rough history.'

'It's not very pretty on the outside.'

'Bombing will do that.'

'I guess you picked the wrong side.'

'Bologna did not.'

No sense refighting the war. They paused as their voices seemed to float up and echo slightly around the dome. Backman's mother had taken him to church a few times each year as a child, but that halfhearted effort at pursuing a faith had been abandoned quickly in high school and totally forgotten over the past forty years. Not even prison could convert him, unlike some of the other inmates. But it was still difficult for a man with no convictions to understand how any style of meaningful worship could be conducted in a such a cold, heartless museum.

'It seems so empty. Does anyone ever worship in this place?'

'There's a daily mass and services on Sunday. I was married here.'

'You're not supposed to talk about yourself. Luigi will get mad.'

'Italian, Marco, no more English.' In Italian, she asked him, 'What did you study this morning with Ermanno?'

'La famiglia.'

'La sua famiglia. Mi dica.' Tell me about your

194

family.

'It's a real mess,' he said in English.

'Sua moglie?' Your wife?

'Which one? I have three.'

'Italian.'

'Quale? Ne ho tre.'

'L'ultima.' The last one.

Then he caught himself. He was not Joel Backman, with three ex-wives and a screwed-up family. He was Marco Lazzeri from Toronto, with a wife, four children, and five grandchildren. 'I was kidding,' he said in English. 'I have one wife.'

'Mi dica, in Italiano, di sua moglie?' Tell me about your wife.

In very slow Italian, Marco described his fictional wife. Her name is Laura. She is fifty-two years old. She lives in Toronto. She works for a small company. She does not like to travel. And so on.

Every sentence was repeated at least three times. Every mispronunciation was met with a grimace and a quick 'Ripeta.' Over and over, Marco went on and on about a Laura who did not exist. And when he finished with her, he was led to his oldest child, another creation, this one named Alex. Thirty years old, a lawyer in Vancouver, divorced with two kids, etc., etc.

Fortunately, Luigi had given him a little biography on Marco Lazzeri, complete with all the data he was now reaching for in the back of a frigid church. She prodded him on, urging perfection, cautioning against speaking too fast, the natural tendency.

'Deve parlare lentamente,' she kept saying. You must speak slowly.

195

She was strict and no fun, but also very motivational. If he could learn to speak Italian half as well as she spoke English, then he would be ahead of the pack. If she believed in constant repetition, then so did he.

As they were discussing his mother, an elderly gentleman entered the church and sat in the pew directly in front of them. He was soon lost in meditation and prayer. They decided to make a quiet exit. A light snow was still falling and they stopped at the first café for espresso and a smoke.

'Adesso, possiamo parlare della sua famiglia?' he asked. Can we talk about your family now?

She smiled, showed teeth, a rarity, and said, 'Benissimo, Marco.' Very good. 'Ma, non possiamo. Mi dispiace.' But, I'm sorry. We cannot.

'Perchè non?' Why not?

'Abbiamo delle regole.' We have rules.

'Dov'è suo marito?' Where is your husband?

'Qui, a Bologna.' Here, in Bologna.

'Dov'è lavora?' Where does he work?

'Non lavora.'

After her second cigarette they ventured back onto the covered sidewalks and began a thorough lesson about snow. She delivered a short sentence in English, and he was supposed to translate it. It is snowing. It never snows in Florida. Maybe it will snow tomorrow. It snowed twice last week. I love the snow. I don't like snow.

They skirted the edge of the main plaza and stayed under the porticoes. On Via Rizzoli they passed the store where Marco bought his boots and his parka and he thought she might like to hear his version of that event. He could handle most of the Italian. He let it pass, though, since she was so

196

engrossed in the weather. At an intersection they stopped and looked at Le Due Torri, the two surviving towers that the Bolognesi were so proud of.

There were once more than two hundred towers, she said. Then she asked him to repeat the sentence. He tried, butchered the past tense and the number, and was then asked to repeat the damn sentence until he got it right.

In medieval times, for reasons present-day Italians cannot explain, their ancestors seized upon the unusual architectural compulsion of building tall slender towers in which to live. Since tribal wars and local hostilities were epidemic, the towers were meant principally for protection. They were effective lookout posts and valuable during attacks, though they proved to be less than practical as living quarters. To protect the food, the kitchens were often on the top floor, three hundred or so steps above the street, which made it difficult to find dependable domestic help. When fights broke out, the warring families were known to simply launch arrows and fling spears at each other from one offending tower to the other. No sense fighting in the streets like common folk.

They also became quite the status symbol. No self-respecting noble could allow his neighbor and/or rival to have a taller tower, so in the twelfth and thirteenth centuries a curious game of one-upmanship raged over the skyline of Bologna as the nobles tried to keep up with the Joneses. The city was nicknamed la turrita, the towered one. An English traveler described it as a 'bed of asparagus.'

By the fourteenth century organized

government was gaining a foothold in Bologna, and those with vision knew that the warring nobles had to be reined in. The city, whenever it had enough muscle to get away with it, tore down many of the towers. Age and gravity took care of others; poor foundations crumbled after a few centuries.

In the late 1800s, a noisy campaign to tear them all down was narrowly approved. Only two survived—Asinelli and Garisenda. Both stand near each other at the Piazza di Porto Ravegnana. Neither stands exactly straight, with Garisenda drifting off to the north at an angle that rivals the more famous, and far prettier, one in Pisa. The two old survivors have evoked many colorful descriptions over the decades. A French poet likened them to two drunk sailors staggering home, trying to lean on one another for support. Ermanno's guidebook referred to them as the 'Laurel and Hardy' of medieval architecture.

La Torre degli Asinelli was built in the early twelfth century, and, at 97.2 meters, is twice as tall as its partner. Garisenda began leaning as it was almost completed in the thirteenth century, and was chopped in half in an effort to stop the tilt. The Garisenda clan lost interest and abandoned the city in disgrace.

Marco had learned the history from Ermanno's book. Francesca didn't know this, and she, like all good guides, took fifteen cold minutes to talk about the famous towers. She formulated a simple sentence, delivered it perfectly, helped Marco stumble through it, then grudgingly went to the next one.

'Asinelli has four hundred and ninety-eight steps to the top,' she said.

'Andiamo,' Marco said quickly. Let's go. They entered the thick foundation through a narrow door, followed a tight circular staircase up fifty feet or so to where the ticket booth had been stuck in a corner. He bought two tickets at three euros each, and they started the climb. The tower was hollow, with the stairs fixed to the outside walls.

Francesca said she hadn't climbed it in at least ten years, and seemed excited about their little adventure. She took off, up the narrow, sturdy oak steps, with Marco keeping his distance behind. An occasional small open window allowed light and cold air to filter in. 'Pace yourself,' she called over her shoulder, in English, as she slowly pulled away from Marco. On that snowy February afternoon there were no others climbing to the top of the city.

He paced himself and she was soon out of sight. About halfway up, he stopped at a large window so the wind could cool his face. He caught his breath, then took off again, even slower now. A few minutes later, he stopped again, his heart pounding away, his lungs working overtime, his mind wondering if he could make it. After 498 steps he finally emerged from the boxlike attic and stepped onto the top of the tower. Francesca was smoking a cigarette, gazing upon her beautiful city, no sign of sweat anywhere on her face.

The view from the top was panoramic. The red tile roofs of the city were covered with two inches of snow. The pale green dome of San Bartolomeo was directly under them, refusing any accumulation. 'On a clear day, you can see the Adriatic Sea to the east, and the Alps to the north,' she said, still in English. 'It's just beautiful, even in the snow.'

'Just beautiful,' he said, almost panting. The wind whipped through the metal bars between the brick posts, and it was much colder above Bologna than on its streets.

'The tower is the fifth-tallest structure in old Italy,' she said proudly. He was certain she could name the other four.

'Why was this tower saved?' he asked.

'Two reasons, I think. It was well designed and well built. The Asinelli family was strong and powerful. And it was used as a prison briefly in the fourteenth century, when many of the other towers were demolished. Truthfully, no one really knows why this one was spared.' Three hundred feet up, and she was a different person. Her eyes were alive, her voice radiant.

'This always reminds me of why I love my city,' she said with a rare smile. Not at him, not at anything he said, but at the rooftops and skyline of Bologna. They stepped to the other side and looked in the distance to the southwest. On a hill above the city they could see the outline of Santuario di San Luca, the guardian angel of the city.

'Have you been there?' she asked.

'No.'

'We'll do it one day when the weather is nice, okay?'

'Sure.'

'We have so much to see.'

Maybe he wouldn't fire her after all. He was so starved for companionship, especially from the opposite sex, that he could tolerate her aloofness and sadness and mood swings. He would study even harder to gain her approval.

If the climb to the top of the Asinelli Tower had buoyed her spirits, the trip down brought back the same old dour demeanor. They had a quick espresso near the towers and said goodbye. As she walked away, no superficial hug, no cheek-pecking, not even a cursory handshake, he decided he would give her one more week.

He put her on secret probation. She had seven days to become nice, or he'd simply stop the lessons. Life was too short.

She was very pretty, though.

*   *   *

The envelope had been opened by his secretary, just like all the other mail from yesterday and the day before. But inside the first envelope was another, this one addressed simply to Neal Backman. In bold print on the front and back were the dire warnings: PERSONAL, CONFIDENTIAL, TO BE OPENED ONLY BY NEAL BACKMAN.

'You might want to look at the one on top,' the secretary said as she hauled in his daily stack of mail at 9:00 a.m. 'The envelope was postmarked two days ago in York, Pennsylvania.' When she closed the door behind her, Neal examined the envelope. It was light brown in color, with no markings other than what had been hand-printed by the sender. The printing looked vaguely familiar.

With a letter opener, he slowly cut along the top of the envelope, then pulled out a single sheet of folded white paper. It was from his father. It was a shock, but then it was not.

Dear Neal: *Feb. 21*

I'm safe for now but I doubt it will last. I need your help. I have no address, no phone, no fax, and I'm not sure I would use them if I could. I need access to e-mail, something that cannot be traced. I have no idea how to do this, but I know you can figure it out. I have no computer and no money. There is a good chance you are being watched, so whatever you do, you must not leave a trail. Cover your tracks. Cover mine. Trust no one. Watch everything. Hide this letter, then destroy it. Send me as much money as possible. You know I'll pay it back. Never use your real name on anything. Use the following address:

Sr. Rudolph Viscovitch, Università degli Studi, University of Bologna, Via Zamboni 22, 44041, Bologna, Italy. Use two envelopes—the first for Viscovitch, the second for me. In your note to him ask him to hold the package for Marco Lazzeri.

Hurry!   *Love, Marco*

Neal placed the letter on his desk and walked over to lock his door. He sat on a small leather sofa and tried to arrange his thoughts. He had already decided his father was out of the country, otherwise he would've made contact weeks earlier. Why was he in Italy? Why was the letter mailed from York, Pennsylvania?

Neal's wife had never met her father-in-law. He'd been in prison for two years when they met and married. They had sent photos of the wedding, and later a photo of their child, Joel's second granddaughter.

Joel was not a topic Neal liked to talk about it. Or think about. He had been a lousy father, absent

202

for most of his childhood, and his astounding plunge from power had embarrassed everyone close to him. Neal had grudgingly sent letters and cards during the incarceration, but he could truthfully say, at least to himself and his wife, that he did not miss his father. He'd rarely been around the man.

Now he was back, asking for money that Neal did not have, assuming with no hesitation that Neal would do exactly as he was instructed, perfectly willing to endanger someone else.

Neal walked to his desk and read the letter again, then again. It was the same scarcely readable chicken scratch he'd seen throughout his life. And it was his same method of operation, whether at home or at the office. Do this, this, and this, and everything will work. Do it my way, and do it now! Hurry! Risk everything because I need you.

And what if everything worked smoothly and the broker came back? He certainly wouldn't have time for Neal and the granddaughter. If given the chance, Joel Backman, fifty-two, would once again rise to glory in the power circles of Washington. He'd make the right friends, hustle the right clients, marry the right woman, find the right partners, and within a year he'd once again work from a vast office where he would charge outrageous fees and bully congressmen.

Life had been much simpler with his father in prison.

What would he tell Lisa, his wife? Honey, that $2,000 we have buried in our savings account has just been spoken for. Plus a few hundred bucks for an encrypted e-mail system. And you and the baby keep the doors locked at all times because life just became much more dangerous.

With the day shot to hell, Neal buzzed his secretary and asked her to hold his calls. He stretched out on the sofa, kicked off his loafers, closed his eyes, and began massaging his temples.

18

In the nasty little war between the CIA and the FBI, both sides often used certain journalists for tactical reasons. Preemptive strikes could be launched, counterattacks blunted, hasty retreats glossed over, even damage control could be implemented by manipulating the press. Dan Sandberg had cultivated sources on both sides for almost twenty years and was perfectly willing to be used when the information was correct, and exclusive. He was also willing to assume the role of courier, cautiously moving between the armies with sensitive gossip to see how much the other side knew. In his effort to confirm the story that the FBI was investigating a cash-for-pardon scandal, he contacted his most reliable source at the CIA. He was met with the usual stonewall, one that lasted less than forty-eight hours.

His contact at Langley was Rusty Lowell, a frazzled career man with shifting titles. Whatever he was paid to do, his real job was watching the press and advising Teddy Maynard on how to use and abuse it. He was not a snitch, not one to pass along anything that wasn't true. After years of working at the relationship, Sandberg was reasonably confident that most of what he got from

Lowell was doled out by Teddy himself.

They met at Tyson's Corner Mall, over in Virginia, just off the Beltway, in the back of a cheap pizzeria on the upper-level food court. They each bought one slice of pepperoni and cheese and a soft drink, then found a booth where no one could see them. The usual rules applied: (1) everything was off the record and deep background; (2) Lowell would give the green light before Sandberg could run any story; and (3) if anything Lowell said was contradicted by another source, he, Lowell, would have the chance to review it and offer the last word.

As an investigative journalist, Sandberg hated the rules. However, Lowell had never been wrong, and he was not talking to anyone else. If Sandberg wanted to mine this rich source, he had to play by the rules.

'They've found some money,' Sandberg began. 'And they think it's linked to a pardon.'

Lowell's eyes always betrayed him because he was never deceitful. They narrowed immediately and it was obvious that this was something new.

'Does the CIA know this?' Sandberg asked.

'No,' Lowell said bluntly. He had never been afraid of the truth. 'We've been watching some accounts offshore, but nothing's happened. How much money?'

'A lot. I don't know how much. And I don't know how they found it.'

'Where did it come from?'

'They don't know for sure, but they're desperate to link it to Joel Backman. They're talking to the White House.'

'And not us.'

'Evidently not. It reeks of politics. They'd love to pin a scandal on President Morgan, and Backman would be the perfect conspirator.'

'Duke Mongo would be a nice target too.'

'Yes, but he's practically dead. He's had a long, colorful career as a tax cheat, but now he's out to pasture. Backman has secrets. They want to haul him back, run him through the grinder over at Justice, blow the top off Washington for a few months. It will humiliate Morgan.'

'The economy's sliding like hell. What a wonderful diversion.'

'Like I said, it's all about politics.'

Lowell finally took a bite of pizza and chewed it quickly as he thought. 'Can't be Backman. They're way off target.'

'You're sure.'

'I'm positive. Backman had no idea a pardon was in the works. We literally yanked him out of his cell in the middle of the night, made him sign some papers, then shipped him out of the country before sunrise.'

'And where did he go?'

'Hell, I don't know. And if I did I wouldn't tell you. The point is that Backman had no time to arrange a bribe. He was buried so deep in prison he couldn't even dream of a pardon. It was Teddy's idea, not his. Backman's not their man.'

'They intend to find him.'

'Why? He's a free man, fully pardoned, not some convict on the run. He can't be extradited, unless of course they squeeze an indictment.'

'Which they can do.'

Lowell frowned at the table for a second or two. 'I can't see an indictment. They have no proof.

They have some suspicious money sitting in a bank, as you say, but they don't know where it came from. I assure you it's not Backman's money.'

'Can they find him?'

'They're gonna put the pressure on Teddy, and that's why I wanted to talk.' He shoved the half-eaten pizza aside and leaned in closer. 'There will soon be a meeting in the Oval Office. Teddy will be there, and he'll be asked by the President to see the sensitive stuff on Backman. He will refuse. Then it's showdown time. Will the Prez have the guts to fire the old man?'

'Will he?'

'Probably. At least Teddy is expecting it. This is his fourth president, which, as you know, is a record, and the first three have all wanted to fire him. Now, though, he's old and ready to go.'

'He's been old and ready to go forever.'

'True, but he's run a tight ship. This time it's different.'

'Why doesn't he just resign?'

'Because he's a cranky, contrary, stubborn old son of a bitch, you know that.'

'That's well established.'

'And if he gets fired, he's not going peacefully. He'd like balanced coverage.'

'Balanced coverage' was their long-standing buzzword for 'slant it our way.'

Sandberg slid his pizza away too and cracked his knuckles. 'Here's the story as I see it,' he said, part of the ritual. 'After eighteen years of solid leadership at the CIA, Teddy Maynard gets sacked by a brand-new president. The reason is that Maynard refused to divulge details of sensitive ongoing operations. He stood his ground to protect national security, and stared down the President, who, along with the FBI, wants classified information so that it, the FBI, can pursue an investigation relating to pardons granted by former president Morgan.'

'You cannot mention Backman.'

'I'm not ready to use names. I don't have confirmation.'

'I assure you the money did not come from Backman. And if you use his name at this point, there's a chance he'll see it and do something stupid.'

'Like what?'

'Like, run for his life.'

'Why is that stupid?'

'Because we don't want him running for his life.'

'You want him dead?'

'Of course. That's the plan. We want to see who kills him.'

Sandberg settled back against the hard plastic bench and looked away. Lowell picked slices of pepperoni off his cold rubbery pizza, and for a long time they thought in silence. Sandberg drained his Diet Coke, and finally said, 'Teddy somehow convinced Morgan to pardon Backman, who's stashed away somewhere as bait for the kill.'

Lowell was looking away but nodding.

'And the killing will answer some questions over at Langley?'

'Perhaps. That's the plan.'

'Does Backman know why he was pardoned?'

'We certainly haven't told him, but he's fairly bright.'

'Who's after him?'

'Some very dangerous people who carry grudges.'

'Do you know who?'

A nod, a shrug, a nonanswer. 'There are several with potential. We'll watch closely and maybe learn something. Maybe not.'

'And why are they carrying grudges?'

Lowell laughed at the ridiculous question. 'Nice try, Dan. You've been asking that for six years now. Look, I gotta go. Work on the balanced piece and let me see it.'

'When is the meeting with the President?'

'Not sure. As soon as he gets back.'

'And if Teddy's terminated?'

'You'll be the first person I call.'

*   *   *

As a small-town lawyer in Culpeper, Virginia, Neal Backman was earning far less than what he had dreamed about in law school. Back then, his father's firm was such a force in D.C. that he could easily see himself making the big bucks after only a few years of practice. The greenest associates at Backman, Pratt & Bolling started at $100,000 a year, and a rising junior partner thirty years of age would earn three times as much. During his second year of law school, a local magazine put the broker on the cover and talked about his expensive toys. His income was estimated at $10 million a year. This had caused quite a stir around law school, something Neal was not uncomfortable with. He could remember thinking how wonderful the future would be with all that earning potential.

However, less than a year after signing on as a

green associate, he was sacked by the firm after his father pled guilty, and was literally thrown out of the building.

But Neal had soon stopped dreaming of the big money and the glitzy lifestyle. He was perfectly content to practice law with a nice little firm on Main Street and hopefully take home $50,000 a year. Lisa stopped working when their daughter was born. She managed the finances and kept their lives on budget.

After a sleepless night, he awoke with a rough idea of how to proceed. The most painful issue had been whether or not to tell his wife. Once he decided not to, the plan began to take shape. He went to the office at eight, as usual, and puttered online for an hour and a half, until he was sure the bank was open. As he walked down Main Street he found it impossible to believe that there might be people lurking nearby watching his movements. Still, he would take no chances.

Richard Koley ran the nearest branch of Piedmont National Bank. They went to church together, hunted grouse, played softball for the Rotary Club. Neal's law firm had banked there forever. The lobby was empty at such an early hour, and Richard was already at his desk with a tall cup of coffee, *The Wall Street Journal,* and evidently very little to do. He was pleasantly surprised to see Neal, and for twenty minutes they talked about college basketball. When they eventually got around to business, Richard said, 'So what can I do for you?'

'Just curious,' Neal said casually, delivering lines he'd been rehearsing all morning. 'How much might I borrow with just my signature?'

'Bit of a jam, huh?' Richard was grabbing the mouse and already glancing at the monitor, where all answers were stored.

'No, nothing like that. Rates are so low and I've got my eye on a hot stock.'

'Not a bad strategy, really, though I certainly can't advertise it. With the Dow at ten thousand again you wonder why more folks don't load up with credit and buy stocks. It would certainly be good for the old bank.' He managed an awkward banker's chuckle at his own quick humor. 'Income range?' he asked, tapping keys, somber-faced now.

'It varies,' Neal said. 'Sixty to eighty.'

Richard frowned even more, and Neal couldn't tell if it was because he was sad to learn his friend made so little, or because his friend earned so much more than he. He'd never know. Small-town banks were not known for overpaying their people.

'Total debts, outside the mortgage?' he asked, tapping again.

'Hmmm, let's see.' Neal closed his eyes and ran through the math again. His mortgage was almost $200,000 and Piedmont held that. Lisa was so opposed to debt that their own little balance sheet was remarkably clean. 'Car loan of about twenty grand,' he said. 'Maybe a thousand or so on the credit cards. Not much, really.'

Richard nodded his approval and never took his eyes off the monitor. When his fingers left the keyboard, he shrugged and turned into the generous banker. 'We could do three thousand on a signature. Six percent interest, for twelve months.'

Since he'd never borrowed with no collateral, Neal wasn't sure what to expect. He had no idea

211

what his signature would command, but somehow $3,000 sounded about right. 'Can you go four thousand?' he asked.

Another frown, another hard study of the monitor, then it revealed the answer. 'Sure, why not? I know where to find you, don't I?'

'Good. I'll keep you posted on the stock.'

'Is this a hot tip, something on the inside?'

'Give me a month. If the price goes up, I'll come back and brag a little.'

'Fair enough.'

Richard was opening a drawer, looking for forms. Neal said, 'Look, Richard, this is just between us boys, okay? Know what I mean? Lisa won't be signing the papers.'

'No problem,' the banker said, the epitome of discretion. 'My wife doesn't know half of what I do on the financial end. Women just don't understand.'

'You got it. And along those lines, would it be possible to get the funds in cash?'

A pause, a puzzled look, but then anything was possible at Piedmont National. 'Sure, give me an hour or so.'

'I need to run to the office and sue a guy, okay? I'll be back around noon to sign everything and get the money.'

Neal hustled to his office, two blocks away, with a nervous pain in his stomach. Lisa would kill him if she found out, and in a small town secrets were hard to bury. In four years of a very happy marriage they had made all decisions together. Explaining the loan would be painful, though she would probably come around if he told the truth.

Repaying the money would pose a challenge.

His father had always been one to make easy promises. Sometimes he came through, sometimes he didn't, and he was never too concerned one way or the other. But that was the old Joel Backman. The new one was a desperate man with no friends, no one to trust.

What the hell. It was only $4,000. Richard would keep it quiet. Neal would worry about the loan later. He was, after all, a lawyer. He could squeeze in some extra fees here and there, put in a few more hours.

His primary concern at that moment was the package to be shipped to Rudolph Viscovitch.

*   *   *

With the cash bulging in his pocket, Neal fled Culpeper during the lunch hour and hurried up to Alexandria, ninety minutes away. He found the store, Chatter, in a small strip mall on Russell Road, a mile or so from the Potomac River. It advertised itself online as the place to go for the latest in telecom gadgetry, and one of the few places in the United States where one could purchase unlocked cell phones that would work in Europe. As he browsed for a few moments, he was astounded at the selection of phones, pagers, computers, satellite phones—everything one could possibly need to keep in touch. He couldn't browse for long—there was a four o'clock deposition in his office. Lisa would be making one of her many daily check-ins to see what, if anything, was happening downtown.

He asked a clerk to show him the Ankyo 850 PC Pocket Smartphone, the greatest technological marvel to hit the market in the past ninety days. The clerk removed it from a display case and, with great enthusiasm, switched languages and described it as 'Full QWERTY keyboard, tri-band operation on five continents, eighty megabyte built-in memory, high-speed data connectivity with EGPRS, wireless LAN access, Bluetooth wireless technology, IPv4 and IPv6 dual stack support, infrared, Pop-Port interface, Symbian operating system version 7.0S, Series 80 platform.'

'Automatic switching between bands?'

'Yes.'

'Covered by European networks?'

'Of course.'

The smartphone was slightly larger than the typical business phone, but it was comfortable in the hand. It had a smooth metallic surface with a rough plastic back cover that prevented sliding when in use.

'It's larger,' the clerk was saying. 'But it's packed with goodies—e-mail, multimedia messaging, camera, video player, complete word processing, Internet browsing—and complete wireless access almost anywhere in the world. Where are you going with it?'

'Italy.'

'It's ready to go. You'll just need to open an account with a service provider.'

Opening an account meant paperwork. Paperwork meant leaving a trail, something Neal was determined not to do. 'What about a prepaid SIM card?' he asked.

'We got 'em. For Italy it's called a TIM—Telecom Italia Mobile. It's the largest provider in Italy, covers about ninety-five percent of the country.'

'I'll take it.'

Neal slid down the lower part of the cover to reveal a full keypad. The clerk explained, 'It's best to hold it with both hands and type with the thumbs. You can't fit all ten fingers on the keypad.' He took it from Neal and demonstrated the preferred method of thumb-typing.

'Got it,' Neal said. 'I'll take it.'

The price was $925 plus tax, plus another $89 for the TIM card. Neal paid in cash as he simultaneously declined the extended warranty, rebate registration, owner's program, anything that would create paperwork and leave a trail. The clerk asked for his name and address and Neal declined. At one point he said, with great irritation, 'Is it possible to simply pay for this and leave?'

'Well, sure, I guess,' the clerk said.

'Then let's do it. I'm in a hurry.'

He left and drove half a mile to a large office supply store. He quickly found a Hewlett-Packard Tablet PC with integrated wireless capability. Another $440 got invested in his father's security, though Neal would keep the laptop and hide it in his office. Using a map he'd downloaded, he found the PackagePost in another strip mall nearby. Inside, at a shipping desk, he hurriedly wrote two pages of instructions for his father, then folded them into an envelope containing a letter and more instructions he'd prepared earlier that morning. When he was certain no one was watching, he wedged twenty $100 bills in the small black carrying case that came with the Ankyo marvel. Then he placed the letter and the instructions, the smartphone, and the case inside a mailing carton from the store. He sealed it tightly, and on the outside he wrote with a black marker PLEASE HOLD FOR MARCO LAZZERI. The carton was then placed inside another, slightly larger one that was addressed to Rudolph Viscovitch at Via Zamboni 22, Bologna. The return address was PackagePost, 8851 Braddock Road, Alexandria, Virginia 22302. Because he had no choice, he left his name, address, and phone number on the registry, in case the package got returned. The clerk weighed the package and asked about insurance. Neal declined, and prevented more paperwork. The clerk added the international stamps, and finally said, 'Total is eighteen dollars and twenty cents.'

Neal paid him and was assured again that it would be mailed that afternoon.

19

In the semidarkness of his small apartment, Marco went through his early-morning routine with his usual efficiency. Except for prison, when he had little choice and no motivation to hit the ground running, he'd never been one to linger after waking. There was too much to do, too much to see. He'd often arrived at his office before 6:00 a.m. breathing fire and looking for the day's first brawl, and often after only three or four hours of sleep.

Those habits were returning now. He wasn't attacking each day, wasn't looking for a fight, but there were other challenges.

He showered in less than three minutes,

another old habit that was aided mightily on Via Fondazza by a severe shortage of warm water. Over the lavatory he shaved and worked carefully around the quite handsome growth he was cultivating on his face. The mustache was almost complete; the chin was solid gray. He looked nothing like Joel Backman, nor did he sound like him. He was training himself to speak much slower and in a softer voice. And of course he was doing so in another language.

His quick morning routine included a little espionage. Beside his bed was a chest of drawers where he kept his things. Four drawers, all the same size, with the last one six inches above the floor. He took a very thin strand of white thread he'd unraveled from a bed sheet; the same thread he used every day. He licked both ends, leaving as much saliva as possible, then stuck one end under the bottom of the last drawer. The other end was stuck to the side brace of the chest, so that when the drawer was opened the invisible thread was pulled out of position.

Someone, Luigi he presumed, entered his room every day while he was studying with either Ermanno or Francesca and went through the drawers.

His desk was in the small living room, under the only window. On it he kept an assortment of papers, notepads, books; Ermanno's guide to Bologna, a few copies of the *Herald Tribune*, a sad collection of free shopping guides he'd gathered from Gypsies who passed them out on the streets, his well-used Italian-English dictionary, and the growing pile of study aids Ermanno was burdening him with. The desk was only moderately well organized, a condition that irritated him. His old lawyer's desk, one that wouldn't fit in his current living room, had been famous for its meticulous order. A secretary fussed over it late every afternoon.

But amid the rubble was an invisible scheme. The desk's surface was some type of hardwood that had been nicked and marked over the decades. One defect was a small stain of some sort—Marco had decided it was probably ink. It was about the size of a small button and was located almost in the dead center of the desk. Every morning, as he was leaving, he placed the corner of a sheet of scratch paper directly in the center of the ink stain. Not even the most diligent of spies would have noticed.

And they didn't. Whoever sneaked in for the daily sweep had never, not once, been careful enough to place the papers and books back in their precise location.

Every day, seven days a week, even on the weekends when he was not studying, Luigi and his gang entered and did their dirty work. Marco was considering a plan whereby he would wake up one Sunday morning with a massive headache, telephone Luigi, still the only person he talked to on the cell phone, and ask him to fetch some aspirin or whatever they used in Italy. He would go through the ruse of nursing himself, staying in bed, keeping the apartment dark, until late in the afternoon when he would call Luigi again and announce he felt much better and needed something to eat. They would walk around the corner, have a quick bite, then Marco would suddenly feel like returning to his apartment. They would be gone for less than an hour.

Would someone else handle the sweep?

The plan was taking shape. Marco wanted to know who else was watching him. How large was the net? If their concern was simply to keep him alive, then why would they sift through his apartment every day? What were they afraid of?

They were afraid he would disappear. And why should that frighten them so? He was a free man, perfectly free to move about. His disguise was good. His language skills were rudimentary but passable and improving daily. Why should they care if he simply drifted away? Caught a train and toured the country? Never came back? Wouldn't that make their lives easier?

And why keep him on such a short leash, with no passport and very little cash?

They were afraid he would disappear.

He turned off the lights and opened the door. It was still dark outside under the arcaded sidewalks of Via Fondazza. He locked the door behind him and hurried away, off in search of another early-morning café.

Through the thick wall, Luigi was awakened by a buzzer somewhere in the distance; the same buzzer that awakened him most mornings at such dreadful hours.

'What's that?' she said.

'Nothing,' he said as he flung the covers in her direction and stumbled, naked, out of the room. He hurried across the den to the kitchen, where he unlocked the door, stepped inside, closed and locked it, and looked at the monitors on a folding table. Marco was leaving through his front door, as usual. And at ten minutes after six, again, nothing unusual about that. It was a very frustrating habit.

Damn Americans.

He pushed a button and the monitor went silent. Procedures required him to get dressed immediately, hit the streets, find Marco, and watch him until Ermanno made contact. But Luigi was growing tired of procedures. And he had Simona waiting.

She was barely twenty, a student from Naples, an absolute doll he'd met a week earlier at a club he'd discovered. Last night had been their first together, and it would not be their last. She was already sleeping again when he returned and buried himself under the blankets.

It was cold outside. He had Simona. Whitaker was in Milan, probably still asleep and probably in bed with an Italian woman. There was absolutely no one monitoring what he, Luigi, would do for the entire day. Marco was doing nothing but drinking coffee.

He pulled Simona close and fell asleep.

*   *   *

It was a clear, sunny day in early March. Marco finished a two-hour session with Ermanno. As always, when the weather cooperated, they walked the streets of central Bologna and spoke nothing but Italian. The verb of the day had been 'fare,' translated as 'to do' or 'to make,' and as far as Marco could tell it was one of the most versatile and overused verbs in the entire language. The act of shopping was 'fare la spesa,' translated as 'to make the expenses, or to do the acquisitions.' Asking a question was 'fare la domanda,' 'to make a question.' Having breakfast was 'fare la

220

colazione,' 'to do breakfast.'

Ermanno signed off a little early, again claiming he had studies of his own to pursue. More often than not, when a strolling lesson came to an end, Luigi made his appearance, taking the handoff from Ermanno, who vanished with remarkable speed. Marco suspected that such coordination was meant to give him the impression that he was always being watched.

They shook hands and said goodbye in front of Feltrinelli's, one of the many bookstores in the university section. Luigi appeared from around a corner and offered the usual hearty 'Buon giorno. Pranziamo?' Are we having lunch?

'Certamente.'

The lunches were becoming less frequent, with Marco getting more chances to dine by himself and handle the menu and the service.

'Ho trovato un nuovo ristorante.' I have found a new restaurant.

'Andiamo.' Let's go.

It wasn't clear what Luigi did with his time during the course of a day, but there was no doubt he spent hours scouring the city for different cafés, trattorias, and restaurants. They had never eaten at the same place twice.

They walked through some narrow streets and came to Via dell' Indipendenza. Luigi did most of the talking, always in very slow, deliberate, precise Italian. He'd forgotten English as far as Marco was concerned.

'Francesca can't study this afternoon,' he said.

'Why not?'

'She has a tour. A group of Australians called her yesterday. Her business is very slow this time of

221

the year. Do you like her?'

'Am I supposed to like her?'

'Well, that would be nice.'

'She's not exactly warm and fuzzy.'

'Is she a good teacher?'

'Excellent. Her perfect English inspires me to study more.'

'She says you study very hard, and that you are a nice man.'

'She likes me?'

'Yes, as a student. Do you think she's pretty?'

'Most Italian women are pretty, including Francesca.'

They turned onto a small street, Via Goito, and Luigi pointed just ahead. 'Here,' Luigi said, and they stopped at the door to Franco Rossi's. 'I've never been here, but I hear it's very good.'

Franco himself greeted them with a smile and open arms. He wore a stylish dark suit that contrasted nicely with his thick gray hair. He took their coats and chatted with Luigi as if they were old friends. Luigi was dropping names and Franco was approving of them. A table near the front window was selected. 'Our best one,' Franco said with a gush. Marco looked around and didn't see a bad table.

'The antipasti here are superb,' Franco said modestly, as if he hated to brag about his food. 'My favorite of the day, however, would be the sliced mushroom salad. Lino adds some truffles, some Parmesan, a few sliced apples . . .' At that point Franco's words faded as he kissed the tips of his fingers. 'Really good,' he managed to say with his eyes closed, dreaming.

They agreed on the salad and Franco was off to

welcome the next guests. 'Who's Lino?' asked Marco.

'His brother, the chef.' Luigi dipped some Tuscan bread in a bowl of olive oil. A waiter stopped by and asked about wine. 'Certainly,' Luigi said. 'I'd like something red, from the region.'

There was no question about it. The waiter stabbed his pen at the wine list and said, 'This one here, a Liano from Imola. It is fantastic.' He took a whiff of air just to emphasize the point. Luigi had no choice. 'We'll try it.'

'We were talking about Francesca,' Marco said. 'She seems so distracted. Is something wrong with her?'

Luigi dipped some bread in the olive oil and chewed on a large bite while debating how much to tell Marco. 'Her husband is not well,' he said.

'Does she have children?'

'I don't think so.'

'What's wrong with her husband?'

'He's very sick. I think he's older. I've never met him.'

Il Signore Rossi was back to guide them through the menus, which wasn't really needed. He explained that the tortellini just happened to be the best in Bologna, and particularly superb that day. Lino would be happy to come out of the kitchen and verify this. After the tortellini, an excellent choice would be the veal filet with truffles.

For more than two hours they followed Franco's advice, and when they left they pushed their stomachs back down Via dell' Indipendenza and discussed their siestas.

*   *   *

He found her by accident at the Piazza Maggiore. He was having an espresso at an outdoor table, braving the chill in the bright sunshine, after a vigorous thirty-minute walk, when he saw a small group of fair-haired seniors coming out of the Palazzo Comunale, the city's town hall. A familiar figure was leading, a thin, slightly built woman who held her shoulders high and straight, her dark hair falling out from under a burgundy beret. He left one euro on the table and headed toward them. At the fountain of Neptune, he eased in behind the group—ten in all—and listened to Francesca at work. She was explaining that the gigantic bronze image of the Roman god of the sea was sculpted by a Frenchman over a three-year period, from 1563 to 1566. It was commissioned by a bishop under an urban beautification program aimed at pleasing the pope. Legend has it that before he began the actual work, the Frenchman was concerned about the ample nudity of the project—Neptune is stark naked—so he sent the design to the pope in Rome for approval. The pope wrote back, 'For Bologna, it's okay.'

Francesca was a bit livelier with the real tourists than she was with Marco. Her voice had more energy, her smile came quicker. She was wearing a pair of very stylish eyeglasses that made her look ten years younger. Hiding behind the Australians, he watched and listened for a long time without being noticed.

She explained that the Fontana del Nettuno is now one of the most famous symbols of the city, and perhaps the most popular backdrop for photos. Cameras were pulled from every pocket, and the tourists took their time posing in front of Neptune. At one point, Marco managed to move close enough to make eye contact with Francesca. When she saw him she instinctively smiled, then said a soft 'Buon giorno.'

'Buon giorno. Mind if I tag along?' he asked in English.

'No. Sorry I had to cancel.'

'No problem. How about dinner?'

She glanced around as if she'd done something wrong.

'To study, of course. Nothing more,' he said.

'No, I'm sorry,' she said. She looked beyond him, across the piazza to the Basilica di San Petronio. 'That little café over there,' she said, 'beside the church, at the corner. Meet me there at five and we'll study for an hour.'

'Va bene.'

The tour continued a few steps to the west wall of the Palazzo Comunale, where she stopped them in front of three large framed collections of black-and-white photos. The history lesson was that during World War II the heart of the Italian Resistance was in and around Bologna. The Bolognesi hated Mussolini and his fascists and the German occupiers, and worked diligently in the underground. The Nazis retaliated with a vengeance—their well-publicized rule was that they would murder ten Italians for every one German soldier killed by the Resistance. In a series of fifty-five massacres in and around Bologna they murdered thousands of young Italian fighters. Their names and faces were on the wall, forever memorialized.

It was a somber moment, and the elderly

225

Australians inched closer to look at the heroes. Marco moved closer too. He was struck by their youthfulness, by their promise that was forever lost—slaughtered for their bravery.

As Francesca moved on with her group, he stayed behind, staring at the faces that covered much of the long wall. There were hundreds, maybe thousands of them. A pretty female face here and there. Brothers. Fathers and sons. An entire family.

Peasants willing to die for their country and their beliefs. Loyal patriots with nothing to give but their lives. But not Marco. No sir. When forced to choose between loyalty and money, Marco had done what he always did. He'd gone for the money. He'd turned his back on his country.

All for the glory of cash.

*   *   *

She was standing inside the door of the café, waiting, not drinking anything but, of course, having a smoke. Marco had decided that her willingness to meet so late for a lesson was further evidence of her need for the work.

'Do you feel like walking?' she said before she said hello.

'Of course.' He'd walked several miles with Ermanno before lunch, then for hours after lunch waiting on her. He'd walked enough for one day, but then what else was there to do? After a month of doing several miles a day he was in shape. 'Where?'

'It's a long one,' she said.

They wound through narrow streets, heading to

the southwest, chatting slowly in Italian, discussing the morning's lesson with Ermanno. She talked about the Australians, always an easy and amiable group. Near the edge of the old city they approached the Porta Saragozza and Marco realized where he was, and where he was going.

'Up to San Luca,' he said.

'Yes. The weather is very clear, the night will be beautiful. Are you okay?'

His feet were killing him but he would never think of declining. 'Andiamo,' he said. Let's go.

Sitting almost one thousand feet above the city on the Colle della Guardia, one of the first foothills of the Apennines, the Santuario di San Luca has, for eight centuries, looked over Bologna as its protector and guardian. To get up to it, without getting wet or sunburned, the Bolognesi decided to do what they'd always done best—build a covered sidewalk. Beginning in 1674, and continuing without interruption for sixty-five years, they built arches; 666 arches over a walkway that eventually runs for 3.6 kilometers, the longest porticoed sidewalk in the world.

Though Marco had studied the history, the details were much more interesting when they came from Francesca. The hike up was a steady climb, and they paced themselves accordingly. After a hundred arches, his calves were screaming for relief. She, on the other hand, glided along as if she could climb mountains. He kept waiting for all that cigarette smoking to slow her down.

To finance such a grandiose and extravagant project, Bologna used its considerable wealth. In a rare display of unity among the feuding factions, each arch of the portico was funded by a different group of merchants, artisans, students, churches, and noble families. To record their achievement, and to secure their immortality, they were allowed to hang plaques opposite their arches. Most had disappeared over time.

Francesca stopped for a brief rest at the 170th arch, where one of the few remaining plaques still hung. It was known as 'la Madonna grassa,' the fat Madonna. There were fifteen chapels en route. They stopped again between the eighth and ninth chapels, where a bridge had been built to straddle a road. Long shadows were falling through the porticoes as they trudged up the steepest part of the incline. 'It's well lighted at night,' she assured him. 'For the trip down.'

Marco wasn't thinking about the trip down. He was still looking up, still gazing at the church, which at times seemed closer and at other times seemed to be sneaking away from them. His thighs were aching now, his steps growing heavier.

When they reached the crest and stepped from under the 666th portico, the magnificent basilica spread before them. Its lights were coming on as darkness surrounded the hills above Bologna, and its dome glowed in shades of gold. 'It's closed now,' she said. 'We'll have to see it another day.'

During the hike up, he'd caught a glimpse of a bus easing down the hill. If he ever decided to visit San Luca again for the sole purpose of wandering through another cathedral, he'd be sure to take the bus.

'This way,' she said softly, beckoning him over. 'I know a secret path.'

He followed her along a gravel trail behind the church to a ledge where they stopped and took in

228

the city below them. 'This is my favorite spot,' she said, breathing deeply, as if trying to inhale the beauty of Bologna.

'How often do you come here?'

'Several times a year, usually with groups. They always take the bus. Sometimes on a Sunday afternoon I'll enjoy the walk up.'

'By yourself?'

'Yes, by myself.'

'Could we sit somewhere?'

'Yes, there is a small bench hidden over there. No one knows about it.' He followed her down a few steps, then along a rocky path to another ledge with views just as spectacular.

'Are your legs tired?' she asked.

'Of course not,' he lied.

She lit a cigarette and enjoyed it as few people could possibly enjoy one. They sat in silence for a long time, both resting, both thinking and gazing at the shimmering lights of Bologna.

Marco finally spoke. 'Luigi tells me your husband is very ill. I'm sorry.'

She glanced at him with a look of surprise, then turned away. 'Luigi told me the personal stuff is off-limits.'

'Luigi changes the rules. What has he told you about me?'

'I haven't asked. You're from Canada, traveling around, trying to learn Italian.'

'Do you believe that?'

'Not really.'

'Why not?'

'Because you claim to have a wife and a family, yet you leave them for a long trip to Italy. And if you're just a businessman off on a pleasure trip,

229

then where does Luigi fit in? And Ermanno? Why do you need those people?'

'Good questions. I have no wife.'

'So it's all a lie.'

'Yes.'

'What's the truth?'

'I can't tell you.'

'Good. I don't want to know.'

'You have enough problems, don't you, Francesca?'

'My problems are my business.'

She lit another cigarette. 'Can I have one of those?' he asked.

'You smoke?'

'Many years ago.' He picked one from the pack and lit it. The lights from the city grew brighter as the night engulfed them.

'Do you tell Luigi everything we do?' he asked.

'I tell him very little.'

'Good.'

20

Teddy's last visit to the White House was scheduled for 10:00 a.m. He planned to be late. Beginning at seven that morning, he met with his unofficial transition team—all four deputy directors and his senior people. In quiet little conferences he informed those he'd trusted for many years that he was on the way out, that it had been inevitable for a long time, that the agency was in good shape and life would go on.

Those who knew him well sensed an air of

230

relief. He was, after all, pushing eighty and his legendary bad health was actually getting worse.

At precisely 8:45, while meeting with William Lucat, his deputy director for operations, he summoned Julia Javier for their Backman meeting. The Backman case was important, but in the scheme of global intelligence it was mid-list.

How odd that an operation dealing with a disgraced former lobbyist would be Teddy's downfall.

Julia Javier sat next to the ever vigilant Hoby, who was still taking notes that no one would ever see, and began matter-of-factly. 'He's in place, still in Bologna, so if we had to activate now we could do so.'

'I thought the plan was to move him to a village in the countryside, someplace where we could watch him more closely,' Teddy said.

'That's a few months down the road.'

'We don't have a few months.' Teddy turned to Lucat and said, 'What happens if we push the button now?'

'It'll work. They'll get him somewhere in Bologna. It's a nice city with almost no crime. Murders are unheard of, so his death will get some attention if his body is found there. The Italians will quickly realize that he's not—what's his name, Julia?'

'Marco,' Teddy said without looking at notes. 'Marco Lazzeri.'

'Right, they'll scratch their heads and wonder who the hell he is.'

Julia said, 'There's no clue as to his real identity. They'll have a body, a fake ID, but no family, no friends, no address, no job, nothing.

231

They'll bury him like a pauper and keep the file open for a year. Then they'll close it.'

'That's not our problem,' Teddy said. 'We're not doing the killing.'

'Right,' said Lucat. 'It'll be a bit messier in the city, but the boy likes to wander the streets. They'll get him. Maybe a car will hit him. The Italians drive like hell, you know.'

'It won't be that difficult, will it?'

'I wouldn't think so.'

'And what are our chances of knowing when it happens?' Teddy asked.

Lucat scratched his beard and looked across the table at Julia, who was biting a nail and looking over at Hoby, who was stirring green tea with a plastic stick. Lucat finally said, 'I'd say fifty-fifty, at the scene anyway. We'll be watching twenty-four/seven, but the people who'll take him out will be the best of the best. There may be no witnesses.'

Julia added, 'Our best chance will be later, a few weeks after they bury the pauper. We have good people in place. We'll listen closely. I think we'll hear it later.'

Lucat said, 'As always, when we're not pulling the trigger, there's a chance we won't know for sure.'

'We cannot screw this up, understand? It'll be nice to know that Backman is dead—God knows he deserves it—but the goal of the operation is to see who kills him,' Teddy said as his white wrinkled hands slowly lifted a paper cup of green tea to his mouth. He slurped it loudly, crudely.

Maybe it was time for the old man to fade away in a retirement home.

'I'm reasonably confident,' Lucat said. Hoby

wrote that down.

'If we leak it now, how long before he's dead?' Teddy asked.

Lucat shrugged and looked away as he pondered the question. Julia was chewing another nail. 'It depends,' she said cautiously. 'If the Israelis move, it could happen in a week. The Chinese are usually slower. The Saudis will probably hire a freelance agent; it could take a month to get one on the ground.'

'The Russians could do it in a week,' Lucat added.

'I won't be here when it happens,' Teddy said sadly. 'And no one on this side of the Atlantic will ever know. Promise me you'll give me a call.'

'This is the green light?' Lucat asked.

'Yes. Careful how you leak it, though. All hunters must be given an equal chance at the prey.'

They gave Teddy their final farewells and left his office. At nine-thirty, Hoby pushed him into the hall and to the elevator. They rode down eight levels to the basement where the bulletproof white vans were waiting for his last trip to the White House.

*　　　*　　　*

The meeting was brief. Dan Sandberg was sitting at his desk at the *Post* when it began in the Oval Office a few minutes after ten. And he hadn't moved twenty minutes later when the call came from Rusty Lowell. 'It's over,' he said.

'What happened?' Sandberg asked, already pecking at his keyboard.

'As scripted. The President wanted to know

233

about Backman. Teddy wouldn't budge. The President said he was entitled to know everything. Teddy agreed but said the information was going to be abused for political purposes and it would compromise a sensitive operation. They argued briefly. Teddy got himself fired. Just like I told you.'

'Wow.'

'The White House is making an announcement in five minutes. You might want to watch.'

As always, the spin began immediately. The somber-faced press secretary announced that the President had decided to 'pursue a fresher course with our intelligence operations.' He praised Director Maynard for his legendary leadership and seemed downright saddened by the prospect of having to find his successor. The first question, shot from the front row, was whether Maynard resigned or had been fired.

'The President and Director Maynard reached a mutual understanding.'

'What does that mean?'

'Just what I said.'

And so it went for thirty minutes.

Sandberg's front-page story the following morning dropped two bombs. It began with the definite confirmation that Maynard had been fired after he refused to divulge sensitive information for what he deemed to be raw political purposes. There was no resignation, no 'reaching of a mutual understanding.' It was an old-fashioned sacking. The second blast announced to the world that the President's insistence on obtaining intelligence data was directly tied to a new FBI investigation into the selling of pardons. The cash-for-pardon scandal had been a distant rumbling until Sandberg opened the door. His scoop practically stopped traffic on the Arlington Memorial Bridge.

While Sandberg was hanging around the press room, reveling in his coup, his cell phone rang. It was Rusty Lowell, who abruptly said, 'Call me on a land line, and do it quickly.' Sandberg went to a small office for privacy and dialed Lowell's number at Langley.

'Lucat just got fired,' Lowell said. 'At eight o'clock this morning he met with the President in the Oval Office. He was asked to step in as the interim director. He said yes. They met for an hour. The President pushed on Backman. Lucat wouldn't budge. Got himself fired, just like Teddy.'

'Damn, he's been there a hundred years.'

'Thirty-eight to be exact. One of the best men here. A great administrator.'

'Who's next?'

'That's a very good question. We're all afraid of the knock on the door.'

'Somebody's got to run the agency.'

'Ever meet Susan Penn?'

'No. I know who she is, but I never met her.'

'Deputy director for science and technology. Very loyal to Teddy, hell we all are, but she's also a survivor. She's in the Oval Office right now. If she's offered the interim, she'll take it. And she'll give up Backman to get it.'

'He is the President, Rusty. He's entitled to know everything.'

'Of course. And it's a matter of principle. Can't really blame the guy. He's new on the job, wants to flex his muscle. Looks like he'll fire us all until he gets what he wants. I told Susan Penn to take the job to stop the bleeding.'

'So the FBI should know about Backman real soon?'

'Today, I would guess. Not sure what they'll do when they find out where he is. They're weeks away from an indictment. They'll probably just screw up our operation.'

'Where is he?'

'Don't know.'

'Come on, Rusty, things are different now.'

'The answer is no. End of story. I'll keep you posted on the bloodletting.'

An hour later, the White House press secretary met with the press and announced the appointment of Susan Penn as interim director of the CIA. He made much of the fact that she was the first female to hold the position, thus proving once again how determined this President was to labor diligently for the cause of equal rights.

*   *   *

Luigi was sitting on the edge of his bed, fully dressed and all alone, waiting for the signal from next door. It came at fourteen minutes after 6:00 a.m.—Marco was becoming such a creature of habit. Luigi walked to his control room and pushed a button to silence the buzzer that indicated that his friend had exited through the front door. A computer recorded the exact time and within seconds someone at Langley would know that Marco Lazzeri had just left their safe house on Via Fondazza at precisely 6:14.

He hadn't trailed him in a few days. Simona had been sleeping over. He waited a few seconds, slipped out his rear door, cut through a narrow alley, then peeked through the shadows of the arcades along Via Fondazza. Marco was to his left, headed south and walking at his usual brisk pace, which was getting faster the longer he stayed in Bologna. He was at least twenty years older than Luigi, but with his penchant for walking miles every day he was in better shape. Plus he didn't smoke, didn't drink much, didn't seem to be interested in ladies and the nightlife, and he'd spent the last six years in a cage. Little wonder he could roam the streets for hours, doing nothing.

He wore the new hiking boots every day. Luigi had not been able to get his hands on them. They remained bug-free, leaving no signal behind. Whitaker worried about this in Milan, but then he worried about everything. Luigi was convinced that Marco might walk for a hundred miles within the city, but he wasn't leaving town. He'd disappear for a while, go exploring or sightseeing, but he could always be found.

He turned onto Via Santo Stefano, a main avenue that ran from the southeast corner of old Bologna into the thick of things around Piazza Maggiore. Luigi crossed over and followed from the other side. As he practically jogged along, he quickly radioed Zellman, a new guy in town, sent by Whitaker to tighten the web. Zellman was waiting on Strada Maggiore, another busy avenue between the safe house and the university.

Zellman's arrival was an indication of the plan moving forward. Luigi knew most of the details now, and was somewhat saddened by the fact that Marco's days were numbered. He wasn't sure who would take him out, and he got the impression that

Whitaker didn't know either.

Luigi was praying that he would not be called upon to do the deed. He'd killed two other men, and preferred to avoid such messes. Plus, he liked Marco.

Before Zellman picked up the trail, Marco vanished. Luigi stopped and listened. He ducked into the darkness of a doorway, just in case Marco had stopped too.

*   *   *

He heard him back there, walking a little too heavily, breathing a little too hard. A quick left on a narrow street, Via Castellata, a sprint for fifty yards, then another left onto Via de' Chiari, and a complete change of direction, from due north to due west, a hard pace for a long time until he came to an opening, a small square called Piazza Cavour. He knew the old city so well now, the avenues, alleys, dead ends, intersections, the endless maze of crooked little streets, the names of every square and many of the shops and stores. He knew which tobacco stores opened at six and which waited until seven. He could find five coffee shops that were filled by sunrise, though most waited until daylight. He knew where to sit in the front window, behind a newspaper, with a view of the sidewalk and wait for Luigi to stroll by.

He could lose Luigi anytime he wanted, though most days he played along and kept his trails wide and easy to follow. But it was the fact that he was being watched so closely that spoke volumes.

They don't want me to disappear, he kept saying to himself. And why? Because I'm here for a reason.

He swung wide to the west of the city, far away from where he might be expected to be. After almost an hour of zigzagging through and looping around dozens of short streets and alleys, he stepped onto Via Irnerio and watched the foot traffic. Bar Fontana was directly across the street. There was no one watching it.

Rudolph was tucked away in the rear, head buried low in the morning paper, pipe smoke rising in a lazy blue spiral. They hadn't seen each other in ten days, and after the usual warm greetings his first question was 'Did you make it to Venice?'

Yes, a delightful visit. Marco dropped the names of all the places he'd memorized from the guidebook. He raved about the beauty of the canals, the amazing variety of bridges, the smothering hordes of tourists. A fabulous place. Couldn't wait to go back. Rudolph added some of his own memories. Marco described the church of San Marco as if he'd spent a week there.

Where to next? Rudolph inquired. Probably south, toward warmer weather. Maybe Sicily, the Amalfi coast. Rudolph, of course, adored Sicily and described his visits there. After half an hour of travel talk, Marco finally got around to business. 'I'm traveling so much, I really have no address. A friend from the States is sending me a package. I gave him your address at the law school. Hope you don't mind.'

Rudolph was relighting his pipe. 'It's already here. Came yesterday,' he said, with heavy smoke pouring out with the words.

Marco's heart skipped a beat. 'Was there a return address?'

'Some place in Virginia.'

'Good.' His mouth was instantly dry. He took a sip of water and tried to conceal his excitement. 'Hope it wasn't a problem.'

'Not at all.'

'I'll swing by later and pick it up.'

'I'm in the office from eleven to twelve-thirty.'

'Good, thanks.' Another sip. 'Just curious, how big is the package?'

Rudolph chewed on the stem of his pipe and said, 'A small cigar box maybe.'

*   *   *

A cold rain started at mid-morning. Marco and Ermanno were walking through the university area and found shelter in a quiet little bar. They finished the lesson early, primarily because the student pushed so hard. Ermanno was always ready to quit early.

Since Luigi had not booked lunch, Marco was free to roam, presumably without being followed. But he was careful just the same. He did his loops and backtracking maneuvers, and felt silly as always. Silly or not, they were now standard procedure. Back on Via Zamboni he drifted behind a group of students strolling aimlessly along. At the door to the law school he ducked inside, bounded up the stairs, and within seconds was knocking on Rudolph's half-opened door.

Rudolph was at his ancient typewriter, hammering away at what appeared to be a personal letter. 'Over there,' he said, pointing to a pile of rubble covering a table that hadn't been cleared in decades. 'That brown thing on top.'

240

Marco picked up the package with as little interest as possible. 'Thanks again, Rudolph,' he said, but Rudolph was typing again and in no mood for a visit. He'd clearly been interrupted.

'Don't mention it,' he said over his shoulder, releasing another cloud of pipe smoke.

'Is there a restroom nearby?' Marco asked.

'Down the hall, on your left.'

'Thanks. See you around.'

There was a prehistoric urinal and three wooden stalls. Marco went into the far one, locked the door, lowered the lid, and took a seat. He carefully opened his package and unfolded the sheets of paper. The first one was plain, white, no letterhead of any kind. When he saw the words 'Dear Marco,' he felt like crying.

Dear Marco:

Needless to say, I was thrilled to hear from you. I thanked God when you were released and I pray for your safety now. As you know, I will do anything to help.

Here is a smartphone, state of the art and all that. The Europeans are ahead of us with cell phone and wireless Internet technology, so this should work fine over there. I've written some instructions on another sheet of paper. I know this will sound like Greek, but it's really not that complicated.

Don't try and call—it's too easy to track. Plus, you would have to use a name and set up an account. E-mail is the way. By using KwyteMail with encryption, it's impossible to track our messages. I suggest that you e-mail only me. I can then handle the relays.

241

On this end I have a new laptop that I keep near me at all times.

This will work, Marco. Trust me. As soon as you're online, e-mail and we can chat.

Good Luck, Grinch (March 5)

Grinch? A code or something. He had not used their real names.

Marco studied the sleek device, thoroughly bewildered by it but also determined to get the damn thing going. He probed its small case, found the cash, and counted it slowly as if it were gold. The door opened and closed; someone was using the urinal. Marco could hardly breathe. Relax, he kept telling himself.

The restroom door opened and closed again, and he was alone. The page of instructions was handwritten, obviously when Neal didn't have a lot of time. It read:

Ankyo 850 PC Pocket Smartphone—fully charged battery—6 hours talk time before recharging, recharger included.

Step 1) Find Internet café with wireless access—list enclosed

Step 2) Either enter café or get within 200 feet of it

Step 3) Turn on, switch is in upper right-hand corner

Step 4) Watch screen for 'Access Area' then the question 'Access Now?' Press 'Yes' under screen; wait.

Step 5) Then push keypad switch, bottom right, and unfold keypad

Step 6) Press Wi-Fi access on screen

Step 7) Press 'Start' for Internet browser

242

Step 8) At cursor, type 'www.kwytemail.com'
Step 9) Type user name 'Grinch456'
Step 10) Type pass phrase 'post hoc ergo propter hoc'
Step 11) Press 'Compose' to bring up New Message Form
Step 12) Select my e-mail address: 123Grinch@kwytemail.com
Step 13) Type your message to me
Step 14) Click on 'Encrypt Message'
Step 15) Click 'Send'
Step 16) Bingo—I'll have the message

More notes followed on the other side, but Marco needed to pause. The smartphone was growing heavier by the minute as it inspired more questions than answers. For a man who'd never been in an Internet café, he could not begin to understand how one could be used from across the street. Or within two hundred feet.

Secretaries had always handled the e-mail flood. He'd been much too busy to sit in front of a monitor.

There was an instruction booklet that he opened at random. He read a few lines and didn't understand a single phrase. Trust Neal, he told himself.

You have no choice here, Marco. You have to master this damn thing.

From a Web site called www.AxEss.com Neal had printed a list of free wireless Internet places in Bologna—three cafés, two hotels, one library, and one bookstore.

Marco folded his cash, stuck it in his pocket, then slowly put his package back together. He stood, flushed the toilet for some reason, and left the restroom. The phone, the papers, the case, and the small recharger were easily buried in the deep pockets of his parka.

The rain had turned to snow when he left the law school, but the covered sidewalks protected him and the crowd of students hurrying to lunch. As he drifted away from the university area, he pondered ways to hide the wonderful little assets Neal had sent him. The phone would never leave his person. Nor would the cash. But the paperwork—the letter, the instructions, the manual—where could he stash them? Nothing was protected in his apartment. He saw in a store window an attractive shoulder bag of some sort. He went and inquired. It was a Silvio brand laptop case, navy blue, waterproof, made of a synthetic fabric that the saleslady could not translate. It cost sixty euros, and Marco reluctantly placed them on the counter. As she finished the sale, he carefully placed the smartphone and its related items into the bag. Outside, he flung it over his shoulder and tucked it snugly under his right arm.

The bag meant freedom for Marco Lazzeri. He would guard it with his life.

He found the bookstore on Via Ugo Bassi. The magazines were on the second level. He stood by the rack for five minutes, holding a soccer weekly while watching the front door for anyone suspicious. Silly. But it was a habit now. The Internet hookups were on the third floor, in a small coffee shop. He bought a pastry and a Coke and found a narrow booth where he could sit and watch everyone going and coming.

No one could find him there.

He pulled out his Ankyo 850 with as much confidence as he could muster and glanced through its manual. He reread Neal's instructions. He followed them nervously, typing on the tiny keypad with both thumbs, the way it was illustrated in the owner's manual. After each step he looked up to check the movements around the café.

The steps worked perfectly. He was online in short order, much to his amazement, and when the codes worked he was looking at a screen that was giving him the okay to write a message. Slowy, he moved his thumbs around and typed his first wireless Internet e-mail:

> *Grinch: Got the package. You'll never know how much it means to me. Thank you for your help. Are you sure our messages are completely secure? If so, I will tell you more about my situation. I fear I am not safe. It's about 8:30 a.m. your time. I'll send this message now, and check back in a few hours. Love, Marco*

He sent the message, turned the machine off, then stayed for an hour poring over the manual. Before he left to meet Francesca, he turned it on again and followed the route to get online. On the screen he tapped 'Google Search,' then typed in 'Washington Post.' Sandberg's story caught his attention, and he scrolled through it.

He'd never met Teddy Maynard, but they had spoken several times by phone. Very tense conversations. The man had been practically dead ten years ago. In his other life Joel had butted heads a few times with the CIA, usually over shenanigans his defense-contractor clients were trying to pull.

Outside the bookstore, Marco sized up the street, saw nothing of interest, and began another long walk.

Cash for pardons? What a sensational story, but it was asking too much to believe that an outgoing president would take bribes like that. During his spectacular fall from power, Joel had read many things about himself, about half of them true. He'd learned the hard way to believe little of what got printed.

21

At an unnamed, unnumbered, nondescript building on Pinsker Street in downtown Tel Aviv, an agent named Efraim entered from the sidewalk and walked past the elevator to a dead-end corridor with one locked door. There was no knob, no handle. He pulled a device that resembled a small television remote from his pocket and aimed it at the door. Thick tumblers fell somewhere inside, a sharp click, and the door opened into one of the many safe houses maintained by the Mossad, the Israeli secret police. It had four rooms—two with bunk beds where Efraim and his three colleagues slept, a small kitchen where they cooked their simple meals, and a large cluttered workroom where they spent hours every day planning an operation that had been practically dormant for six years but was suddenly one of the Mossad's highest priorities.

The four were members of *kidon,* a small, tight

unit of highly skilled field agents whose primary function was assassination. Quick, efficient, silent killing. Their targets were enemies of Israel who could not be brought to trial because its courts could not get jurisdiction. Most targets were in Arab and Islamic countries, but *kidon* were often used in the former Soviet bloc, Europe, Asia, even North Korea and the United States. They had no boundaries, no restraints, nothing to stop them from taking out those who wanted to destroy Israel. The men and women of *kidon* were fully licensed to kill for their country. Once a target was approved, in writing, by the current prime minister, an operation plan was put into place, a unit was organized, and the enemy of Israel was as good as dead. Obtaining such approval at the top had rarely been difficult.

Efraim tossed a bag of pastries onto one of the folding tables where Rafi and Shaul were plowing through research. Amos was in a corner at the computer, studying maps of Bologna, Italy.

Most of their research was stale; it included pages of mainly useless background on Joel Backman, information that had been collected years ago. They knew everything about his chaotic personal life—the three ex-wives, the three children, the former partners, the girlfriends, the clients, the old lost friends from the power circles in D.C. When his killing had been approved six years earlier, another *kidon* had worked urgently putting together the background on Backman. A preliminary plan to kill him in a car accident in D.C. had been jettisoned when he suddenly pled guilty and fled to prison. Not even a *kidon* could reach him in protective custody at Rudley.

The background was important now only because of his son. Since his surprise pardon and disappearance seven weeks earlier, the Mossad had kept two agents close to Neal Backman. They rotated every three or four days so no one in Culpeper, Virginia, would get suspicious; small towns with their nosy neighbors and bored cops presented enormous challenges. One agent, a pretty lady with a German accent, had actually chatted with Neal on Main Street. She claimed to be a tourist and needed directions to Montpelier, the nearby home of President James Madison. She flirted, or tried her best to, and was perfectly willing go further. He didn't take the bait. They'd bugged his home and office, and they listened to cell phone conversations. From a lab in Tel Aviv, they read every one of his office e-mails and those from home as well. They monitored his bank account and his credit card spending. They knew he'd made a quick trip to Alexandria six days earlier, but they did not know why.

They were watching Backman's mother too, in Oakland, but the poor lady was fading fast. For years they had debated the idea of slipping her one of the poison pills from their amazing arsenal. They would then ambush her son at her funeral. However, the *kidon* manual on assassination prohibited the killing of family members unless said members were also involved in threats to Israeli security.

But the idea was still debated, with Amos being its most vocal proponent.

They wanted Backman dead, but they also wanted him to live a few hours before passing on. They needed to chat with him, to ask some questions, and if the answers weren't forthcoming they knew how to make him talk. Everyone talked when the Mossad really wanted answers.

'We have found six agents who speak Italian,' Efraim said. 'Two will be here this afternoon at three, for a meeting.' None of the four spoke Italian, but all spoke perfect English, as well as Arabic. Among them there were eight other languages.

Each of the four had combat experience, extensive computer training, and were skilled at crossing borders (with and without paperwork), interrogation, disguises, and forgery. And they had the ability to kill in cold blood with no regrets. The average age was thirty-four, and each had been involved with at least five successful *kidon* assassinations.

When fully operational, their *kidon* would have twelve members. Four would carry out the actual killing, and the other eight would provide cover, surveillance, and tactical support, and would clean up after the hit.

'Do we have an address?' Amos asked from the computer.

'No, not yet,' said Efraim. 'And I'm not sure we'll get one. This is coming through counterintelligence.'

'There are half a million people in Bologna,' Amos said almost to himself.

'Four hundred thousand,' said Shaul. 'And a hundred thousand of those are students.'

'We're supposed to get a picture of him,' Efraim said, and the other three stopped what they were doing and looked up. 'There's a photo of Backman somewhere, one taken recently, after prison. Getting a copy is a possibility.'

'That would certainly be helpful,' Rafi said.

They had a hundred old photos of Joel Backman. They had studied every square centimeter of his face, every wrinkle, every vein in his eyes, every strand of hair on his head. They had counted his teeth, and they had copies of his dental records. Their specialists across town at the headquarters of Israel's Central Institute for Intelligence and Special Duties, better known as Mossad, had prepared excellent computer images of what Backman would look like now, six years after the world last saw him. There was a series of digital projections of Backman's face at a hefty 240 pounds, his weight when he pled guilty. And another series of Backman at 180, his rumored weight now. They had worked with his hair, leaving it natural, and predicting its color for a fifty-two-year-old man. They colored it black and red and brown. They cut it and left it longer. They put a dozen different pairs of glasses on his face, then added a beard, first a dark one, then a gray one.

It all came back to the eyes. Study the eyes.

Though Efraim was the leader of the unit, Amos had seniority. He had been assigned to Backman in 1998 when the Mossad first heard rumors of the JAM software that was being shopped around by a powerful Washington lobbyist. Working through their ambassador in Washington, the Israelis pursued the purchase of JAM, thought they had a deal, but were stiff-armed when Backman and Jacy Hubbard took their goods elsewhere.

The selling price was never made known. The deal was never consummated. Some money changed hands, but Backman, for some reason, did not deliver the product.

Where was it now? Had it ever existed in the first place?

Only Backman knew.

The six-year hiatus in the hunt for Joel Backman had given Amos ample time to fill in some gaps. He believed, as did his superiors, that the so-called Neptune satellite system was a Red Chinese creation; that the Chinese had spent a hefty chunk of their national treasury in building it; that they had stolen valuable technology from the Americans to do so; that they had brilliantly disguised the launching of the system and fooled U.S., Russian, and Israeli satellites; and that they had been unable to reprogram the system to override the software JAM had uploaded. Neptune was useless without JAM, and the Chinese would give up their Great Wall to get their hands on it and Backman.

Amos, and Mossad, also believed that Farooq Khan, the last surviving member of the trio and the principal author of the software, had been tracked down by the Chinese and murdered eight months ago. Mossad was on his trail when he disappeared.

They also believed the Americans were still not sure who built Neptune, and this intelligence failure was an ongoing, almost permanent embarrassment. American satellites had dominated the skies for forty years and were so effective they could see through clouds, spot a machine gun under a tent, intercept a wire transfer from a drug dealer, eavesdrop on a conversation in a building, and find oil under the desert with infrared imagery. They were vastly superior to anything the Russians

251

had put up. For another system of equal or better technology to be designed, built, launched, and to become operational without the knowledge of the CIA and the Pentagon had been unthinkable.

Israeli satellites were very good, but not as good as the Americans'. Now it appeared to the intelligence world that Neptune was more advanced than anything the United States had ever launched.

These were only assumptions; little had been confirmed. The only copy of JAM had been hidden. Its creators were dead.

Amos had lived the case for almost seven years, and he was thrilled to have a new *kidon* in place and was urgently making plans. Time was very short. The Chinese would blow up half of Italy if they thought Backman would end up in the rubble. The Americans might try and get him too. On their soil he was protected by their Constitution, with its layers of safeguards. The laws required that he be treated fairly then tucked away in prison and protected around the clock. But on the other side of the world he was fair game.

Kidon had been used to neutralize a few wayward Israelis, but never at home. The Americans would do the same.

*   *   *

Neal Backman kept his new, very thin laptop in the same old battered briefcase he hauled home every night. Lisa had not noticed it because he never took it out. He kept it close, always within a step or two.

He changed his morning routine slightly. He'd bought a card from Jerry's Java, a fledgling coffee and doughnut chain that was trying to lure customers with fancy coffee and free newspapers, magazines, and wireless Internet access. The franchise had converted an abandoned drive-through taco hut at the edge of town, jazzed it up with funky decor, and in its first two months was doing a booming business.

There were three cars in front of him at the drive-through window. His laptop was on his knees, just under the steering wheel. At the curb, he ordered a double mocha, no whipped cream, and waited for the cars in front to inch forward. He pecked away with both hands as he waited. Once online, he quickly went to KwyteMail. He typed in his user name—Grinch123—then his pass phrase—post hoc ergo propter hoc. Seconds later there it was—the first message from his father.

Neal held his breath as he read, then exhaled mightily and eased forward in line. It worked! The old man had figured it out!

Quickly, he typed:

Marco: Our messages cannot be traced. You can say anything you want, but it's always best to say as little as possible. Delighted you're there and out of Rudley. I'll go online each day at this time—at precisely 7:50 a.m. EST. Gotta run. Grinch

He placed the laptop in the passenger seat, lowered his window, and paid almost four bucks for a cup of coffee. As he pulled away, he kept glancing at the computer to see how long the access signal would last. He turned onto the street, drove no more than two hundred feet, and the signal

253

was gone.

*   *   *

Last November, after Arthur Morgan's astounding defeat, Teddy Maynard began devising his Backman pardon strategy. With his customary meticulous planning, he prepared for the day when moles would leak the word of Backman's whereabouts. To tip the Chinese, and do so in a manner that would not arouse suspicion, Teddy began looking for the perfect snitch.

Her name was Helen Wang, a fifth-generation Chinese American who'd worked for eight years at Langley as an analyst on Asian issues. She was very smart, very attractive, and spoke passable Mandarin Chinese. Teddy got her a temporary assignment at the State Department, and there she began cultivating contacts with diplomats from Red China, some of whom were spies themselves and most of whom were constantly on the prowl for new agents.

The Chinese were notorious for their aggressive tactics in recruiting spies. Each year 25,000 of their students were enrolled in American universities, and the secret police tracked them all. Chinese businessmen were expected to cooperate with central intelligence when they returned home. The thousands of American companies doing business on the mainland were constantly monitored. Their executives were researched and watched. The good prospects were sometimes approached.

When Helen Wang 'accidentally' let it slip that her background included a few years at the CIA, and that she hoped to return soon, she quickly had the attention of intelligence chiefs in Beijing. She accepted an invitation from a new friend to have lunch at a swanky D.C. restaurant, then dinner. She played her role beautifully, always reticent about their overtures but always reluctantly saying yes. Her detailed memos were hand delivered to Teddy after every encounter.

When Backman was suddenly freed from prison, and it became apparent he'd been stashed away and would not surface, the Chinese put tremendous pressure on Helen Wang. They offered her $100,000 for information about his location. She appeared to be frightened by the offer, and for a few days broke off contact. With perfect timing, Teddy got her assignment at State canceled and called her back to Langley. For two weeks she had nothing to do with her old friends undercover at the Chinese embassy.

Then she called them and the payoff soon climbed to $500,000. Helen turned nasty and demanded $1 million, claiming that she was risking her career and her freedom and it was certainly worth more money than that. The Chinese agreed.

The day after Teddy was fired, she called her handler and requested a secret meeting. She gave him a sheet of paper with wiring instructions to a bank account in Panama, one that was secretly owned by the CIA. When the money was received, she said, they would meet again and she would have the location of Joel Backman. She would also give them a recent photo of Joel Backman.

The drop was a 'brush by,' an actual physical meeting between mole and handler, done in such a way that no one would notice anything unusual.

After work, Helen Wang stopped at a Kroger store in Bethesda. She walked to the end of aisle twelve, where the magazines and paperbacks were displayed. Her handler was loitering at the rack with a copy of *Lacrosse Magazine*. Helen picked up another copy of the same magazine and quickly slid an envelope into it. She flipped pages with passable boredom, then put the magazine back on the rack. Her handler was shuffling through the sports weeklies. Helen wandered away, but only after she saw him take her copy of *Lacrosse Magazine*.

For a change, the cloak-and-dagger routine wasn't needed. Helen's friends at the CIA weren't watching because they had arranged the drop. They'd known her handler for many years.

The envelope contained one sheet of paper—an eight-by-ten color xerox photo of Joel Backman as he was apparently walking down the street. He was much thinner, had the beginnings of a grayish goatee, European-style eyeglasses, and was dressed like a local. Handwritten at the bottom of the page was: Joel Backman, Via Fondazza, Bologna, Italy. The handler gawked at it as he sat in his car, then he sped away to the embassy of the People's Republic of China on Wisconsin Avenue NW in Washington.

*　　　*　　　*

At first the Russians seemed to have no interest in the whereabouts of Joel Backman. Their signals were read a variety of ways at Langley. No early conclusions were made, none were possible. For years the Russians had secretly maintained that the so-called Neptune system was one of their own, and this had contributed mightily to the confusion at the CIA.

Much to the surprise of the intelligence world, Russia was managing to keep aloft about 160 reconnaissance satellites a year, roughly the same number as the former Soviet Union. Its robust presence in space had not diminished, contrary to what the Pentagon and the CIA had predicted.

In 1999, a defector from the GRU, the Russian military's intelligence arm and successor to the KGB, informed the CIA that Neptune was not the property of the Russians. They had been caught off guard as badly as the Americans. Suspicion was focused on the Red Chinese, who were far behind in the satellite game.

Or were they?

The Russians wanted to know about Neptune, but they were not willing to pay for information about Backman. When the overtures from Langley were largely ignored, the same color photo sold to the Chinese was anonymously e-mailed to four Russian intelligence chiefs operating under diplomatic cover in Europe.

*   *   *

The leak to the Saudis was handled through an executive of an American oil company stationed in Riyadh. His name was Taggett and he'd lived there for more than twenty years. He was fluent in Arabic and moved in the social circles as easily as any foreigner. He was especially close to a mid-level bureaucrat in the Saudi Foreign Ministry office, and over late-afternoon tea he told him that his company had once been represented by Joel

Backman. Further, and much more important, Taggett claimed to know where Backman was hiding.

Five hours later, Taggett was awakened by a buzzing doorbell. Three young gentlemen in business suits pushed their way into his apartment and demanded a few moments of his time. They apologized, explained that they were with some branch of the Saudi police, and really needed to talk. When pressed, Taggett reluctantly passed on the information he had been coached to disclose.

Joel Backman was hiding in Bologna, Italy, under a different name. That was all he knew.

Could he find out more? they asked.

Perhaps.

They asked him if he would leave the next morning, return to his company's headquarters in New York, and dig for more information about Backman. It was very important to the Saudi government and the royal family.

Taggett agreed to do so. Anything for the king.

22

Every year in May, just before Ascension Day, the people of Bologna march up the Colle della Guardia from the Saragozza gate, along the longest continuous arcade in the world, through all 666 arches and past all fifteen chapels, to the summit, to the Santuario di San Luca. In the sanctuary they remove their Madonna and proceed back down to the city, where they parade her through the crowded streets and finally place her in the

Cathedral of San Pietro, where she stays for eight days until another parade takes her home. It's a festival unique to Bologna, and has gone on uninterrupted since 1476.

As Francesca and Joel sat in the Santuario di San Luca, Francesca was describing the ritual and how much it meant to the people of Bologna. Pretty, but just another empty church as far as Marco was concerned.

They had taken the bus this time, thus avoiding the 666 arches and the 3.6-kilometer hike up the hill. His calves still hurt from the last visit to San Luca, three days ago.

She was so distracted by weightier matters that she was lapsing into English and didn't seem to realize it. He did not complain. When she finished with the festival, she began pointing to the interesting elements in the cathedral—the architecture and construction of the dome, the painting of the frescoes. Marco was fighting desperately to pay attention. The domes and faded frescoes and marble crypts and dead saints were all running together now in Bologna, and he caught himself thinking of warmer weather. Then they could stay outdoors and talk. They could visit the city's lovely parks and if she so much as mentioned a cathedral he would revolt.

She wasn't thinking of warmer weather. Her thoughts were elsewhere.

'You've already done that one,' he interrupted when she pointed at a painting above the baptistery.

'I'm sorry. Am I boring you?'

He started to blurt out the truth, but instead said, 'No, but I've seen enough.'

259

They left the sanctuary and sneaked around behind the church, to her secret pathway that led down a few steps to the best view of the city. The last snow was melting quickly on the red tiled roofs. It was the eighteenth of March.

She lit a cigarette and seemed content to loiter in silence and admire Bologna. 'Do you like my city?' she asked, finally.

'Yes, very much.'

'What do you like about it?'

After six years in prison, any city would do. He thought for a moment, then said, 'It's a real city, with people living where they work. It's safe and clean, timeless. Things haven't changed much over the centuries. The people enjoy their history and they're proud of their accomplishments.'

She nodded slightly, approving of his analysis. 'I'm baffled by Americans,' she said. 'When I guide them through Bologna they're always in a hurry, always anxious to see one sight so they can cross it off the list and move on to the next. They're always asking about tomorrow, and the next day. Why is this?'

'I'm the wrong person to ask.'

'Why?'

'I'm Canadian, remember?'

'You're not Canadian.'

'No, I'm not. I'm from Washington.'

'I've been there. I've never seen so many people racing around, going nowhere. I don't understand the desire for such a hectic life. Everything has to be so fast—work, food, sex.'

'I haven't had sex in six years.'

She gave him a look that conveyed many questions. 'I really don't want to talk about that.'

'You brought it up.'

She puffed on the cigarette as the air cleared. 'Why haven't you had sex in six years?'

'Because I was in prison, in solitary confinement.'

She flinched slightly and her spine seemed to straighten. 'Did you kill someone?'

'No, nothing like that. I'm pretty harmless.'

Another pause, another puff. 'Why are you here?'

'I really don't know.'

'How long will you stay?'

'Maybe Luigi can answer that.'

'Luigi,' she said as if she wanted to spit. She turned and began walking. He followed along because he was supposed to. 'What are you hiding from?' she asked.

'It's a very, very long story, and you really don't want to know.'

'Are you in danger?'

'I think so. I'm not sure how much, but let's just say that I'm afraid to use my real name and I'm afraid to go home.'

'Sounds like danger to me. Where does Luigi fit in?'

'He's protecting me, I think.'

'For how long?'

'I really don't know.'

'Why don't you simply disappear?'

'That's what I'm doing now. I'm in the middle of my disappearance. And from here, where would I go? I have no money, no passport, no identification. I don't officially exist.'

'This is very confusing.'

'Yes. Why don't we drop it.'

261

He glanced away for a second and did not see her fall. She was wearing black leather boots with low heels, and the left one twisted violently on a rock in the narrow pathway. She gasped and fell hard onto the walkway, bracing herself at the last second with both hands. Her purse flew forward. She shrieked something in Italian. Marco quickly knelt down to grab her.

'It's my ankle,' she said, grimacing. Her eyes were already moist, her pretty face twisted in pain.

He gently lifted her from the wet pathway and carried her to a nearby bench, then retrieved her purse. 'I must've tripped,' she kept saying. 'I'm sorry.' She fought the tears but soon gave up.

'It's okay, it's okay,' Marco said, kneeling in front of her. 'Can I touch it?'

She slowly lifted her left leg, but the pain was too great.

'Let's leave the boot on,' Marco said, touching it with great care.

'I think it's broken,' she said. She pulled a tissue from her purse and wiped her eyes. She was breathing heavy and gritting her teeth. 'I'm sorry.'

'It's okay.' Marco looked around; they were very much alone. The bus up to San Luca had been virtually empty, and they had seen no one in the past ten minutes. 'I'll, uh, go inside and find help.'

'Yes, please.'

'Don't move. I'll be right back.' He patted her knee and she managed a smile. Then he hustled away, almost falling himself. He ran to the rear of the church and saw no one. Where, exactly, does one find an office in a cathedral? Where is the curator, administrator, head priest? Who's in charge of this place? Outside, he circled San Luca twice before he saw a custodian emerge from a partially hidden door by the gardens.

'Mi può aiutare?' he called out. Can you help me?

The custodian stared and said nothing. Marco was certain he had spoken clearly. He walked closer and said, 'La mia amica si é fatta male.' My lady friend is hurt.

'Dov'è?' the man grunted. Where?

Marco pointed and said, 'Lì, dietro alla chiesa.' Over there, behind the church.

'Aspetti.' Wait. He turned and walked back to the door and opened it.

'Si sbrighi, per favora.' Please hurry.

A minute or two dragged by, with Marco waiting nervously, wanting to dash back and check on Francesca. If she'd broken a bone, then shock might set in quickly. A larger door below the baptistery opened, and a gentleman in a suit came rushing out with the custodian behind him.

'La mia amica è caduta,' Marco said. My friend fell.

'Where is she?' asked the gentleman in excellent English. They were cutting across a small brick patio, dodging unmelted snow.

'Around back, by the lower ledge. It's her ankle; she thinks she broke it. We might need an ambulance.'

Over his shoulder the gentleman snapped something at the custodian, who disappeared.

Francesca was sitting on the edge of the bench with as much dignity as possible. She held the tissue at her mouth; the crying had stopped. The gentleman didn't know her name, but he had obviously seen her before at San Luca. They

263

chatted in Italian, and Marco missed most of it.

Her left boot was still on, and it was agreed that it should remain so, to prevent swelling. The gentleman, Mr. Coletta, seemed to know his first aid. He examined her knees and hands. They were scratched and sore, but there was no bleeding. 'It's just a bad sprain,' she said. 'I really don't think it's broken.'

'An ambulance will take forever,' the gentleman said. 'I'll drive you to the hospital.'

A horn honked nearby. The custodian had fetched a car and pulled up as close as possible.

'I think I can walk,' Francesca said gamely, trying to stand.

'No, we'll help you,' Marco said. Each grabbed an elbow and slowly raised her to her feet. She grimaced when she put pressure on the foot, but said, 'It's not broken. Just a sprain.' She insisted on walking. They half carried her toward the car.

Mr. Coletta took charge and arranged them in the backseat so that her feet were in Marco's lap, elevated, and her back was resting against the left rear door. When his passengers were properly in place, he jumped behind the wheel and shifted gears. They crawled in reverse along a shrub-lined alley, then onto a narrow paved road. Soon, they were moving down the hill, headed for Bologna.

Francesca put on her sunglasses to cover her eyes. Marco noticed a trickle of blood on her left knee. He took the tissue from her hand and began to dab it. 'Thank you,' she whispered. 'I'm sorry I've ruined your day.'

'Please stop that,' he said with a smile.

It was actually the best day with Francesca. The fall was humbling her and making her seem human.

It was evoking, however unwilling, honest emotions. It was allowing sincere physical contact, one person genuinely trying to help another. It was shoving him into her life. Whatever happened next, whether at the hospital or at her home, he would at least be there for a moment. In the emergency, she was needing him, though she certainly didn't want that.

As he held her feet and stared blankly out the window, Marco realized how desperately he craved a relationship of any kind, with any person.

Any friend would do.

At the foot of the hill, she said to Mr. Coletta, 'I would like to go to my apartment.'

He looked in the rearview mirror and said, 'But I think you should see a doctor.'

'Maybe later. I'll rest for a bit and see how it feels.' The decision was made; arguing would've been useless.

Marco had some advice too, but he held it. He wanted to see where she lived.

'Very well,' said Mr. Coletta.

'It's Via Minzoni, near the train station.'

Marco smiled to himself, quite proud that he knew the street. He could picture it on a map, at the northern edge of the old city, a nice section but not the high-rent district. He had walked it at least once. In fact, he'd found an early-hours coffee bar at a spot where the street ended at the Piazza dei Martiri. As they zipped along the perimeter, in the mid-afternoon traffic, Marco glanced at every street sign, took in every intersection, and knew exactly where he was at all times.

Not another word was spoken. He held her feet, her stylish but well-used black boots slightly soiling his wool slacks. At that moment, he couldn't have cared less. When they turned onto Via Minzoni, she said, 'Down about two blocks, on the right.' A moment later she said, 'Just ahead. There's a spot behind that green BMW.'

They gently extracted her from the rear seat and got her to the sidewalk, where she shook free for a second and tried to walk. The ankle gave way; they caught her. 'I'm on the second floor,' she said, gritting her teeth. There were eight apartments. Marco watched carefully as she pushed the button next to the name of Giovanni Ferro. A female voice answered.

'Francesca,' she said, and the door clicked. They stepped into a foyer that was dark and shabby. To the right was an elevator with its door open, waiting. The three of them filled it tightly. 'I'm really fine now,' she said, obviously trying to lose both Marco and Mr. Coletta.

'We need to get some ice on it,' Marco said as they began a very slow ride up.

The elevator made a noisy stop, its door finally opened, and they shuffled out, both men still holding Francesca by the elbows. Her apartment was only a few steps away, and when they arrived at the door Mr. Coletta had gone far enough.

'I'm very sorry about this,' he said. 'If there are medical bills, would you please call me?'

'No, you're very kind. Thank you so much.'

'Thank you,' Marco said, still attached to her. He pushed the doorbell and waited as Mr. Coletta ducked back in the elevator and left them. She pulled away and said, 'This is fine, Marco. I can manage from here. My mother is house-sitting today.'

He was hoping for an invitation inside, but he was in no position to push on. The episode had run its course as far as he was concerned, and he had learned much more than he could have expected. He smiled, released her arm, and was about to say goodbye when a lock clicked loudly from inside. She turned toward the door, and in doing so put pressure on her wounded ankle. It buckled again, causing her to gasp and reach for him.

The door opened just as Francesca fainted.

*   *   *

Her mother was Signora Altonelli, a seventyish lady who spoke no English and for the first few hectic minutes thought Marco had somehow harmed her daughter. His bumbling Italian proved inadequate, especially under the pressure of the moment. He carried Francesca to the sofa, raised her feet, and conveyed the concept of 'Ghiaccio, ghiaccio.' Ice, get some ice. She reluctantly backed away, then disappeared into the kitchen.

Francesca was stirring by the time her mother returned with a wet washcloth and a small plastic bag of ice.

'You fainted,' Marco said, hovering over her. She clutched his hand and looked about wildly.

'Chi è?' her mother said suspiciously. Who's he?

'Un amico.' A friend. He patted her face with the washcloth and she rallied quickly. In some of the fastest Italian he had yet to experience, she explained to her mother what had happened. The machine-gun bursts back and forth made him dizzy as he tried to pick off an occasional word, then he simply gave up. Suddenly, Signora Altonelli smiled

267

and patted him on the shoulder with great approval. Good boy.

When she disappeared, Francesca said, 'She's gone to make coffee.'

'Great.' He had pulled a stool next to the sofa, and he sat close by, waiting. 'We need to get some ice on this thing,' he said.

'Yes, we should.'

They both looked at her boots. 'Will you take them off?' she asked.

'Sure.' He unzipped the right boot and removed it as though that foot had been injured too. He went even slower with the left one. Every little movement caused pain, and at one point he said, 'Would you prefer to do it?'

'No, please, go ahead.' The zipper stopped almost exactly at the ankle. The swelling made it difficult to ease the boot off. After a few long minutes of delicate wiggling, while the patient suffered with clenched teeth, the boot was off.

She was wearing black stockings. Marco studied them, then announced, 'These have to come off.'

'Yes, they do.' Her mother returned and fired off something in Italian. 'Why don't you wait in the kitchen?' Francesca said to Marco.

The kitchen was small but impeccably put together, very modern with chrome and glass and not a square inch of wasted space. A high-tech coffeepot gurgled on a counter. The walls above a small breakfast nook were covered in bright abstract art. He waited and listened to both of them chatter at once.

They got the stockings off without further injury. When Marco returned to the living room, Signora Altonelli was arranging the ice around the left ankle.

'She says it's not broken,' Francesca said to him. 'She worked in a hospital for many years.'

'Does she live in Bologna?'

'Imola, a few miles away.'

He knew exactly where it was, on the map anyway. 'I guess I should be going now,' he said, not really wanting to go but suddenly feeling like a trespasser.

'I think you need some coffee,' Francesca said. Her mother darted away, back into the kitchen.

'I feel like I'm intruding,' he said.

'No, please, after all you've done today, it's the least I can do.'

Her mother was back, with a glass of water and two pills. Francesca gulped it all down and propped her head up on some pillows. She exchanged short sentences with her mother, then looked at him and said, 'She has a chocolate torta in the refrigerator. Would you like some?'

'Yes, thank you.'

And her mother was off again, humming now and quite pleased that she had someone to care for and someone to feed. Marco resumed his place on the stool. 'Does it hurt?'

'Yes, it does,' she said, smiling. 'I cannot lie. It hurts.'

He could think of no appropriate response, so he ventured back to common ground. 'It all happened so fast,' he said. They spent a few minutes rehashing the fall. Then they were silent. She closed her eyes and appeared to be napping. Marco crossed his arms over his chest and stared at a huge, very odd painting that covered almost an entire wall.

The building was ancient, but from the inside Francesca and her husband had fought back as determined modernists. The furniture was low, sleek black leather with bright steel frames, very minimalist. The walls were covered with baffling contemporary art.

'We can't tell Luigi about this,' she whispered.

'Why not?'

She hesitated, then let it go. 'He is paying me two hundred euros a week to tutor you, Marco, and he's complaining about the price. We've argued. He has threatened to find someone else. Frankly, I need the money. I'm getting one or two jobs a week now; it's still the slow season. Things will pick up in a month when the tourists come south, but right now I'm not earning much.'

The stoic façade was long gone. He couldn't believe that she was allowing herself to be so vulnerable. The lady was frightened, and he would break his neck to help her.

She continued: 'I'm sure he will terminate my services if I skip a few days.'

'Well, you're about to skip a few days.' He glanced at the ice wrapped around her ankle.

'Can we keep it quiet? I should be able to move around soon, don't you think?'

'We can try to keep it quiet, but Luigi has a way of knowing things. He follows me closely. I'll call in sick tomorrow, then we'll figure out something the next day. Maybe we could study here.'

'No. My husband is here.'

Marco couldn't help but glance over his shoulder. 'Here?'

'He's in the bedroom, very ill.'

'What's—'

'Cancer. The last stages. My mother sits with him when I'm working. A hospice nurse comes in each afternoon to medicate him.'

'I'm sorry.'

'So am I.'

'Don't worry about Luigi. I'll tell him I'm thrilled with your teaching style, and that I will refuse to work with anyone else.'

'That would be a lie, wouldn't it?'

'Sort of.'

Signora Altonelli was back with a tray of torta and espresso. She placed it on a bright red coffee table in the middle of the room and began slicing. Francesca took the coffee but didn't feel like eating. Marco ate as slowly as humanly possible and sipped from his small cup as if it might be his last. When Signora Altonelli insisted on another slice, and a refill, he grudgingly accepted.

Marco stayed about an hour. Riding down in the elevator, he realized that Giovanni Ferro had not made a sound.

23

Red China's principal intelligence agency, the Ministry of State Security, or MSS, used small, highly trained units to carry out assassinations around the world, in much the same manner as the Russians, Israelis, British, and Americans.

One notable difference, though, was that the Chinese had come to rely upon one unit in particular. Instead of spreading the dirty work around like other countries, the MSS turned first to a young man the CIA and Mossad had been watching with great admiration for several years. His name was Sammy Tin, the product of two Red Chinese diplomats who were rumored to have been selected by the MSS to marry and reproduce. If ever an agent were perfectly cloned, it was Sammy Tin. Born in New York City and raised in the suburbs around D.C., he'd been educated by private tutors who bombarded him with foreign languages from the time he left diapers. He entered the University of Maryland at the age of sixteen, left it with two degrees at the age of twenty-one, then studied engineering in Hamburg, Germany. Somewhere along the way he picked up bomb-making as a hobby. Explosives became his passion, with an emphasis on controlled explosions from odd packages—envelopes, paper cups, ballpoint pens, cigarette packages. He was an expert marksman, but guns were simple and bored him. The Tin Man loved his bombs.

He then studied chemistry under an assumed name in Tokyo, and there he mastered the art and science of killing with poisons. By the time he was twenty-four he had a dozen different names, about that many languages, and crossed borders with a vast array of passports and disguises. He could convince any customs agent anywhere that he was Japanese, Korean, or Taiwanese.

To round out his education, he spent a grueling year in training with an elite Chinese army unit. He learned to camp, cook over a fire, cross raging rivers, survive in the ocean, and live in the wilderness for days. When he was twenty-six, the MSS decided the boy had studied enough. It was time to start killing.

As far as Langley could tell, he began notching his astounding body count with the murders of three Red Chinese scientists who'd gotten too cozy with the Russians. He got them over dinner at a restaurant in Moscow. While their bodyguards waited outside, one got his throat slit in the men's room while he finished up at the urinal. It took an hour to find his body, crammed in a rather small garbage can. The second made the mistake of worrying about the first. He went to the men's room, where the Tin Man was waiting, dressed as a janitor. They found him with his head stuffed down the toilet, which had been clogged and was backing up. The third died seconds later at the table, where he was sitting alone and becoming very worried about his two missing colleagues. A man in a waiter's jacket hurried by, and without slowing thrust a poison dart into the back of his neck.

As killings go, it was all quite sloppy. Too much blood, too many witnesses. Escape was dicey, but the Tin Man got a break and managed to dash through the busy kitchen unnoticed. He was on the loose and sprinting through a back alley by the time the bodyguards were summoned. He ducked into the dark city, caught a cab, and twenty minutes later entered the Chinese embassy. The next day he was in Beijing, quietly celebrating his first success.

The audacity of the attack shocked the intelligence world. Rival agencies scrambled to find out who did it. It ran so contrary to how the Chinese normally eliminated their enemies. They were famous for their patience, the discipline to wait and wait until the timing was perfect. They would chase until their prey simply gave up. Or they would ditch one plan and go to the next, carefully waiting for their opportunity.

When it happened again a few months later in Berlin, the Tin Man's legend was born. A French executive had handed over some bogus high-tech secrets dealing with mobile radar. He got flung from the balcony of a fourteenth-floor hotel room, and when he landed beside the pool it upset quite a few sunbathers. Again, the killing was much too visible.

In London, the Tin Man blew a man's head off with a cell phone. A defector in New York's Chinatown lost most of his face when a cigarette exploded. Sammy Tin was soon getting credit for most of the more dramatic intelligence killings in that underworld. The legend grew rapidly. Though he kept four or five trusted members in his unit, he often worked alone. He lost a man in Singapore when their target suddenly emerged with some friends, all with guns. It was a rare failure, and the lesson from it was to stay lean, strike fast, and don't keep too many people on the payroll.

As he matured, the hits became less dramatic, less violent, and much easier to conceal. He was now thirty-three, and without a doubt the most feared agent in the world. The CIA spent a fortune trying to track his movements. They knew he was in Beijing, hanging around his luxurious apartment. When he left, they tracked him to Hong Kong. Interpol was alerted when he boarded a nonstop flight to London, where he changed passports and at the last moment boarded an Alitalia flight to Milan.

Interpol could only watch. Sammy Tin often traveled with diplomatic cover. He was no criminal; he was an agent, a diplomat, a businessman, a professor, anything he needed to be.

A car was waiting for him at Milan's Malpensa airport, and he vanished into the city. As far as the CIA could tell, it had been four and a half years since the Tin Man had set foot in Italy.

*　　　*　　　*

Mr. Elya certainly looked the part of a wealthy Saudi businessman, though his heavy wool suit was almost black, a little too dark for Bologna, and its pinstripes were much too thick for anything designed in Italy. And his shirt was pink, with a glistening white collar, not a bad combo, but, well, it was still pink. Through the collar was a gold bar, also too thick, that pushed the knot of the tie up tightly for the choking look, and at each end of the bar was a diamond. Mr. Elya was into diamonds—a large one on each hand, dozens of smaller ones clustered in his Rolex, a couple more in the gold cuffs of his shirt. The shoes appeared to Stefano to be Italian, brand new, brown, but much too light to go with the suit.

As a whole, the package simply wasn't working. It was trying mightily, though. Stefano had time to analyze his client while they rode in virtual silence from the airport, where Mr. Elya and his assistant had arrived by private jet, to the center of Bologna. They were in the rear of a black Mercedes, one of Mr. Elya's conditions, with a driver who was silent in the front seat along with the assistant, who evidently spoke only Arabic. Mr. Elya's English was passable, quick bursts of it, usually followed with something in Arabic to the assistant, who felt compelled to write down everything his master

275

said.

After ten minutes in the car with them, Stefano was already hoping they would finish well before lunch.

The first apartment he showed them was near the university, where Mr. Elya's son would soon arrive to study medicine. Four rooms on the second floor, no elevator, solid old building, nicely furnished, certainly luxurious for any student— 1,800 euros a month, one year's lease, utilities extra. Mr. Elya did nothing but frown, as if his spoiled son would require something much nicer. The assistant frowned too. They frowned all the way down the stairs, into the car, and said nothing as the driver hurried to the second stop.

It was on Via Remorsella, one block west of Via Fondazza. The flat was slightly larger than the first, had a kitchen the size of a broom closet, was badly furnished, had no view whatsoever, was twenty minutes away from the university, cost 2,600 euros a month, and even had a strange odor to it. The frowning stopped, they liked the place. 'This will be fine,' Mr. Elya said, and Stefano breathed a sigh of relief. With a bit of luck, he wouldn't have to entertain them over lunch. And he'd just earned a nice commission.

They hurried over to the office of Stefano's company, where paperwork was produced at a record pace. Mr. Elya was a busy man with an urgent meeting in Rome, and if the rental couldn't be completed right then, on the spot, then forget everything!

The black Mercedes sped them back to the airport, where a rattled and exhausted Stefano said thanks and farewell and hurried away as quickly as possible. Mr. Elya and his assistant walked across the tarmac to his jet and disappeared inside. The door closed.

The jet didn't move. Inside, Mr. Elya and his assistant had ditched their business garb and were dressed casually. They huddled with three other members of their team. After waiting for about an hour, they finally left the jet, hauled their substantial baggage to the private terminal, then into waiting vans.

*　　　　*　　　　*

Luigi had become suspicious of the navy blue Silvio bag. Marco never left it in his apartment. It was never out of his sight. He carried it everywhere, strapped over his shoulder and tucked tightly under his right arm as if it contained gold.

What could he possibly possess now that required such protection? He rarely carried his study materials anywhere. If he and Ermanno studied inside, they did so in Marco's apartment. If they studied outside, it was all conversation and no books were used.

Whitaker in Milano was suspicious too, especially since Marco had been spotted in an Internet café near the university. He sent an agent named Krater to Bologna to help Zellman and Luigi keep a closer eye on Marco and his troublesome bag. With the noose tightening and fireworks expected, Whitaker was asking Langley for even more muscle on the streets.

But Langley was in chaos. Teddy's departure, though certainly not unexpected, had turned the place upside down. The shock waves from Lucat's sacking were still being felt. The President was threatening a major overhaul, and the deputy directors and high-level administrators were spending more time protecting their butts than watching their operations.

It was Krater who got the radio message from Luigi that Marco was drifting toward Piazza Maggiore, probably in search of his late-afternoon coffee. Krater spotted him as he strode across the square, dark blue bag under his right arm, looking very much like a local. After studying a rather thick file on Joel Backman, it was nice to finally lay eyes on him. If the poor guy only knew.

But Marco wasn't thirsty, not yet anyway. He passed the cafés and shops, then suddenly, after a furtive glance, stepped into Albergo Nettuno, a fifty-room boutique hotel just off the piazza. Krater radioed Zellman and Luigi, who was particularly puzzled because Marco had no reason whatsoever to be entering a hotel. Krater waited five minutes, then walked into the small lobby, absorbing everything he saw. To his right was a lobby area with some chairs and a few travel magazines strewn over a wide coffee table. To his left was a small empty phone room with its door open, then another room that was not empty. Marco sat there, alone, hunched over the small table under the wall-mounted phone, his blue bag open. He was too busy to see Krater walk by.

'May I help you, sir?' the clerk said from the front desk.

'Yes, thanks, I wanted to inquire about a room,' Krater said in Italian.

'For when?'

'Tonight.'

'I'm sorry, but we have no vacancies.'

Krater picked up a brochure at the desk. 'You're always full,' he said with a smile. 'It's a popular place.'

'Yes, it is. Perhaps another time.'

'Do you by chance have Internet access?'

'Of course.'

'Wireless?'

'Yes, the first hotel in the city.'

He backed away and said, 'Thanks. I'll try again another time.'

'Yes, please.'

He passed the phone room on the way out. Marco had not looked up.

*　　　*　　　*

With both thumbs he was typing his text and hoping he would not be asked to leave by the clerk at the front desk. The wireless access was something the Nettuno advertised, but only for its guests. The coffee shops, libraries, and one of the bookstores offered it free to anyone who ventured in, but not the hotels.

His e-mail read:

> *Grinch: I once dealt with a banker in Zurich, name of Mikel Van Thiessen, at Rhineland Bank, on Bahnhofstrasse, downtown Zurich. See if you can determine if he's still there. If not, who took his place? Do not leave a trail!*
> *Marco*

He pushed Send, and once again prayed that he'd done things right. He quickly turned off the

Ankyo 850 and tucked it away in his bag. As he left, he nodded at the clerk, who was on the phone.

Two minutes after Krater came out of the hotel, Marco made his exit. They watched him from three different points, then followed him as he mixed easily with the late-afternoon rush of people leaving work. Zellman circled back, entered the Nettuno, went to the second phone room on the left, and sat in the seat where Marco had been less than twenty minutes earlier. The clerk, puzzled now, pretended to be busy behind his desk.

An hour later, they met in a bar and retraced his movements. The conclusion was obvious, but still hard to swallow—since Marco had not used the phone, he was freeloading on the hotel's wireless Internet access. There was no other reason to randomly enter the hotel lobby, sit in a phone room for less than ten minutes, then abruptly leave. But how could he do it? He had no laptop, no cell phone other than the one Luigi had loaned him, an outdated device that would only work in the city and could in no way be upgraded to go online. Had he obtained some high-tech gadget? He had no money.

Theft was a possibility.

They kicked around various scenarios. Zellman left to e-mail the disturbing news to Whitaker. Krater was dispatched to begin window shopping for an identical blue Silvio bag.

Luigi was left to contemplate dinner.

His thoughts were interrupted by a call from Marco himself. He was in his apartment, not feeling too well, his stomach had been jumpy all afternoon. He'd canceled his lesson with Francesca, and now he was begging off dinner.

24

If Dan Sandberg's phone rang before 6:00 a.m., the news was never good. He was a night owl, a nocturnal creature who often slept until it was time to have breakfast and lunch together. Everyone who knew him also knew that it was pointless to phone early.

It was a colleague at the *Post*. 'You got scooped, buddy,' he announced gravely.

'What?' Sandberg snapped.

'The *Times* just wiped your nose for you.'

'Who?'

'Backman.'

'What?'

'Go see for yourself.'

Sandberg ran to the den of his messy apartment and attacked his desk computer. He found the story, written by Heath Frick, a hated rival at *The New York Times*. The front-page headline read FBI PARDON PROBE SEARCHES FOR JOEL BACKMAN.

Citing a host of unnamed sources, Frick reported that the FBI's cash-for-pardon investigation had intensified and was expanding to include specific individuals who were granted reprieves by former president Arthur Morgan. Duke Mongo was named as a 'person of interest,' a euphemism often tossed about when the authorities wanted to taint a person they were unable to formally indict. Mongo, though, was hospitalized and rumored to be gasping for his last breath.

The probe was now focusing its attention on

Joel Backman, whose eleventh-hour pardon had shocked and outraged many, according to Frick's gratuitous analysis. Backman's mysterious disappearance had only fueled the speculation that he'd bought himself a pardon and fled to avoid the obvious questions. Old rumors were still out there, Frick reminded everyone, and various unnamed and supposedly trustworthy sources hinted that the theory about Backman burying a fortune had not been officially laid to rest.

'What garbage!' Sandberg snarled as he scrolled down the screen. He knew the facts better than anyone. This crap could not be substantiated. Backman had not paid for a pardon.

No one even remotely connected with the former president would say a word. For now, the probe was just a probe, with no formal investigation under way, but the heavy federal artillery was not far away. An eager U.S. attorney was clamoring to get started. He didn't have his grand jury yet, but his office was sitting on go, waiting on word from the Justice Department.

Frick wrapped it all up with two paragraphs about Backman, historical rehash that the paper had run before.

'Just filler!' Sandberg fumed.

* * *

The President read it too but had a different reaction. He made some notes and saved them until seven-thirty, when Susan Penn, his interim director of the CIA, arrived for the morning briefing. The PDB—president's daily briefing— had historically been handled by the director himself, always in the Oval Office and normally the first item of the day's business. But Teddy Maynard and his rotten health had changed the routine, and for the past ten years the briefings had been done by someone else. Now traditions were being honored again.

An eight- to ten-page summary of intelligence matters was placed on the President's desk precisely at 7:00 a.m. After almost two months in office, he had developed the habit of reading every word of it. He found it fascinating. His predecessor had once boasted that he read hardly anything— books, newspapers, magazines. Certainly not legislation, policies, treaties, or daily briefings. He'd often had trouble reading his own speeches. Things were much different now.

Susan Penn was driven in an armored car from her Georgetown home to the White House, where she arrived each morning at 7:15. Along the way she read the daily summary, which was prepared by the CIA. On page four that morning was an item about Joel Backman. He was attracting the attention of some very dangerous people, perhaps even Sammy Tin.

The President greeted her warmly and had coffee waiting by the sofa. They were alone, as always, and they went right to work.

'You've seen *The New York Times* this morning?' he asked.

'Yes.'

'What are the chances that Backman paid for a pardon?'

'Very slim. As I've explained before, he had no idea one was in the works. He didn't have time to arrange things. Plus, we're quite confident he didn't have the money.'

'Then why was Backman pardoned?'

Susan Penn's loyalty to Teddy Maynard was fast becoming history. Teddy was gone, and would soon be dead, but she, at the age of forty-four, had a career left. Perhaps a long one. She and the President were working well together. He seemed in no hurry to appoint his new director.

'Frankly, Teddy wanted him dead.'

'Why? What is your recollection of why Mr. Maynard wanted him dead?'

'It's a long story—'

'No, it's not.'

'We don't know everything.'

'You know enough. Tell me what you know.'

She tossed her copy of the summary on the sofa and took a deep breath. 'Backman and Jacy Hubbard got in way over their heads. They had this software, JAM, that their clients had stupidly brought to the United States, to their office, looking for a fortune.'

'These clients were the young Pakistanis, right?'

'Yes, and they're all dead.'

'Do you know who killed them?'

'No.'

'Do you know who killed Jacy Hubbard?'

'No.'

The President stood with his coffee and walked to his desk. He sat on the edge and glared across the room at her. 'I find it hard to believe that we don't know these things.'

'Frankly, so do I. And it's not because we haven't tried. It's one reason Teddy worked so hard to get Backman pardoned. Sure, he wanted him dead, just on general principle—the two have a history and Teddy has always considered Backman to be a traitor. But he also felt strongly that Backman's murder might tell us something.'

'What?'

'Depends on who kills him. If the Russians do it, then we can believe the satellite system belonged to the Russians. Same for the Chinese. If the Israelis kill him, then there's a good chance Backman and Hubbard tried to sell their product to the Saudis. If the Saudis get to him, then we can believe that Backman double-crossed them. We're almost certain that the Saudis thought they had a deal.'

'But Backman screwed them?'

'Maybe not. We think Hubbard's death changed everything. Backman packed his bags and ran away to prison. All deals were off.'

The President walked back to the coffee table and refilled his cup. He sat across from her and shook his head. 'You expect me to believe that three young Pakistani hackers tapped into a satellite system so sophisticated that we didn't even know about it?'

'Yes. They were brilliant, but they also got lucky. Then they not only hacked their way in, but they wrote some amazing programs that manipulated it.'

'And that's JAM?'

'That's what they called it.'

'Has anybody ever seen the software?'

'The Saudis. That's how we know that it not only exists but probably works as well as advertised.'

'Where is the software now?'

'No one knows, except, maybe, Backman himself.'

285

A long pause as the President sipped his lukewarm coffee. Then he rested his elbows on his knees and said, 'What's best for us, Susan? What's in our best interests?'

She didn't hesitate. 'To follow Teddy's plan. Backman will be eliminated. The software hasn't been seen in six years, so it's probably gone too. The satellite system is up there, but whoever owns it can't play with it.'

Another sip, another pause. The President shook his head and said, 'So be it.'

*　　　*　　　*

Neal Backman didn't read *The New York Times*, but he did a quick search each morning for his father's name. When he ran across Frick's story, he attached it to an e-mail and sent it with the morning message from Jerry's Java.

At his desk, he read the story again, and relived the old rumors of how much money the broker had buried while the firm was collapsing. He'd never asked his father the question point-blank, because he knew he would not get a straight answer. Over the years, though, he had come to accept the common belief that Joel Backman was as broke as most convicted felons.

Then why did he have the nagging feeling that the cash-for-pardon scheme could be true? Because if anyone buried so deep in a federal prison could pull off such a miracle, it was his father. But how did he get to Bologna, Italy? And why? Who was after him?

The questions were piling up, the answers more elusive than ever.

As he sipped his double mocha and stared at his locked office door, he once again asked himself the great question: How does one go about locating a certain Swiss banker without the use of phones, faxes, regular mail, or e-mail?

He'd figure it out. He just needed time.

*   *   *

The *Times* story was read by Efraim as he rode the train from Florence to Bologna. A call from Tel Aviv had alerted him, and he found it online. Amos was four seats behind him, also reading it on his laptop.

Rafi and Shaul would arrive early the next morning, Rafi on a flight from Milan, Shaul on a train from Rome. The four Italian-speaking members of the *kidon* were already in Bologna, hurriedly putting together the two safe houses they would need for the project.

The preliminary plan was to grab Backman under the darkened porticoes along Via Fondazza or another suitable side street, preferably early in the morning or after dark. They would sedate him, shove him in a van, take him to a safe house, and wait for the drugs to wear off. They would interrogate him, eventually kill him with poison, and drive his body two hours north to Lake Garda where he'd be fed to the fish.

The plan was rough and fraught with pitfalls, but the green light had been given. There was no turning back. Now that Backman was getting so much attention, they had to strike quickly.

The race was also fueled by the fact that the Mossad had good reason to believe that Sammy

287

Tin was either in Bologna, or somewhere close.

*   *   *

The nearest restaurant to her apartment was a lovely old trattoria called Nino's. She knew the place well and had known the two sons of old Nino for many years. She explained her predicament, and when she arrived both of them were waiting and practically carried her inside. They took her cane, her bag, her coat, and walked her slowly to their favorite table, which they'd moved closer to the fireplace. They brought her coffee and water, and offered anything else she could possibly want. It was mid-afternoon, the lunch crowd was gone. Francesca and her student had Nino's to themselves.

When Marco arrived a few minutes later, the two brothers greeted him like family. 'La professoressa la sta aspettando,' one of them said. The teacher is waiting.

The fall on the gravel at San Luca and the sprained ankle had transformed her. Gone was the frosty indifference. Gone was the sadness, at least for now. She smiled when she saw him, even reached up, grabbed his hand, and pulled him close so they could blow air kisses at both cheeks, a custom Marco had been observing for two months but had yet to engage in. This was, after all, his first female acquaintance in Italy. She waved him to the chair directly across from her. The brothers swarmed around, taking his coat, asking him about coffee, anxious to see what an Italian lesson would look and sound like.

'How's your foot?' Marco asked, and made the

288

mistake of doing so in English. She put her finger to her lips, shook her head, and said, 'Non inglese, Marco. Solamente Italiano.'

He frowned and said, 'I was afraid of that.'

Her foot was very sore. She had kept it on ice while she was reading or watching television, and the swelling had gone down. The walk to the restaurant had been slow, but it was important to move about. At her mother's insistence, she was using a cane. She found it both useful and embarrassing.

More coffee and water arrived, and when the brothers were convinced that things were perfect with their dear friend Francesca and her Canadian student, they reluctantly retreated to the front of the restaurant.

'How is your mother?' he asked in Italian.

Very well, very tired. She has been sitting with Giovanni for a month now, and it's taking a toll.

So, thought Marco, Giovanni is now available for discussion. How is he?

Inoperable brain cancer, she said, and it took a few tries to get the translation right. He has been suffering for almost a year, and the end is quite close. He is unconscious. It's a pity.

What was his profession, what did he do?

He taught medieval history at the university for many years. They met there—she was a student, he was her professor. At the time he was married to a woman he disliked immensely. They had two sons. She and her professor fell in love and began an affair which lasted almost ten years before he divorced his wife and married Francesca.

Children? No, she said with sadness. Giovanni had two, he didn't want any more. She had regrets,

289

many regrets.

The feeling was clear that the marriage had not been a happy one. Wait till we get around to mine, thought Marco.

It didn't take long. 'Tell me all about you,' she said. 'Speak slowly. I want the accents to be as good as possible.'

'I'm just a Canadian businessman,' Marco began in Italian.

'No, really. What's your real name?'

'No.'

'What is it?'

'For now it's Marco. I have a long history, Francesca, and I can't talk about it.'

'Very well, do you have children?'

Ah, yes. For a long time he talked about his three children—their names, ages, occupations, residences, spouses, children. He added some fiction to move along his narrative, and he pulled off a small miracle by making the family sound remotely normal. Francesca listened intently, waiting to pounce on any wayward pronunciation or improperly conjugated verb. One of Nino's boys brought some chocolates and lingered long enough to say, with a huge smile, 'Parla molto bene, signore.' You speak very well, sir.

She began to fidget after an hour and Marco could tell she was uncomfortable. He finally convinced her to leave, and with great pleasure he walked her back down Via Minzoni, her right hand tightly fixed to his left elbow while her left hand worked the cane. They walked as slowly as possible. She dreaded the return to her apartment, to the deathwatch, the vigil. He wanted to walk for miles, to cling to her touch, to feel the hand of someone who needed him.

At her apartment they traded farewell kisses and made arrangements to meet at Nino's tomorrow, same time, same table.

Jacy Hubbard spent almost twenty-five years in Washington; a quarter of a century of major-league hell-raising with an astounding string of disposable women. The last had been Mae Szun, a beauty almost six feet tall with perfect features, deadly black eyes, and a husky voice that had no trouble at all getting Jacy out of a bar and into a car. After an hour of rough sex, she had delivered him to Sammy Tin, who finished him off and left him at his brother's grave.

When sex was needed to set up a kill, Sammy preferred Mae Szun. She was a fine MSS agent in her own right, but the legs and face added a dimension that had proved deadly on at least three occasions. He summoned her to Bologna, not to seduce but to hold hands with another agent and pretend to be happily married tourists. Seduction, though, was always a possibility. Especially with Backman. Poor guy had just spent six years locked up, away from women.

Mae spotted Marco as he moved in a crowd down Strada Maggiore, headed in the general direction of Via Fondazza. With amazing agility, she picked up her pace, pulled out a cell phone, and managed to gain ground on him while still looking like a bored window shopper.

Then he was gone. He suddenly took a left, turned down a narrow alley, Via Begatto, and headed north, away from Via Fondazza. By the time she made the turn, he was out of sight.

25

Spring was finally arriving in Bologna. The last flurries of snow had fallen. The temperature had approached fifty degrees the day before, and when Marco stepped outside before dawn he thought about swapping his parka for one of the other jackets. He took a few steps under the dark portico, let the temperature sink in, then decided it was still chilly enough to keep the parka. He'd return in a couple of hours and he could switch then if he wanted. He crammed his hands in his pockets and took off on the morning hike.

He could think of nothing but the *Times* story. To see his name plastered across the front page brought back painful memories, and that was unsettling enough. But to be accused of bribing the President was actionable at law, and in another life he would have started the day by shotgunning lawsuits at everyone involved. He would have owned *The New York Times*.

But what kept him awake were the questions. What would the attention mean for him now? Would Luigi snatch him again and run away?

And the most important: Was he in more danger today than yesterday?

He was surviving nicely, tucked away in a lovely city where no one knew his real name. No one recognized his face. No one cared. The Bolognesi went about their lives without disturbing others.

Not even he recognized himself. Each morning when he finished shaving and put on his glasses and his brown corduroy driver's cap, he stood at the mirror and said hello to Marco. Long gone were the fleshy jowls and puffy dark eyes, the thicker, longer hair. Long gone was the smirk and the arrogance. Now he was just another quiet man on the street.

Marco was living one day at a time, and the days were piling up. No one who read the *Times* story knew where Marco was or what he was doing.

He passed a man in a dark suit and instantly knew he was in trouble. The suit was out of place. It was a foreign variety, something bought off the rack in a low-end store, one he'd seen every day in another life. The white shirt was the same monotonous button-down he'd seen for thirty years in D.C. He'd once considered floating an office memo banning blue-and-white cotton button-downs, but Carl Pratt had talked him out of it.

He couldn't tell the color of the tie.

It was not the type of suit you'd ever see under the porticoes along Via Fondazza before dawn, or at any other time for that matter. He took a few steps, glanced over his shoulder, and saw that the suit was now following him. White guy, thirty years old, thick, athletic, the clear winner in a footrace or a fistfight. So Marco used another strategy. He suddenly stopped, turned around, and said, 'You want something?'

To which someone else said, 'Over here, Backman.'

Hearing his name stopped him cold. For a second his knees were rubbery, his shoulders sagged, and he told himself that no, he was not dreaming. In a flash he thought of all the horrors the word 'Backman' brought with it. How sad to be so terrified of your own name.

293

There were two of them. The one with the voice arrived on the scene from the other side of Via Fondazza. He had basically the same suit, but with a bold white shirt with no buttons on the collar. He was older, shorter, and much thinner. Mutt and Jeff. Thick 'n' Thin.

'What do you want?' Marco said.

They were slowly reaching for their pockets. 'We're with the FBI,' the thick one said. American English, probably Midwest.

'Sure you are,' Marco said.

They went through the required ritual of flashing their badges, but under the darkness of the portico Marco could read nothing. The dim light over an apartment door helped a little. 'I can't read those,' he said.

'Let's take a walk,' said the thin one. Boston, Irish. 'Walk' came out 'wok.'

'You guys lost?' Marco said without moving. He didn't want to move, and his feet were quite heavy anyway.

'We know exactly where we are.'

'I doubt that. You got a warrant?'

'We don't need one.'

The thick one made the mistake of touching Marco's left elbow, as if he would help him move along to where they wanted to go. Marco jerked away. 'Don't touch me! You boys get lost. You can't make an arrest here. All you can do is talk.'

'Fine, let's go have a chat,' said the thin one.

'I don't have to talk.'

'There's a coffee shop a couple of blocks away,' said the thick one.

'Great, have some coffee. And a pastry. But leave me alone.'

Thick 'n' Thin looked at each other, then glanced around, not sure what to do next, not sure what plan B entailed.

Marco wasn't moving; not that he felt very safe where he was, but he could almost see a dark car waiting around the corner.

Where the hell is Luigi right now? he asked himself. Is this part of his conspiracy?

He'd been discovered, found, unmasked, called by his real name on Via Fondazza. This would certainly mean another move, another safe house.

The thin one decided to take control of the encounter. 'Sure, we can meet right here. There are a lot of folks back home who'd like to talk to you.'

'Maybe that's why I'm over here.'

'We're investigating the pardon you bought.'

'Then you're wasting a helluva lot of time and money, which would surprise no one.'

'We have some questions about the transaction.'

'What a stupid investigation,' Marco said, spitting the words down at the thin one. For the first time in many years he felt like the broker again, berating some haughty bureaucrat or dim-witted congressman. 'The FBI spends good money sending two clowns like you all the way to Bologna, Italy, to tackle me on a sidewalk so you can ask me questions that no fool in his right mind would answer. You're a couple of dumbasses, you know that? Go back home and tell your boss that he's a dumbass too. And while you're talking to him, tell him he's wasting a lot of time and money if he thinks I paid for a pardon.'

'So you deny—'

'I deny nothing. I admit nothing. I say nothing, except that this is the FBI at its absolute worst. You boys are in deep water and you can't swim.'

Back home they'd slap him around a little, push him, curse him, swap insults. But on foreign soil they weren't sure how to behave. Their orders were to find him, to see if he did in fact live where the CIA said he was living. And if found, they were supposed to jolt him, scare him, hit him with some questions about wire transfers and offshore accounts.

They had it all mapped out and had rehearsed it many times. But under the porticoes of Via Fondazza, Mr. Lazzeri was annihilating their plans.

'We're not leaving Bologna until we talk,' said the thick one.

'Congratulations, you're in for a long vacation.'

'We have our orders, Mr. Backman.'

'And I've got mine.'

'Just a few questions, please,' said the thin one.

'Go see my lawyer,' Marco said, and began to walk away, in the direction of his apartment.

'Who's your lawyer?'

'Carl Pratt.'

They weren't moving, weren't following, and Marco picked up his pace. He crossed the street, glanced quickly at his safe house, but didn't slow down. If they wanted to follow, they waited too long. By the time he darted onto Via del Piombo, he knew they could never find him. These were his streets now, his alleys, his darkened doorways to shops that wouldn't open for three more hours.

They found him on Via Fondazza only because they knew his address.

At the southwestern edge of old Bologna, near the Porto San Stefano, he caught a city bus and rode it for half an hour, until he stopped near the train station at the northern perimeter. There he caught another bus and rode into the center of the city. The buses were filling; the early risers were getting to work. A third bus took him across the city again to the Porta Saragozza, where he began the 3.6-kilometer hike up to San Luca. At the four-hundredth arch he stopped to catch his breath, and between the columns he looked down and waited for someone to come sneaking up behind him. There was no one back there, as he expected.

He slowed his pace and finished the climb in fifty-five minutes. Behind the Santuario di San Luca he followed the narrow pathway where Francesca had fallen, and finally parked himself on the bench where she had waited. From there, his early-morning view of Bologna was magnificent. He removed his parka to cool off. The sun was up, the air was as light and clear as any he'd ever breathed, and for a long time Marco sat very much alone and watched the city come to life.

He treasured the solitude, and the safety of the moment. Why couldn't he make the climb every morning, and sit high above Bologna with nothing to do but think, and maybe read the newspapers? Perhaps call a friend on the phone and catch up on the gossip?

He'd have to find the friends first.

It was a dream that would not come true.

With Luigi's very limited cell phone he called Ermanno and canceled their morning session.

Then he called Luigi and explained that he didn't feel like studying.

'Is something wrong?'

'No. I just need a break.'

'That's fine, Marco, but we're paying Ermanno to teach you, okay? You need to study every day.'

'Drop it, Luigi. I'm not studying today.'

'I don't like this.'

'And I don't care. Suspend me. Kick me out of school.'

'Are you upset?'

'No, Luigi, I'm fine. It's a beautiful day, springtime in Bologna, and I'm going for a long walk.'

'Where?'

'No thanks, Luigi. I don't want company.'

'What about lunch?'

Hunger pains shot through Marco's stomach. Lunch with Luigi was always delicious and he always grabbed the check. 'Sure.'

'Let me think. I'll call you back.'

'Sure, Luigi. Ciao.'

They met at twelve-thirty at Caffè Atene, an ancient dive in an alley, down a few steps from street level. It was a tiny place, with small square tables practically touching each other. The waiters jostled around with trays of food held high overhead. Chefs yelled from the kitchen. The cramped dining room was smoky, loud, and packed with hungry people who enjoyed talking at full volume as they ate. Luigi explained that the restaurant had been around for centuries, tables were impossible to get, and the food was, of course, superb. He suggested they share a plate of calamari to get things started.

After a morning of arguing with himself up at San Luca, Marco had decided not to tell Luigi about his encounter with the FBI. At least not then, not that morning. He might do it the next day, or the next, but for the moment he was still sorting things out. His principal reason for holding back was that he did not want to pack up and run again, not on Luigi's terms.

If he ran, he would be alone.

He couldn't begin to imagine why the FBI would be in Bologna, evidently without the knowledge of Luigi and whoever he was working for. He was assuming Luigi knew nothing of their presence. He certainly seemed to be much more concerned with the menu and the wine list. Life was good. Everything was normal.

The lights went out. Suddenly, Caffè Atene was completely dark, and in the next instant a waiter with a tray of someone's lunch came crashing across their table, yelling and cursing and spilling himself onto both Luigi and Marco. The legs of the antique table buckled and its edge crashed hard onto Marco's lap. At about the same time, a foot or something hit him hard on the left shoulder. Everyone was yelling. Glass was breaking. Bodies were getting shoved, then from the kitchen someone screamed, 'Fire!'

The scramble outside and onto the street was completed without serious injury. The last person out was Marco, who ducked low to avoid the stampede while searching for his navy blue Silvio bag. As always, he had hung its strap over the back of his chair, with the bag resting so close to his body he could usually feel it. It had disappeared in the melee.

299

The Italians stood in the street and stared in disbelief at the café. Their lunch was in there, half eaten and now being ruined. Finally, a thin light puff of smoke emerged and made its way through the door and into the air. A waiter could be seen running by the front tables with a fire extinguisher. Then some more smoke, but not much.

'I lost my bag,' Marco said to Luigi as they watched and waited.

'The blue one?'

How many bags do I carry around, Luigi? 'Yes, the blue one.' He already had suspicions that the bag had been snatched.

A small fire truck with an enormous siren arrived, slid to a stop, and kept wailing as the firemen raced inside. Minutes passed, and the Italians began to drift away. The decisive ones left to find lunch elsewhere while there was still time. The others just kept gawking at this horrible injustice.

The siren was finally neutralized. Evidently the fire was too, and without the need for water being sprayed all over the restaurant. After an hour of discussion and debate and very little firefighting, the situation was under control. 'Something in the restroom,' a waiter yelled to one of his friends, one of the few remaining weakened and unfed patrons. The lights were back on.

They allowed them back inside to get their coats. Some who'd left in search of other meals were returning to get their things. Luigi became very helpful in the hunt for Marco's bag. He discussed the situation with the headwaiter, and before long half the staff was scouring the restaurant. Among the excited chatter, Marco heard a waiter say something about a 'smoke bomb.'

The bag was gone, and Marco knew it.

They had a panino and a beer at a sidewalk café, under the sun where they could watch pretty girls stroll by. Marco was preoccupied with the theft, but he worked hard to appear unconcerned.

'Sorry about the bag,' Luigi said at one point.

'No big deal.'

'I'll get you another cell phone.'

'Thanks.'

'What else did you lose?'

'Nothing. Just some maps of the city, some aspirin, a few euros.'

In a hotel room a few blocks away, Zellman and Krater had the bag on the bed, its contents neatly arranged. Other than the Ankyo smartphone, there were two maps of Bologna, both well marked and well used but revealing little, four $100 bills, the cell phone Luigi had loaned him, a bottle of aspirin, and the owner's manual for the Ankyo.

Zellman, the more agile computer whiz of the two, plugged the smartphone into an Internet access jack and was soon fiddling with the menu. 'This is good stuff,' he was saying, quite impressed with Marco's gadget. 'The absolute latest toy on the market.'

Not surprisingly, he was stopped by the password. They would have to dissect it at Langley. With his laptop, he e-mailed a message to Julia Javier, passing along the serial number and other information.

Within two hours of the theft, a CIA agent was sitting in the parking lot outside Chatter in suburban Alexandria, waiting for the store to open.

26

From a distance he watched her shuffle along gamely, bravely, with her cane down the sidewalk beside Via Minzoni. He followed and was soon fifty feet away. Today she wore brown suede boots, no doubt for the support. The boots had low heels. Flat shoes would've been more comfortable, but then she was Italian and fashion always took priority. The light brown skirt stopped at her knees. She was wearing a tight wool sweater, bright red in color, and it was the first time he'd seen her when she wasn't bundled up for cold weather. No overcoat to hide her really nice figure.

She was walking cautiously and limping slightly, but with a determination that gave him heart. It was just coffee at Nino's, for an hour or two of Italian. And it was all for him!

And the money.

For a moment he thought about her money. Whatever the dire situation with her poor husband, and her seasonal work as a tour guide, she managed to dress stylishly and live in a beautifully decorated apartment. Giovanni had been a professor. Perhaps he'd saved carefully over the years, and now his illness was straining their budget.

Whatever. Marco had his own problems. He'd just lost $400 in cash and his only lifeline to the outside world. People who weren't supposed to know his whereabouts now knew his exact address. Nine hours earlier he'd heard his real name used on Via Fondazza.

He slowed and allowed her to enter Nino's, where she was again greeted like a beloved member of the family by Nino's boys. Then he circled the block to give them time to get her situated, to fuss over her, bring her coffee, chat for a moment and catch up on the neighborhood gossip. Ten minutes after she arrived, he walked through the door and got bear-hugged by Nino's youngest son. A friend of Francesca's was a friend for life.

Her moods changed so much that Marco did not know what to expect. He was still touched by the warmth of yesterday, but he knew that the indifference could return today. When she smiled and grabbed his hand and started all the cheek pecking he knew instantly the lesson would be the highlight of a rotten day.

When they were finally alone he asked about her husband. Things had not changed. 'It's only a matter of days,' she said with stiff lip, as if she'd already accepted death and was ready for the grieving.

He asked about her mother, Signora Altonelli, and got a full report. She was baking a pear torta, one of Giovanni's favorites, just in case he got a whiff of it from the kitchen.

'And how was your day?' she asked.

It would be impossible to fictionalize a worse set of occurrences. From the shock of hearing his real name barked through the darkness, to being the victim of a carefully staged theft, he couldn't imagine a worse day.

'A little excitement during lunch,' he said.

'Tell me about it.'

He described his hike up to San Luca, to the

spot where she fell, her bench, the views, the canceled session with Ermanno, lunch with Luigi, the fire but not the loss of his bag. She had not noticed the absence of it until he told the story.

'There's so little crime in Bologna,' she said, half apologetic. 'I know Caffè Atene. It's not a place for thieves.'

These were probably not Italians, he wanted to say, but managed to nod gravely as if to say: Yes, yes, what's the world coming to?

When the small talk was over, she switched gears like a stern professor and said she was in the mood to tackle some verbs. He said he was not, but his moods were unimportant. She drilled him on the future tense of abitare (to live) and vedere (to see). Then she made him weave both verbs in all tenses into a hundred random sentences. Far from being distracted, she pounced on any wayward accent. A grammatical mistake prompted a quick reprimand, as if he'd just insulted the entire country.

She had spent the day penned up in her apartment, with a dying husband and a busy mother. The lesson was her only chance to release some energy. Marco, however, was exhausted. The stress of the day was taking its toll, but Francesca's high-octane demands took his mind off his fatigue and confusion. One hour passed quickly. They recharged with more coffee, and she launched into the murky and difficult world of the subjunctive— present, imperfect, and past perfect. Finally, he began to founder. She tried to prop him up with reassurances that the subjunctive sinks a lot of students. But he was tired and ready to sink.

He surrendered after two hours, thoroughly

304

drained and in need of another long walk. It took fifteen minutes to say goodbye to Nino's boys. He happily escorted her back to her apartment. They hugged and pecked cheeks and promised to study tomorrow.

If he walked as directly as possible, his apartment was twenty-five minutes away. But he had not walked directly to any place in more than a month.

He began to wander.

*   *   *

At 4:00 p.m., eight of the *kidon* were on Via Fondazza, at various points—one drinking coffee at a sidewalk café, three strolling aimlessly a block apart, one cruising back and forth on a scooter, and one looking out a window from the third floor.

Half a mile away, outside the central city, on the second floor above a flower shop owned by an elderly Jew, the four other members of the *kidon* were playing cards and waiting nervously. One, Ari, was one of the top English interrogators within the Mossad.

They played with little conversation. The night ahead would be long and unpleasant.

*   *   *

Throughout the day, Marco had struggled with the question of whether to return to Via Fondazza. The FBI boys could still be there, ready for another ugly confrontation. He felt sure they would not be stiff-armed so easily. They wouldn't simply call it quits and catch a plane. They had superiors back home who demanded results.

Though far from certain, he had a strong hunch that Luigi was behind the theft of his Silvio bag. The fire had not really been a fire; it was more of a diversion, a reason for the lights to go off and a cover for someone to grab the bag.

He didn't trust Luigi because he trusted no one.

They had his cute little smartphone. Neal's codes were in there somewhere. Could they be broken? Could the trail lead to his son? Marco had not the slightest idea how those things worked, what was possible, what was impossible.

The urge to leave Bologna was overwhelming. Where to go and how to get there were questions he had not sorted out. He was rambling now, and he felt vulnerable, almost helpless. Every face glancing at him was someone else who knew his real name. At a crowded bus stop he cut the line and climbed on, not sure where he was going. The bus was packed with weary commuters, shoulder to shoulder as they bounced along. Through the windows he watched the foot traffic under the marvelous crowded porticoes of the city center.

At the last second he jumped off, then walked three blocks along Via San Vitale until he saw another bus. He rode in circles for almost an hour, then finally stepped off near the train station. He drifted with another crowd, then darted across Via dell' Indipendenza to the bus station. Inside he found the departures, saw that one was leaving in ten minutes for Piacenza, an hour and a half away with five stops in between. He bought a ticket for thirty euros and hid in the restroom until the last minute. The bus was almost full. The seats were wide with high headrests, and as the bus moved slowly through heavy traffic, Marco almost nodded off. Then he caught himself. Sleeping was not permissible.

This was it—the escape he'd been contemplating since the first day in Bologna. He'd become convinced that to survive he would be forced to disappear, to leave Luigi behind and make it on his own. He had often wondered exactly how and when the flight would begin. What would trigger it? A face? A threat? Would he take a bus or train, cab or plane? Where would he go? Where would he hide? Would his rudimentary Italian get him through it? How much money would he have at the time?

This was it. It was happening. There was no turning back now.

The first stop was the small village of Bazzano, fifteen kilometers west of Bologna. Marco got off the bus and did not get back on. Again, he hid in the restroom of the station until the bus was gone, then crossed the street to a bar where he ordered a beer and asked the bartender about the nearest hotel.

Over his second beer he asked about the train station, and learned that Bazzano did not have one. Only buses, said the bartender.

Albergo Cantino was near the center of the village, five or six blocks away. It was dark when he arrived at the front desk, with no bags, something that did not go unnoticed by the signora who handled things.

'I'd like a room,' he said in Italian.

'For how many nights?'

'Only one.'

'The rate is fifty-five euros.'

'Fine.'

'Your passport, please.'

'Sorry, but I lost it.'

Her plucked and painted eyebrows arched in great suspicion, then she began shaking her head. 'Sorry.'

Marco laid two hundred-euro bills on the counter in front of her. The bribe was obvious— just take the cash, no paperwork, and give me a key.

More shaking, more frowning.

'You must have a passport,' she said. Then she folded her arms across her chest, jerked her chin upward, braced for the next exchange. There was no way she was going to lose.

Outside, Marco walked the streets of the strange town. He found a bar and ordered coffee; no more alcohol, he had to keep his wits.

'Where can I find a taxi?' he asked the bartender.

'At the bus station.'

*   *   *

By 9:00 p.m. Luigi was walking the floors of his apartment, waiting for Marco to return next door. He called Francesca and she reported that they had studied that afternoon; in fact they'd had a delightful lesson. Great, he thought.

His disappearance was part of the plan, but Whitaker and Langley thought it would take a few more days. Had they lost him already? That quickly? There were now five agents very close by—Luigi, Zellman, Krater, and two others sent from Milano.

Luigi had always questioned the plan. In a city the size of Bologna it was impossible to maintain physical surveillance of a person twenty-four hours a day. Luigi had argued almost violently that the only way for the plan to work was to stash Backman away in a small village where his movements were limited, his options few, and his visitors much more visible. That had been the original plan, but the details had been abruptly changed in Washington.

At 9:12, a buzzer quietly went off in the kitchen. He hurried to the monitors in the kitchen. Marco was home. His front door was opening. Luigi stared at the digital image from the hidden camera in the ceiling of the living room next door.

Two strangers—not Marco. Two men in their thirties, dressed like regular guys. They closed the door quickly, quietly, professionally, then began looking around. One carried a small black bag of some sort.

They were good, very good. To pick the lock of the safe house they had to be very good.

Luigi smiled with excitement. With a little luck, his cameras were about to record Marco getting nabbed. Maybe they would kill him right there in the living room, captured on film. Perhaps the plan would work after all.

He flipped the audio switches and increased the volume. Language was crucial here. Where were they from? What was their tongue? There were no sounds, though, as they moved about silently. They whispered once or twice, but he could barely hear it.

27

The taxi made an abrupt stop on Via Gramsci, near the bus and train stations. From the backseat, Marco handed over enough cash, then ducked between two parked cars and was soon lost in the darkness. His escape from Bologna had been very brief indeed, but then it wasn't exactly over. He zigzagged out of habit, looping back, watching his own trail.

On Via Minzoni he moved quickly under the porticoes and stopped at her apartment building. He didn't have the luxury of second thoughts, of hesitating or guessing. He rang twice, desperately hoping that Francesca, and not Signora Altonelli, would answer.

'Who is it?' came that lovely voice.

'Francesca, it's me, Marco. I need some help.'

A very slight pause, then, 'Yes, of course.'

She met him at her door on the second floor and invited him in. Much to his dismay, Signora Altonelli was still there, standing in the kitchen door with a hand towel, watching his entrance very closely.

'Are you all right?' Francesca asked in Italian.

'English, please,' he said, looking and smiling at her mother.

'Yes, of course.'

'I need a place to stay tonight. I can't get a room because I have no passport. I can't even bribe my way into a small hotel.'

'That's the law in Europe, you know.'

'Yes, I'm learning.'

She waved at the sofa, then turned to her mother and asked her to make some coffee. They sat down. He noticed she was barefoot and moving about without the cane, though she still needed it. She wore tight jeans and a baggy sweater and looked as cute as a coed.

'Why don't you tell me what's going on?' she said.

'It's a complicated story and I can't tell you most of it. Let's just say that I don't feel very safe right now, that I really need to leave Bologna, as soon as possible.'

'Where are you going?'

'I'm not sure. Somewhere out of Italy, out of Europe, to a place where I'll hide again.'

'How long will you hide?'

'A long time. I'm not sure.'

She stared at him coldly, without blinking. He stared back because even when cold, the eyes were beautiful. 'Who are you?' she asked.

'Well, I'm certainly not Marco Lazzeri.'

'What are you running from?'

'My past, and it's rapidly catching up with me. I'm not a criminal, Francesca. I was once a lawyer. I got in some trouble. I served my time. I've been fully pardoned. I'm not a bad guy.'

'Why is someone after you?'

'It was a business deal six years ago. Some very nasty people are not happy with how the deal was finished. They blame me. They would like to find me.'

'To kill you?'

'Yes. That's what they'd like to do.'

'This is very confusing. Why did you come here? Why did Luigi help you? Why did he hire me

311

and Ermanno? I don't understand.'

'And I can't answer those questions. Two months ago I was in prison, and I thought I would be there for another fourteen years. Suddenly, I'm free. I was given a new identity, brought here, hidden first in Treviso, now Bologna. I think they want to kill me here.'

'Here! In Bologna!'

He nodded and looked toward the kitchen as Signora Altonelli appeared with a tray of coffee, and also a pear torta that had not yet been sliced. As she placed it delicately on a small plate for Marco, he realized that he had not eaten since lunch.

Lunch with Luigi. Lunch with the fake fire and the stolen smartphone. He thought of Neal again and worried about his safety.

'It's delicious,' he said to her mother in Italian. Francesca was not eating. She watched every move he made, every bite, every sip of coffee. When her mother went back to the kitchen, she said, 'Who does Luigi work for?'

'I'm not sure. Probably the CIA. You know the CIA?'

'Yes. I read spy novels. The CIA put you here?'

'I think the CIA got me out of prison, out of the country, and here to Bologna where they've hidden me in a safe house while they try and figure out what to do with me.'

'Will they kill you?'

'Maybe.'

'Luigi?'

'Possibly.'

She placed her cup on the table and fiddled with her hair for a while. 'Would you like some water?' she asked as she got to her feet.

'No thanks.'

'I need to move a little,' she said as she carefully placed weight on her left foot. She walked slowly into the kitchen, where things were quiet for a moment before an argument broke out. She and her mother were disagreeing rather heatedly, but they were forced to do so in loud, tense whispers.

It dragged on for a few minutes, died down, then flared up as neither side seemed ready to yield. Finally, Francesca came limping back with a small bottle of San Pellegrino and took her place on the sofa.

'What was that all about?' he asked.

'I told her you wanted to sleep here tonight. She misunderstood.'

'Come on. I'll sleep in the closet. I don't care.'

'She's very old-fashioned.'

'Is she staying here tonight?'

'She is now.'

'Just give me a pillow. I'll sleep on the kitchen table.'

Signora Altonelli was a different person when she returned to remove the coffee tray. She glared at Marco as if he'd already molested her daughter. She glared at Francesca as if she wanted to slap her. She huffed around the kitchen for a few minutes, then retired somewhere back in the apartment.

'Are you sleepy?' Francesca asked.

'No. You?'

'No. Let's talk.'

'Okay.'

'Tell me everything.'

                    *   *   *

He slept a few hours on the sofa, and was awakened by Francesca tapping on his shoulder. 'I have an idea,' she said. 'Follow me.'

He followed her to the kitchen, where a clock read 4:15. On the counter by the sink was a disposable razor, a can of shaving cream, a pair of eyeglasses, and a bottle of hair something or other—he couldn't translate it. She handed him a small burgundy leather case and said, 'This is a passport. Giovanni's.'

He almost dropped it. 'No, I can't—'

'Yes, you can. He won't be needing it. I insist.'

Marco slowly opened it and looked at the distinguished face of a man he'd never meet. The expiration date was seven months away, so the photo was almost five years old. He found the birthday—Giovanni was now sixty-eight years old, a good twenty years older than his wife.

During the cab ride back from Bazzano, he'd thought of nothing but a passport. He'd thought about stealing one from an unsuspecting tourist. He'd thought about buying one somewhere on the black market but had no idea where to go. And he'd pondered Giovanni's, one that, sadly, was about to be useless. Null and void.

But he'd dismissed the thought for fear of endangering Francesca. What if he got caught? What if an immigration guard at an airport got suspicious and called his supervisor over? But his biggest fear was getting caught by the people who were chasing him. The passport could implicate her, and he would never do that.

'Are you sure?' he asked. Now that he was

314

holding the passport he really wanted to keep it.

'Please, Marco, I want to help. Giovanni would insist.'

'I don't know what to say.'

'We have work to do. There's a bus for Parma that leaves in two hours. It would be a safe way out of town.'

'I want to get to Milano,' he said.

'Good idea.'

She took the passport and opened it. They studied the photo of her husband. 'Let's start with that thing around your mouth,' she said.

Ten minutes later the mustache and goatee were gone, his face completely shaven. She held a mirror for him as he hovered over the kitchen sink. Giovanni at sixty-three had less gray hair than Marco at fifty-two, but then he'd not had the experience of a federal indictment and six years in prison.

He assumed the hair coloring was something she used, but he was not about to ask. It promised results in an hour. He sat in a chair facing the table with a towel draped over his shoulders while she gently worked the solution through his hair. Very little was said. Her mother was asleep. Her husband was still and quiet and heavily medicated.

Not long ago Giovanni the professor had worn round tortoiseshell eyeglasses, light brown, quite the academic look, and when Marco put them on and studied his new look he was startled at the change. His hair was much darker, his eyes much different. He hardly recognized himself.

'Not bad' was her assessment of her own work. 'It will do for now.'

She brought in a navy corduroy sports coat,

315

with well-worn patches on the elbows. 'He's about two inches shorter than you,' she said. The sleeves needed another inch, and the jacket would've been tight through the chest, but Marco was so thin these days that anything would swallow him.

'What's your real name?' she said as she tugged on the sleeves and adjusted the collar.

'Joel.'

'I think you should travel with a briefcase. It will look normal.'

He couldn't argue. Her generosity was overwhelming, and he needed every damned bit of it. She left, then came back with a beautiful old briefcase, tan leather with a silver buckle.

'I don't know what to say,' Marco mumbled.

'It's Giovanni's favorite, a gift from me twenty years ago. Italian leather.'

'Of course.'

'If you get caught somehow with the passport, what will you say?' she asked.

'I stole it. You're my tutor. I was in your home as a guest. I managed to find the drawer with your documents, and I stole your husband's passport.'

'You're a good liar.'

'At one time, I was one of the best. If I get caught, Francesca, I will protect you. I promise. I will tell lies that will baffle everyone.'

'You won't get caught. But use the passport as little as possible.'

'Don't worry. I'll destroy it as soon as I can.'

'Do you need money?'

'No.'

'Are you sure? I have a thousand euros here.'

'No, Francesca, but thanks.'

'You'd better hurry.'

He followed her to the front door where they stopped and looked at each other. 'Do you spend much time online?' he asked.

'A little each day.'

'Check out Joel Backman, start with *The Washington Post*. There's a lot of stuff there, but don't believe everything you read. I'm not the monster they've created.'

'You're not a monster at all, Joel.'

'I don't know how to thank you.'

She took his right hand and squeezed it with both of hers. 'Will you ever return to Bologna?' she asked. It was more of an invitation than a question.

'I don't know. I really don't have any idea what's about to happen. But, maybe. Can I knock on your door if I make it back?'

'Please do. Be careful out there.'

He stood in the shadows of Via Minzoni for a few minutes, not wanting to leave her, not ready to begin the long journey.

Then there was a cough from under the darkened porticoes across the street, and Giovanni Ferro was on the run.

28

As the hours passed with excruciating slowness, Luigi gradually moved from worry to panic. One of two things had happened: either the hit had already occurred, or Marco had gotten wind of something and was trying to flee. Luigi worried about the stolen bag. Was it too strong a move? Had it scared Marco to the point of disappearing?

317

The expensive smartphone had shaken everyone. Their boy had been doing much more than studying Italian, walking the streets, and sampling every café and bar in town. He'd been planning, and communicating.

The smartphone was in a lab in the basement of the American embassy in Milan, where, according to the latest from Whitaker, and they were talking every fifteen minutes, the technicians had been unable to crack its codes.

A few minutes after midnight, the two intruders next door evidently got tired of waiting. As they were making their exit, they spoke a few words loud enough to be recorded. It was English with a trace of an accent. Luigi had immediately called Whitaker and reported that they were probably Israeli.

He was correct. The two agents were instructed by Efraim to leave the apartment and take up other positions.

When they left, Luigi decided to send Krater to the bus station and Zellman to the train station. With no passport, Marco could not buy a plane ticket. Luigi decided to ignore the airport. But, as he told Whitaker, if their boy can somehow buy a state-of-the-art cell phone PC that cost about a thousand bucks, maybe he could also find himself a passport.

By 3:00 a.m. Whitaker was yelling in Milano and Luigi, who couldn't yell for security reasons, could only curse, which he was doing in English and Italian and holding his own in both languages.

'You've lost him, dammit!' Whitaker screeched.

'Not yet!'

'He's already dead!'

Luigi hung up again, for the third time that morning.

The *kidon* pulled back around 3:30 a.m. They would all rest for a few hours, then plan the day ahead.

*   *   *

He sat with a wino on a bench in a small park, not far down Via dell' Indipendenza from the bus station. The wino had been nursing a jug of pink fluid for most of the night, and every five minutes or so he managed to lift his head and utter something at Marco, five feet away. Marco mumbled back, and whatever he said seemed to please the wino. Two of his colleagues were completely comatose and were huddled nearby like dead soldiers in a trench. Marco didn't feel exactly safe, but then he had more serious problems.

A few people loitered in front of the bus station. Around five-thirty activity increased when a large group of what appeared to be Gypsies came bustling out, all speaking loudly at once, obviously delighted to be off the bus after a long ride from somewhere. More departing passengers were arriving, and Marco decided it was time to leave the wino. He entered the station behind a young couple and their child and followed them to the ticket counter where he listened as they bought tickets to Parma. He did the same, then hurried to the restroom and again hid in a stall.

Krater was sitting in the station's all-night diner, drinking bad coffee behind a newspaper while he watched the passengers come and go. He watched Marco walk by. He noted his height, build,

319

age. The walk was familiar, though much slower. The Marco Lazzeri he'd been following for weeks could walk as fast as most men could jog. This fellow's pace was much slower, but then there was nowhere to go. Why hurry? On the streets Lazzeri was always trying to lose them, and at times he was successful.

But the face was very different. The hair was much darker. The brown corduroy cap was gone, but then it was an accessory and easy to lose. The tortoiseshell eyeglasses caught Krater's attention. Glasses were wonderful diversions but so often they were overplayed. Marco's stylish Armani frames had fit him perfectly, slightly altering his appearance without calling attention to his face. The round glasses on this guy begged for attention.

The facial hair was gone; a five-minute job, something anyone would do. The shirt was not one Krater had seen before, and he'd been in Marco's apartment with Luigi during sweeps when they looked at every item of clothing. The faded jeans were very generic, and Marco had purchased a similar pair. The blue sports coat with worn elbow patches, along with the handsome attaché, kept Krater in his chair. The jacket had many miles on it, something Marco could not have acquired. The sleeves were a bit short, but that was not uncommon. The briefcase was made of fine leather. Marco might somehow find and spend some cash on a smartphone, but why waste it on such an expensive briefcase? His last bag, the navy blue Silvio he'd owned until about sixteen hours ago when Krater grabbed it during the melee at Caffè Atene, had cost sixty euros.

Krater watched him until he rounded a corner

and was out of sight. A possibility, nothing more. He sipped his coffee and for a few minutes contemplated the gentleman he'd just seen.

Marco stood in the stall with his jeans bunched around his ankles, feeling quite silly but much more concerned with a good cover at this point. The door opened. The wall to the left of the door had four urinals; across were six lavatories, and next to them were the four stalls. The other three were empty. There was very little traffic at the moment. Marco listened carefully, waiting to hear the sounds of human relief—the zipper, the jangle of a belt buckle, the deep sigh men often make, the spray of urine.

Nothing. There was no noise from the lavatories, no one washing their hands. The doors to the other three stalls did not open. Maybe it was the custodian making his rounds, and doing so very quietly.

In front of the lavatories, Krater bent low and saw the jeans around the ankles in the last stall. Next to the jeans was the fine briefcase. The gentleman was taking care of his business and in no hurry about it.

The next bus left at 6:00 a.m. for Parma; after that there was a 6:20 departure for Florence. Krater hurried to the booth and bought tickets for both. The clerk looked at him oddly, but Krater couldn't have cared less. He went back to the restroom. The gentleman in the last stall was still there.

Krater stepped outside and called Luigi. He gave a description of the man, and explained that he appeared to be in no hurry to leave the men's room.

'The best place to hide,' Luigi said.

'I've done it many times.'

'Do you think it's Marco?'

'I don't know. If it is, it's a very good disguise.'

Rattled by the smartphone, the $400 in American cash, and the disappearance, Luigi was not taking chances. 'Follow him,' he said.

At 5:55, Marco pulled up his jeans, flushed, grabbed his briefcase, and took off for the bus. Waiting on the platform was Krater, nonchalantly eating an apple with one hand and holding a newspaper with the other. When Marco headed for the bus to Parma, so did Krater.

A third of the seats were empty. Marco took one on the left side, halfway back, by a window. Krater was looking away when he passed by, then found a seat four rows behind him.

*   *   *

The first stop was Modena, thirty minutes into the trip. As they entered the city, Marco decided to take stock of the faces behind him. He stood and made his way to the rear, to the restroom, and along the way gave a casual glance to each male.

When he locked himself in the restroom, he closed his eyes and said to himself, 'Yes, I've seen that face before.'

Less than twenty-four hours earlier, in Caffè Atene, just a few minutes before the lights went out. The face had been in a long mirror that lined the wall with an old coatrack, above the tables. The face had been seated nearby, behind him, with another man.

It was a familiar face. Maybe he'd even seen it

before somewhere in Bologna.

Marco returned to his seat as the bus slowed and approached the station. Think quickly, man, he kept telling himself, but keep your cool. Don't panic. They've followed you out of Bologna; you can't let them follow you out of the country.

As the bus stopped, the driver announced their arrival in Modena. A brief stop; a departure in fifteen minutes. Four passengers waddled down the aisle and got off. The others kept their seats; most were dozing anyway. Marco closed his eyes and allowed his head to drift to his left, against the window, fast asleep now. A minute passed and two peasants climbed aboard, wild-eyed and clutching heavy cloth bags.

When the driver returned and was situating himself behind the wheel, Marco suddenly eased from his seat, slid quickly along the aisle, and hopped off the bus just as the door was closing. He walked quickly into the station, then turned around and watched the bus back away. His pursuer was still on board.

Krater's first move was to sprint off the bus, perhaps arguing with the driver in the process, but then no driver will fight to keep someone on board. He caught himself, though, because Marco obviously knew he was being followed. His last-second exit only confirmed what Krater had suspected. It was Marco all right, running like a wounded animal.

Problem was, he was loose in Modena and Krater was not. The bus turned onto another street, then stopped for a traffic light. Krater rushed to the driver, holding his stomach, begging to get off before he vomited all over the place. The door flew open, Krater jumped off and ran back toward the station.

Marco wasted no time. When the bus was out of sight, he hurried to the front of the station where three taxis were lined up. He jumped into the backseat of the first one and said, 'Can you take me to Milano?' His Italian was very good.

'Milano?'

'Sì, Milano.'

'È molto caro!' It's very expensive.

'Quanto?'

'Duecento euro.' Two hundred euros.

'Andiamo.'

*   *   *

After an hour of scouring the Modena bus station and the two streets next to it, Krater called Luigi with the news that was not all good, and not all bad. He'd lost his man, but the mad dash for freedom confirmed that it was indeed Marco.

Luigi's reaction was mixed. He was frustrated that Krater had been outfoxed by an amateur. He was impressed that Marco could effectively change his appearance and elude a small army of assassins. And he was angry at Whitaker and the fools in Washington who kept changing the plans and had now created an impending disaster for which he, Luigi, would no doubt get the blame.

He called Whitaker, yelled and cursed some more, then headed for the train station with Zellman and the two others. They'd meet up with Krater in Milano, where Whitaker was promising a full-court press with all the muscle he could pull in.

Leaving Bologna on the direct Eurostar, Luigi

had a wonderful idea, one he could never mention. Why not just simply call the Israelis and the Chinese and tell them that Backman was last seen in Modena, headed west to Parma and probably Milano? They wanted him much more than Langley did. And they could certainly do a better job of finding him.

But orders were orders, even though they kept changing.

All roads led to Milano.

29

The cab stopped a block away from the Milano central train station. Marco paid the driver, thanked him more than once, wished him well back home in Modena, then walked past a dozen more taxis that were waiting for arriving passengers. Inside the mammoth station, he drifted with the crowd, up the escalators, into the controlled frenzy of the platform area where a dozen tracks brought the trains. He found the departure board and studied his options. A train left for Stuttgart four times a day, and its seventh stop was Zurich. He picked up a schedule, bought a cheap city guide with a map, then found a table at a café among a row of shops. Time could not be wasted, but he needed to figure out where he was. He had two espressos and a pastry while his eyes watched the crowd. He loved the mob, the throng of people coming and going. There was safety in those numbers.

His first plan was to take a walk, about thirty

minutes, to the center of the city. Somewhere along the way he would find an inexpensive clothing store and change everything—jacket, shirt, pants, shoes. They had spotted him in Bologna. He couldn't risk it again.

Surely, somewhere in the center of the city, near the Piazza del Duomo, there was an Internet café where he could rent a computer for fifteen minutes. He had little confidence in his ability to sit in front of a strange machine, turn the damn thing on, and not only survive the jungle of the Internet but get a message to Neal. It was 10:15 a.m. in Milan, 4:15 a.m. in Culpeper, Virginia. Neal would be checking in live at 7:50.

Somehow he'd make the e-mail work. He had no choice.

The second plan, the one that was looking better and better as he watched a thousand people casually hop on trains that would have them scattered throughout Europe in a matter of hours, was to run. Buy a ticket right now and get out of Milano and Italy as soon as possible. His new hair color and Giovanni's eyeglasses and old professor's jacket had not fooled them in Bologna. If they were that good, they would surely find him anywhere.

He compromised with a walk around the block. The fresh air always helped, and after four blocks his blood was pumping again. As in Bologna, the streets of Milano fanned out in all directions like a spiderweb. The traffic was heavy and at times hardly moved. He loved the traffic, and he especially loved the crowded sidewalks that gave him cover.

The shop was called Roberto's, a small haberdashery wedged between a jewelry store and a bakery. The two front windows were packed with clothing that would hold up for about a week, which fit Marco's time frame perfectly. A clerk from the Middle East spoke worse Italian than Marco, but he was fluent in pointing and grunting and he was determined to transform his customer. The blue jacket was replaced with a dark brown one. The new shirt was a white pullover with short sleeves. The slacks were low-grade wool, very dark navy. Alterations would take a week, so Marco asked the clerk for a pair of scissors. In the mildewy dressing room, he measured as best he could, then cut the pants off himself. When he walked out in his new ensemble, the clerk looked at the ragged edges where the cuffs should have been and almost cried.

The shoes Marco tried on would have crippled him before he made it back to the train station, so he stayed with his hiking boots for the moment. The best purchase was a tan straw hat that Marco bought because he'd seen one just before entering the store.

What did he care about fashion at this point?

The new getup cost him almost four hundred euros, money he hated to part with, but he had no choice. He tried to swap Giovanni's briefcase, which was certainly worth more than everything he was wearing, but the clerk was too depressed over the butchered slacks. He was barely able to offer a weak thanks and goodbye. Marco left with the blue jacket, faded jeans, and the old shirt folded up in a red shopping bag; again, something different to carry around.

He walked a few minutes and saw a shoe store. He bought a pair of what appeared to be slightly modified bowling shoes, without a doubt the ugliest items in what turned out to be a very nice store. They were black with some manner of burgundy striping, hopefully built for comfort and not attractiveness. He paid 150 euros for them, only because they were already broken in. It took two blocks before he could muster the courage to look down at them.

*   *   *

Luigi got himself followed out of Bologna. The kid on the scooter saw him leave the apartment next to Backman's, and it was the manner in which he left that caught his attention. He was jogging, and gaining speed with each step. No one runs under the porticoes on Via Fondazza. The scooter hung back until Luigi stopped and quickly crawled into a red Fiat. He drove a few blocks, then slowed long enough for another man to jump into the car. They took off at breakneck speed, but in city traffic the scooter had no trouble keeping up. When they wheeled into the train station and parked illegally, the kid on the scooter saw it all and radioed Efraim again.

Within fifteen minutes, two Mossad agents dressed as traffic policemen entered Luigi's apartment, setting off alarms—some silent, some barely audible. While three agents waited on the street, providing cover, the three inside kicked open the kitchen door and found the astounding collection of electronic surveillance equipment.

When Luigi, Zellman, and a third agent stepped onto the Eurostar to Milano, the kid on the scooter had a ticket too. His name was Paul, the youngest member of the *kidon* and the most fluent speaker of Italian. Behind the bangs and baby face was a twenty-six-year-old veteran of half a dozen killings. When he radioed that he was on the train and it was moving, two more agents entered Luigi's apartment to help dissect the equipment. One alarm, though, could not be silenced. Its steady ring penetrated the walls just enough to attract attention from a few neighbors along the street.

After ten minutes, Efraim called a halt to the break-in. The agents scattered, then regrouped in one of their safe houses. They had not been able to determine who Luigi was or who he worked for, but it was obvious he'd been spying on Backman around the clock.

As the hours passed with no sign of Backman, they began to believe that he had fled. Could Luigi lead them to him?

*   *   *

In central Milano, at the Piazza del Duomo, Marco gawked at the mammoth Gothic cathedral that took only three hundred years to complete. He strolled along the Galleria Vittorio Emanuele, the magnificent glass-domed gallery that Milano is famous for. Lined with cafés and bookshops, the gallery is the center of the city's life, its most popular meeting place. With the temperature approaching sixty degrees, Marco had a sandwich and a cola outdoors where the pigeons swarmed every wayward crumb. He watched elderly Milanesi stroll through the gallery, women arm in arm, men stopping to chat as if time was irrelevant. To be so

329

lucky, he thought.

Should he leave immediately, or should he lay low for a day or two? That was the new urgent question. In a crowded city of four million people, he could vanish for as long as he wanted. He'd get a map, learn the streets, spend hours hiding in his room and hours walking the alleys.

But the bloodhounds behind him would have time to regroup.

Shouldn't he leave now, while they were back there scrambling and scratching their heads?

Yes he should, he decided. He paid the waiter and glanced down at his bowling shoes. They were indeed comfortable but he couldn't wait to burn them. On a city bus he saw an ad for an Internet café on Via Verri. Ten minutes later he entered the place. A sign on the wall gave the rates—ten euros per hour, minimum of thirty minutes. He ordered an orange juice and paid for half an hour. The clerk nodded in the general direction of a table where a bunch of computers were waiting. Three of the eight were being used by people who obviously knew what they were doing. Marco was already lost.

But he faked it well. He sat down, grabbed a keyboard, stared at the monitor and wanted to pray, but plowed ahead as if he'd been hacking for years. It was surprisingly easy; he went to the KwyteMail site, typed his user name, 'Grinch456,' then his pass phrase, 'post hoc ergo propter hoc,' waited ten seconds, and there was the message from Neal:

Marco: Mikel Van Thiessen is still with Rhineland Bank, now the vice president of client services. Anything else? Grinch.

At exactly 7:50 EST, Marco typed a message:

Grinch: Marco here—live and in person. Are you there?

He sipped his juice and stared at the screen. Come on, baby, make this thing work. Another sip. A lady across the table was talking to her monitor. Then the message:

I'm here, loud and clear. What's up?

Marco typed: *They stole my Ankyo 850. There's a good chance the bad guys have it and they're picking it to pieces. Any chance they can discover you?*
Neal: *Only if they have the user name and pass phrase. Do they?*
Marco: *No, I destroyed them. There's no way they can get around a password?*
Neal: *Not with KwyteMail. It's totally secure and encrypted. If they have the PC and nothing more, then they're out of luck.*
Marco: *And we're completely safe now?*
Neal: *Yes, absolutely. But what are you using now?*
Marco: *I'm in an Internet café, renting a computer, like a real hacker.*
Neal: *Do you want another Ankyo smartphone?*
Marco: *No, not now, maybe later. Here's the deal. Go see Carl Pratt. I know you don't like him,*

331

but at this point I need him. Pratt was very close to former senator Ira Clayburn from North Carolina. Clayburn ruled the Senate Intelligence Committee for many years. I need Clayburn now. Go through Pratt.

Neal: *Where's Clayburn now?*

Marco: *I don't know—I just hope he's still alive. He came from the Outer Banks of NC, some pretty remote place. He retired the year after I went to federal camp. Pratt can find him.*

Neal: *Sure, I'll do it as soon as I can sneak away.*

Marco: *Please be careful. Watch your back.*

Neal: *Are you okay?*

Marco: *I'm on the run. I left Bologna early this morning. I'll try to check in the same time tomorrow. Okay?*

Neal: *Keep your head down. I'll be here tomorrow.*

Marco signed off with a smug look. Mission accomplished. Nothing to it. Welcome to the age of high-tech wizardry and gadgetry. He made sure his exit was clean from KwyteMail, then finished his orange juice and left the café. He headed in the direction of the train station, stopping first at a leather shop where he managed an even swap of Giovanni's fine briefcase for a black one of patently inferior quality; then at a cheap jewelry store where he paid eighteen euros for a large round-faced watch with a bright red plastic band, something else to distract anyone looking for Marco Lazzeri, formerly of Bologna; then at a used-book shop where he spent two euros on a well-worn hardback containing the poetry of Czeslaw Milosz, all in Polish of course, anything to confuse the bloodhounds; and, finally, at a secondhand

332

accessory store where he bought a pair of sunglasses and a wooden cane, which he began using immediately on the sidewalk.

The cane reminded him of Francesca. It also slowed him down, changed his gait. With time to spare he shuffled into Milano Centrale and bought a ticket for Stuttgart.

*   *   *

Whitaker got the urgent message from Langley that Luigi's safe house had been broken into, but there was absolutely nothing he could do about it. All the agents from Bologna were now in Milano, scrambling frantically. Two were at the train station, looking for the needle in the haystack. Two were at Malpensa airport, twenty-seven miles from downtown. Two were at Linate airport, which was much closer and handled primarily European flights. Luigi was at the central bus station, still arguing by cell phone that perhaps Marco wasn't even in Milano. Just because he took the bus from Bologna to Modena, and headed in the general direction of northwest, didn't necessarily mean he was going to Milano. But Luigi's credibility at the moment was somewhat diminished, at least in Whitaker's substantial opinion, so he was banished to the bus station where he watched ten thousand people come and go.

Krater got closest to the needle.

For sixty euros, Marco purchased a first-class ticket in hopes that he could avoid the exposure of traveling by coach. For the ride north, the first-class car was the last one, and Marco climbed aboard at five-thirty, forty-five minutes before departure. He settled into his seat, hid his face as much as possible behind the sunglasses and the tan straw hat, opened the book of Polish poetry, and gazed out at the platform where passengers walked by his train. Some were barely five feet away, all in a hurry.

Except one. The guy on the bus was back; the face from Caffè Atene; probably the sticky-fingered thug who'd grabbed his blue Silvio bag; the same bloodhound who'd been a step too slow off the bus in Modena about eleven hours ago. He was walking but not going anywhere. His eyes were squinted, his forehead wrinkled in a deep frown. For a professional, he was much too obvious, thought Giovanni Ferro, who, unfortunately, now knew much more than he wanted to know about ducking and hiding and covering tracks.

Krater had been told that Marco would probably head either south to Rome, where he had more options, or north to Switzerland, Germany, France—virtually the entire continent to choose from. For five hours Krater had been strolling along the twelve platforms, watching as the trains came and went, mixing with the crowds, not concerned at all with who was getting off but paying desperate attention to who was getting on. Every blue jacket of any shade or style got his attention, but he had yet to see one with the worn elbow patches.

It was in the cheap black briefcase wedged between Marco's feet, in seat number seventy of the first-class car to Stuttgart. Marco watched Krater amble along the platform, paying very close attention to the train whose final destination was Stuttgart. He was holding what appeared to be a ticket, and as he walked out of sight Marco could swear that he got on the train.

Marco fought the urge to get off. The door to his cabin opened, and Madame entered.

30

Once it was determined that Backman had disappeared, and was not finally dead at the hands of someone else, a frenetic five hours passed before Julia Javier found the information that should've been close by. It was found in a file that had been locked away in the director's office, and once guarded by Teddy Maynard himself. If Julia had ever seen the information, she could not remember. And, in the chaos, she was certainly not going to admit anything.

The information had come, reluctantly, from the FBI years earlier when Backman was being investigated. His financial dealings were under great scrutiny because the rumors were wild that he'd bilked a client and buried a fortune. So where was the money? In search of it, the FBI had been piecing together his travel history when he abruptly pled guilty and was sent away. The guilty plea didn't close the Backman file, but it certainly removed the pressure. With time, the travel research was completed, and eventually sent over to Langley.

In the month before Backman was indicted, arrested, and released on a very restricted bail arrangement, he had made two quick trips to Europe. For the first one, he'd flown Air France business class with his favorite secretary to Paris, where they frolicked for a few days and saw the sights. She later told investigators that Backman had spent one long day dashing off to Berlin for some quick business, but made it back in time for dinner at Alain Ducasse. She did not accompany him.

There were no records of Backman traveling by a commercial airliner to Berlin, or anywhere else within Europe, during that week. A passport would've been required, and the FBI was positive he had not used his. A passport would not have been required for a train ride. Geneva, Bern, Lausanne, and Zurich are all within four hours of Paris by train.

The second trip was a seventy-two-hour sprint from Dulles, first class on Lufthansa to Frankfurt, again for business, though no business contacts had been discovered there. Backman had paid for two nights in a luxury hotel in Frankfurt, and there was no evidence that he had slept elsewhere. Like Paris, the banking centers of Switzerland are within a few hours' train ride from Frankfurt.

When Julia Javier finally found the file and read the report, she immediately called Whitaker and said, 'He's headed for Switzerland.'

*　　　*　　　*

Madame had enough luggage for an affluent family of five. A harried porter helped her haul the heavy suitcases on board and into the first-class car, which she consumed with herself, her belongings, and her perfume. The cabin had six seats, at least four of which she laid claim to. She sat in one across from Marco and wiggled her ample rear as if to make it expand. She glanced at him, cowering against the window, and gushed over a sultry 'Bonsoir.' French, he thought, and since it didn't seem right to respond in Italian, he relied on old faithful. 'Hello.'

'Ah, American.'

With languages, identities, names, cultures, backgrounds, lies, lies, and more lies all swirling around, he managed to say with no conviction whatsoever, 'No, Canadian.'

'Ah, yes,' she said, still arranging bags and settling in. Evidently American would've been more welcome than Canadian. Madame was a robust woman of sixty, with a tight red dress, thick calves, and stout black pumps that had traveled a million miles. Her heavily decorated eyes were puffy, and the reason was soon evident. Long before the train moved, she pulled out a large flask, unscrewed its top which became a cup, and knocked back a shot of something strong. She swallowed hard, then smiled at Marco and said, 'Would you like a drink?'

'No thanks.'

'It's a very good brandy.'

'No thanks.'

'Very well.' She poured another one, drained it, then put away the flask.

A long train ride just got longer.

'Where are you going?' she asked in very good English.

'Stuttgart. And you?'

'Stuttgart, then on to Strasbourg. Can't stay too long in Stuttgart, you know.' Her nose wrinkled as if the entire city was swimming in raw sewage.

'I love Stuttgart,' Marco said, just to watch it unwrinkle.

'Oh, well.' Her shoes caught her attention. She kicked them off with little regard as to where they might land. Marco braced for a jolt of foot odor but then realized it had little chance of competing with the cheap perfume.

In self-defense, he pretended to nod off. She ignored him for a few minutes, then said loudly, 'You speak Polish?' She was looking at his book of poetry.

He jerked his head as if he'd just been awakened. 'No, not exactly. I'm trying to learn it, though. My family is Polish.' He held his breath as he finished, half expecting her to unleash a torrent of proper Polish and bury him with it.

'I see,' she said, not really approving.

At exactly 6:15, an unseen conductor blew a whistle and the train started to move. Fortunately, there were no other passengers assigned to Madame's car. Several had walked down the aisle and stopped, glanced in, seen the congestion, then moved on to another cabin where there was more room.

Marco watched the platform intensely as they began moving. The man from the bus was nowhere to be seen.

Madame worked the brandy until she began snoring. She was awakened by the conductor who punched their tickets. A porter came through with a pushcart loaded with drinks. Marco bought a beer and offered one to his cabinmate. His offer was greeted with another mammoth wrinkle of the nose, as if she'd rather drink urine.

Their first stop was Como/San Giovanni, a two-minute break during which no one got on. Five minutes later they stopped at Chiasso. It was almost dark now, and Marco was pondering a quick exit. He studied the itinerary; there were four more stops before Zurich, one in Italy and three in Switzerland. Which country would work best?

He couldn't risk being followed now. If they were on the train, then they had stuck to him from Bologna, through Modena and Milano, through various disguises. They were professionals, and he was no match for them. Sipping his beer, Marco felt like a miserable amateur.

Madame was staring at the butchered hems of his slacks. Then he caught her glancing down at the modified bowling shoes, and for that he didn't blame her at all. Then the bright red watchband caught her attention. Her face conveyed the obvious—she did not approve of his low sense of fashion. Typical American, or Canadian, or whatever he was.

He caught a glimpse of lights shimmering off Lake Lugano. They were snaking through the lake region, gaining altitude. Switzerland was not far away.

An occasional drifter moved down the darkened aisle outside their cabin. They would look in, through the glass door, then move along toward the rear, where there was a restroom. Madame had plopped her large feet in the seat opposite her, not too far from Marco. An hour into the trip, and she had managed to spread her boxes and magazines and clothing throughout the entire cabin. Marco was afraid to leave his seat.

Fatigue finally set in, and Marco fell asleep. He was awakened by the racket at the Bellinzona station, the first stop in Switzerland. A passenger entered the first-class car and couldn't find the right seat. He opened the door to Madame's cabin, looked around, didn't like what he saw, then went off to yell at the conductor. They found him a spot elsewhere. Madame hardly looked up from her fashion magazines.

The next stretch was an hour and forty minutes, and when Madame went back to her flask Marco said, 'I'll try some of that.' She smiled for the first time in hours. Though she certainly didn't mind drinking alone, it was always more pleasant with a friend. A couple of shots, though, and Marco was nodding off again.

*   *   *

The train jerked as it slowed for the stop at Arth-Goldau. Marco's head jerked too, and his hat fell off. Madame was watching him closely. When he opened his eyes for good, she said, 'A strange man has been looking at you.'

'Where?'

'Where? Here, of course, on this train. He's been by at least three times. He stops at the door, looks closely at you, then sneaks away.'

Maybe it's my shoes, thought Marco. Or my slacks. Watchband? He rubbed his eyes and tried to act as though it happened all the time.

'What does he look like?'

'Blond hair, about thirty-five, cute, brown jacket. Do you know him?'

'No, I have no idea.' The man on the bus at Modena had neither blond hair nor a brown jacket, but those minor points were irrelevant now. Marco was frightened enough to switch plans.

Zug was twenty-five minutes away, the last stop before Zurich. He could not run the risk of leading them to Zurich. Ten minutes out, he announced he needed to use the restroom. Between his seat and the door was Madame's obstacle course. As he began stepping through it, he placed his briefcase and cane in his seat.

He walked past four cabins, each with at least three passengers, none of whom looked suspicious. He went to the restroom, locked the door, and waited until the train began to slow. Then it stopped. Zug was a two-minute layover, and the train so far had been ridiculously on time. He waited one minute, then walked quickly back to his cabin, opened the door, said nothing to Madame, grabbed his briefcase and his cane, which he was perfectly prepared to use as a weapon, and raced to the rear of the train where he jumped onto the platform.

It was a small station, elevated with a street below. Marco flew down the steps to the sidewalk where a lone taxi sat with a driver unconscious behind the wheel. 'Hotel, please,' he said, startling the driver, who instinctively grabbed the ignition key. He asked something in German and Marco tried Italian. 'I need a small hotel. I don't have a reservation.'

'No problem,' the driver said. As they pulled away, Marco looked up and saw the train moving. He looked behind him, and saw no one giving chase.

The ride took all of four blocks, and when they stopped in front of an A-frame building on a quiet side street the driver said in Italian, 'This hotel is

341

very good.'

'Looks fine. Thanks. How far away is Zurich by car?'

'Two hours, more or less. Depends on the traffic.'

'Tomorrow morning, I need to be in downtown Zurich at nine o'clock. Can you drive me there?'

The driver hesitated for a second, his mind thinking of cold cash. 'Perhaps,' he said.

'How much will it cost?'

The driver rubbed his chin, then shrugged and said, 'Two hundred euros.'

'Good. Let's leave here at six.'

'Six, yes, I'll be here.'

Marco thanked him again and watched as he drove away. A bell rang when he entered the front door of the hotel. The small counter was deserted, but a television was chattering away somewhere close by. A sleepy-eyed teenager finally appeared and offered a smile. 'Guten abend,' he said.

'Parla inglese?' Marco asked.

He shook his head, no.

'Italiano?'

'A little.'

'I speak a little too,' Marco said in Italian. 'I'd like a room for one night.'

The clerk pushed over a registration form, and from memory Marco filled in the name on his passport, and its number. He scribbled in a fictional address in Bologna, and a bogus phone number as well. The passport was in his coat pocket, close to his heart, and he was prepared to reluctantly pull it out.

But it was late and the clerk was missing his television show. With atypical Swiss inefficiency, he said, also in Italian, 'Forty-two euros,' and didn't mention the passport.

Giovanni laid the cash on the counter, and the clerk gave him a key to room number 26. In surprisingly good Italian, he arranged a wake-up call for 5:00 a.m. Almost as an afterthought, he said, 'I lost my toothbrush. Would you have an extra?'

The clerk reached into a drawer and pulled out a box full of assorted necessities—toothbrushes, toothpaste, disposable razors, shaving cream, aspirin, tampons, hand cream, combs, even condoms. Giovanni selected a few items and handed over ten euros.

A luxury suite at the Ritz could not have been more welcome than room 26. Small, clean, warm, with a firm mattress, and a door that bolted twice to keep away the faces that had been haunting him since early morning. He took a long, hot shower, then shaved and brushed his teeth forever.

Much to his relief, he found a minibar in a cabinet under the television. He ate a packet of cookies, washed them down with two small bottles of whiskey, and when he crawled under the covers he was mentally drained and physically exhausted. The cane was on the bed, nearby. Silly, but he couldn't help it.

31

In the depths of prison he'd dreamed of Zurich, with its blue rivers and clean shaded streets and modern shops and handsome people, all proud to be Swiss, all going about their business with a pleasant seriousness. In another life he'd ridden the quiet electric streetcars with them as they headed into the financial district. Back then he'd been too busy to travel much, too important to leave the fragile workings of Washington, but Zurich was one of the few places he'd seen. It was his kind of city: unburdened by tourists and traffic, unwilling to spend its time gawking at cathedrals and museums and worshiping the last two thousand years. Not at all. Zurich was about money, the refined management of it as opposed to the naked cash grab Backman had once perfected.

He was on a streetcar again, one he'd caught near the train station, and was now moving steadily along Bahnhofstrasse, the main avenue of downtown Zurich, if in fact it had one. It was almost 9:00 a.m. He was among the last wave of the sharply dressed young bankers headed for UBS and Credit Suisse and a thousand lesser-known but equally rich institutions. Dark suits, shirts of various colors but not many white ones, expensive ties with thicker knots and fewer designs, dark brown shoes with laces, never tassels. The styles had changed slightly in the past six years. Always conservative, but with some dash. Not quite as stylish as the young professionals in his native Bologna, but quite attractive.

Everyone was reading something as they moved along. Streetcars passed from the other direction. Marco pretended to be engrossed in a copy of *Newsweek*, but he was really watching everyone else.

No one was watching him. No one seemed offended by his bowling shoes. In fact, he'd seen another pair on a casually dressed young man near the train station. His straw hat was getting no attention. The hems of his slacks had been repaired slightly after he'd purchased a cheap sewing kit from the hotel desk, then spent half an hour trying to tailor his pants without drawing blood. His outfit cost a fraction of those around him, but what did he care? He'd made it to Zurich without Luigi and all those others, and with a little more luck he'd make it out.

At Paradeplatz the streetcars wheeled in from east and west and stopped. They emptied quickly as the young bankers scattered in droves and headed for the buildings. Marco moved with the crowd, his hat now left behind under the seat in the streetcar.

Nothing had changed in seven years. The Paradeplatz was still the same—an open plaza lined with small shops and cafés. The banks around it had been there for a hundred years; some announced their names from neon signs, others were hidden so well they couldn't be found. From behind his sunglasses he soaked in as much of the surroundings as he could while sticking close to three young men with gym bags slung over their shoulders. They appeared to be headed for Rhineland Bank, on the east side. He followed them inside, into the lobby, where the fun began.

The information desk hadn't moved in seven years; in fact, the well-groomed lady sitting behind it looked vaguely familiar. 'I'd like to see Mr. Mikel Van Thiessen,' he said as softly as possible.

'And your name?'

'Marco Lazzeri.' He would use 'Joel Backman' later, upstairs, but he was hesitant to use it here. Hopefully, Neal's e-mails to Van Thiessen had alerted him to the alias. The banker had been asked to remain in town, if at all possible, for the next week or so.

She was on the phone and also pecking at a keyboard. 'It will be just a moment, Mr. Lazzeri,' she said. 'Would you mind waiting?'

'No,' he said. Waiting? He'd been dreaming of this for years. He took a chair, crossed his legs, saw the shoes, then put his feet under the chair. He was certain that he was being watched from a dozen different camera angles now, and that was fine. Maybe they would recognize Backman sitting in the lobby, maybe they wouldn't. He could almost see them up there, gawking at the monitors, scratching their heads, saying, 'Don't know, he's much thinner, gaunt, even.'

'And the hair. It's obviously a bad coloring job.'

To help them Joel removed Giovanni's tortoiseshell glasses.

Five minutes later, a stern-faced security type in a much lesser suit approached him from nowhere and said, 'Mr. Lazzeri, would you follow me?'

They rode a private elevator up to the third floor where Marco was led into a small room with thick walls. All the walls seemed to be thick at Rhineland Bank. Two other security agents were waiting. One actually smiled, the other did not.

They asked him to place both hands on a biometric fingerprint scanner. It would compare his fingerprints to the ones he left behind almost seven years ago, at this same place, and when the perfect match was made there would be more smiles, then a nicer room, a nicer lobby, the offer of coffee or juice. Anything, Mr. Backman.

He asked for orange juice because he'd had no breakfast. The security agents were back in their cave. Mr. Backman was now being serviced by Elke, one of Mr. Van Thiessen's shapely assistants. 'He'll be out in just a minute,' she explained. 'He wasn't expecting you this morning.'

Kinda hard to make appointments when you're hiding in toilet stalls. Joel smiled at her. Ol' Marco was history now. Finally laid to rest after a good two-month run. Marco had served him well, kept him alive, taught him the basics of Italian, walked him around Treviso and Bologna, and introduced him to Francesca, a woman he would not soon forget.

But Marco would also get him killed, so he ditched him there on the third floor of the Rhineland Bank, while looking at Elke's black stiletto heels and waiting on her boss. Marco was gone, never to return.

Mikel Van Thiessen's office was designed to smack his visitors with a powerful right hook. Power in the massive Persian rug. Power in the leather sofa and chairs. Power in the ancient mahogany desk that wouldn't have fit in the cell at Rudley. Power in the array of electronic gadgets at his disposal. He met Joel at the powerful oak door and they shook hands properly, but not like old friends. They had met exactly once before.

If Joel had lost sixty pounds since their last visit, Van Thiessen had found most of it. He was much grayer too, not nearly as crisp and sharp as the younger bankers Joel had seen on the streetcar. Van Thiessen directed his client to the leather chairs while Elke and another assistant scurried around to fetch coffee and pastries.

When they were alone, with the door shut, Van Thiessen said, 'I've been reading about you.'

'Oh really. And what have you read?'

'Bribing a president for a pardon, come on, Mr. Backman. Is it really that easy over there?'

Joel couldn't tell if he was joking or not. Joel was in an upbeat mood, but he didn't exactly feel like swapping one-liners.

'I didn't bribe anyone, if that's what you're suggesting.'

'Yes, well, the newspapers are certainly filled with speculation.' His tone was more accusatory than jovial, and Joel decided not to waste time. 'Do you believe everything you read in the newspapers?'

'Of course not, Mr. Backman.'

'I'm here for three reasons. I want access to my security box. I want to review my account. I want to withdraw ten thousand dollars in cash. After that, I may have another favor or two.'

Van Thiessen shoved a small cookie in his mouth and chewed rapidly. 'Yes, of course. I don't think we'll have a problem with any of that.'

'Why should you have a problem?'

'Not a problem, sir. I'll just need a few minutes.'

'For what?'

'I'll need to consult with a colleague.'

'Can you do so quickly?'

Van Thiessen practically bolted from the room and slammed the door behind him. The pain in Joel's stomach was not from hunger. If the wheels came off now, he had no plan B. He'd walk out of the bank with nothing, hopefully make it across the Paradeplatz to a streetcar, and once on board he would have no place to go. The escape would be over. Marco would be back, and Marco would eventually get him killed.

As time came to an abrupt halt, he kept thinking about the pardon. With it, his slate was wiped clean. The U.S. government was in no position to pressure the Swiss to freeze his account. The Swiss didn't freeze accounts! The Swiss were immune from pressure! That's why their banks were filled with loot from around the world.

They were the Swiss!

Elke retrieved him and asked if he would follow her downstairs. In other days, he would've followed Elke anywhere, but now it was only downstairs.

He'd been to the vault during his prior visit. It was in the basement, several levels below ground, though the clients never knew how deep into Swiss soil they were descending. Every door was a foot thick, every wall appeared to be made of lead, every ceiling had surveillance cameras. Elke handed him off to Van Thiessen again.

Both thumbs were scanned for matching prints. An optical scanner took his photo. 'Number seven,' Van Thiessen said, pointing. 'I'll meet you there,' he said, and left through a door.

Joel walked down a short hallway, passing six windowless steel doors until he came to the seventh. He pushed a button, all sorts of things tumbled and clicked inside, and the door finally opened. He stepped inside, where Van Thiessen was waiting.

The room was a twelve-foot square, with three walls lined with individual vaults, most about the size of a large shoe box.

'Your vault number?' he asked.

'L2270.'

'Correct.'

Van Thiessen stepped to his right, bent slightly to face L2270. On the vault's small keypad he punched some numbers, then straightened himself and said, 'If you wish.'

Under Van Thiessen's watchful eyes, Joel stepped to his vault and entered the code. As he did so, he softly whispered the numbers, forever seared in his memory: 'Eighty-one, fifty-five, ninety-four, ninety-three, twenty-three.' A small green light began blinking on the keypad. Van Thiessen smiled and said, 'I'll be waiting at the front. Just ring when you're finished.'

When he was alone, Joel removed the steel box from his vault and pulled open the top. He picked up the padded mailing envelope and opened it. There were the four two-gigabyte Jaz disks that had once been worth $1 billion.

He allowed himself a moment, but no more than sixty seconds. He was, after all, very safe at that time, and if he wanted to reflect, what was the harm?

He thought of Safi Mirza, Fazal Sharif, and Farooq Khan, the brilliant boys who'd discovered Neptune, then wrote reams of software to manipulate the system. They were all dead now, killed by their naïve greed and their choice of lawyer. He thought of Jacy Hubbard, the brash, gregarious, infinitely charismatic crook who had snowed the voters for an entire career and finally gotten much too greedy. He thought of Carl Pratt and Kim Bolling and dozens of other partners he'd brought into their prosperous firm, and the lives that had been wrecked by what he was now holding in his hand. He thought of Neal and the humiliation he'd caused his son when the scandal engulfed Washington and prison became not only a certainty but a sanctuary.

And he thought of himself, not in selfish terms, not in pity, not passing the blame to anyone else. What a miserable mess of a life he'd lived, so far anyway. As much as he'd like to go back and do it differently, he had no time to waste on such thoughts. You've only got a few years left, Joel, or Marco, or Giovanni, or whatever the hell your name is. For the first time in your rotten life, why don't you do what's right, as opposed to what's profitable?

He put the disks in the envelope, the envelope in his briefcase, then replaced the steel box in the vault. He rang for Van Thiessen.

*   *   *

Back in the power office, Van Thiessen handed him a file with one sheet of paper in it. 'This is a summary of your account,' he was saying. 'It's very straightforward. As you know, there's been no activity.'

'You guys are paying one percent interest,' Joel said.

351

'You were aware of our rates when you opened the account, Mr. Backman.'

'Yes, I was.'

'We protect your money in other ways.'

'Of course.' Joel closed the file and handed it back. 'I don't want to keep this. Do you have the cash?'

'Yes, it's on the way up.'

'Good. I need a few things.'

Van Thiessen pulled over his writing pad and stood ready with his fountain pen. 'Yes,' he said.

'I want to wire a hundred thousand to a bank in Washington, D.C. Can you recommend one?'

'Certainly. We work closely with Maryland Trust.'

'Good, wire the money there, and with the wire open a generic savings account. I will not be writing checks, just making withdrawals.'

'In what name?'

'Joel Backman and Neal Backman.' He was getting used to his name again, not ducking when he said it. Not cowering in fear, waiting for gunfire. He liked it.

'Very well,' Van Thiessen said. Anything was possible.

'I need some help in getting back to the U.S. Could your girl check the Lufthansa flights to Philadelphia and New York?'

'Of course. When, and from where?'

'Today, as soon as possible. I'd like to avoid the airport here. How far away is Munich by car?'

'By car, three to four hours.'

'Can you provide a car?'

'I'm sure we can arrange that.'

'I prefer to leave from the basement here, in a

car driven by someone not dressed like a chauffeur. Not a black car either, something that will not attract attention.'

Van Thiessen stopped writing and shot a puzzled look. 'Are you in danger, Mr. Backman?'

'Perhaps. I'm not sure, and I'm not taking chances.'

Van Thiessen pondered this for a few seconds, then said, 'Would you like for us to make the airline reservations?'

'Yes.'

'Then I need to see your passport.'

Joel pulled out Giovanni's borrowed passport. Van Thiessen studied it for a long time, his stoic banker's face betraying him. He was confused and worried. He finally managed, 'Mr. Backman, you will be traveling with someone else's passport.'

'That's correct.'

'And this is a valid passport?'

'It is.'

'I assume you do not have one of your own.'

'They took it a long time ago.'

'This bank cannot take part in the commission of a crime. If this is stolen, then—'

'I assure you it's not stolen.'

'Then how did—'

'Let's just say it's borrowed, okay?'

'But using someone else's passport is a violation of the law.'

'Let's not get hung up on U.S. immigration policy, Mr. Van Thiessen. Just get the schedules. I'll pick the flights. Your girl makes the reservations using the bank's account. Deduct it from my balance. Get me a car and a driver. Deduct that from my balance, if you wish. It's all very simple.'

It was just a passport. Hell, other clients had three or four of them. Van Thiessen handed it back to Joel and said, 'Very well. Anything else?'

'Yes, I need to go online. I'm sure your computers are secure.'

'Absolutely.'

*   *   *

His e-mail to Neal read:

> *Grinch—With a bit of luck, I should arrive in U.S. tonight. Get a new cell phone today. Don't let it out of your sight. Tomorrow morning call the Hilton, Marriott, and Sheraton, in downtown Washington. Ask for Giovanni Ferro. That's me. Call Carl Pratt first thing this morning, on the new phone. Push hard to get Senator Clayburn in D.C. We will cover his expenses. Tell him it's urgent. A favor to an old friend. Don't take no for an answer. No more e-mails until I get home. Marco*

After a quick sandwich and a cola in Van Thiessen's office, Joel Backman left the bank building riding shotgun in a shiny green BMW four-door sedan. For good measure, he kept a Swiss newspaper in front of his face until they were on the autobahn. The driver was Franz. Franz fancied himself a Formula One hopeful, and when Joel let it be known that he was in somewhat of a hurry, Franz slipped into the left lane and hit 150 kilometers per hour.

32

At 1:55 p.m., Joel Backman was sitting in a lavishly large seat in the first-class section of a Lufthansa 747 as it began its push back from the gate at the Munich airport. Only when it started to move did he dare pick up the glass of champagne he'd been staring at for ten minutes. The glass was empty by the time the plane stopped at the end of the runway for its final check. When the wheels lifted off the pavement, Joel closed his eyes and allowed himself the luxury of a few hours of relief.

*   *   *

His son, on the other hand, and at exactly the same moment, 7:55 Eastern Standard time, was stressed to the point of throwing things. How the hell was he supposed to go buy a new cell phone immediately, then call Carl Pratt again and solicit old favors that did not exist, and somehow cajole a retired and cantankerous old senator from Ocracoke, North Carolina, to drop what he was doing and return immediately to a city he evidently disliked immensely? Not to mention the obvious: he, Neal Backman, had a rather full day at the office. Nothing as pressing as rescuing his wayward father, but still a pretty full docket with clients and other important matters.

He left Jerry's Java, but instead of going to the office he went home. Lisa was bathing their daughter and was surprised to see him. 'What's wrong?' she said.

'We have to talk. Now.'

He began with the mysterious letter postmarked from York, Pennsylvania, and went through the $4,000 loan, as painful as it was, then the smartphone, the encrypted e-mails, pretty much the entire story. She took it calmly, much to his relief.

'You should've told me,' she said more than once.

'Yes, and I'm sorry.'

There was no fight, no arguing. Loyalty was one of her strongest traits, and when she said, 'We have to help him,' Neal hugged her.

'He'll pay back the money,' he assured her.

'We'll worry about the money later. Is he in danger?'

'I think so.'

'Okay, what's the first step?'

'Call the office and tell them I'm in bed with the flu.'

*   *   *

Their entire conversation was captured live and in perfect detail by a tiny mike planted by the Mossad in the light fixture above where they were sitting. It was wired to a transmitter hidden in their attic, and from there it was relayed to a high-frequency receiver a quarter of a mile away in a seldom-used retail office space recently leased for six months by a gentleman from D.C. There, a technician listened to it twice, then quickly e-mailed his field agent in the Israeli embassy in Washington.

Since Backman's disappearance in Bologna more than twenty-four hours ago, the bugs planted around his son had been monitored even more closely.

The e-mail to Washington concluded with 'JB's coming home.'

Fortunately, Neal did not mention the name 'Giovanni Ferro' during the conversation with Lisa. Unfortunately, he did mention two of the three hotels—the Marriott and the Sheraton.

Backman's return was given the highest priority possible. Eleven Mossad agents were located on the East Coast; all were ordered to D.C. immediately.

*   *   *

Lisa dropped their daughter off at her mother's, then she and Neal sped south to Charlottesville, thirty minutes away. In a shopping center north of town they found the office for U.S. Cellular. They opened an account, bought a phone, and within thirty minutes were back on the road. Lisa drove while Neal tried to find Carl Pratt.

*   *   *

Aided by generous helpings of champagne and wine, Joel managed to sleep for several hours over the Atlantic. When the plane landed at JFK at 4:30 p.m., the relaxation was gone, replaced by uncertainties and a compulsion to look over his shoulder.

At immigration, he at first stepped into line with the returning Americans, a much shorter line. The mob waiting across the way for non-U.S. was embarrassing. Then he caught himself, glanced

357

around, began cursing under his breath, and hustled over to the foreigners.

How stupid can you be?

A thick-necked uniformed kid from the Bronx was yelling at people to follow this line, not that one, and hurry up while you're at it. Welcome to America. Some things he had not missed.

The passport officer frowned at Giovanni's passport, but then he'd frowned at all the others too. Joel had been watching him carefully from behind a pair of cheap sunglasses.

'Could you remove your sunglasses, please?' the officer said.

'Certamente,' Joel said loudly, anxious to prove his Italianness. He took off the sunglasses, squinted as if blinded, then rubbed his eyes while the officer tried to study his face. Reluctantly, he stamped the passport and handed it over without a word. With nothing to declare, the customs officials barely looked at him. Joel hustled through the terminal and found the line at the taxi stand. 'Penn Station,' he said. The driver resembled Farooq Khan, the youngest of the three, just a boy, and as Joel studied him from the backseat he pulled his briefcase closer.

Moving against the rush hour traffic, he was at Penn Station in forty-five minutes. He bought an Amtrak ticket to D.C., and at 7:00 left New York for Washington.

*   *   *

The taxi parked on Brandywine Street in northwest Washington. It was almost eleven, and most of the fine homes were dark. Backman spoke to the driver, who was already reclining and ready for a nap.

Mrs. Pratt was in bed and struggling with sleep when she heard the doorbell. She grabbed her robe and hurried down the stairs. Her husband slept in the basement most nights, mainly because he snored but also because he was drinking too much and suffering from insomnia. She presumed he was there now.

'Who is it?' she asked through the intercom.

'Joel Backman,' came the answer, and she thought it was a prank.

'Who?'

'Donna, it's me, Joel. I swear. Open the door.'

She peeped through the hole in the door and did not recognize the stranger. 'Just a minute,' she said, then ran to the basement where Carl was watching the news. A minute later he was at the door, wearing a Duke sweat suit and holding a pistol.

'Who is it?' he demanded through the intercom.

'Carl, it's me, Joel. Put the gun down and open the door.'

The voice was unmistakable. He opened the door and Joel Backman walked into his life, an old nightmare back for more. There were no hugs, no handshakes, hardly a smile. The Pratts quietly examined him because he looked so different— much thinner, hair darker and shorter, strange clothing. He got a 'What are you doing here?' from Donna.

'That's a good question,' he said coolly. He had the advantage of planning. They were caught completely off guard. 'Will you put that gun down?'

Pratt put the gun on a side table.

'Have you talked to Neal?' Backman asked.

'All day long.'

'What's going on, Carl?' Donna asked.

'I don't really know.'

'Can we talk? That's why I'm here. I don't trust phones anymore.'

'Talk about what?' she demanded.

'Could you make us some coffee, Donna?' Joel asked pleasantly.

'Hell no.'

'Scratch the coffee.'

Carl had been rubbing his chin, assessing things. 'Donna, we need to talk in private. Old law firm stuff. I'll give you the rundown later.'

She shot them both a look that clearly said, Go straight to hell, then stomped back up the stairs. They stepped into the den. Carl said, 'Would you like something to drink?'

'Yes, something strong.'

He went to a small wet bar in a corner and poured single malts—doubles. He handed Joel a drink and without the slightest effort at a smile said, 'Cheers.'

'Cheers. It's good to see you, Carl.'

'I bet it is. You weren't supposed to see anyone for another fourteen years.'

'Counting the days, huh?'

'We're still cleaning up after you, Joel. A bunch of good folks got hurt. I'm sorry if Donna and I aren't exactly thrilled to see you. I can't think of too many people in this town who'd like to give you a hug.'

'Most would like to shoot me.'

Carl gave a wary look over at the pistol.

'I can't worry about that,' Backman continued. 'Sure, I'd like to go back and change some things, but I don't have that luxury. I'm running for my life now, Carl, and I need some help.'

'Maybe I don't want to get involved.'

'I can't blame you. But I need a favor, a big one. Help me now, and I promise I'll never show up on your doorstep again.'

'I'll shoot the next time.'

'Where's Senator Clayburn? Tell me he's still alive.'

'Yes, very much so. And you caught some luck.'

'What?'

'He's here, in D.C.'

'Why?'

'Hollis Maples is retiring, after a hundred years in the Senate. They had a bash for him tonight. All the old boys are in town.'

'Maples? He was drooling in his soup ten years ago.'

'Well, now he can't see his soup. He and Clayburn were as tight as ticks.'

'Have you talked to Clayburn?'

'Yes.'

'And?'

'It might be a tough one, Joel. He didn't like the sound of your name. Something about being shot for treason.'

'Whatever. Tell him he can broker a deal that will make him feel like a real patriot.'

'What's the deal?'

'I have the software, Carl. The whole package. Picked it up this morning from a vault in a bank in Zurich where it's been sitting for more than six years. You and Clayburn come to my room in the morning, and I'll show it to you.'

'I really don't want to see it.'

'Yes you do.'

Pratt sucked down two ounces of scotch. He walked back to the bar and refilled his glass, took another toxic dose, then said, 'When and where?'

'The Marriott on Twenty-second Street. Room five-twenty. Nine in the morning.'

'Why Joel? Why should I get involved?'

'A favor to an old friend.'

'I don't owe you any favors. And the old friend left a long time ago.'

'Please, Carl. Bring in Clayburn, and you'll be out of the picture by noon tomorrow. I promise you'll never see me again.'

'That is very tempting.'

*   *   *

He asked the driver to take his time. They cruised through Georgetown, along K Street, with its late-night restaurants and bars and college hangouts all packed with people living the good life. It was March 22 and spring was coming. The temperature was around sixty-five and the students were anxious to be outside, even at midnight.

The cab slowed at the intersection of I Street and 14th and Joel could see his old office building in the distance on New York Avenue. Somewhere in there, on the top floor, he'd once ruled his own little kingdom, with his minions running behind him, jumping at every command. It was not a nostalgic moment. Instead he was filled with regret for a worthless life spent chasing money and buying friends and women and all the toys a serious big shot could want. They drove on, past the countless office buildings, government on one side, lobbyists on the other.

He asked the driver to change streets, to move on to more pleasant sights. They turned onto Constitution and drove along the Mall, past the Washington Monument. His youngest child, Anna Lee, had begged him for years to take her for a springtime walk along the Mall, like the other kids in her class. She wanted to see Mr. Lincoln and spend a day at the Smithsonian. He'd promised and promised until she was gone. Anna Lee was in Denver now, he thought, with a child he'd never seen.

As the dome of the Capitol drew nearer, Joel suddenly had enough. This little trip down memory lane was depressing. The memories in his life were too unpleasant.

'Take me to the hotel,' he said.

33

Neal made the first pot of coffee, then stepped outside onto the cool bricks of the patio and admired the beauty of an early-spring daybreak.

If his father had indeed arrived back in D.C., he would not be asleep at six-thirty in the morning. The night before, Neal had coded his new phone with the numbers of the Washington hotels, and as the sun came up he started with the Sheraton. No Giovanni Ferro. Then the Marriott.

'One moment, please,' the operator said, then the phone to the room began ringing. 'Hello,' came a familiar voice.

'Marco, please,' Neal said.

'Marco here. Is this the Grinch?'

'It is.'

'Where are you right now?'

'Standing on my patio, waiting for the sun.'

'And what type of phone are you using?'

'It's a brand-new Motorola that I've kept in my pocket since I bought it yesterday.'

'You're sure it's secure.'

'Yes.'

A pause as Joel breathed deeply. 'It's good to hear your voice, son.'

'And yours as well. How was your trip?'

'Very eventful. Can you come to Washington?'

'When?'

'Today, this morning.'

'Sure, everybody thinks I have the flu. I'm covered at the office. When and where?'

'Come to the Marriott on Twenty-second Street. Walk in the lobby at eight forty-five, take the elevator to the sixth floor, then the stairs down to the fifth. Room five-twenty.'

'Is all this necessary?'

'Trust me. Can you use another car?'

'I don't know. I'm not sure who—'

'Lisa's mother. Borrow her car, make sure no one is following you. When you get to the city, park it at the garage on Sixteenth then walk to the Marriott. Watch your rear at all times. If you see anything suspicious, then call me and we'll abort.'

Neal glanced around his backyard, half expecting to see agents dressed in black moving in on him. Where did his father pick up the cloak-and-dagger stuff? Six years in solitary maybe? A thousand spy novels?

'Are you with me?' Joel snapped.

'Yeah, sure. I'm on my way.'

*   *   *

Ira Clayburn looked like a man who'd spent his life on a fishing boat, as opposed to one who'd served thirty-four years in the U.S. Senate. His ancestors had fished the Outer Banks of North Carolina, around their home at Ocracoke, for a hundred years. Ira would've done the same, except for a sixth-grade math teacher who discovered his exceptional IQ. A scholarship to Chapel Hill pulled him away from home. Another one to Yale got him a master's. A third, to Stanford, placed the title of 'Doctor' before his name. He was happily teaching economics at Davidson when a compromise appointment sent him to the Senate to fill an unexpired term. He reluctantly ran for a full term, and for the next three decades tried his best to leave Washington. At the age of seventy-one he finally walked away. When he left the Senate, he took with him a mastery of U.S. intelligence that no politician could equal.

He agreed to go to the Marriott with Carl Pratt, an old friend from a tennis club, only out of curiosity. The Neptune mystery had never been solved, as far as he knew. But then he'd been out of the loop for the last five years, during which time he'd been fishing almost every day, happily taking his boat out and trolling the waters from Hatteras to Cape Lookout.

During the twilight of his Senate career, he had watched Joel Backman become the latest in a long line of hotshot lobbyists who perfected the art of twisting arms for huge fees. He was leaving Washington when Jacy Hubbard, another cobra who got what he deserved, was found dead.

He had no use for their ilk.

When the door to room 520 opened, he stepped inside behind Carl Pratt and came face-to-face with the devil himself.

But the devil was quite pleasant, remarkably gracious, a different man. Prison.

Joel introduced himself and his son Neal to Senator Clayburn. All hands were properly shaken, all thanks duly given. The table in the small suite was covered with pastries, coffee, and juice. Four chairs had been pulled around in a loose circle, and they sat down.

'This shouldn't take long,' Joel said. 'Senator, I need your help. I don't know how much you know about the rather messy affair that sent me away for a few years . . .'

'I know the basics, but there have always been questions.'

'I'm pretty sure I know the answers.'

'Whose satellite system is it?'

Joel couldn't sit. He walked to the window, looked out at nothing, then took a deep breath. 'It was built by Red China, at an astronomical cost. As you know, the Chinese are far behind us in conventional weapons, so they're spending heavily on the high-tech stuff. They stole some of our technology, and they successfully launched the system—nicknamed Neptune—without the knowledge of the CIA.'

'How did they do that?'

'Something as low-tech as forest fires. They

torched twenty thousand acres one night in a northern province. It created an enormous cloud and in the middle of it they launched three rockets, each with three satellites.'

'The Russians did that once,' Clayburn said.

'And the Russians got fooled by their own trick. They missed Neptune too—everybody did. No one in the world knew it existed until my clients stumbled across it.'

'Those Pakistani students.'

'Yes, and all three are dead.'

'Who killed them?'

'I suspect agents of Red China.'

'Who killed Jacy Hubbard?'

'Same.'

'And how close are these people to you?'

'Closer than I would like.'

Clayburn reached for a doughnut and Pratt drained a glass of orange juice. Joel continued, 'I have the software—JAM as they called it. There was only one copy.'

'The one you tried to sell?' Clayburn said.

'Yes. And I really want to get rid of it. It's proving to be quite deadly, and I'm desperate to hand it over. I'm just not sure who should get it.'

'What about the CIA?' Pratt said, because he had yet to say anything.

Clayburn was already shaking his head no.

'I can't trust them,' Joel said. 'Teddy Maynard got me pardoned so he could sit back and watch someone else kill me. Now there's an interim director.'

'And a new President,' Clayburn said. 'The CIA is a mess right now. I wouldn't go near it.' And with that Senator Clayburn stepped over the line, becoming an advisor, not just a curious spectator.

'Who do I talk to?' Joel asked. 'Who can I trust?'

'DIA, the Defense Intelligence Agency,' Clayburn said without hesitation. 'The head guy there is Major Wes Roland, an old friend.'

'How long has he been there?'

Clayburn thought for a second, then said, 'Ten, maybe twelve years. He has a ton of experience, smart as hell. And an honorable man.'

'And you can talk to him?'

'Yes. We've kept in touch.'

'Doesn't he report to the director of the CIA?' Pratt asked.

'Yes, everyone does. There are now at least fifteen different intelligence agencies—something I fought against for twenty years—and by law they all report to the CIA.'

'So Wes Roland will take whatever I give him and tell the CIA?' Joel asked.

'He has no choice. But there are different ways to go about it. Roland is a sensible man, and he knows how to play the politics. That's how he's survived this long.'

'Can you arrange a meeting?'

'Yes, but what will happen at the meeting?'

'I'll throw JAM at him and run out of the building.'

'And in return?'

'It's an easy deal, Senator. I don't want money. Just a little help.'

'What?'

'I prefer to discuss it with him. With you in the room, of course.'

There was a gap in the conversation as

Clayburn stared at the floor and weighed the issues. Neal walked to the table and selected a croissant. Joel poured more coffee. Pratt, obviously hungover, worked another tall glass of orange juice.

Finally, Clayburn sat back in his chair and said, 'I assume this is urgent.'

'Worse than urgent. If Major Roland is available, I would meet with him right now. Anywhere.'

'I'm sure he'll drop whatever he's doing.'

'The phone's over there.'

Clayburn stood and stepped toward the desk. Pratt cleared his throat and said, 'Look, fellas, at this point in the game, I'd like to check out. I don't want to hear any more. Don't want to be a witness, or a defendant, or another casualty. So if you'll just excuse me, I'll be heading back to the office.'

He didn't wait for a response. He was gone in an instant, with the door closing hard behind him. They watched it for a few seconds, somewhat taken aback by the abrupt exit.

'Poor Carl,' Clayburn said. 'Always afraid of his shadow.' He picked up the phone and went to work.

In the middle of the fourth call, and the second straight to the Pentagon, Clayburn placed his hand over the receiver and said to Joel, 'They prefer to meet at the Pentagon.'

Joel was already shaking his head. 'No. I'm not going in there with the software until there's a deal. I'll leave it behind and give it to them later, but I'm not walking in there with it.'

Clayburn relayed this, then listened for a long time. When he covered the receiver again he asked,

'The software, what's it on?'

'Four disks,' Joel said.

'They have to verify it, you understand?'

'Okay, I'll take two disks with me into the Pentagon. That's about half of it. They can take a quick look.'

Clayburn huddled over the receiver and repeated Joel's conditions. Again, he listened for a long time, then he asked Joel, 'Will you show me the disks?'

'Yes.'

He placed the call on hold while Joel picked up his briefcase. He removed the envelope, then the four disks, and placed them on the bed for Neal and Clayburn to gawk at. Clayburn went back to the phone and said, 'I'm looking at four disks. Mr. Backman assures me it is what it is.' He listened for a few minutes, then punched the hold button again.

'They want us at the Pentagon right now,' he said.

'Let's go.'

Clayburn hung up and said, 'Things are hopping over there. I think the boys are excited. Shall we go?'

'I'll meet you in the lobby in five minutes,' Joel said.

When the door closed behind Clayburn, Joel quickly gathered the disks and stuck two of them into his coat pocket. The other two—numbers three and four—were placed back in the briefcase, which he handed to Neal as he said, 'After we leave, go to the front desk and get another room. Insist on checking in now. Call this room, leave me a message and tell me where you are. Stay there until you hear from me.'

'Sure, Dad. I hope you know what you're doing.'

'Just cutting a deal, son. Like in the old days.'

*　　　*　　　*

The taxi dropped them at the south lot of the Pentagon, near the Metro stop. Two uniformed members of Major Roland's staff were waiting with credentials and instructions. They walked them through the security clearances and got their photos made for their temporary ID cards. The entire time Clayburn was griping about how easy it was back in the old days.

Old days or not, he had made a quick transition from the skeptical critic to a major player, and he was thoroughly engaged in Backman's plot. As they hiked along the wide corridors of the second floor, he reminisced about how simple life had been when there were two superpowers. We always had the Soviets. The bad guys were easy to identify.

They took the stairs to the third floor, C wing, and were led by the staffers through a set of doors and into a suite of offices where they were obviously expected. Major Roland himself was standing by, waiting. He was about sixty, still looking trim and fit in his khaki uniform. Introductions were made, and he invited them into his conference room. At one end of the long, wide center table, three technicians were busy checking out a large computer that had evidently just been rolled in.

Major Roland asked Joel's permission to have two assistants present. Certainly. Joel had no objection.

'Would you mind if we video the meeting?' Roland asked.

'For what purpose?' Joel asked.

'Just to have it on film in case someone higher up wants to see it.'

'Such as?'

'Perhaps the President.'

Joel looked at Clayburn, his only friend in the room, and a tenuous one at best.

'What about the CIA?' Joel asked.

'Maybe.'

'Let's forget the video, at least initially. Maybe at some point during the meeting, we'll agree to switch on the camera.'

'Fair enough. Coffee or soft drinks?'

No one was thirsty. Major Roland asked the computer technicians if their equipment was ready. It was, and he asked them to step outside the room.

Joel and Clayburn sat on one side of the conference table. Major Roland was flanked by his two deputies on the opposite side. All three had pens and notepads ready to go. Joel and Clayburn had nothing.

'Let's start and finish a conversation about the CIA,' Backman began, determined to be in charge of the proceedings. 'As I understand the law, or at least the way things once worked around here, the director of the CIA is in charge of all intelligence activities.'

'That's correct,' Roland said.

'What will you do with the information I am about to give you?'

The major glanced to his right, and the look that passed between him and the deputy there conveyed a lot of uncertainty. 'As you said, sir, the director is entitled to know and have everything.'

Backman smiled and cleared his throat. 'Major, the CIA tried to get me killed, okay? And, as far as I know, they're still after me. I don't have much use for the guys over at Langley.'

'Mr. Maynard's gone, Mr. Backman.'

'And someone took his place. I don't want money, Major. I want protection. First, I want my own government to leave me alone.'

'That can be arranged,' Roland said with authority.

'And I'll need some help with a few others.'

'Why don't you tell us everything, Mr. Backman? The more we know, the more we can help you.'

With the exception of Neal, Joel Backman didn't trust another person on the face of the earth. But the time had come to lay it all on the table and hope for the best. The chase was over; there was no place else to run.

He began with Neptune itself, and described how it was built by Red China, how the technology was stolen from two different U.S. defense contractors, how it was launched under cover and fooled not only the U.S. but also the Russians, the British, and the Israelis. He narrated the lengthy story of the three Pakistanis—their ill-fated discovery, their fear of what they found, their curiosity at being able to communicate with Neptune, and their brilliance in writing software that could manipulate and neutralize the system. He spoke harshly of his own giddy greed in shopping JAM to various governments, hoping to make more money than anyone could dream of. He pulled no punches when recalling the recklessness of Jacy Hubbard, and the foolishness of their schemes to peddle their product. Without hesitation, he admitted his mistakes and took full responsibility for the havoc he'd caused. Then he pressed on.

No, the Russians had no interest in what he was selling. They had their own satellites and couldn't afford to negotiate for more.

No, the Israelis never had a deal. They were on the fringes, close enough to know that a deal with the Saudis was looming. The Saudis were desperate to purchase JAM. They had a few satellites of their own, but nothing to match Neptune.

Nothing could match Neptune, not even the latest generation of American satellites.

The Saudis had actually seen the four disks. In a tightly controlled experiment, two agents from their secret police were given a demonstration of the software by the three Pakistanis. It took place in a computer lab on the campus of the University of Maryland, and it had been a dazzling, very convincing display. Backman had watched it, as had Hubbard.

The Saudis offered $100 million for JAM. Hubbard, who fancied himself a close friend of the Saudis, was the point man during the negotiations. A 'transaction fee' of $1 million was paid, the money wired to an account in Zurich. Hubbard and Backman countered with half a billion.

Then all hell broke loose. The feds attacked with warrants, indictments, investigations, and the Saudis got spooked. Hubbard got murdered. Joel fled to the safety of prison, leaving a wide path of destruction behind and some angry people with serious grudges.

*   *   *

The forty-five-minute summary ended without a single interruption. When Joel finished, none of the three on the other side of the table was taking notes. They were too busy listening.

'I'm sure we can talk to the Israelis,' Major Roland said. 'If they're convinced the Saudis will never get their hands on JAM, then they'll rest much easier. We've had discussions with them over the years. JAM has been a favorite topic. I'm quite sure they can be placated.'

'What about the Saudis?'

'They've asked about it too, at the highest levels. We have a lot of common interests these days. I'm confident they'll relax if they know that we have it and no one else will get it. I know the Saudis well, and I think they'll write it off as a bad deal. There is the small matter of the transaction fee.'

'A million bucks is chump change to them. It's not negotiable.'

'Very well. I guess that leaves the Chinese.'

'Any suggestions?'

Clayburn had yet to speak. He leaned forward on his elbows and said, 'In my opinion, they'll never forget it. Your clients basically hijacked a zillion-dollar system and rendered it useless without their homemade software. The Chinese have nine of the best satellites ever built floating around up there and they can't use them. They are not going to forgive and forget, and you really can't blame them. Unfortunately, we have little leverage with Beijing on delicate intelligence matters.'

Major Roland was nodding. 'I'm afraid I must agree with the senator. We can let them know that we have the software, but this is something they'll never forget.'

'I don't blame them. I'm just trying to survive, that's all.'

'We'll do what we can with the Chinese, but it may not be much.'

'Here's the deal, gentlemen. You give me your word that you'll get the CIA out of my life, and that you'll act quickly to appease the Israelis and the Saudis. Do whatever is possible with the Chinese, which I understand may be very little. And you give me two passports—one Australian and one Canadian. As soon as they're ready, and this afternoon would not be too soon, you bring them to me and I'll hand over the other two disks.'

'It's a deal,' Roland said. 'But, of course, we need to have a look at the software.'

Joel reached into his pocket and removed disks one and two. Roland called the computer technicians back in, and the entire group huddled around the large monitor.

*   *   *

A Mossad agent with the code name of Albert thought he saw Neal Backman enter the lobby of the Marriott on 22nd Street. He called his supervisor, and within thirty minutes two other agents were inside the hotel. Albert again saw Neal Backman an hour later, as he left an elevator carrying a briefcase that he had not carried into the hotel, went to the front desk, and appeared to fill out a registration form. Then he pulled out his wallet and handed over a credit card.

He returned to the elevator, where Albert missed him by a matter of seconds.

The knowledge that Joel Backman was probably staying at the Marriott on 22nd Street was extremely important, but it also posed enormous problems. First, the killing of an American on American soil was an operation so delicate that the prime minister would have to be consulted. Second, the actual assassination itself was a logistical nightmare. The hotel had six hundred rooms, hundreds of guests, hundreds of employees, hundreds of visitors, no less than five conventions in progress. Thousands of potential witnesses.

However, a plan came together quickly.

34

They had lunch with the senator in the rear of a Vietnamese deli near Dupont Circle, a place they judged to be safe from lobbyists and old-timers who might see them together and start one of the hot rumors that kept the city alive and gridlocked. For an hour, as they struggled with spicy noodles almost too hot to eat, Joel and Neal listened as the fisherman from Ocracoke regaled them with endless stories of his glory days in Washington. He said more than once that he did not miss politics, yet his memories of those days were filled with intrigue, humor, and many friendships.

Clayburn had started the day thinking that a bullet in the head would've been too good for Joel Backman, but when they said goodbye on the sidewalk outside the café he was begging him to please come see his boat, and bring Neal too. Joel had not been fishing since childhood, and he knew he would never make it to the Outer Banks, but out of gratitude he promised to try.

Joel came closer to a bullet in the head than he would ever know. As he and Neal strolled along Connecticut Avenue after lunch, they were closely watched by the Mossad. A sharpshooter was ready in the rear of a rented panel truck. Final approval, though, was still hung up in Tel Aviv. And the sidewalk was very crowded.

Using the yellow pages in his hotel room, Neal had found a men's shop that advertised overnight alterations. He was anxious to help—his father desperately needed some new clothes. Joel bought a navy three-piece suit, a white dress shirt, two ties, some chinos and casual clothes, and, thankfully, two pairs of black dress shoes. The total was $3,100, and he paid in cash. The bowling shoes were left in a wastebasket, though the salesman had been somewhat complimentary of them.

At exactly 4:00 p.m., while sitting in a Starbucks coffee shop on Massachusetts Avenue, Neal took his cell phone and dialed the number given by Major Roland. He handed the phone to his father.

Roland himself answered. 'We're on our way,' he said.

'Room five-twenty,' Joel said, eyes watching the other coffee drinkers. 'How many are coming?'

'It's a nice group,' Roland said.

'I don't care how many you bring, just leave everybody else in the lobby.'

'I can do that.'

They forgot the coffee and walked ten blocks

back to the Marriott, with every step watched closely by well-armed Mossad agents. Still no action in Tel Aviv.

The Backmans were in the room for a few minutes when there was a knock on the door.

Joel shot a nervous glance at his son, who froze and looked as anxious as his father. This could be it, Joel said to himself. The epic journey that began on the streets of Bologna, on foot, then a cab, then a bus to Modena, a taxi all the way to Milan, more little hikes, more cabs, then the train destined for Stuttgart, but with an unexpected detour in Zug, where another driver took the cash and hauled him into Zurich, two streetcars, then Franz and the green BMW doing 150 kilometers all the way to Munich, where the warm and welcome arms of Lufthansa brought him home. This could be the end of the road.

'Who is it?' Joel asked as he stepped to the door.

'Wes Roland.'

Joel looked through the peephole, saw no one. He took a deep breath and opened the door. The major was now wearing a sports coat and tie, and he was all alone and empty-handed. At least he appeared to be alone. Joel glanced down the hall and saw people trying to hide. He quickly closed the door and introduced Roland to Neal.

'Here are the passports,' Roland said, reaching into his coat pocket and pulling out two broken-in passports. The first had a dark blue cover with AUSTRALIA in gold letters. Joel opened it and looked at the photo first. The technicians had taken the Pentagon security photo, lightened the hair considerably, removed the eyeglasses and a few of the wrinkles, and produced a pretty good image. His name was Simon Wilson McAvoy. 'Not bad,' Joel said.

The second was bound in navy blue, with CANADA in gold letters on the outside. Same photo, and the Canadian name of Ian Rex Hatteboro. Joel nodded his approval and handed both to Neal for his inspection.

'There is some concern about the grand jury investigation into the pardon scandal,' Roland said. 'We didn't discuss it earlier.'

'Major, you and I both know I'm not involved in that affair. I expect the CIA to convince the boys over at Hoover that I'm clean. I had no idea a pardon was in the works. It's not my scandal.'

'You may be called to appear before a grand jury.'

'Fine. I'll volunteer. It'll be a very short appearance.'

Roland seemed satisfied. He was just the messenger. He began to look around for his end of the bargain. 'Now, about that software,' he said.

'It's not here,' Joel said, with unnecessary drama. He nodded at Neal, who left the room. 'Just a minute,' he said to Roland, whose eyebrows were arching up while his eyes grew narrow.

'Is there a problem?' he said.

'Not at all. The package is in another room. Sorry, but I've been acting like a spy for too long.'

'Not a bad practice for a man in your position.'

'I guess it's now a way of life.'

'Our technicians are still playing with the first two disks. It's really an impressive piece of work.'

'My clients were smart boys, and good boys. Just got greedy, I guess. Like a few others.'

There was a knock on the door, and Neal was back. He handed the envelope to Joel, who removed the two disks, then gave them to Roland. 'Thanks,' he said. 'It took guts.'

'Some people have more guts than brains, I guess.'

The exchange was over. There was nothing left to say. Roland made his way to the door. He grabbed the doorknob, then thought of something else. 'Just so you know,' he said gravely, 'the CIA is reasonably certain that Sammy Tin landed in New York this afternoon. The flight came from Milan.'

'Thanks, I guess,' Joel said.

When Roland left the hotel room with the envelope, Joel stretched out on the bed and closed his eyes. Neal found two beers in the minibar and fell into a nearby chair. He waited a few minutes, sipped his beer, then finally said, 'Dad, who is Sammy Tin?'

'You don't want to know.'

'Oh, yeah. I want to know everything. And you're going to tell me.'

*   *   *

At 6:00 p.m., Lisa's mother's car stopped outside a hair salon on Wisconsin Avenue in Georgetown. Joel got out and said goodbye. And thanks. Neal sped away, anxious to get home.

Neal had made the appointment by phone a few hours earlier, bribing the receptionist with the promise of $500 in cash. A stout lady named Maureen was waiting, not too happy to be working late but nonetheless anxious to see who would drop that kind of money on a quick coloring job.

Joel paid first, thanked both the receptionist and Maureen for their flexibility, then sat in front of a mirror.

'You want it washed?' Maureen said.

'No. Let's hurry.'

She put her fingers in his hair and said, 'Who did this?'

'A lady in Italy.'

'What color do you have in mind?'

'Gray, solid gray.'

'Natural?'

'No, beyond natural. Let's get it almost white.'

She rolled her eyes at the receptionist. We get all kinds in here.

Maureen went to work. The receptionist went home, locking the door behind her. A few minutes into the project, Joel asked, 'Are you working tomorrow?'

'Nope, it's my day off. Why?'

'Because I need to come in around noon for another session. I'll be in the mood for something darker tomorrow, something to hide the gray you're doing now.'

Her hands stopped. 'What's with you?'

'Meet me here at noon, and I'll pay a thousand bucks in cash.'

'Sure. What about the next day?'

'I'll be fine when some of the gray is gone.'

*   *   *

Dan Sandberg had been loafing at his desk at the *Post* late in the afternoon when the call came. The gentleman on the other end identified himself as Joel Backman, said he wanted to talk. Sandberg's caller ID showed an unknown number.

'The real Joel Backman?' Sandberg said, scrambling for his laptop.

'The only one I know.'

'A real pleasure. Last time I saw you, you were in court, pleading guilty to all sorts of bad stuff.'

'All of which was wiped clean with a presidential pardon.'

'I thought you were tucked away on the other side of the world.'

'Yeah, I got tired of Europe. Kinda missed my old stomping grounds. I'm back now, ready to do business again.'

'What kind of business?'

'My specialty, of course. That's what I wanted to talk about.'

'I'd be delighted. But I'll have to ask questions about the pardon. Lots of wild rumors out there.'

'That's the first thing we'll cover, Mr. Sandberg. How about tomorrow morning at nine?'

'I wouldn't miss it. Where do we meet?'

'I'll have the presidential suite at the Hay-Adams. Bring a photographer if you like. The broker is back in town.'

Sandberg hung up and called Rusty Lowell, his best source at the CIA. Lowell was out, and as usual no one had any idea where he was. He tried another source at Langley, but found nothing.

*   *   *

Whitaker sat in the first-class section of the Alitalia flight from Milano to Dulles. Up front, the booze was free and free-flowing, and Whitaker tried his best to get hammered. The call from Julia Javier had been a shock. She had begun pleasantly enough with the question 'Anyone seen Marco over there, Whitaker?'

'No, but we're looking.'

'Do you think you'll find him?'

'Yes, I'm quite sure he'll turn up.'

'The director is very anxious right now, Whitaker. She wants to know if you're going to find Marco.'

'Tell her yes, we'll find him!'

'And where are you looking, Whitaker?'

'Between here, in Milano, and Zurich.'

'Well, you're wasting your time, Whitaker, because ol' Marco has popped up here in Washington. Met with the Pentagon this afternoon. Slipped right through your fingers, Whitaker, made us look stupid.'

'What!'

'Come home, Whitaker, and get here quickly.'

Twenty-five rows back, Luigi was crouching low in coach, rubbing knees with a twelve-year-old girl who was listening to some of the raunchiest rap he'd ever heard. He was on his fourth drink himself. It wasn't free and he didn't care what it cost.

He knew Whitaker was up there making notes on exactly how to pin all the blame on Luigi. He should be doing the same, but for the moment he just wanted to drink. The next week in Washington would be quite unpleasant.

*　　　*　　　*

At 6:02 p.m., eastern standard time, the call came from Tel Aviv to halt the Backman killing. Stand down. Abort. Pack up and withdraw, there would be no dead body this time.

For the agents it was welcome news. They were trained to move in with great stealth, do their deed, disappear with no clues, no evidence, no trail. Bologna was a far better place than the crowded streets of Washington, D.C.

An hour later, Joel checked out of the Marriott and enjoyed a long walk through the cool air. He stayed on the busy streets, though, and didn't waste any time. This wasn't Bologna. This city was far different after hours. Once the commuters were gone and the traffic died down, things got dangerous.

The clerk at the Hay-Adams preferred credit, something plastic, something that would not upset the bookkeeping. Rarely did a client insist on paying in cash, but this client wouldn't take no for an answer. The reservation had been confirmed, and with a proper smile he handed over a key and welcomed Mr. Ferro to their hotel.

'Any bags, sir?'

'None.'

And that was the end of their little conversation.

Mr. Ferro headed for the elevators carrying only a cheap black-leather briefcase.

35

The presidential suite at the Hay-Adams was on the eighth floor, with three large windows overlooking H Street, then Lafayette Park, then the White House. It had a king-size bedroom, a bathroom well appointed with brass and marble, and a sitting room with period antiques, a slightly out-of-date television and phones, and a fax machine that was seldom used. It went for $3,000 a night, but then what did the broker care about such things?

When Sandberg knocked on the door at nine, he waited only a second before it was yanked open and a hearty 'Morning, Dan!' greeted him. Backman lunged for his right hand and as he pumped it furiously he dragged Sandberg into his domain.

'Glad you could make it,' he said. 'Would you like some coffee?'

'Yeah, sure, black.'

Sandberg dropped his satchel onto a chair and watched Backman pour from a silver coffeepot. Much thinner, with hair that was shorter and almost white, gaunt through the face. There was a slight resemblance to defendant Backman, but not much.

'Make yourself at home,' Backman was saying. 'I've ordered some breakfast. Should be up in a minute.'

He carefully set two cups with saucers on the coffee table in front of the sofa, and said, 'Let's work here. You plan to use a recorder?'

'If that's all right.'

'I prefer it that way. Eliminates misunderstandings.' They took their positions. Sandberg placed a small recorder on the table, then got his pad and pen ready. Backman was all smiles as he sat low in his chair, legs casually crossed, the confident air of a man who wasn't afraid of any question. Sandberg noticed the shoes, hard rubber soles that had barely been used. Not a scuff or speck of dirt anywhere on the black leather. Typically, the lawyer was put together—navy suit, bright white shirt with cuffs, gold links, a collar bar, a red-and-gold tie that begged for attention.

'Well, the first question is, where have you been?'

'Europe, knocking about, seeing the Continent.'

'For two months?'

'Yep, that's enough.'

'Anyplace in particular?'

'Not really. I spent a lot of time on the trains over there, a marvelous way to travel. You can see so much.'

'Why have you returned?'

'This is home. Where else would I go? What else would I do? Bumming around Europe sounds like great fun, and it was, but you can't make a career out of it. I've got work to do.'

'What kind of work?'

'The usual. Government relations, consulting.'

'That means lobbying, right?'

'My firm will have a lobbying arm, yes. That will be a very important part of our business, but by no means the centerpiece.'

'And what firm is that?'

'The new one.'

'Help me out here, Mr. Backman.'

'I'm opening a new firm, the Backman Group, offices here, New York, and San Francisco. We'll have six partners initially, should be up to twenty in a year or so.'

'Who are these people?'

'Oh, I can't name them now. We're hammering out the details, negotiating the fine points, pretty sensitive stuff. We plan to cut the ribbon on the first of May, should be a big splash.'

'No doubt. This will not be a law firm?'

'No, but we plan to add a legal section later.'

'I thought you lost your license when . . .'

'I did, yes. But with the pardon, I'm now eligible to sit for the bar exam again. If I get a hankering to start suing people, then I'll brush up on the books and get a license. Not in the near future, though, there's just too much work to do.'

'What kind of work?'

'Getting this thing off the ground, raising capital, and, most important, meeting with potential clients.'

'Could you give me the names of some clients?'

'Of course not, but just hang on for a few weeks and that information will be available.'

The phone on the desk rang, and Backman frowned at it. 'Just a second. It's a call I've been waiting on.' He walked over and picked it up. Sandberg heard, 'Backman, yes, hello, Bob. Yes, I'll be in New York tomorrow. Look, I'll call you back in an hour, okay? I'm in the middle of something.' He hung up and said, 'Sorry about that.'

It was Neal, calling as planned, at exactly 9:15,

and he would call every ten minutes for the next hour.

'No problem,' said Sandberg. 'Let's talk about your pardon. Have you seen the stories about the alleged buying of presidential pardons?'

'Have I seen the stories? I have a defense team in place, Dan. My guys are all over this. If and when the feds manage to put together a grand jury, if they ever get that far, I've informed them that I want to be the first witness. I have absolutely nothing to hide, and the suggestion that I paid for a pardon is actionable at law.'

'You plan to sue?'

'Absolutely. My lawyers are preparing a massive libel action now against *The New York Times* and that hatchet man, Heath Frick. It'll be ugly. It'll be a nasty trial, and they're gonna pay me a bunch of money.'

'You're sure you want me to print that?'

'Hell yes! And while we're at it, I commend you and your newspaper for the restraint you've shown so far. It's rather unusual, but admirable nonetheless.'

Sandberg's story of this visit to the presidential suite was big enough to begin with. Now, however, it had just been thrust onto the front page, tomorrow morning.

'Just for the record, you deny paying for the pardon?'

'Categorically, vehemently denied. And I'll sue anybody who says I did.'

'So why were you pardoned?'

Backman reshifted his weight and was about to launch into a long one when the door buzzer erupted. 'Ah, breakfast,' he said, jumping to his feet. He opened the door and a white-jacketed waiter pushed in a cart holding caviar and all the trimmings, scrambled eggs with truffles, and a bottle of Krug champagne in a bucket of ice. While Backman signed the check the waiter opened the bottle.

'One glass or two?' the waiter asked.

'A glass of champagne, Dan?'

Sandberg couldn't help but glance at his watch. Seemed a bit early to start with the booze, but then why not? How often would he be sitting in the presidential suite looking over at the White House sipping on bubbly that cost $300 a bottle? 'Sure, but just a little.'

The waiter filled two glasses, put the Krug back in the ice, and left the room just as the phone rang again. This time it was Randall from Boston, and he'd have to sit by the phone for another hour while Backman finished his business.

He slammed down the receiver and said, 'Eat a bite, Dan, I ordered enough for the both us.'

'No, thanks, I had a bagel earlier.' He took the champagne and had a drink.

Backman dipped a wafer into a $500 pile of caviar and stuck it in his mouth, like a teenager with a corn chip and salsa. He chomped on it as he paced, glass in hand.

'My pardon?' he said. 'I asked President Morgan to review my case. Frankly, I didn't think he had any interest, but he's a very astute person.'

'Arthur Morgan?'

'Yes, very underrated as a president, Dan. He didn't deserve the shellacking he got. He will be missed. Anyway, the more Morgan studied the case, the more concerned he became. He saw through the government's smoke screen. He caught their lies. As an old defense lawyer himself, he understood the power of the feds when they want to nail an innocent person.'

'Are you saying you were innocent?'

'Absolutely. I did nothing wrong.'

'But you pled guilty.'

'I had no choice. First, they indicted me and Jacy Hubbard on bogus charges. We didn't budge. "Bring on the trial," we said. "Give us a jury." We scared the feds so bad that they did what they always do. They went after our friends and families. Those gestapo idiots indicted my son, Dan, a kid fresh out of law school who knew nothing about my files. Why didn't you write about that?'

'I did.'

'Anyway, I had no choice but to take the fall. It became a badge of honor for me. I pled guilty so all charges would be dropped against my son and my partners. President Morgan figured this out. That's why I was pardoned. I deserved it.'

Another wafer, another mouthful of gold, another slurp of Krug to wash it all down. He was pacing back and forth, jacket off now, a man with many burdens to unload. Then he suddenly stopped and said, 'Enough about the past, Dan. Let's talk about tomorrow. Look at that White House over there. Have you ever been there for a state dinner, black tie, marine color guard, slinky ladies in beautiful gowns?'

'No.'

Backman was standing in the window, gazing at the White House. 'Twice I've done that,' he said with a trace of sadness. 'And I'll be back. Give me two, maybe three years, and one day they'll hand deliver a thick invitation, heavy paper, gold embossed lettering: The President and First Lady request the honor of your presence . . .'

He turned and looked smugly at Sandberg. 'That's power, Dan. That's what I live for.'

Good copy, but not exactly what Sandberg was after. He jolted the broker back to reality with a sharp 'Who killed Jacy Hubbard?'

Backman's shoulders dropped and he walked to the ice bucket for another round. 'It was a suicide, Dan, plain and simple. Jacy was humiliated beyond belief. The feds destroyed him. He just couldn't handle it.'

'Well, you're the only person in town who believes it was a suicide.'

'And I'm the only person who knows the truth. Print that, would you.'

'I will.'

'Let's talk about something else.'

'Frankly, Mr. Backman, your past is much more interesting than your future. I have a pretty good source that tells me that you were pardoned because the CIA wanted you released, that Morgan caved under pressure from Teddy Maynard, and that they hid you somewhere so they could watch and see who nailed you first.'

'You need new sources.'

'So you deny—'

'I'm here!' Backman spread his arms so Sandberg could see everything. 'I'm alive! If the CIA wanted me dead, then I'd be dead.' He swallowed some champagne, and said, 'Find a better source. You want some eggs? They're getting cold.'

'No thanks.'

Backman scooped a large serving of scrambled eggs onto a small plate and ate them as he moved around the room, from window to window, never too far away from his view of the White House. 'They're pretty good, got truffles.'

'No thanks. How often do you have this for breakfast?'

'Not often enough.'

'Did you know Bob Critz?'

'Sure, everybody knew Critz. He'd been around as long as I had.'

'Where were you when he died?'

'San Francisco, staying with a friend, saw it on the news. Really sad. What's Critz got to do with me?'

'Just curious.'

'Does this mean you're out of questions?'

Sandberg was flipping back through his notes when the phone rang again. It was Ollie this time, and Backman would have to call him back.

'I have a photographer downstairs,' Sandberg said. 'My editor would like some photos.'

'Of course.'

Joel put on his jacket, checked his tie, hair, and teeth in a mirror, then had another scoop of caviar while the photographer arrived and unloaded some gear. He fiddled with the lighting while Sandberg kept the recorder on and tossed up a few questions.

The best shot, according to the photographer, but also one that Sandberg thought was quite nice, was a wide one of Joel on the burgundy leather sofa, with a portrait on the wall behind him. He posed for a few by the window, trying to get the White House in the distance.

The phone kept ringing, and Joel finally ignored it. Neal was supposed to call back every five minutes in the event a call went unanswered, ten if Joel picked up. After twenty minutes of shooting, the phone was driving them crazy.

The broker was a busy man.

The photographer finished, collected his gear, and left. Sandberg hung around for a few minutes, then finally headed for the door. As he was leaving he said, 'Look, Mr. Backman, this will be a big story tomorrow, no doubt about that. But just so you know, I don't buy half the crap you've told me today.'

'Which half?'

'You were guilty as hell. So was Hubbard. He didn't kill himself, and you ran to prison to save your ass. Maynard got you pardoned. Arthur Morgan didn't have a clue.'

'Good. That half is not important.'

'What is?'

'The broker is back. Make sure that's on the front page.'

*   *   *

Maureen was in a much better mood. Her day off had never been worth a thousand bucks. She escorted Mr. Backman to a private parlor in the rear, away from the gaggle of ladies getting worked on in the front of the salon. Together, they studied colors and shades, and finally selected one that would be easy to maintain. To her, 'maintain' meant the hope of $1,000 every five weeks.

Joel really didn't care. He'd never see her again.

394

She turned the white into gray and added enough brown to take five years off his face. Vanity was not at stake here.

Youth didn't matter. He just wanted to hide.

36

His last guests in the suite made him cry. Neal, the son he hardly knew, and Lisa, the daughter-in-law he'd never met, handed him Carrie, the two-year-old granddaughter he'd only dreamed about. She cried too, at first, but then settled down as her grandfather walked her around and showed her the White House just over there. He walked her from window to window, from room to room, bouncing her and chatting away as if he'd had experience with a dozen grandkids. Neal took more photos, but these were of a different man. Gone was the flashy suit; he was wearing chinos and a plaid button-down. Gone were the bluster and arrogance; he was a simple grandfather clinging to a beautiful little girl.

Room service delivered a late lunch of soups and salads. They enjoyed a quiet family meal, Joel's first in many, many years. He ate with only one hand because the other balanced Carrie on his knee, which never stopped its steady bounce.

He warned them of tomorrow's story in the *Post*, and explained the motives behind it. It was important for him to be seen in Washington, and in the most visible way possible. It would buy him some time, confuse everyone who might still be looking for him. It would create a splash, and be talked about for days, long after he was gone.

Lisa wanted answers as to how much danger he was in, and Joel confessed that he wasn't sure. He would drop out for a while, move around, always being careful. He'd learned a lot in the past two months.

'I'll be back in a few weeks,' he said. 'And I'll drop in from time to time. Hopefully, after a few years things will be safer.'

'Where are you going now?' Neal asked.

'I'm taking the train to Philly, then I'll catch a flight to Oakland. I would like to visit my mother. It would be nice if you'd drop her a card. I'll take my time, eventually end up somewhere in Europe.'

'Which passport will you use?'

'Not the ones I got yesterday.'

'What?'

'I'm not about to allow the CIA to monitor my movements. Barring an emergency, I'll never use them.'

'So how do you travel?'

'I have another passport. A friend loaned it to me.'

Neal gave him a look of suspicion, as if he knew what 'friend' meant. Lisa missed it, though, and little Carrie picked that moment to relieve herself. Joel was quick to hand her to her mother.

While Lisa was in the bathroom changing the diaper, Joel lowered his voice and said, 'Three things. First, get a security firm to sweep your home, office, and cars. You might be surprised. It'll cost about ten grand, and it must be done. Second, I'd like for you to locate an assisted-living place somewhere close to here. My mother, your grandmother, is stuck out there in Oakland with no one to check on her. A good place will cost three to four thousand a month.'

'I take it you have the money.'

'Third, yes, I have the money. It's in an account here at Maryland Trust. You're listed as one of the owners. Withdraw twenty-five thousand to cover the expenses you've incurred so far, and keep the rest close by.'

'I don't need that much.'

'Well, spend some, okay? Loosen up a little. Take the girl to Disney World.'

'How will we correspond?'

'For now, e-mail, the Grinch routine. I'm quite the hacker, you know.'

'How safe are you, Dad?'

'The worst is over.'

Lisa was back with Carrie, who wanted to return to the bouncing knee. Joel held her for as long as he could.

* * *

Father and son entered Union Station together while Lisa and Carrie waited in the car. The bustle of activity made Joel anxious again; old habits would be hard to break. He pulled a small carry-on bag, loaded with all of his possessions.

He bought a ticket to Philadelphia, and as they slowly made their way to the platform area Neal said, 'I really want to know where you're going.'

Joel stopped and looked at him. 'I'm going back to Bologna.'

'There's a friend there, right?'

'Yes.'

'Of the female variety?'

'Oh yes.'
'Why am I not surprised?'
'Can't help it, son. It was always my weakness.'
'She's Italian?'
'Very much so. She's really special.'
'They were all special.'
'This one saved my life.'
'Does she know you're coming back?'
'I think so.'
'Please be careful, Dad.'
'I'll see you in a month or so.'
They hugged and said goodbye.

AUTHOR'S NOTE

My background is law, certainly not satellites or espionage. I'm more terrified of high-tech electronic gadgets today than a year ago. (These books are still written on a thirteen-year-old word processor. When it stutters, as it seems to do more and more, I literally hold my breath. When it finally quits, I'm probably done too.)

It's all fiction, folks. I know very little about spies, electronic surveillance, satellite phones, smartphones, bugs, wires, mikes, and the people who use them. If something in this novel approaches accuracy, it's probably a mistake.

Bologna, however, is very real. I had the great luxury of tossing a dart at a map of the world to find a place to hide Mr. Backman. Almost anywhere would work. But I adore Italy and all things Italian, and I have to confess that I was not blindfolded when I threw the dart.

My research (too severe a word) led me to Bologna, a delightful old city that I immediately came to adore. My friend Luca Patuelli showed me around. He knows all the chefs in Bologna, no small feat, and in the course of our tedious work I put on about ten pounds.

Thanks to Luca, to his friends, and to their warm and magical city. Thanks also to Gene McDade, Mike Moody, and Bert Colley.